BY JACK CURTIS

Point of Impact
Glory
Crows' Parliament

Jack
Curtis

SIMON & SCHUSTER

POINT OF IMPACT

A NOVEL

NEW YORK   LONDON   TORONTO   SYDNEY   TOKYO   SINGAPORE

SIMON & SCHUSTER
SIMON & SCHUSTER BUILDING
ROCKEFELLER CENTER
1230 AVENUE OF THE AMERICAS
NEW YORK, NEW YORK 10020

DESIGNED BY EVE METZ
MANUFACTURED IN THE UNITED STATES OF AMERICA

1 2 3 4 5 6 7 8 9 10

LIBRARY OF CONGRESS CATALOGING IN PUBLICATION DATA
CURTIS, JACK, DATE
POINT OF IMPACT: A NOVEL/JACK CURTIS.
P. CM.
I. TITLE.
PS3503.U866P6 1991
813'.54—DC20   90-27221
CIP
ISBN 0-671-73640-X

TO DON AND ENID WATSON

ONE

ONE

Dartmoor
1971

A FARMER HAD SHOT THE FOX two days earlier, peppering the creature with pellets from an over-and-under shotgun. Now it was almost ready to die; nothing kept it moving but instinct. In truth, it should have died hours before, but it was a strong dog-fox— young, free of worm and other weakening parasites, not able to prevent its own death, but able to make the dying take longer.

On the northern horizon, clouds were pushing in from the sea —acres of cumulo-nimbus, black with the rain they carried, a dark canopy over the moor. The fox had lapped at the dewpool, then sunk down beside it, the rufous flank heaving with effort. Its pelt was scabrous and torn from the shotgun wounds, most of which were seeping a clear poison, like resin. Now, as if sensing the coming storm, it tried to rise, but its legs were a nerveless tangle, its eyes fogged by septicemia. Three more wrenching attempts had it upright and it stood awhile, its sharp mask lowered to the ground, its limbs quivering. From its lolling tongue, three or four small, bright clots of blood slid onto the furze.

A murmur of thunder rolled over from seaward and a wind flashed the grass. The flat, ragged surface of the dewpool puckered as it took the first spattering of rain. Then everything was still once more. The fox trotted forward about ten yards or so, behaving for the moment, as if nothing were wrong. Then it stopped, took another half-dozen paces, and died on its feet.

Soon crows would have its eyes. Soon its paunch would be opened up like an overfull bag by the moorland scavengers. Soon it would be nothing but a few scattered bones and a rag of pelt melding with the dark earth. The fox had traveled many miles during the days of its dying, but hadn't come far. It had circled all the time, staying within its own territory. At no time had the creature been out of sight of the massive outcrop of Bethel Tor.

The two men could see the rain coming across the moor like a purple curtain. They could have moved to the southern, leeward side of the tor and hunkered in against the jut of granite there, but they chose not to. Instead, they pulled waterproof capes over their heads, helping each other to get the stiff, camouflage-dappled material down over their packs and rifles. They looked toward the storm clouds expectantly, as if glad of the creeping downpour. One of them noticed, a half-mile away, black birds flocking and landing close to the dewpool.

It was late autumn, not more than an hour from dusk, and the men had been out on the moor for as long as it had taken the fox to die. They had started out with basic rations, which were pretty much used up. They were equipped with maps and map references which were supposed to take them to a certain destination, but it had never been their intention to arrive there. They carried standard-issue SLR rifles and five rounds each of live ammunition that one of them had stolen from stores on the day they'd set out.

The man watching the birds as they circled pulled off his beret and smoothed his dark, spiky hair before settling the leather band low on his forehead once more. He had a lean, rather mournful face and a long, narrow nose that had once been broken and later set very slightly out of true. His companion had the ruddy complexion of a country boy, made to seem raw, now, by the growing flurries of rain. He crouched under his cape, head cocked to one side, listening along the wind.

Five minutes later, he heard what he was listening for. The dark man saw his friend's head turn toward the sound and they both remained still until it came again. A shout of command. They stood up, bringing their weapons from beneath their capes and releasing the safety catches. The dark man was smiling slightly, like someone suddenly taken by a pleasant memory. In that moment, the storm hit them, breaking on the gray stone of the tor.

It was good cover. The men stood patiently, enduring the wind-driven downpour, each holding in his mind's eye an image of the group that would soon come into view. Another shout—and the dark man edged around the boss of granite to look up the bracken-covered slope that he and his friend had descended an hour or so earlier. A minute passed; then several figures, dim outlines, could be seen breasting the hill. They were moving at the trot, six of them running in ranks of two, the seventh flanking them like an outrider. They came like shadows through the rain, gray and blurred; the only sharpness was the sound of the flanking man's voice—a litany of insults as constant as the wind.

The dark man moved back and nodded to his companion. Together, they edged to the far side of the rock and waited, expressionless, rainwater sluicing their faces before being whipped off their chins in rivulets.

As the group grew level, they could hear—beneath the bellowing of the flanker—the thud of boots landing in unison, and the runners' grunts of effort. In the same moment, their timing perfect, the two men stepped clear of the sheltering rock. The runners were past: twenty feet ahead, maybe thirty. The flanker was still yelling.

The dark man raised his rifle and fired almost without hesitation. The voice stopped—everything seemed to stop, as if the wind had died, as if the rain had been siphoned off. The runners turned—not to the noise of the gunshot but to the seventh man as he pitched forward. Carried on by his own momentum, he seemed to scramble, traveling rapidly on all fours, but the wound quickly sapped him and he went down on his face.

The bullet had taken him at the base of the spine, giving him only a few seconds before the nerve complex to his legs stopped functioning. He didn't know what was happening; the shock had blotted his mind. Like the fox, he functioned wholly on instinct. As if it might help, as if some hope lay in the action, he levered himself up on his elbows and used what strength there was in his biceps and shoulders to work his body forward, dragging the dead weight of his paralyzed legs.

The ruddy-faced man stepped outward slightly and took steady aim. The flanker wasn't moving far or fast; he had all the time in the world for this. His first shot smashed the flanker's right shoulder blade and the man grunted, rearing up like a seal. The second was copybook—directly to the back of the cranium, just above the neck.

It had taken twenty seconds. The six runners had scattered—not seeking cover but, after the first shot, they had moved rapidly

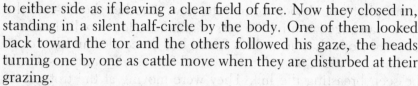

to either side as if leaving a clear field of fire. Now they closed in, standing in a silent half-circle by the body. One of them looked back toward the tor and the others followed his gaze, the heads turning one by one as cattle move when they are disturbed at their grazing.

The men by the rock didn't stir at first. The runners saw two outlines, raveled by rain and stock-still. No one moved or spoke. Then the two figures slid away, their gray shapes melding with the gray of the tor as if they were shouldering their way into the granite itself.

The runners looked down at the dead man. One of them got the toe of his boot under the body and heaved, turning it. There was pulp, livid and purple, low down on the torso where the first bullet had found its exit. Most of the face had gone. When they first looked, the shattered features were loud with blood; but as they continued to stare, the rainstorm hosed it off, cleaning the ragged edges of flesh, polishing the smashed teeth, the nose bone, the cheekbone, as if the broken head were already becoming skull-like.

Somebody laughed. After a moment, they were all laughing.

It's easy to join the army. A couple of tests that wouldn't tax a twelve-year-old, a physical, and you're in. Basic training teaches recruits to follow orders without question. Drill is about obedience and stamina. You take abuse and hardship. You're broken down, then put back together the way the army wants you. After that, life gets a little easier.

That's standard. The SAS requires more of you. It's an elite, not interested in second-raters. When you take their selection course, the first thing you're likely to hear is someone telling you that you won't make it. After that, they'll try as hard as they know how to make sure you don't. There's a method for this, a series of what the selectors call "sickeners."

Sickener 1

A recruit will have been on a few cross-country marches over rough terrain. Each day the distance increases; each day his pack is made heavier.

At one stage, he'll have to crawl along a gully that has been filled with mud, the rotting guts of animals, and human shit.

When he reaches the end of the march, the lorry waiting to collect him will drive off before he can reach it.

Sickener 2

On combat survival courses, recruits spend days living off the land while being hunted by soldiers from other regiments. The hunters are under instruction to give recruits a bad time. Bones get broken.

Days begin before dawn and end well after dark. Endurance marches take place in impossible weather. The minimum distance to be covered is forty-five miles in twenty-four hours over ground that is, in effect, wilderness. People die.

Sickener 3

Recruits have to be able to withstand interrogation techniques. Exhausted by exercises that have stretched them to their physical limits, they undergo sensory deprivation—hooded and hearing only white noise. Someone will ask, "What's your regiment? What is your objective?"

They'll be tied across a pole and immersed in water to the point of drowning. Someone will ask, "What's your regiment? What is your objective?"

They'll be manacled in a cell, naked, while from the next room come the sounds of flogging, screams, vomiting. Someone will ask, "What's your regiment? What is your objective?"

Many break. The SAS is glad of that. They don't want those men.

There are other sickeners. You'd have to allow that the men who devise them and put them into practice are a strange breed, but they're only doing their jobs. Most of them. Some—very few—take pleasure in what they're doing. They don't want to let up. They like the control they wield, and the power. More than that, they enjoy seeing men suffer. Their brutality isn't simulated, it's real; and it goes on outside the training sessions, the marches, the interrogations.

The men who don't qualify can afford to forget those sadists. It might take time, but it's possible. The men who are accepted can't forget because they must still live with their tormentors. They might want to kill those men—those few sadists. They might dream of doing it; and that wouldn't be surprising, since killing is what they've been trained for. They might devise a method for it —when and where. It might become a desire so strong that it scarcely seems possible to resist.

A desire just like that had pushed Eric Ross and Martin Jackson off their scheduled route on the moor and into the lee of Bethel Tor. It had led to the death of Sergeant Joseph Halliday, smashing his spine and blowing half his face away. Ross and Jackson didn't feel bad about that. And they didn't much care what might happen next.

There was an officer called Gilbey and a rather more senior officer called Morgan. They were together in Gilbey's office, though Morgan had commandeered the comfortable desk chair. Gilbey sat in a small armchair facing the window. He didn't like the fact that Morgan's face was put into heavy shadow by the light at his back. He also didn't like the fact that Morgan was smoking, since Gilbey made it a general rule that his office was a smoke-free zone. An ADC brought an ashtray, then left as instructed.

"How?" Morgan asked.

"Army-issue rifle. The rounds must have been stolen from stores." It was an admission that Gilbey hadn't wanted to make but couldn't avoid.

"Who?"

"There were twelve pairs out on the moor. The usual sort of exercise. They're all confined to barracks. Thus far, we haven't questioned any of them. That was what . . ."

Morgan nodded. "Why?" he asked.

"Halliday was . . ." A long pause followed. Finally, Gilbey said, "Zealous."

"A thug," Morgan suggested.

"A bit of a thug, yes."

Morgan swiveled slightly in his chair, so that his profile was picked out by the backlight. "We've made some inquiries, Geoffrey. Checked a few things. You understand?"

Gilbey nodded.

"Reports of something rather more than zealotry, it seems. During survival courses. The sickeners. Especially during the interrogation sessions. And not only then. In barracks too." Morgan swiveled back and flipped open a folder that lay on the desk.

"A man roped to his bed, Geoffrey, and flogged across the buttocks. Yes?" Morgan raised his eyebrows. "Another manacled, sitting in a puddle, left there overnight. A man—" he hesitated, "buggered by an NCO under Halliday's instructions." He paused. "Something about a broomstick, Geoffrey." The voice was eerily gentle. "Now that must have been painful, wouldn't you say? And not very nice, really."

Gilbey shrugged. "We hear rumors of bullying, of course."

"Bullying . . . yes." Morgan smiled. "Sounds a bit like something from *Tom Brown's School Days*, doesn't it? Regrettable, perhaps, but nothing a chap shouldn't be able to take." His smile broadened, but Gilbey wasn't taken in by that. "Did you go to public school, Geoffrey?"

Gilbey was growing impatient and risked showing a little of his annoyance. "I imagine that someone, somewhere, has reached a decision," he said.

Morgan made a show of lighting a fresh cigarette, extinguishing the match by holding it in the gentle exhalation of smoke so that it fluttered awhile before dying.

"Yes," he said finally. "Do nothing. An accident. An official accident." There was silence for a full minute. "What of the men who saw it happen?"

"I don't suppose," Gilbey said, "that they'll demand an inquiry."

"What of the officers on the exercise?"

"They'll do as ordered, of course."

"What of Halliday's relatives?"

"They'll believe what they're told, I expect."

"No wife."

"As you know." Gilbey was tired of facing the window; he felt exposed and disadvantaged. He got up and paced to the door, then went back to the chair he'd been sitting in, laying his hands on its back. It didn't help. He felt like an anxious interviewee. "That's what you—"

The other man's voice cut across. "There won't be any problems, will there, Geoffrey? An accident. We can make that stick?"

Gilbey persisted. "That's what the Home Office wants?"

"We can't afford this kind of thing, Geoffrey. We're becoming a nation of protest groups. Pacifists, nuclear disarmers, hippies, druggies, people banging on about love and peace. Parading around pop festivals with flowers up their arses. Taking drugs. Talking about the Establishment as if it were some sort of wog junta. I can think of a dozen commie politicians who'd love to get

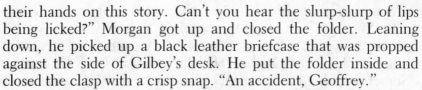

their hands on this story. Can't you hear the slurp-slurp of lips being licked?" Morgan got up and closed the folder. Leaning down, he picked up a black leather briefcase that was propped against the side of Gilbey's desk. He put the folder inside and closed the clasp with a crisp snap. "An accident, Geoffrey."

"And the man who killed him?" Gilbey asked. "Men . . ."

Morgan walked to the door. "Why talk of who killed him? It was an accident, wasn't it? The Home Office statement has already been issued." Morgan checked his watch. "Half an hour ago."

Eric Ross stroked his nose alongside the bony wen of the badly set break; then he smiled, much as he'd smiled on the day when Sergeant Halliday had been killed.

There was a raw, flexing light over the moor—white, unless it filtered through bracken or fern, when it took on a green glow, like isinglass. Ross and Jackson were sitting a little above the steep that rolled down to Belstone Tor. Not far away lay the remnant of the fox: a smudge, a dampness, a hank of hair.

They had gone back, as people will often go back to a place where they have been particularly sad or particularly happy; to a place that has changed their lives. A week had passed since the killing. It was clear to them that nothing was going to happen. The army was not so much protecting its own as protecting itself. Part of what had drawn them back to the moor was an indelible sense of strangeness. Life had remained normal. People ate, talked, shared a joke, went about their business. The training depot continued to function as it always had. It wouldn't have taken much effort to pretend that the incident had simply never taken place. Except for the dreams of it; except for the recollection of excitement, like a lit nerve.

Neither man had spoken much on the walk to the tor; and they had maintained a silence while they sat, as if keeping vigil, until Ross turned to his friend and spoke his name.

"Martin?" He meant: What are you thinking?

Jackson reached out and touched Ross's mouth with his index finger. Be quiet, the gesture said. Don't ask. It was a curious motion, both swift and tender. After a while the men rose and began the walk downhill. Nearby, a kestrel quivered just above head height, rocking slightly in the wind and making the hundreds of tiny adjustments to wing and tail feathers that would keep the head motionless.

Ross and Jackson passed the tor without a second glance. Behind them lay the moor's life and litter. The hawk, suspended in air. The rag of fox pelt. Seven rounds of live ammunition on the bed of the dewpool.

TWO

1

THE HOUSE HAD NEITHER a name nor a street address. To reach it, you'd travel southwest from Tucson on Interstate 10, then swing north after a few miles, then west, then north again. It was possible to come across the place by accident; a few travelers, a few tourists, had done that, but it was very clear to them that a casual visit wouldn't have been welcomed.

From a distance, you could see only a blaze of color. It was so bright, so startling, that the eye would swing to it at once. Desert colors are sere, burned hues—ocher, dull red, hot yellows, the matt greens of the saguaro and organ-pipe cactus. The brilliance that lay around the house—an acre all told—was a mosaic of sharp, singing color that seemed to float and flow in the warp of a heat haze. An irrigation system had been used to create a vast rose garden.

If you got closer, you'd see some native intruders among the blooms—Mexican poppies, owl clover, Indian paintbrush, and the white, bugle-shaped flowers of the ajo lily, surprised into existence by the constant source of water. But their delicate shades were swamped by the roses, red roses, foreign and bizarre and utterly out of place. Hugo Kemp liked red roses.

First you'd see that blaze. Then you'd see the house, long and low and unobtrusive. If you got down there, drawn by the oddness of it, you'd come to a wire fence. On the fence, you'd see a plaque decorated with two red flashes topped by a death's head and a brief description of the number of volts that ran through the wire. If you stayed there long enough, you might meet a man in blue jeans, a T-shirt, and a straw Stetson. The man would ask you to leave, and you'd almost certainly do that, since the man would be carrying a rifle slung in the crook of his arm.

Well, thought Nina Kemp, a little bit of this, a little bit of that. She took two capsules, yellow and black, red and black, and set them toward the back of the table. The floor was paved with Mexican terra-cotta tiles which gave the table a slight forward slope, and the capsules rolled toward her, each taking a mazy, idiosyncratic route to her hand. She enjoyed that little ritual, though she couldn't have said why. It had become part of the day.

The red and black reached her first. She swallowed it quickly in order to be ready for the arrival of the yellow and black. She cupped her hand by the lip of the table and let the second capsule drop into her palm, then put it between her lips and held it there, half-in, half-out, as a lizard savors a bug. She seemed almost to forget it, gazing out at the roses. A wash; a blur. If she slitted her eyes, the blooms seemed to swim at her and she felt heady, as if she were standing among them and taking their scent. Then she sucked the capsule in, swilling it down with a mouthful of orange juice. A little bit of this, a little bit of that.

Nina was an attractive woman, but there were things you had to look past in order to find that. Her narrow face was made striking by the bas-relief of high cheekbones; a thick sweep of black hair fell to her shoulders; pale skin, green eyes. And it was the eyes, really, that you had to get past. They seemed always slightly unfocused, as if her gaze were out of true, or as if she were looking beyond what other people might be seeing. When she moved, she moved slowly, warily, and on the few occasions when she spoke she seemed to have difficulty with the words, as if overcoming a great reluctance to say anything at all.

Nina didn't notice these things in herself. Of the world, she noticed less and less. What slowed her movements and slowed her speech was the sheet anchor of depression that had become her second nature.

She got up from the table, leaving behind a litter of uneaten breakfast food, coffee spillage, a half-empty jug of juice, and went out to the terrace at the front of the house. A man passed by carrying a cellular phone and a batch of documents, but they didn't speak. Hugo Kemp's workers had long since given up on attempts at conversation with Nina. She was a flake; they knew that.

She lowered herself into a sun-bleached cane chair and looked over the foam of roses to a distant butte flanked by pillars of out-crop rock. She saw it, but didn't think about it. At one time, it would have occurred to her to go there; to want to go there. At one time, her thoughts might have taken her as far as Benson, or Pantano, or even Tucson itself. Not now. She was twenty-nine years old, and she lived at home with her father because he wanted it that way. She had almost come to believe that she wanted it that way, too.

The man who had passed Nina on the terrace entered the house and walked through the dining area where Nina's uneaten break-fast was being cleared by a Navajo woman. He continued through an elegant drawing room, low and framed by glass walls, then came into a long, cool passageway that led directly to the back of the house. Doors off the corridor opened onto a library, a study, and several bedrooms. One door, though, led to a flight of steps that went directly downward. Given the construction of the house, and its location, that shouldn't have happened.

Glinwood pressed a button alongside the door and spoke his name into an intercom. An answering buzz let him in. The under-ground room was well lit and cleverly air-conditioned; you might almost have looked for the view. It was nearly the size of the entire floor space of the house, apart from a row of vaults at one end.

Hugo Kemp turned as Glinwood approached and took the pa-pers that were being offered to him. He glanced at them, then asked, "What do you think?"

Glinwood nodded. "It seems right," he said. "It looks okay to me."

Kemp took the papers to a desk at one side of the room and spread them out. Together, the two men scanned the documents. From time to time, Glinwood went to a bookshelf and brought back to the desk some work of reference or another.

Just above their heads, Nina dozed in the cane chair. It was mid-morning and the sun, directly on her, was growing hot. She might have been more comfortable if she'd dragged the chair into a piece of shade, but it didn't occur to her to do that. She felt heavy from the effect of the pills; her head lolled, lifted suddenly as if to a sharp sound, then dropped again. She was wearing baggy white cotton pants, caught at the ankle, and a loose white shirt, the sleeves buttoned at the wrist. She never wore shorts or a T-shirt; her arms and legs were always covered.

Someone standing in front of her, looking closely at her while she slept, would have seen that, even in sleep, her face was still clouded, and that her hands jumped from time to time in her lap, as if her dreams were tugging at her. As her head drooped, a fall of hair gathered and slid past her cheek, darkly, layer by layer, until she was masked on that side. Her breathing seemed remote.

On her shirt sleeve, on one leg of her pants, just below the knee, were small, red blots where the blood hadn't quite stopped.

2

LINDA BOWMAN OFTEN WALKED down Oxford Street during her lunch break. Her budget for clothes was severely limited, but she liked to check out the changing displays and the new fashions. It was a warm day in summer, and the London streets had a bleached look about them. Oxford Street was a canyon walled by glass; the sun threw a white sheen of reflected light that tailed off as it ran along the line of perspective.

Linda was wearing a pale blue, sleeveless dress that she'd bought two years ago when she and Pete were first married. It was a good marriage; she was made happy by it; and she knew that Pete felt the same. All in all, Linda should have been contented. But there were a couple of things that troubled her most of the time. One was a shortage of money—a constant struggle with bills, the mortgage, housekeeping expenses. Linda and Pete would often talk about this, trying to devise ways to make ends meet. Pete was worried about it too. He'd given up smoking and drank only the occasional beer on Saturday nights. It was clear that the problem humiliated and depressed him; he wanted to be able to provide for his wife.

The second thing that troubled Linda was closely connected to the first. It was something she'd never discussed with Pete. In fact, she lived in fear of the possibility of his ever finding out about it. That problem was on her mind as she strolled from window to window, pausing to look in at the unaffordable dresses.

The street was packed with people, all of them anonymous, all of them just faces in a crowd. Nothing special about any of them. Nothing special about Linda, either, except that someone, just a moment or two before, had picked her out. Chosen her. Perhaps it was the blue dress, or the fact that she was moving slowly as she gazed at the displays. It made no matter.

From his vantage point, the man watched her approach. She passed into the shadow of an awning, then disappeared for a while beneath the green canvas. The man had observed this pattern and knew that she would emerge quite soon. Beyond the awning was a road junction, an open space bathed in bright sunlight, where she would have to pause before crossing. He shifted his position slightly and brought the butt of a .308 target rifle up to his shoulder, sighting the cross hairs of the scope on a telephone booth a few feet from the junction. Everything was in crisp focus. He could read the dialing instructions inside the booth. He lowered the gun, waiting, and brought his hand away from the trigger guard to stroke his nose, fingering the nodule of bone that bulged on one side.

He saw Linda's feet first—white sandals—then the fullness of her dress; and then she was clear, strolling toward the junction. As she stopped and waited for the lights to change, the cross hairs quartered her. A taxi went past, and a bus that took her out of his vision for a moment. Then came a gap in the traffic.

Ross squeezed off a single shot, knowing it was all he needed. It took him fifteen seconds to break the gun down, stow it in a sports bag, and get off the roof.

At first, no one noticed. Some had heard the shot, some hadn't, but few had taken any notice of it. London is full of sudden noises. No one expects them to be gunshots. Only those standing closest to Linda saw that something was wrong, although to begin with they didn't know what had happened. Linda gasped and went backward on her heels. Hands went out to aid her, but the force of the bullet took her too fast. She cannoned into a woman laden with store bags, sending bags and purchases spilling into the street. She hit the plate glass of a shopfront, turned, then stood still a moment as if gazing in. The lights changed and people began to cross the road.

Those who had turned to help Linda stopped in the act, balked by the sight of the exit wound, a ragged hole in her back just below the shoulder blade. Their faces were blank with shock, as if their features had been wiped.

Linda slid down the glass, seeming as if she might kneel; then her legs gave way and she tumbled, falling onto her back. The pale blue dress, from neckline to waist, was heavy with blood.

3

ROBIN CULLEY WAS SITTING close to an open window. The bang and blare of the city at his back made his words scarcely audible. He said, "I don't know either." Then he said it again, a little louder.

"I heard you." Helen Blake smiled at him. It was a smile of acknowledgment, nothing more.

"Neither of us knows. It's a risk. Life's full of them." He waited for a response. When none came, he said, "Don't you think?"

Helen nodded. She was lying on the bed, naked, where he had left her. It didn't seem to concern her that he had gotten dressed and perched on a chair across the room in order to talk to her. He looked for a power-play interpretation of this, found one, and decided he didn't like it.

"I've taken risks," she said. "I've fallen on my ass. The crash was audible to just about everyone I knew."

"I know that." Culley half-turned to look out of the window: busy people, refuse, daytime neon. When he turned back, Helen had risen from the bed and was making for the bathroom. His eyes went over her body, covertly, as if she were showing no more than a curve of breast or a length of thigh. She passed him and paused by the bathroom door, her back to him. He could still feel the nodules of her spine under his tongue, the diminishing undulation, the nap of down in the small of her back.

"Listen," she said, "I don't know what to think, okay? I mean I don't really know *what* I'm thinking. Maybe I don't want to. But here we are, here am I, bare-assed and liking it and feeling a bit shaky and a bit . . ." She paused, then shrugged and turned to face him. "A bit embarrassed. Not coy, I don't mean that. Just . . . as if it were the first time. Excited and uncertain and vulnerable." As she went into the bathroom, she added, "Accent on the vulnerable. You see?"

Culley waited until he heard the water running in the shower, then collected his coat and left. The street was all clamor and heat. Three guys stood outside a small theater-front that advertised a live stage show, all nude, girls and men, girls and girls, continuous performances, don't enter if you are easily shocked. Outside a Greek restaurant, a deal was going down—coke or crack; these days, soft drugs were just back-up. Culley ignored it. As he came close to his car, he could hear the radio squawking.

He took the call and swung the car toward Oxford Street. He was less than half a mile away from the incident, but London traffic moves slowly, slower than the horse-drawn carriages of a century ago. Culley swore at the line of vehicles ahead of him, caught up by his anger for a while. Then Helen's fragrance swamped him, stronger than recollection, and his mind went back to the room he'd just left.

She would be out of the shower by now, standing in front of the long mirror that fronted the pine wardrobe, squirting little gobbets of moisturizing cream into her palm and massaging it into her skin. She would sit cross-legged on the bed, not knowing how indecorous and inviting the pose was, leaning forward so that her hair fell down to dry evenly. Because she found the process boring, she would have a book in the angle of her knees.

He couldn't be sure of these things, of course; couldn't guaran-

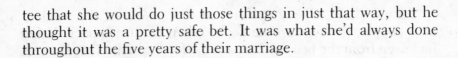

tee that she would do just those things in just that way, but he thought it was a pretty safe bet. It was what she'd always done throughout the five years of their marriage.

Culley showed his ID and ducked under the tape that cordoned off a section of the street. At the intersection, screens had been thrown up around the body of Linda Bowman. Mike Dawson saw Culley approaching and walked partway up the street to meet him.

"Where the fuck were you?"

Culley was looking toward the screens. "Stopped off for a cup of coffee," he said. "Who's been down here?"

"Protheroe," Dawson told him. "Who noticed your absence."

"And?"

"I fed him a line. That won't stop him asking questions later, though."

"Okay." Culley was too preoccupied to say thanks. They reached the screens and Culley went in first. A photographer was in there, together with a civilian doctor. Both had just finished their work. Culley knew them. He nodded to the doctor. "Have you spoken to my sergeant?"

"He knows all there is to know at this stage." The doctor snapped the clasp on his bag. "Single gunshot wound. Death pretty much instantaneous, I'm sure of that. We'll get more later."

Culley looked down at the girl for a moment, the clutter of limbs, the dress caked with a brown stain. He went back into the street, taking Dawson with him. "Who is she?" He looked along the length of the street as he spoke, his head tilted back.

"Linda Bowman," Dawson told him. "Twenty-four, a secretary. Worked in the rag trade. A place called Riches. It's a pun—you know? Rags to riches. It's also the owner's name: Charles Rich."

"It's wonderful to hear of someone with a sense of humor," Culley observed. "What happened?"

"About one-fifteen. She was shot as she was crossing the road. From above—the entry and exit wounds show that; and with a high-velocity rifle, if you want my guess. Still, we'll—"

"Wait to hear what the butchers say. Yes." Culley asked, "Where exactly? Do we know?"

Dawson sighed. "Dozens of witnesses, of course. Hundreds. No one told us anything we wanted to hear. Plenty heard the shot; no one realized what it was, or that the girl had been hit. Not at first.

We've got a fistful of them making statements, but I wouldn't call them eyewitnesses. Apart from the girl falling—how that happened—there was fuck-all to see so far as I can judge."

"He shot from cover."

"Sure."

Culley's eyes went back to the rooftops. Dawson said, "She's married. They live in north London. Apparently her husband's got a small building business. Nothing much; just him and a couple of laborers—"

Culley interrupted. "How did you get this?"

"There was a payslip in her bag. Her office is just a couple of streets from here. I sent someone around. There's a woman works there—" Dawson looked at his notebook. "Peggy Harrison. She and the Bowman girl were friends. She was told there'd been an accident. They got the information out of her before she was told the truth. Wasn't much good for anything after that."

"The husband?"

"Out on a job. We're tracking him down." Dawson paused. "The thing is, Robin . . . There's nothing here that makes any sense. The girl, her husband, they're as normal as bread and cheese. Mr. and Mrs. Ordinary."

"We'll see," Culley said. There was a sharpness in his voice.

"Think about it," Dawson said. His tone of voice meant, motiveless, senseless, just for its own sake. For fun.

Culley shook his head. "We'll see."

They drove back separately, but arrived within a few minutes of each other. Culley was scanning the messages on his desk when Dawson walked in. He closed the door and leaned against it— deferential for not coming all the way in, aggressive for denying Culley a way out.

"I'm the sergeant, you're the inspector. Rank has its privileges. Tell me what to think."

"What did you say to Protheroe?"

"That you were pursuing inquiries. He likes that kind of jargon. It makes him feel like a policeman."

Culley sifted the message slips. He said, "We have to be sure."

"Okay," Dawson agreed. "Just don't tell me that people killing people for no good reason is unheard of." As if it were part of the same conversation, the same challenge, he added, "You were seeing Helen, were you?"

Culley looked up at the stocky figure lodged against the door frame; Dawson was offering a tiny smile of encouragement.

"I wouldn't take this detection business too seriously, Mike. It's just a way of making a living."

Dawson shrugged. "You know best." Without pausing, he added, "How long has it been? Eighteen months? Two years? I thought you were beginning to enjoy the freelance life."

Culley gave him a look that said *Stop*.

"The triumph of hope over experience." Dawson shouldered himself off the door frame, but didn't step much farther into the room. He looked like someone allowing for a quick getaway. "It happens, of course. The question is: how often. If you gave yourself odds, what do you think you'd get? Better than ten-to-one?"

"I'm assuming your heart is in the right place," Culley told him. "Shut up."

"I had this terrific girl once. The trouble was that I was drinking a bit at the time, and she'd had a mother who'd had to dry out on a fairly regular basis, so I made her edgy. We saw each other—oh —more or less every night for a year. Then we lived together for a few months. She had this strawberry mark right here," Dawson pointed, "half-hidden. Very sexy. Anyway, the boozing was too much for her, and she left. I went apeshit. Begged, pleaded, threatened, promised to go on the wagon for life. So she decided to give me another try. It wasn't the same. I thought it would be, but it wasn't. Too much had gone . . . you know—between her leaving and coming back." Dawson's gaze went over Culley's head, as if he'd spotted something intriguing in one of the windows opposite. "Sally, her name was. Susan. Something like that."

Culley put his papers down on the desk with tremendous care. He said, "I don't want to talk about it."

"No, okay." Dawson smiled. "I just think it might be a bad move, you know? I mean, if she says no, you'll be fucked-over; if she says yes, and it turns out to be the wrong thing, you'll be fucked-over. There must have been reasons for the split-up in the first place. Who's to say they've gone away? It's like a time warp. You think you've advanced by several months, years, of experience and self-knowledge, suddenly you're back in the old routine: 'I did, you didn't, why do you always have to—' You know that stuff. I'm simply wondering whether people actually change that much. Shouldn't you call Protheroe?"

Culley lifted the phone. "You're a bastard, Dawson," he observed evenly.

Dawson nodded. "Never said otherwise."

Lionel Protheroe liked rank. He liked the concept, and he liked the fact that he'd got some. When Culley walked into the office and sat down, he was looking at the back of Protheroe's head, which was just above the back of Protheroe's chair.

"What have we got here, Culley?" He left a second's pause before swinging around to bring them face to face.

I don't believe you just did that, Culley thought. He said, "A shooting in Oxford Street." Carefully avoiding the "sir."

"A girl," Protheroe observed. "Anonymous and blameless."

"So far as we know."

"Please." Protheroe held up a hand. "What do you expect to find? She was a drug baron? Triad member? Lynchpin of organized crime?"

"We haven't looked yet. We don't know what we'll find, because we haven't—"

"Maybe it was a domestic. She burned the old man's toast. Bought the wrong brand of coffee. He staked out a rooftop in Oxford Street, bided his time, then arrived with a high-velocity rifle and blew a fist-sized hole in her back. No more decaf for me, you bitch." Culley waited. "Random. She was random. Ted Latimer's been on the phone. He thinks so, too."

Sir Edward Latimer, Chief Constable. He had the kind of rank that Protheroe really liked. "Well," Culley said, "he could be right."

"You don't think so." Protheroe had a habit of running a finger under his mustache so that the hairs lifted, bristling like a yard-broom; then he'd smooth it on the backstroke.

Culley looked away. "I'll know more when I've talked to some people. The husband. People at the place where she worked. Neighbors."

"Don't waste too much time," said Protheroe. "I think I know what we've got here." He paused. "What does Dawson think? He took the call, yes?" Culley nodded. "What does he think?"

"He thinks what you think."

"Sir," Protheroe said.

4

$\longrightarrow$

H ERE THEY WERE, leaving the house. First, Daddy laden with suitcases. Then Mummy carrying the cooler and a big straw bag that contained whatever might be needed for the journey.

Here they were, getting into the car: Mummy, Anthony, and Lynne; here they were arriving; and here they were on the beach. Fishing in rock pools with a net; digging for sand crabs; burying Daddy in the sand; having a picnic.

Here they were. Happy families.

Eric Ross sat in the dark and watched the video, his wife beside him on the sofa, the heads of the kids bobbing in front of the screen. He'd seen it before; they'd all seen it before; but they'd watch it from time to time—this one, or another one. This holiday or some other. When it finished, the kids made him run the beach sequence backward because it looked as if they were digging him up. While Anthony and Lynne were having their baths, Ross went out into the back garden. His neighbor was hoeing between some bean rows and they exchanged a few words. He circled the garden, his suburban demesne, sipping his drink, pausing to take the scent from some nicotiana.

A man walks into a filling station with a gun and walks out with the contents of the cash register. He goes home. He was looking forward to watching the game that night, but his girlfriend wants to go out for a meal. He records the game. They go to an Italian place in the neighborhood. She has the tagliatelli.

A hooker decides to call it a night. Enough's enough. The last trick took forever, goddammit. She tried all the things you do to make them come, but this son of a bitch held out. When she gets back, her husband fixes her a drink. She smiles at him. She says, "Listen, let's get laid."

34

A man shoots a girl dead in a London street. He takes care to make sure the gun is locked in the trunk of his car. Later, when the kids are asleep, he'll put it in a cupboard in the basement and snap the padlock home. He watches a home movie. He takes a turn around the garden.

It's just a job. Just business. If you saw them in the street, how would you know? If you sat opposite to them on a train, stood behind them in a movie line, met them at a party, how would you know?

The people at home, the people they come back to, never ask "How was your day?" Never, "How did it go?" That way, they can stay ignorant if they want to. Or they can pretend if they must.

Angie Ross never asked.

5

MIKE DAWSON WAS ONE of the people who didn't have anyone to go home to. He brought in a bottle of red wine, two hamburgers medium-to-rare, fries, and some completely inedible coleslaw. He dumped them on Culley's desk.

"What do we know?" Culley asked.

Dawson was stocky, built like a fighter, a flat, broad brow and a big smile. He hooked with his right, bringing his hamburger around for a bite. "A foot patrol got there first. All he saw was blood and panic. The girl . . . lived in Finchley. Married, as we know. They don't have any children. Building-to-building search —nothing. We interviewed people in the street—nothing. It's not surprising. Lots of little firms, lots of little offices, lots of people minding their own business, visitors in and out all day. Some people at their desks, others taking an early lunch. It's a nightmare."

35

"They found the husband?"

"An hour ago. Every bit as ordinary as she seemed to be. He's called Peter. His firm does contract work. Nothing shady. The doctor pumped a few ccs of Valium into the back of his hand, and he's still thumping his head against the wall, poor bastard."

"The girl's office?" It occurred to Culley that Dawson had a coy look about him. He'd said, "As she *seemed* to be."

"We took statements from her boss and the woman she shared an office with. Peggy . . ." Dawson searched for it. "Harrison. Nothing much there. Then someone looked through her desk. There was a locked drawer." Dawson took a bite of hamburger and chewed enthusiastically.

Culley watched him a moment, then said, "Don't fuck me about, Mike."

"Black leather miniskirt, garter belt, a pair of stockings, high-heeled shoes." Dawson swallowed, reached into his pocket, and took out a bankbook. He tossed it onto the desk. "And this."

Culley flipped through the receipt stubs. "Not the branch she and her husband use, I imagine."

"Not even the same bank. Look at the running total."

Culley looked. Then he went back to the first stub. "Over— what?—eight months or so." Dawson nodded, still eating. "So we've got a part-time whore."

"Hostessing," Dawson said, "topless waitress: something like that."

"We'll have to see the husband again," Culley observed. "He'll have to know about this."

"They hadn't been married two years," Dawson said.

"Do you suppose that makes any difference?"

"God," Dawson said, "some women are cows."

"I've met some who didn't have too high an opinion of you. *Jesus Christ.*" Culley peeled the bun back from his hamburger and peered at it. "This isn't dead."

Dawson smiled. "Bring it to forensic," he said. "Billy will check it out."

Billy Knowle was an elegant man. It was the first thing you noticed about him: carefully combed hair, polished shoes, a collar and tie beneath the white laboratory coat. Most of all, you noticed his fingers. They were long and slender, well cared-for. If you looked at the dapper appearance, you might think: a banker, perhaps a lawyer. If you looked at the hands: a musician, or a painter. When Culley and Dawson walked in, he was wedging the last third of a hamburger into his mouth and raising a beer can as he chewed.

Dawson looked at Culley. "He's making his own decisions," he said.

Knowle walked to a workbench and lifted some papers from it, glanced at them, then took the delayed swallow of beer.

"It was a .308. Probably a Lee Enfield, maybe a Parker Hale. I'm guessing. Powerful rifle, a .308. Very accurate. Muzzle velocity, two thousand, seven hundred feet per second. Effective range better than eight thousand feet. The bullet will travel four miles or more. I think your—" He broke off.

"Linda Bowman," said Culley.

"—was hit from four hundred feet or so. The autopsy will tell you more. It was a center shot, I'm told. She'd have been dead before she fell."

"So he's a marksman," Culley asked.

"Well, he only bothered to shoot once."

"What about the gun?"

"Custom-built, for sure. Something that'll break down. Easy to pack away. No one's going to wander around toting a bloody great gun case without causing suspicion. It's like having your car customized. You just need the basic weapon."

"And you think he's a good shot?"

"Oh, yeah . . . Looking at the reports. Took her right over the heart. Why?"

Dawson said, "We wondered if he might've missed. I mean, whether he was really going for someone else and the girl got in the way."

"She's not a likely candidate?" Knowle asked.

"Not really." Dawson paused. "She might have been whoring on the side."

Knowle looked at Culley. "That's something, isn't it?"

"I don't think so, Billy. When did you last hear of a ponce carrying a target rifle? If she'd been poaching, she might have got kicked or cut. Nothing like this."

"No connection at all?"

"Not so far," Dawson said. "I don't think there will be."

Again, Knowle looked at Culley. "That's a bit worrying, isn't it?"

"Perhaps." Culley sounded peevish.

Knowle shuffled through the reports again, but wasn't really reading them. "No," he said. "It was a peach of a shot. I'd say he really wanted her. Custom-built. Telescopic sight." He tossed the papers aside and took another slug of beer. "He can probably shoot the balls off a gnat."

From the bedroom window of Culley's apartment, you could see a bend in the river, a broad sweep followed by a stretch of water that was soon afterward obscured by buildings. He sat in the bow of the window, his knees drawn up, sipping a drink. Boats came and went, their lights shedding a yellow curtain that seemed to go fathoms deep, trailing and wafting like weed.

Culley was given to a betting system that relied on two boats drawing level on the crown of the bend. When this happened, the reflection of their lights would blend and drag against each other, then slowly separate. If it happened on a third time, or a seventh, or an eleventh, it brought luck. That was the theory.

After the separation, Culley had moved rapidly and self-indulgently, buying this apartment, overspending to give himself a view of the river. He'd bought low Rajastani tables, some bowls, African pots, and more kitchen equipment than he'd ever need. Most of the ideas came from magazines.

Helen had visited him a couple of months after the place was finished. She'd seemed neither amused nor impressed by what he'd done. He'd realized afterward, not without shame, that he had wanted her to be proud of him.

"I'll stay at the house until it's sold," she'd said. "If that's okay. Then find a place."

Straight to business. Culley had hoped that the two months of silence between them might have bred changes. He'd guessed that the worst thing to do was ask a question about that very possibility, so of course he'd asked it.

"Changes?" She'd smiled. "Now and then, we'd meet. Now and then, we'd screw. I'd get home from the gallery, the place would be empty. Maybe you'd arrive a couple of hours before I left the next morning; or I'd hear you undressing in the dark. All that will have changed—right?"

Culley had shrugged. "Do you want a beer?" He'd wanted a drink himself but, more than that, he hadn't wanted to hear the rest.

"Your other world," Helen said. "Your daytime, nighttime,

dawn, dusk, Saturday, Sunday, eating, sleeping world. Your territory. Your *patch*. Not the way ordinary people live. Not places that ordinary people see. Not people that ordinary people know. You said that to me once. I remember—"

Culley had left the room to fetch his beer. When he'd returned she'd simply gone back to the beginning of her sentence, like someone picking up stitches.

"I remember the look on your face when you said it. I remember your smile. You like it. There's a darkness you like." Helen had paused. "I should—"

Culley had taken on the remark for her. "You should have said all this before."

It had been a Sunday afternoon, about two-thirty, when they might have been ending a late lunch. As she'd made for the door, the phone had rung. Helen had paused, half-in, half-out of the room.

"You see?" she'd said.

6

UNDER OTHER CIRCUMSTANCES, Peggy Harrison would have felt uneasy. The nick; an interview room; a copper asking her questions; a policewoman sitting silently in one corner, making notes but also there to chaperone . . . who? Herself? This guy Dawson? Both.

Peggy came from a south London family whose male members had been used to minor brushes with the law. Peggy had grown up laughing at coppers, and fearing them. Right now, though, she was too sad and bewildered to pay much attention to where she was.

Dawson was asking about Charles Rich. "Was he much of a bother to you, then?"

Peggy was dabbing a cigarette at her lips, taking tiny plumes of smoke back into her lungs in a series of fast, identical gasps. "Not really. He had his bits on the side, you know, but not at work. It was just dirty talk—double meanings and such. He used to do a bit of groping in the packing room, or pat my bum occasionally, but he'd never have gone for an affair. Too much of a bloody snob."

"How many?" Dawson asked. "Bits on the side."

"There was a woman called Joanna, used to phone. She was in London. I don't know where. Then there was some toffee-nosed cow who used to call him from the country. Claire." Peggy gave her version of a county accent. "Joanna and Claire." She laughed. "He goes hunting, you know? Comes in on a Monday, about lunchtime, with a lot of guff about the number of times he fell off. Pity he doesn't break his bloody neck."

"You don't like him," Dawson suggested.

Peggy shrugged. "It's a job. They're not that easy to come by."

"He never had a go at Linda?"

"I expect he told her she'd got nice tits, or something. Wouldn't have impressed Linda."

"She didn't like him either."

"He's a creep."

Dawson had been standing in a corner of the room, propped into the angle, his arms folded. Now he crossed the room and sat down opposite Peggy. Between them was a plain, badly scabbed pine table. Peggy's face was narrow, oddly birdlike. As Dawson sat, she looked sideways, away from him, and lowered her head slightly. For a moment, she looked as if she might mantle her features with a wing.

"What about it, Peggy?" Dawson waited a moment, then: "The stuff in her desk drawer."

"I don't know." Dawson tried to read the tremble in her voice. "I don't know what it was for."

"Miniskirt, garter belt, sexy stockings . . ."

Peggy shook her head. She was crying, biting her lip in an attempt to limit the tears.

Dawson tried again. "There's got to be a reason, hasn't there?" He offered her a lead—something she'd said earlier. "Linda used to stay late some nights; after you'd left the office."

"She used to go to night school." Dawson's silence was a provocation. Angrily, Peggy added, "To improve her typing speed." She took another cigarette and suffered Dawson to light it for her. Eventually, she said, "I don't . . . I can't work it out," dabbing the cigarette against her lips. "*How* much was in the bankbook?"

Dawson told her. He decided it was time to push. "What would it have been? Whoring?"

"No."

"Using the office telephone, giving that number, maybe—"

"No."

"—call after six, make some dates—what? Two or three a night before she had to get back to—"

"*No*." Peggy yelled it. She was staring at Dawson, hating him, wondering if he could be right.

"What then?" His voice was gentle, as if truth stood at the doorway and had to be coaxed over the threshold. "The clothes—why were they there?"

Peggy nodded. It was a gesture that meant, Yes, they were there, weren't they? Those things were actually there. As if all that had gone before, all they'd said, had disputed it. As if the contents of Linda's locked drawer might have been argued away. She was saying, *I believe they were there*. She wasn't saying, *And I know why*. She didn't. Dawson could see that.

And now she'd made that admission, Peggy could ask questions of her own. Her relationship with Dawson, for that moment, had become close and collusive. Because neither of them knew the answers, she could ask the very questions that Dawson had taxed her with a moment before.

"Why? What for? They were very happy. We all went on holiday last year. The four of us. They hadn't long been married. She couldn't . . . I mean, Pete was all over her, bringing her drinks, holding hands, you know; same with her. Why would she?"

The recollection brought her to a question she hadn't thought of before; a question of her own. She looked at Dawson sharply, her eyes bright with shock because she already knew the answer.

"He'll have to know, will he? Pete?"

Dawson held her look but didn't speak.

"Oh, Christ," she said, and turned her face away.

Eric Ross put his foot flat against the base of the door by the hinge and pushed. The door was locked, but he knew it would give on the opposite side. He'd spent a short while, three days before, pulling the rusty screws on the hinges, then pushing them back into the rotten cavities to make things look secure. Over compensating, probably, but why narrow the odds? The wood grated against fragments of rubble. He eased it back to allow enough space to go in at the crouch, then pushed it back once he was inside.

The building hadn't been used for years. There was a smell of rot and, underneath that, something acidic—the odor of things that had gone beyond the bad.

He climbed from level to level. More than half the glass in the steel frames had been broken. The concrete floors were pitted where machines had been unbolted. On one landing was a small, glass office, bare except for some steel bookshelves and a calendar girl who smiled and pointed her breasts at him while cupping the palm of one hand coyly between her legs. You can have this, but you can't have that.

Three levels farther and he stopped. The window was a tall arch, the frame corroded by rust. Only the glass under the uppermost section was left. He put down his case and looked out.

Sixty feet below and thirty feet beyond were four sets of tracks, brown with disuse, sprouts of coarse grass growing between the ties. Then some shunting tracks and an engine shed. Then the main-line station. Travelers were striding up and down platforms and boarding trains. The concourse was thick with people buying tickets, buying newspapers, scanning the arrival and departure boards, drinking outside the cafeteria or the pub, waiting to leave, waiting for someone to arrive.

They all had histories. They all had people who knew them. They were all at just this moment in their lives. Ross didn't think these thoughts. He looked at them as if he were shopping.

The concourse only held his attention for a moment. He stooped and assembled the gun, rapidly, not really having to concentrate on the task, then glanced at his watch. People were hurrying along the platform nearest to him, glancing into carriages to find those that were least crowded.

Perfect timing.

A man carrying a black briefcase was trotting across the concourse toward the barrier; he showed a season ticket as he went through to the train.

Ross hefted the gun and slid the barrel partway through the third vertical window space. There was a sill to brace his elbow. He tracked the platform.

A young man with an instrument case appeared in the scope. Ross held him until he passed beyond a comfortable angle of fire. He was looking for a seat in the foremost carriage.

A girl walked through the cross hairs, then came back. She was wearing a suit. Her hair was caught up in a plait and she had an expensive satchel slung over her shoulder. Ross swung the gun away from her. He'd seen the reports of Linda Bowman's death and noticed the nearness of her name to his daughter's. It disturbed him. He didn't like the color of luck in it.

The man with the black briefcase appeared in a window seat pretty much halfway down the train. He settled himself in his seat, then turned his face to the view of tall derelict buildings on the station's southern side. In the same moment, the train began to move.

"She didn't know."

Culley was about to make a call. He put the phone down when Dawson walked in. "What?"

"I've just been with the other secretary. Peggy Harrison. She didn't know."

"You don't surprise me." Culley sighed. "We'll have to see the husband again."

"We?"

"One of us."

Dawson lodged on a corner of Culley's desk. Culley said, "I was about to make a phone call."

"Go ahead." Dawson nudged the phone. At the same time, he said, "It's nothing, is it? You said so yourself. If she'd been on someone else's patch, some other tom, she might have got roughed up. Not this. Whatever use she found for the naughty underwear, it can't have been serious enough to make someone shoot her tit off in the middle of Oxford Street."

"We still need to know."

"Oh, sure. I think her old man'll go through a lot of grief for nothing, though." Dawson shook his head. "They make clowns of us, don't they?" He nudged the phone again. "Are you going to make that call?" When Culley didn't respond, Dawson reached out; the phone rang before he could get to it.

Culley took the call. It was plain that the voice on the line was giving information without expecting any in return. Culley simply offered a string of Yes, *yes, okay, yes,* and *when?* It took about sixty seconds. He stood up, pulling his jacket from the back of the chair. He said, "We've got another one." His voice was low, almost as though he were talking to himself.

Mike Dawson could have said, "I told you so." He didn't. He said, "Oh, Christ, no." Because all the time, despite what he thought, despite what he knew he knew, Dawson had hoped he might be wrong.

The carriage was a mess. Culley sat down by the window and looked toward the disused workshops. The bullet hole in the glass was very close to his face. It radiated a spider's web, mosaic spangles, with longer lines of fracture reaching for the furthest corners. He could hear Dawson's voice climbing in volume.

"I want the station cleared. Completely." Another voice, less audible, said something. Then Dawson again: "I don't give a flying fuck. Clear it." He appeared at the carriage door and paused a moment.

"It's all shit and feathers in here, isn't it?" He sat down and followed the direction of Culley's gaze. "Up there?"

"Must have been." Culley looked sideways along the bench seat to where it was dark and glutinous with blood. The stain had a dull sheen on it, like gelatin.

"We've got it cordoned," Dawson told him. "No one's getting in. The passengers are being bottlenecked and questioned as they leave. Nod and a wink stuff; I don't suppose we'll learn much."

"What about the guy they stretchered out?"

"Not good. Heart attack, apparently. Hardly surprising. One minute you're about to tackle the crossword, the next you've got a lap full of someone else's brains." He paused. "What do you think?"

Culley had gone back to looking out of the window. "He could have had someone on the concourse. He could have had someone on the platform. But he picked someone who was sitting on a train; and waited until the train began to move."

"It gives him more time," Dawson offered.

"Yes."

"Because someone in the concourse, someone on a platform—that's obvious right away. With his method—the people in the carriage have to stop panicking, pull the stop cord, wait for someone to come. Then the train has to be backed up into the station."

"Yes."

44

Dawson tried to read Culley's expression. "That doesn't mean
. . . You're not still thinking there was a choice here? That he
wanted this guy in particular?"

"I'm not, no. I'm saying that he understands how to be cautious.
There's no rashness about what he's doing."

Dawson grimaced. "Apart from the rashness involved in shooting people at random."

"Well . . . You know how it is. Some of them walk down a main
street looking like extras from the A-Team and shoot anything that
comes into view. Others don't. This guy's anxious not to be
caught."

"Which tells us what?" Dawson asked, then answered his own
question. "That he's not an obvious lunatic: doesn't gibber in public; doesn't act the part.

"He plans things."

"He's foxy."

Culley nodded. "He wants it to last."

"You think that's it?" Helen asked.

Culley had been running the notion for a few hours and it still
seemed right. "Yes," he said, "I think that *has* to be it."

Helen held up a cellophane package containing two steaks.
"This, baked potato, green salad, or send out for pizza, or a bowl
of pasta at the trattoria two doors down."

"That," Culley told her.

She stripped the wrapping from the steaks and went into the
kitchen—a journey that removed her no more than five paces.
Her flat was fashionably central; the compromise was that the
largest of its three rooms was small and the smallest was a cubicle.
She said, "Which means there'll be more."

More. More "incidents." It might seem coy to some, that euphe-
mism. Culley knew better. It was aggressive. It was police language
for "ours," "not your business," "you don't need to know." More
incidents, more problems. More victims, but that went without
saying. People died prematurely all the time—fires, car crashes,
falls from high places. That they died didn't matter much. *How*
they died, that was the issue. He said, "Yes. I would think there
are bound to be."

"Why?"

"Will there be—?"

"No. Why does he . . . What makes them do it?"

"What makes them—?"

"Well, he doesn't know, I mean, if Mike Dawson's right, if Protheroe's right, this guy doesn't know the people. He didn't know the girl in Oxford Street, he didn't know the man on the train." She was standing at the sink, working with her back to him. Her shoulders rose in a shrug. "What is it? Power? Excitement?"

"Shall I make the salad?" Culley asked.

"I'd like to say yes. It would mean the kitchen was big enough for two. Don't worry."

"Who knows?" he said. "You'd have to ask him. I suspect it's different in each case."

"But there's some sort of pattern, isn't there. People who kill for no reason must have something in common."

"Well, that's the point. It's not for no reason. It's for a reason that no one else would understand. The pattern is likely to be that there's no pattern." He recalled having said just the same thing to Protheroe a couple of hours before.

As if she'd read his mind, Helen asked, "What's Protheroe doing?"

"Protheroe," he said, "doesn't know which end is up. He's managed to get himself a slot on the late news bulletin; an attempt to counteract what the papers will be saying."

"Maniac killer slays two," Helen offered.

"Something like that. They'll love it."

Helen coordinated the meal with three swift, seamless movements. Potatoes into the microwave, steaks under the grill, salad spinner to "on." "How do you find him," she asked, "if there's no pattern?"

"That's why it's frightening. Criminals are a bit like a race—a nation. They have a language, recognizable characteristics. We know where to look for them. Largely speaking, we know who they are. If someone turns over a wages van on my patch, I can put it down to one of three or four firms. With this . . . ." Culley gestured toward the window. "It's anyone. Anyone out there."

"What will you do?"

"Fuck knows." He walked over to a small sideboard and took out a bottle of wine, then found a corkscrew in the left hand drawer, where they'd always kept it. The light had just begun to fail. He uncorked the wine without paying attention to the task, staring out of the window at the darkening sky and the growing vibrancy of neon script. *All nude . . . girls . . . live.* The evening was getting into its stride. Streetlife was picking up. People strolling, hailing taxis, hesitating outside restaurants; people heading for theaters, hurrying to keep a date, slipping into one of the strip clubs.

Anyone. Anyone out there.

He took the wine to the table as Helen came in with the food. When he cut the steak, a tiny seepage of pink ran onto the plate.

"Just the way I like it." As if she might have forgotten. It wasn't a very good joke, but it allowed her to know what he was going to say. "If you sold this, and I sold mine, we'd have enough for a kitchen we could both use."

"Don't push," she said. Then, "What *will* you do?"

Culley sighed. "There won't be a victim pattern—if it continues . . ."

"Will it?"

"Probably. I expect so. But there'll be a method. There already is, to some extent. It's *his* method. The way people do things—you know—put the milk in first or last; sleep on the left or the right; use a comb or a hairbrush." He paused. "I have to get to know him."

"Domestic details."

"Yes, well, we're domestic creatures, really; most of us."

"Don't push," she said.

A running tide made the river look heavy and sleek. Half-light and a mackerel sky turned the surface a matt silver, dull, as if some vast caldron had been tilted to release a molten flow that was setting as it cooled.

Eric Ross stood on the walkway of the bridge and looked over the rail while the traffic at his back inched past. Directly below, a tangle of twigs had lodged against the center stanchion; it split the water's skin, but gave no sense of movement; the ripple either side appeared sculpted and still.

He was waiting for the light to go. On one bank, there were lights and voices; people were gathering at a riverside pub, some of them making use of the trestle tables and benches on the paved area close to the water. He was waiting for business to pick up.

It was warm, and already a few drinkers had drifted out to the paved area, but there were seats for all of them, at present; no one was standing up.

"I'll be late," he'd said to Angie.

"What time?"

"I'm not sure," he'd said. "It's difficult to tell."

People sitting and chatting at the tables, nursing their drinks, some on their own, probably expecting friends to show up. He was waiting for the time to be right.

This one was strange. Jobs varied, of course—degrees of difficulty, degrees of risk. Most often, he was concerned to do his work efficiently. Efficient meant safe. From time to time, he'd worked abroad. A week was usually long enough to size things up and find a way, but he had never liked the forced separation from Angie and the kids. Now he felt oddly estranged from them, from the life he shared with them.

He gazed steadily at the snag of twigs and the sinuous shape it gathered from the water, though he'd stopped seeing it long before. It would only have caught his eye if he'd looked away. This one was different. He felt like an actor who had walked on stage with no script and no direction, save "Do as you please." He could be anyone: a soldier trapped behind enemy lines; a poacher; a lethal mathematician with a plan. He could invent a purpose for himself, or simply make the whole business a spectacular whim. He could amble through his task with a slow smile, or become a man driven by some fierce purpose. God's Huntsman. The Demon of the Stairs.

But he needed time on his own to learn the role, and he needed a stage on which to play the part. Not just the moments of high drama, but all of it—the times of planning, the times of preparation, the times when he was doing nothing in particular; he needed to be in character to make it real. Whoever that character was, or might become.

The man with a sense of humor and a gun. The final critic. The Avenging Angel.

He could be anyone.

The last of the light gleamed on the water and was gone. Ross pushed himself away from the rail, turned his back on the neon and the people outside the pub, and began to stroll toward the dark, tree-lined bank on the opposite side, his hands in his pockets, his head hung slightly as if in thought.

Once off the bridge, he walked half a mile to a quiet side street where his car was parked. He took the gun case out of the trunk and walked back to the south side of the bridge. He didn't hurry.

The tall trees on both sides of the towpath filtered the slight breeze, hissing like foam in a weir. They blotted the glow from the city's lights, leaving the space between—the path Ross walked along—utterly dark. He seemed to be moving through a tunnel hung with thick, black flock.

Less than two minutes and he was opposite the pub. He stepped off the path, pushing between scrub trees and undergrowth, until he reached the water's edge. He could hear the voices of the people at the trestle tables: a hum, sometimes a voice lifting and coming clear, now and then a shout of laughter.

The night scope showed him everything. The upper windows of the pub and the tops of people's heads as they walked by and a number of drinkers standing on the flights of stone steps built into the river wall where rowers would launch their skiffs. Some were sitting on the wall itself.

The girl would have been about twenty; the boy a couple of years older, perhaps. They were standing quite close to one another; that's why he chose them. They came within the circumference of the scope, their heads lying along the horizontal hair. Both blond. They could have been brother and sister, except you could tell from the way their bodies balanced that they weren't; from the way they turned their heads from time to time, not always looking at one another when they spoke. Sometimes, when he leaned forward slightly, her head would sway away, just a touch, to draw him on, or gently fend him off; it amounted to the same thing. Her glass stood on the wall. Now and then, she would reach for it, sip, then set it down in the same place. He must have wondered, each time, whether she was about to touch his arm, briefly, pretending that the gesture was for emphasis. She must have wondered, each time, whether he would turn, only fractionally, to intercept the gesture.

They had met that evening, introduced by friends who were sitting below them on the steps, and already they liked one another a lot. They had been standing at the bar getting their drinks when the friends had said, "This is—" and he thought he'd heard "Susie." In fact, her name was Lucy. He'd already called her Susie half a dozen times, and she was planning to set him straight about that.

Ross breathed in, exhaled steadily, and shot her on the out-breath. She had been reaching for her drink and really thought that this time she might rest her hand on his forearm a second before collecting her glass. He thought she might, too. Then she was gone, as if some vast, unseen hand had plucked her away.

The boy had time to be aware of her disappearance; he almost had time to register her absence and to wonder what in God's name could have— And then he was dead.

First her body, then his, coming off the uppermost step like divers racing one another for the water, except that they turned the wrong way. The girl arched onto a table, smashing glasses, spilling beer, going the table's length and off the end. She bowled over twice on the paved area, a spray of blood lifting and turning with her, going everywhere like the jet from a dropped hosepipe.

The boy hit the edge of the table and dropped onto the knees of three people sharing a bench.

A young woman got to her feet and looked down at the white shirt she was wearing; licks of red ran up it to the shoulder; her face was stippled with red, as if a painter had flicked his brush.

A man pushed away from the head that lay in his lap; a gobbet of matter, pink and gray, slipped to his thigh, then dropped onto his shoe.

No one knew what had happened. And then they did.

As Culley got into bed, Helen said, "I don't want this to become a habit." It was one of their jokes from back then, but she'd drunk the better part of a bottle of wine and it seemed funnier, now; entirely appropriate.

He drew tracks up and down her body with his fingertips, missing, touching, missing, and she blushed on her throat and her collarbones. She felt him knock her thigh.

There was a white glare in the corner of her vision. Without obstructing him, without turning away, she lifted the bedside table lamp and lowered it to the floor. His lips moved in little swoops, shoulder to breast, breast to haunch, and he ducked and licked her open.

She sighed. "Who knows you're here?"

"No one," he told her. Then, "Maybe Mike."

Helen reached out again, careful not to disturb him, and took the phone off the hook.

Identical doors, identical pediments; a dip in the curb, asphalt, a garage door. Identical French windows, a patio, a lawn. Flower beds and a fence, topped off with trellis. Eric Ross drove down the street to his home.

Angie was watching TV. He said, "Any good?"

"No." She shook her head, but continued to watch because she already knew more than half the story.

Ross went into the kitchen and cut himself some bread and cheese. He took a beer out of the fridge and went back to join Angie. They sat together in silence for ten minutes or so while Angie saw the program out. Ross cleared his plate, drank the beer, and fetched another. He said, "I might have to go away for a bit. Short trip."

Angie nodded. "Short?"

He smiled. "Short."

She didn't ask. Later, he watched her as she went from closet to dressing table, as she stepped out of her skirt, as she wiped her face with cream and a tissue. She was less slender now; a thickening at the waist and broader hips. Her breasts had settled on the ribcage. Twelve years.

Never before had he wanted to be away. He did the job, he took the money, and he came back with no thought in his mind other than the pleasure that returning afforded him.

Somewhere to be. Somewhere to grow into the role. It couldn't be here. At home, everyone knows who you are.

A place to rehearse in. A place where he could become anyone.

7

THERE WERE THREE MEN in the room: Protheroe, Sir Edward Latimer, and the minister.

The minister had just said, "I want it stopped." Latimer and Protheroe were thinking of ways to come to terms with that notion.

Eventually, Latimer said, "You can see how difficult it is, Minister. We have people who advise; people who are specialists in this sort of thing. But in the end . . . ."

Protheroe said, "A profile. We have to look for a pattern of some kind. Victims, places, a time of day, perhaps. So far . . . ."

The minister nodded. "I see the difficulties," he said. "I want it stopped."

Dawson caught the policewoman's eye. She looked away immediately, her face impassive, and studied a cheap, framed print that hung above the fireplace. She could have named, without pausing, every item in the room; every piece of furniture, ornament, utensil. She knew all the titles of the videos racked alongside the TV. She knew how the rose pattern on the curtains repeated, and she knew the faces in the family snapshots.

Pete Bowman looked at the flimsy clutter that Dawson had dropped onto the table. "They're not Linda's," he said.

His hand went out, retreated, went out again, and gathered one of the stockings, tuck by tuck, until it slithered out of the pile. A tiny run near the toe had been stopped with nail varnish.

"Not Linda's," he said. He looked toward the policewoman, who wouldn't accept his gaze, then at Dawson. "Are they?"

"Yes," Dawson told him.

"Not hers," said Bowman.

The policewoman counted the roses, bottom to top.

"Not Linda's," Bowman said. "Not Linda's, not Linda's, not Linda's."

The bar had once been an honest spit and sawdust pub. Now it was decked out with ferns and cane chairs and brass fans. On the walls were photographs salvaged from God knows where, in which sahibs and memsahibs took tea while turbaned servants stood at attention in the overfurnished drawing rooms.

Culley looked around, saw Sandra Ellis at once. He raised a hand, then pointed at the bar. She mouthed the word "gin."

He collected a beer for himself and took the drinks to her table.

"Are you sure you don't want some tonic with that?"

She smiled. "Spoils the taste of the gin." She looked around. "I remember this place. What in God's name have they done to it?"

"There's a cocktail list on the bar," Culley told her. "Sundowners, planter's punch. Sad tatters of the British raj."

"English raj," said Sandra. The lilt of her Edinburgh accent seemed stronger for a moment. She sipped her gin. "You think she might have been freelance?"

"Well, it occurred to me, obviously."

"What did you find, exactly?"

Culley shrugged. "Sexy underwear, short skirt, tarty stockings . . ."

"Locked away in her desk."

"Yes."

"She's a secretary."

"Endless check lists and advice notes on a word processor."

"Secret software under lock and key."

Culley grinned. "What do you think?"

"It's possible. Not likely, though." Sandra grimaced. "Just about everyone is being run these days. The ponces are too well organized. Even the away-day girls get netted eventually. Silly wee cows. It's difficult to go it alone. You need capital, for one thing; unless you're going to hang out at main-line stations and do it in the punter's car. She could have been using phone boxes, I suppose—writing her number up and waiting for a call. Did she live in the suburbs?"

"Why?" Culley asked.

"There are some houses outside central London—mostly part-timers; housewives earning some pocket money and whiling away a dull afternoon. They're usually run by some respectable middle-aged lady—"

"With a Morningside accent," Culley suggested.

Sandra gave him a level look. She seemed amused. "I don't need to go into management with a bevy of wee slags, Robin. I may be forty, but it would still cost you a week's pay to see me step out of my drawers."

"In that case," Culley told her, "you can buy the next round." He shook his head. "I don't see it—the suburban whorehouse. No time, really; she was at work all day."

"Stripping," Sandra suggested, "or given the bits and pieces you found, a massage parlor would be more likely. What are you looking for?"

"Nothing. Anything. God knows."

"It's a crazy—isn't that right? The TV and the newspapers have got it that way."

"I've read the newspapers," Culley said. " 'Mad jackal.' Very inventive." He shrugged. "I don't know. If she'd been Miss Clean . . . But she had something to hide. It's a lead. And leads are for coppers to follow; it's the way of the world."

"And the guy on the train?" Sandra asked. "The kids at the riverside pub?"

"Sure. I know. I'm wasting my time. It's a lunatic with a map, a pin, and a gun. But something to go on is better than nothing to go on, so I'm looking at what I've got."

"Which isn't much. If she was a stripper, she could have been any man's dirty story. Massage parlor? Well, the girls work in shifts; the traffic's pretty heavy."

"Where do I start?"

"Ask the girls," said Sandra. "Ask the other girls. And lots of luck." She swallowed her drink and stood up.

They left the bar together. Sandra walked to the edge of the curb.

"Can I give you a lift?" Culley asked.

Sandra smiled. She started to walk toward the yellow light of an approaching taxi. "I've got a reputation to maintain."

She was already a few paces ahead of Culley, staring the cab down, her hand raised. He said, "Thanks, Sandy."

Without turning, she said, "Auld lang syne."

8

THE DESERT SANG in the heat, white rocks, baked earth, the untouchable canyon walls, releasing a note too soft for the ear to hear unless you found a different way of listening. In the middle distance, two quarter horses were picking their way between scrub and clumps of cholla. A Harris hawk turned in a thermal, then canted and slipped along the dry duct of the wind.

Nina Kemp's room was cool. White light banged at the windows. The slat blinds were tilted to turn away all but the merest glow and the whisper of air-conditioning sounded like an echo reaching a cave mouth from far back in the cave.

Nina sat cross-legged on the floor. Directly in front of her was a satchel. Across the fringed flap, a string of woven figures stood hand in hand—part of the endless chain of the "friendship design." Tourists bought the satchels and never used them.

The blinds admitted six thin strips of sunlight, clean and hard as tungsten. There was enough light. She didn't want any more light than this. She sat near the mouth of the cave, just back from the bars of light, as if that was as close as she would ever get to the world. She opened the satchel and took out a square linen napkin, which she spread out on the floor. Next she took out a roll of muslin bandage, a bottle of antiseptic fluid, and a hand mirror. She put the bandage on the floor, just beyond the edge of the napkin, and propped the mirror up against a small vanity box set on the floor for just that purpose.

She unfastened the sleeve buttons of her shirt, then two at the neck, and drew it over her head. Her naked torso was pale in the half-dark.

The last object in the satchel was a straight-edged razor. Nina laid it across her hand, from Mount of Venus to fingertip, the tortoiseshell smooth and bowed, then drew the blade until it dog-legged back over her knuckles.

Bad blood between them. Blood relative. Blood feud. Always the notion of something inescapable. *It's in the blood. Of the same blood.* It goes to your heart. *Blood wedding.* It flushes your cheek. It draws a thread across your eye.

She held her left arm straight, the underside uppermost. Her breath was shallow, her gaze fixed on the place. She had left it alone for weeks and everything was clear there, though her right arm was a web of thin scars waiting to heal.

She pulled the blade across, not pressing, giving it no more than its own weight. Her stomach muscles tensed a little, then relaxed as she schooled herself to the pain.

Blood beads appeared as if she had sweated them.

She made another cut, tilting the razor slightly, and the skin parted.

Three more, and then she put the razor down. She watched it

well and trickle either side and down to her wrist. She spread her fingers, making conduits between them. A rivulet from the elbow, a delta over her palm.

Two or three slow drops plashed onto the stiff linen of the napkin, sudden blooms; then more; then a rapid patter like the first rush of raindrops before a storm.

Ira Sanchez lifted his right hand a fraction and let his pony feel the bit. When it stopped, he turned in the saddle and looked back.

Hugo Kemp was watching the Harris hawk. It had put up a rabbit and was cruising behind the creature, feinting at it from time to time, but making no effort to strike. Kemp knew what was going to happen. Each time the rabbit swerved, the hawk would dart in to correct the creature's line, pushing it toward a tall saguaro some eighty yards away. It got into some brush and the hawk made a couple of rapid passes, flushing its prey, then swooped again to put it back on course. Another thirty yards, and another hawk came off the saguaro and flew straight at the rabbit, yellow legs stretched, talons out. The impact raised a small pillar of dust. The second bird stood on the kill, wings spread, as the first came down to feed.

Kemp neck-reined his horse, bringing it around, and trotted up the slight slope to where Ira was waiting.

"Did you see that?" Ira nodded. "The perfect ambush. That tactic's been in use a million years."

"I know," said Ira. "Apache used to take out a whole column that way." Ira was half Pima Indian, named for the tribesman who hoisted the flag on Iwo Jima. His father had been Mexican. When he was a child, Ira's mother used to tell him about his father. She said he was a nice guy and always smiled when she spoke of him.

The two men watched the hawks feasting on the rabbit carcass. Ira smiled. "Works for General Motors, too," he said, and touched his horse with a heel.

Henry Glinwood was standing on the terrace as they rode in. He walked toward them, looking only at Kemp, the afternoon sun a double image on the lenses of his dark glasses. Kemp swung down, throwing the reins to Ira.

"It's started," Glinwood told him.

As they approached the house, a woman came out with a cold beer on a tray. Kemp took it without seeing her.

"How much time do we have?" he asked.

"Ten days . . . two weeks."

"Enough?"

"Oh, yes. We can hold things off till then."

"We've expressed an interest?"

"Of course. Tentatively. I sounded curious; they made a note or two. Nothing heavy."

"The response?"

"Well . . ." Glinwood pursed his lips. "We're not first choice; you know that."

"We will be." They entered the house. "Ten days," said Kemp. "Not two weeks. Ten days."

Nina wiped her arm with antiseptic, then bound it with the bandage and lay on her bed.

She felt light. Not from the blood loss; it wasn't enough for that. From the pain; from the ritual. For a short while, now, she could feel less soiled inside. Less black. She could hate herself less. Some of the badness had leached out with the blood. Emptier was better.

The feeling of faintness would sustain her for a while. It was like living on the edge of sleep and not knowing whether the dream was real, reality a dream, or each a part of the other.

She half-closed her eyes, languorous, slightly flushed, as if she'd just had sex. The partly shaded windows culled the light, admitting a nacreous glow, the color of sun-blindness.

She drifted. If someone had entered the room now, while she rested there unable to care, he would have lain beside her, stroking her breasts as he might have stroked the hair of a child, and loosened the waistband of her pants, and drawn them down as he might undress a child, stroking her, easing her legs, his face appearing above her, the pearly glow from the windows making a halo of his hair.

Nina. She heard his whisper; a voice from an old dream. *Nina.*

9

CULLEY HAD A TREMENDOUS URGE to call Edward Latimer Sir-Sir, once for his knighthood and once for his rank. Protheroe had laid on biscuits with the tea, as if he were a housewife out to impress. No one had touched them.

"C-11 is on alert," said Culley, "though they won't be much use unless we find the guy."

"What else?" asked Latimer.

"I've been given extra people—for the paperwork and screening, mostly. Dozens of witnesses to be interviewed, house-to-house to be done; we're broadcasting appeals, though I don't hold out much hope."

"What else?"

"We've covered all the possible vantage points in Oxford Street and found nothing. We've sifted everything, top to bottom, in the only two buildings he could have shot from at the station. Nothing —so I've told them to look again; I wouldn't think it'll make any difference, though. We've quartered the riverbank over a two-hundred-yard stretch—a string-and-peg grid—and done a walk-through a dozen times or more a hundred yards either side of that. We've had divers in the river. Pretty much of a forlorn hope, but we did it anyway. We'll take another look at low tide today; we're having a dry spell, so the river will recede a good fifty yards from either bank. We've called in favors from every grass in the manor. Where they weren't helpful, we've threatened. No one knows a thing. If the popular theories are correct, and this guy's barking mad, then none of that is any surprise. He wouldn't be on the party list of any of the local firms."

Protheroe took a breath and raised a finger—about to make a point. "Is there anything else you need?" Latimer asked.

"Luck," Culley told him.

"How badly?"

"Badly enough. You know how it goes. Murders are generally domestic, linked to other crime, or it's one lot of villains tearing into another lot. Domestic is easy. You know who it is and ninety percent of the time, you know where to find him. Crime-related: well, if you solve the crime, you catch the killer. Local warfare usually sorts itself out. As often as not, we're given a sacrificial lamb. But someone we can't get close to, killing just anyone for no discernible motive . . . It's next to impossible."

"Is there nothing at all?" As he asked the question, Latimer shook his head, almost as if anticipating the reply.

"Well, there's little enough MO," Culley observed. "He shoots from cover with what we think is a Parker Hale. He doesn't miss. Thus far, we've got four shots and four dead people. That aside, the only consistent thing is the lack of consistency. Different locations, different times of day, no reason anyone can think of behind the selection of targets. Of course, it might be that there is a pattern that simply hasn't emerged yet. I mean, that there's not enough of it to view."

"The girl," Latimer said.

"That's nothing," Protheroe said. "That's—"

"What have you got so far?" asked Latimer.

Culley shrugged. "A bit of freelance whoring, perhaps, or something a lot like that. Mike Dawson is touring Soho with her picture."

"Not much."

"It's all there is."

Protheroe found a way in. "Not connected."

"It's all there is," Culley said.

Latimer had made a few notes. He tapped his teeth with his pen, looking away from the other two men.

Protheroe said, "I'm taking a personal—"

"Somehow, it's got to stop." Latimer capped his pen, as if to signal that he wouldn't hear more. "Already it's gone too far. I know what you're going to say. In theory, it could go on forever, because there's no method for ending it, for finding this man. But somehow, it's got to stop. I've spent a good deal of the last twenty-four hours listening to the Home Secretary and the Prime Minister. I don't suppose that comes as any surprise to you. They're not stupid. They see the problem. But we can't . . ." Latimer broke off, as if seeking a better means of expression; something less petulant. He failed. "We can't have someone shooting citizens at will, no motive, no reason, no way of catching him. People are frightened. Television and the papers aren't helping matters much, and we're doing something about that, but the fact remains that anyone could be a victim and everyone knows it." He paused. A thought had struck him. "Where did he get the gun?"

Culley shook his head. "We've tried that. All gun clubs; all gun club members. That's Greater London, of course. We're going farther afield. It doesn't look good so far. No surprise, really. Our forensic guy suggested that it would be custom-built. I checked that with C-11 and they thought the same. Probably imported. Unless it was bought especially for the job—bought recently, that is—we don't expect to find its origin."

"Anything you need," Latimer assured him. "Anything."

"I've told—" Protheroe began.

"I want you to report directly to me. File your reports in the normal way, but copy me at all times. If there are corners you need to cut, warrants issued immediately, official-secrets act waived, whatever, talk to me."

"Thanks," Culley said. He got up. "I can't think what it might be, but if I find it, I'll ask."

"Culley." Latimer stopped him at the door.

"Yes?"

"You're supposed to call me sir."

In the first club, there were three girls backstage and one out front, stripping. Dawson had waved his ID at the doorman; as he'd walked through into the semidarkness, he'd heard the guy spit.

The manager took him to a dressing room the size of a phone booth, opened the door, and pushed in. One of the girls was sitting on a low stool, naked, her left leg lifted and thrust out so that the ankle rested on her right knee. She was paring her nails. Another was holding one of her breasts and peering down at it as she fixed a red rhinestone pastie. The third was about to go on and was more or less fully clothed. They looked at Dawson with expressions of amused curiosity. He caught sight of himself in the dressing-table mirror and took a moment to recover.

None of them knew Linda Bowman. The manager took Dawson along a corridor that smelled of perfume and mildew and waited with him, close to the wings and in sight of the stage. The girl was almost done. She rolled her crotch along a feather boa, humped the air a few times, turned, flicked out of her G-string, showed them her ass, turned again with both hands on her pubis, then flung her arms up as someone cut the lights. That's it, boys. It's only snatch. Seem familiar, or was it too long ago for you to remember?

She paused in the wings and looked at the photograph. When Dawson asked, she said her name was Mandy, giving the surname after a tiny pause for consideration. She stood with one knee slightly bent and the boa thrown over her shoulder. The stage lights caught her cheek, her shoulder, her hip, the brisk sprout of hairs in her groin. Droplets of sweat dribbled down the slopes of her breasts and dropped from the nipples. She had the unstudied, casual air of an athlete after the race.

"No." She handed the photo back. "Don't know her." As she walked away, she said, "Gerry, there's some bastard out there with a camera. You can hear the fucking motor drive."

In the second club, there were two girls. The management was no friendlier. By the time Dawson had been told no twice, the girl with the boa showed up, wearing a duster coat over her costume.

She grinned at Dawson. "It's a relay," she said. "Surely you knew that. We go to and fro. I spend half my day crossing the street."

In the third club, the girl on stage was working with fire, wiping the flame over her body. She came off holding the torches. A light, tart smell of paraffin and scorch surrounded her.

"No," she said.

As Dawson was leaving, a new girl was coming in. "Hullo, Mandy," he said.

He worked his way through Soho, hearing no. Then he went back and started on the massage parlors. In the sixth, someone said, "Yes."

Dawson showed her another photograph. She said, "Yes," again.

The place had a reception area with a desk and behind the desk a middle-aged woman, looking apprehensive. Beyond that was a lobby that led to a maze of corridors and cubicles. When Culley arrived, Dawson was waiting in the lobby. A girl was with him, and a man in a navy St. Laurent suit. The girl was wearing a garter belt and seamed stockings, and a silk blouson jacket that she'd thrown on over her shoulders. Her hands, half-hidden, were pulling it across her breasts.

The man stepped forward to intercept Culley. "This is well out of order. You know that, do you?"

Culley ignored him. To Dawson, he said, "Who's this?"

"Her name's Jeanette. That's as far as we've got."

The man circled, wanting to face Culley. He said, "I'm talking to you."

"The other girls recognized the photo?"

Dawson nodded. "Oh, yeah. This one was more of a friend."

The man switched targets. He leaned forward and put his face close to Jeanette's. "You say nothing, slag. There's a brief on his way down here."

"She used to do two sessions a week," Dawson said.

"Bowman."

"Yes."

The man touched Culley on the arm. "You're paid-for, you know. Your lot have had the bloody dropsy."

Culley turned and hit him all in one movement, aiming low and getting there. The man went to the wall, bending to clutch himself. After a moment, he coughed and slid into a sitting position. Culley watched him. When it was clear that the man wouldn't get up for a while, Culley said, "Shut up. Okay?" To Dawson, he said, "What about the punters?"

"Having their names and addresses taken. They're not happy. We've got a JP and the headmaster of a private school—among others."

Culley smiled. He turned to Jeanette.

"I didn't know her, not really. We had a drink together once or twice." She was slight and fake blonde. There was a big blue and yellow bruise on her thigh, just above the stocking top.

"It's all right," Culley said.

"They were short of cash—you know. Pete. That his name? She wasn't going to make it a way of life. Lots do it. Part-timers." She looked nervously past Culley's shoulder as she spoke.

Culley didn't follow the look, but knew where it had gone. "Don't worry," he said. "We'll keep an eye on you." It was an empty promise.

There was a small sofa against the far wall. Culley steered her toward it. She sat down, loosing her grip on the front of the jacket. It didn't matter to her what Culley saw. She spent her working day with her tits in men's faces.

"She wasn't a brass." Jeanette seemed anxious to make the distinction.

"What then?"

"Just hand relief. Suck if you have to."

Culley allowed the difference. "Twice a week?" he asked.

"Usually. Never more."

"Did she have regulars?"

Jeanette lifted a shoulder. "I expect so."

"Do you?"

"Yes." Culley waited. Jeanette said, "She would have, yes. We all have regulars."

Culley reached out and Dawson put the second photograph into his hand. He showed it to Jeanette.

"It's possible."

Culley pointed at Dawson. "You told him yes."

"I know I did." She looked briefly at the photo again, then shrugged. "I think so. I'm not sure."

"Nothing will happen to you," Culley assured her. "It's not to do with this place—anything like that. This guy's dead. No connection with you, anyone you work for, okay?"

Jeanette looked at Culley. She smiled, but the expression on her face seemed not to change. Her eyes didn't change.

"No," she said, "it's not that. Just—I'm really not sure. I try not to look at their faces."

10

THE BEST PLACE TO BECOME anyone is anywhere, and that's what Ross had chosen.

He'd rented the apartment in the name of a company that didn't

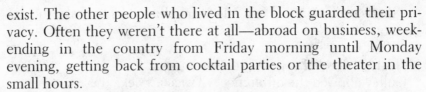

exist. The other people who lived in the block guarded their privacy. Often they weren't there at all—abroad on business, weekending in the country from Friday morning until Monday evening, getting back from cocktail parties or the theater in the small hours.

"Long . . . ?" Angie had asked him.

"I'll call you." He'd allowed her to think that the job was in another country. In a sense, it was. He was on territory he'd never occupied before.

From the broad window in the living room, he looked across hilly parkland to where the lights of the city were beginning to come on. He went into the bedroom, opened his gun case, and returned with the telescopic sight. Close-to, the streets were lined with expensive cars; a man and woman were walking up the hill, he still worrying an argument, she ignoring him and peering at house numbers; a child was walking a dog. Beyond them, darkening treetops; then the sickly pink flush of neon, a luminous fallout, settling on London's roofscape.

He pulled a chair up to the window and pointed the scope at the distant city. A rush of excitement hit him, tightening his gut and fizzing out to his finger ends; a cocktail of lust and fear. It brought him to his feet, and a kaleidoscope of lights, trees, people, window-borne reflections, tumbled through the cross hairs.

He walked into the bedroom again and unpacked the few clothes he'd brought with him, hanging them in one of the oversized closets.

He went to a local store and bought whiskey. On his way back, he collected a pizza he'd ordered earlier.

He made up the bed with linen he found in the linen closet and laid out his shaving gear in the bathroom, then reheated the pizza in the oven.

He marveled that such ordinary things were possible.

And throughout the evening, between this task and that, he went to the window, drawn there as a philosopher might be drawn to some overwhelming idea.

At three A.M., he was there still, the scope held steady, the vision more in his mind than in his eye—a grid of streets, a map of parks, of highways, of suburban roads, shopping malls, cemeteries, wharves, cinemas.

The city. The whole city a killing ground.

.   .   .

"What about the kids?" Dawson asked. He added, "The kids he shot—"

"I know which kids you're talking about," Culley snapped.

"Sure. Okay. Well, where do you suppose they figure?"

"It's a connection."

"Is it? A girl is shot, apparently at random. She makes a little extra cash jerking off the sad and lonely. A man is shot, apparently at random. There's a small chance that she occasionally did it for him. You want that to be significant. Why should it be? It's barely a coincidence."

"You think so."

Dawson had driven Culley to Helen Blake's flat. They had been sitting in the car, talking, for the better part of an hour. Culley was looking up at the lighted window of Helen's living room.

"Yes," Dawson replied. "Listen, for the last three years I've been having my hair cut by the same guy. What?—every couple of months for three years. Say he gets shot and I get shot. Would you want to make a link there?"

"You can't tell a haircut from a handjob?" Culley asked.

"It's coincidence, Robin. Christ, she's not even—what's her name? Jeanette—not even sure."

"If it wasn't—"

"Hookers and clients, dentists and patients, chefs and hungry people, everyone goes to someone for something."

"If it wasn't for the kids at the river, what would you think?"

"The same."

"You'd only have two dead people; and you'd be looking at one connection between them. If there's a reason for the deaths—"

"Okay, I'm not sure. But it—"

"Which is why it's possible."

"But it isn't like that. The kids make the theory wrong." Dawson paused to remember. "Lucy Pearson. Duncan Something . . . Crawford. Yes? She was doing a graduate course at Birkbeck, he was a city broker. I mean, what do you want it to be? Someone inside-trading history degrees?"

Culley saw the light go out in Helen's living room. The bedroom light came on.

"We're wasting time," Dawson said.

"We can look. Why not look?"

"I just told you. Apart from which, a grieving widow in the gin-and-tonic belt is going to have to hear that her late husband liked having his dick sucked by bottle blondes in garter belts."

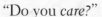

"Do you *care?*"

Dawson thought about it. "Not really. But the kids—"

"Look," Culley said, "I'll bet you're right. Okay? I'm sure you're right. To be truthful, I thought so when I got the report on Bowman. I don't like the idea, and I wish it were otherwise, but that's not going to stop it being true."

He looked up, his eye snagged by a flicker. The bedroom light had gone out.

"I want us to look at the link between Bowman and her client because we can't afford to make a mistake, because it's there—coincidence or not—and because it's the only fucking thing there is to look at."

"You mean, it's something to do," Dawson said.

Culley's voice was low with restrained anger. "I've already told you—I'm assuming you're right. What's happening is that someone has decided that it would be a hell of a lot of fun to slope around London killing people. It makes him feel good. He likes the whole process. Stalking his victims. Watching them behave as if they had a future. Then *bam.* Chaos. Okay. I expect that's how it is. It certainly sounds right to me. But it's a mystery. It's his mystery. I don't know anything about it except that part of the pattern is a probable coincidence that I expect to get me nowhere, but I'm looking at it because it *is* part of the pattern. Now, either give me an alternative or drive me home."

Dawson said, "Aren't you staying here?"

"Drive me home," Culley told him.

Fifteen minutes later, Dawson eased the car into the curb outside Culley's apartment. As if he'd been rehearsing it, he said, "I'm glad you think I'm right."

Culley turned his head to conceal a smile. He got out of the car, then ducked to the open window. "Mike," his voice was level, "aren't you supposed to call me sir?"

Dawson nodded. He said, "Fuck off."

There were three messages on the machine, the last of them from Helen.

The voice was low and sweetly even-tempered: "My name is Helen Blake. My number is unlisted. The time of my call is eleven-twenty and my message is that you are a grade-A son of a bitch."

Culley dialed her number. After two rings, the tape cut in. Helen's voice said, "I can't take your call, I'm afraid. Please

66

leave a message, unless you're Robin Culley, in which case, fuck off."

Not an original concept, Culley thought. He waited for the beep, and said, "I'm sorry. You know how it is. Except that's the problem, of course. I'm sorry."

He hung up and fetched himself a brandy, then dialed the number again. He said, "You shouldn't say fuck on your tape. It contravenes the public broadcasting act." He didn't expect the joke to bail him out.

11

THE NEXT MORNING, early, Eric Ross shot a man who was riding to work on a motorcycle. The sun was barely up and there was no other traffic in the street. The man was only a few yards from his own front door. His wife heard the crash and came out of the house at a sprint. She thought her husband had hit a patch of oil, or some loose gravel. There was blood, though she couldn't find the site of the injury. He seemed to be unconscious.

When the ambulance arrived, they told her that her husband was dead. Because he was DOA, the manner of his death wasn't discovered for some while.

Later the same day, he shot a man who was playing tennis at an expensive club in Richmond. The score was thirty-love and one set all. The man threw the ball up, brought his racquet arm around, and began to bend into the serve. The bullet took him precisely over the heart and flipped him backward like a fish. There

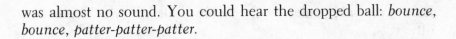

was almost no sound. You could hear the dropped ball: *bounce, bounce, patter-patter-patter.*

Almost on the bip of midnight, he shot Sally Redmond. It had been a tough night for Sally—every table in the restaurant had been booked from seven o'clock through to ten. No one wanted the special. A guy had gotten drunk and knocked wine across three tables on his way back from the men's room—and what was in *there* didn't bear thinking about. The chef took a steam scald on the arm and bitched about it nonstop.

She lived a couple of streets away: five minutes' walk. Ross saw the cross hairs dead center, on the bridge of her nose. He breathed in, breathed out slowly, and shot half her face away.

12

IT ISN'T USUAL for people to feel at risk. They are, of course. Crossing the road, driving a car, taking the train, walking alongside scaffolding; but few people think about it.

Now, everyone thought about it. Not because the television news had given over half an hour to the story every night. Not because the tabloids carried page-sized headlines—TERROR, DEATH CITY—together with lip-licking reports. Not because senior policemen, appearing on TV and being quoted in the papers, were talking a lot but saying very little.

They thought about it because it could be anyone. Any one of them.

People went from house to car, darting looks above, or to left and right. No one walked who didn't have to. Absenteeism was rife. Commuter trains arrived at main-line stations carrying half, sometimes a third, of the normal passenger load. Restaurants, pubs, theaters, cinemas, were taking enormous losses. No office worker would sit at a desk near a window. Supermarket shelves were emptied as people stocked for weeks, rather than days; the sale of chest freezers trebled. Away from the main highways, midday was the same as midnight—quiet, few people on the street. Whoever could leave was leaving.

Like a war. Like a city under siege.

Robin Culley had lots of help, now. He had so much help that he couldn't really have claimed to be leading the investigation anymore.

Advisers from C-11, from the serious crimes department, from anti-terrorist squads, from the Secret Service, from the SAS, and by telephone from two American SWAT squads.

He'd had lengthy sessions with two psychiatrists. They had spouted psychobabble and Culley had grown quickly impatient with them. A third had yet to keep his appointment.

One of the phones on Culley's desk was an open line to Sir Edward Latimer. He was working, now, with senior men from three other divisions and from central HQ.

No one was getting anywhere.

"It's not real life," Culley told Helen. "Surely you can see that. It's exceptional."

"So is the business of two people trying to resurrect a marriage, if that's what we're still doing." Her voice was faint, then loud again, then faint.

"You keep coming and going."

"Cordless phone. I'm moving around."

"Doing what?"

"Cooking."

Culley had tried her half a dozen times at the gallery where she worked; on each occasion, he'd been told that she was unable to take the call. Eventually, he'd gone to her apartment and waited outside until she returned. They'd had dinner in a local restaurant, but she hadn't let him back into her bed.

"I could come over."

"No kidding."

"Loosen up, Helen. The city's like a fucking war zone. Everyone's stretched. I've got guys down here who go to sleep if they stop moving. I want to see you."

"I'm cooking for one," she said. "You'd better pick something up on the way."

He arrived with chop suey, water chestnuts, beef in oyster sauce, and egg-fried rice. Helen ate the soup she'd been making, then fetched a fork and picked some of the choicer pieces off his plate. It was a habit that had always annoyed him, and he assumed she was doing it to test his good humor.

"I'm used to it," she said. "I live alone, I work harder than I once did, I read a lot of books; sometimes I even watch TV."

"There must be things you've missed," Culley said.

"What? Sex?" She shrugged. "I've had my moments."

He really didn't want to hear about that. It was a question he'd decided not to ask, no matter what eventually happened between them. The guesswork was bad enough; evidence would be close to unbearable.

He said, "I was thinking more—lonely evenings, going to the movies, holidays. Someone to do things with."

"Not really," she said.

"Well, it's not the issue, anyway, is it?"

"No."

"The issue is, do you love me, shall we be together?"

"The issue," she reminded him, "is whether I can take it if we are."

"It's exceptional; you must see that. We've had seven deaths in eight days; a sniper, killing indiscriminately. Politicians are calling it an emergency. I can't—"

Helen got up from the table. "I know. The fact remains that your job causes you to be involved; it's all a matter of degree."

She started to make coffee. Culley watched her reflection floating over the windowpane, taking the light then losing it. Narrow face, long aristocratic nose, wide-apart almond eyes, her hair layered but long, tawny with blond streaks, and falling to below her shoulders. She saw he was looking not beyond the window but into it, and waved as if she were outside.

"What's the thinking," she asked, "will he stop?"

"There's no reason why he should . . . except that there was a time before he started."

"What chance of actually catching him?"

Culley adopted the tone of embattled officialdom. "We are making inquiries and hope to see some positive results before long."

"That bad?"

"There's nothing to get hold of. It's the recipe for a perfect crime. Think about it. You decide you'd like to commit a murder. Not for gain. Not out of hatred, jealousy, idealism; but for no other reason than that you'd simply like to do it. Just once. Never again. You're a model citizen. No petty villainy, no association with anyone or anything unlawful. You select a victim wholly at random. Someone you've never met; no connection between you at all. One way or another, you kill this person without being seen. Either there are no witnesses, or you do what this guy does and shoot from cover . . . however you do it, no one *sees* you. Then you go home and live a blameless life. You can't be caught. There's nothing to detect. No history; no motive; no chain of circumstance; no kind of link between you and what you've done. Do you see? No *reason*."

Helen brought the coffee to the table. "But this guy's done it more than once. Isn't that the flaw?"

"Not really. If I give you a problem you can't solve, it doesn't become easier if I then set you another six."

"What will you do?"

"Wait, I suppose."

"What for?"

"Luck."

"What would that be?"

"He makes a mistake—gets seen, leaves something behind, gets sloppy, overconfident . . . I don't know. Gives me something I can recognize. Come to bed."

She went to a small cabinet at one side of the room. "Would you like a brandy or anything?"

"Helen?"

"What chance you'll be called out before morning?"

"I had to leave this number. You can see that."

"What chance?"

"Evens, I should think."

She poured two brandies. A nightcap, or one for the road. After a moment, she said, "I get to come first: just in case."

13

AFTER A WEEK, Eric Ross telephoned his wife.

"Where are you?" Angie asked. Not meaning "Which country" —that was a question that couldn't be asked—but meaning "Have you landed or are you about to take off?" She assumed the job had ended. Nothing had ever taken more than five days before; three would be more usual.

He said, "There's a bit of a problem this end. Things'll take longer."

"How long?"

A silence on the line, then, "It's difficult to say."

They had the sort of aimless domestic conversation that all people have under such circumstances. Ross said, "Kiss the children for me." Angie said she would.

Afterward, she went into the kitchen and poured more coffee into her breakfast cup. It was Saturday. Lynne was still asleep. Anthony had loaded a new game into his computer; Angie could hear him as he beeped some intrepid warrior through a maze guarded by hydras and gryphons.

She raised the cup to her lip. Her eyes met the rack of plates and cups, the jars of spice on their little carousel, the terra-cotta pot by the window planted with parsley and chives. She saw them and didn't see them; she held the cup, but forgot to drink.

She had known when he said, "Kiss the children."

She had known when she heard him thinking of things to ask: about the house, about household affairs, about herself.

She had known when he told her, "There's a bit of a problem."

Or that was the knowledge she was prepared to admit to herself. Each day, she had read the papers; each day, she had watched the TV news at lunchtime, at six o'clock, at ten o'clock. She'd taken the kids to school, then fetched the shopping, and hadn't been afraid to be on the street or in the supermarket parking lot, out there in plain view, although she'd watched other people being afraid.

72

One night, she'd had a dream in which Eric appeared as a figure in a crowd. She'd called to him, but he either hadn't heard or wouldn't reply. He'd walked through a great gathering of people, though none had been able to see him apart from Angie. From time to time, he would tap someone on the shoulder, then pass on. His eyes were burning.

It wasn't the phone call. In truth, it wasn't the dream. Angie had known almost from the start.

The Demon of the Stairs. God's Huntsman.

He sat by the window, the scope on a coffee table close to hand. For a couple of days now it hadn't occurred to him to eat, and he felt light-headed, like someone who has just received exhilarating news. He was loud with power.

It was the beginning of the weekend. He didn't go out that day.

At first, he'd simply done what was necessary, taking little interest in the effect it had. After a while, though, he'd begun to buy the papers and watch the news bulletins. It was odd to read of "panic" and "fear," to listen to phrases like "city under siege" and "reign of terror," and to know that he had provoked them. He watched faces on television—people who talked about him in the abstract; in particular, he watched Robin Culley, liking his sharp, dark good looks and the fact that his hair was too long and too touseled to make him a standard-issue copper.

Ross was Culley's mystery but, at that time, Ross was also becoming a mystery to himself: feared, but unknowable; famous, but anonymous. He felt as if he had invented himself.

Now, he had stopped buying the papers or switching on the TV. It no longer puzzled or excited him to know what people might be thinking. The task had become everything. It was a discipline, like music or mathematics. He could see, now, that what he was doing would be visible, in the end, as some great design, though its true nature wasn't yet clear to him. He realized that to discover it would take time.

He had almost forgotten its original purpose, just as he was beginning to forget his life with Angie and the children.

And he'd completely forgotten that he was supposed to stop.

On the evening of the next day, he went out again.

He drove to a small park in the center of a residential area. It was closed at that time of night, the gates locked. He hoisted himself over the railings and walked half a mile through fussy gardens and lime tree avenues. A wind stirred the leaves. Night creatures rattled the undergrowth.

Beyond the southern entrance to the park was a street of shops and restaurants; and directly opposite, a cinema. Ross lined up on one of the sets of double doors. The movie had ended. People were beginning to leave.

A middle-aged couple, arm in arm. A man on his own, looking for a cab. Two girls together, a younger couple, four kids debating something. Pick and choose; pick and choose.

A girl, laughing. A man, holding her hand. A blue coat, a white sweater, a gray suit, fair hair, dark hair, tall, short.

Pick. Choose. *Bang.*

14

Sᴛᴜᴀʀᴛ ᴋᴇʟꜱᴏ ᴡᴀꜱɴ'ᴛ ʟɪᴋᴇ the other shrinks Culley had met. At first, when he walked into the office, Culley had trouble making a connection between the name and the man's reason for being there. "Kelso . . ." he said.

"I was going to come in last Friday; I had to cancel."

Then Culley remembered. He ordered coffee and sized the other man up while making the call. Kelso was wearing jeans, sneakers, a black T-shirt, and an Armani jacket. His hair had a few lines of gray and was drawn back in a ponytail. He was toothpick-thin. He smiled at Culley and said, "You must want to nail this creep pretty badly."

It was so unexpected that Culley laughed out loud. "Well, he is making life difficult for us, yes."

"I've read the reports," Kelso said. "All the accounts of all the attacks so far. There's not much for you to get hold of, is there?"

"Next to nothing."

"Which is why you're talking to me."

"Any help we can get at the moment . . . ."

"Have you seen others? Shrinks, I mean."

"Two."

"And?"

Culley looked evasive. "Well, I'm not sure . . ." He broke off, looking for the best way of saying it.

Kelso helped him out. "They were fuck-all use."

Culley grinned. "They seemed to be saying that our sniper might not be entirely at peace with his fellow man. The fact is, I think I'd worked that out already."

"How did they wrap that up?"

"Paranoiac self-deception?" Culley was thinking back. "Delusional structures. Ontological insecurity."

"Yep," Kelso nodded. "That's a way of putting it."

"What would yours be?"

"I'd say he was nuts."

"Would you?"

"Probably."

Culley became wary. "You mean, that's what you'd say to me."

"No." Kelso smiled and shook his head. "I'm not trying to patronize you. Technical terms might well give some sort of a profile of the man, but I don't see how it's any help if you know that he might have been mother-dominated, or suffer from some chemical imbalance—according to which theory you'd like to support. As I understand it, you don't have a single lead on the guy, so knowing that he was quite possibly tortured by sibling rivalry isn't going to get you a lot further, is it? If I can assist at all, then it's likely to be by guessing at what he'll do."

"Yes." The coffee was brought in and Culley paused. "And what do you think he'll do?"

"It depends why he's behaving the way he's behaving."

"Sorry?"

"If it's to do with a crisis—I mean, if something specific has made him want to shoot people—then it'll depend on the way the crisis is resolved. The theory here is that he's killing for no reason. That can't be true. He's killing for no *apparent* reason. That is, the reason isn't apparent to us. You have to assume that the potential for this has existed for a while. Perhaps a long while. Something gave him a push. A lot depends on the something. How deep, how resolvable."

"What sort of a something?"

"God knows. It could be a major trauma—someone dying, someone rejecting him in other ways."

"Other ways?" Culley hadn't made the connection.

"Death can be seen as an extreme form of rejection by some people. They want to punish the person who spurned them, but that person isn't around anymore, so someone else catches the crap. A sister refuses to speak to her brother for years after their father's death; a child suddenly finds itself coming in for beatings; a husband and wife divorce. Funerals are an ending for some, a starting point for others."

"Or?"

"Or it could be an event so trivial that you'd never guess, from knowing about it, what the sequence of events turned out to be. A man sees something in a store window that he wants to buy; it's the last item, and the sales assistant won't break the window display for it. The man comes back with a hatchet, kills the assistant, kills the store manager, kills a woman who happened to be standing nearby." Kelso shrugged. "A woman wants to watch a certain TV show. Her husband wants to watch the game. They argue about it. He switches on the game, tells her to shut up, commandeers an armchair in front of the screen. She goes to the kitchen, returns with a hammer, hits him eight times on the head with all her strength."

"These things happened," Culley guessed.

"Oh, yes."

"If it's not a crisis."

"Then it has to do with something less easily understood and a good deal more sinister."

"What?"

"Ambition."

"I don't—"

"It has to do with something he wants to be, wants to become . . . is becoming. A fantasy that he's learned to love. The crisis is probably still there, but not so easily traceable. It might have to do with an accumulation of things. Pressure. A long, slow build-up. What makes them suddenly murder?—The Yorkshire Ripper; the Son of Sam—what makes the time right?"

"Probably," Culley said.

"What?"

"Something you said earlier. He's nuts—*probably*."

"I was going to ask you about the girl," Kelso said, "and the commuter who was shot on the train. You were looking at a connection between them. It was in the report."

"Coincidence," said Culley.

"You're sure?"

"No doubt about it. As it happens, we're not even sure that he was a client. Even so, we looked very carefully—nothing there. Then came the subsequent killings, of course . . ." Culley waited. Finally, he added, "Why?"

"Well, I'm all too aware that seriously disturbed people can act as if they were as normal as the man next door. In fact, some of them *are* the man next door. I wouldn't expect this guy to go running around the streets gibbering with his gun slung over his shoulder. I mean, that's clearly not his style. Still . . ." Kelso spread his fingers and clenched them, as if attempting to capture a meaning. "You've been presented with absolutely nothing, so far as I can see. No slips, no errors, no wrong moves. He knows how to find cover; he knows how to get clear; he knows how to do that without leaving a trace. He doesn't miss, either. You'd think he might've shot wide, just once, or merely wounded someone. What I'm saying . . . He's very good at what he does."

"You mean he's a pro."

"Yes."

"We've thought of that. It doesn't make sense. There would have to be a purpose in what he's doing. The victims don't allow that."

Kelso nodded. "I know." He paused. "I'm sure there are a lot of people who know how to shoot—who can do it accurately time after time. It's just . . . As I went through the reports, I was struck by the sheer efficiency of the man."

"Couldn't the efficiency be part of the madness?" Culley asked.

Kelso looked impressed. "Could be. Could be." He stood up. "That's probably the best I can do for you, at the moment. Call me if you think I might do better."

"I will."

Kelso paused in the act of leaving. "There's another possibility." Culley waited. "You're right, in a sense," Kelso said. "It won't really do simply to say 'He's nuts,' because that makes it sound as though he didn't exist before the first person died."

"What other possibility?" Culley prompted.

"That he wasn't nuts when it started."

. . .

Culley repeated the notion to Helen Blake. A waiter poured chianti into her glass, then picked up her empty plate. She glanced up, smiling.

The waiter smiled back and said, "Enjoy your meal?"

"Yes," she said. Then, "What?"

Culley sighed and told her again.

"Does it make a difference?" Helen plucked a wooden toothpick from a small silver flute and worried at a molar. After a minute, she broke the scrap of wood and took another.

"If it does," Culley said, "I can't work out what it might be."

"Then why worry?" Helen tried to sound amused and a little bored. In truth, she was growing increasingly irritated. They had come to the restaurant—neutral ground, if such a thing existed for them—to talk about themselves. The fact that it had been Helen's suggestion only served to put an edge on her ill-humor. Culley had talked about the sniper pretty much nonstop.

"It could be the first day," he told her. "The first killing. We're no closer than that."

She made a triangle of toothpicks, then snapped them and made an oblong with diagonal facings.

"Protheroe squawks. Latimer squawks. It's not as if either of them had an idea in his head."

She destroyed the oblong and built a house with a little path of broken fragments leading away across the tablecloth.

"Without a reason, without a purpose, there's nothing to calculate."

His images and hers. She had stopped trying to drag the conversation back to its original purpose, but her thoughts circled their marriage, settling on good things and settling on bad. Now and then, his voice pulled her attention back to his own problems: No reason. No purpose. The unpredictability of madness.

She took the house apart, *snap, snap, snap,* and scraped the pieces into a pile along with the rest. She had a tremendous desire to start a little bonfire on the table.

Something he said came through to her, like a sudden nudge. For a moment, she thought he must have been talking about her and she hadn't noticed; then she realized that his topic hadn't changed. But something. It had to do with purpose; hidden purpose.

His luck, the luck he'd been looking for, arrived because Helen's thoughts had been largely somewhere else. She was tired and her mind was switching focus; not concentrating.

She didn't really give a damn, so she found a solution, the way you remember a name after you've stopped trying. It didn't occur to her at first that she was saying anything important. He was posing a problem; she was weary of hearing about it; the answer jumped up at her. It was almost academic and she spoke with a sigh in her voice.

"Suppose I only really wanted to break one of these." Her finger nudged the pyramid of segments; he watched as the scattered pattern littered the cloth. "Only *needed* to break one. How would you know which one it was?"

As if she had just heard herself, just startled herself, she looked at him and they both realized she was right. "You can't even tell which piece belongs to which. How would you know?"

15

T HEY STARTED again.

The victims weren't statistics now, they were candidates. Culley asked Latimer for extra men and was given them. They went back to see widows and widowers, orphans and bereaved parents. They asked different kinds of questions. They turned over the lives of the dead as a gardener turns a midden with a fork, and found rot, damp darkness, things going to the bad. They found things that no one had known about. People were hurt. Memories were soured.

And largely it was all for nothing. Tax evasions, drug habits, drink habits, money salted away, gambling debts, single sins that should never have been found out.

Sally Redmond had a child conceived, born, and adopted during a twelve-month period when her husband had been working as a rigger in Saudi to raise enough for their first mortgage. The contract had prevented him from getting home. He'd tried to persuade her to visit for a holiday. He remembered her excuses about the cost of such a trip: how he would have had to stay longer to earn back the money.

The man who had died on the train hadn't been one of Linda Bowman's clients. Not that; but he'd had a mistress his wife had never known about. She lived in a comfortable apartment in west London and the man had spent every Tuesday and Thursday night with her for twenty years. They had taken a holiday every summer —a regular "business trip" that the man's wife had ceased even to notice after the first five years. In the woman's flat were photographs of them together over two decades, clothes the man's wife had never seen, items he and his lover had bought to replace other, worn-out, items that they had also bought. It had started less than a year after his marriage.

The information was recorded on computer for Culley and others to sift through. Mike Dawson was looking over Culley's shoulder when Culley underlined a name with his finger and said, "What do you think?" The name was Susan Court. Ross had chosen her from the crowd leaving the cinema.

Dawson read off the relevant information. "Daughter of financier, publisher, and entrepreneur James Court. For publisher," he added, "read press baron." He scanned the printout. "Minor convictions: speeding, uninsured motor vehicle. Arrested twice at Greenham Common women's camp—obstruction of vehicles, trespass on Ministry of Defense property, willful damage. Possession of cannabis, possession of cocaine, the latter not prosecuted." He added his own rider: "Rich-bitch daughter of influential father ducks rap. Father increases contribution to campaign funds."

"Good guess," Culley told him.

"Known associates include IRA sympathizers, Marxists, Greenpeace saboteurs. Member of the Workers' Revolutionary Party."

Culley flicked to another tear sheet. "Forget her for a moment," he said. "Look at the father."

Dawson read in silence for a minute or two. "Well, he's got fingers in many a pie. What am I looking at in particular?"

"Newspapers and a couple of TV stations seem to be the indulgences. Largely speaking, they cost money; they don't make it. Here's where the profit is," Culley tapped the printout, "international finance. He's a kind of broker cum matchmaker. Spots the possibility for a deal—someone over here who wants something, someone over here who can supply it, or the money for it—then puts the two interests together; not forgetting to take a piece of the action, of course. Most of the deals he's shepherded recently—within the last eighteen months or so—have been for weaponry. All on the up and up—government contracts."

"So he must have spent a lot of time heads-down with various Defense Ministers," Dawson observed.

"Yes."

"Being told things that most of us don't get to hear about."

"Secrets; yes."

"And his daughter, well, in shorthand terms, was a commie agitator—"

"Just the sort of term his newspapers would have used."

"—who was close to the source." Dawson hesitated. "You're not suggesting that she took the opportunity to rifle her old man's desk drawers, came across some juicy tidbits, and he had her killed?"

"Was that a brief commercial for fatherly love?" Culley asked. "Because I don't think it applied in this case. He bailed her out from time to time, but I gather that was more for his protection than hers. I don't think there was much love lost between them. But, actually, no; I don't necessarily think that. If she'd known things she shouldn't have known, there are people other than her father who might have found her annoying. He organized a deal for Iraq not long ago; Swiss money. He also took a fair profit out of a massive order for South Africa."

"Deep water," Dawson said.

"Worth a look, then."

Dawson nodded, though it didn't register as a gesture of agreement. He said, "Anybody else like your theory? Helen's theory."

Culley laughed. "I think the best I got was 'interesting.' That was Latimer."

"But he didn't say forget it?"

"It seems he thinks I might as well be chasing shadows as chasing my ass, like everyone else. What do you think?"

"I think what I've always thought." Dawson pointed toward the window. "There's a crazy out there shooting people for fun. Still, I've spent as much time as anyone sprinting to get nowhere. Goading the high and mighty will make a change."

"We've been told to proceed with caution."

"Protheroe does love a good cliché." Dawson chuckled. "Will we?"

"To begin with," Culley told him. "Why not?"

Someone who wants something; someone who can supply it. Two halves that make a whole. Product and customer. Army and armorer. Cash and investor. Labor and laborer. Lust and pimp. Dope and addict. Death and executioner. So the world turns.

There were two men in the room, customer and supplier. The place belonged to the supplier—a discreet apartment in a soon-to-be fashionable district. He poured whiskies for both of them, handing a glass to the customer, who had just asked three questions in rapid succession, the last of which was, "What in hell is he doing?"

The supplier raised his eyebrows. "Killing people. That was the brief."

"Don't be arch with me. You know damn well what I mean."

"You mean, *why* is he doing it. Why is he *still* doing it."

"Yes."

"I don't know."

"Let's try another question. When will he stop?"

"I think that's more, *will* he stop?"

"And?"

"Difficult to say. Since I don't know why he hasn't. I also don't know where he is, which means I can't ask him."

The customer drank his whiskey in one and held out his glass for a refill. "Speculate."

"He's having fun."

"You find the whole thing amusing. Is that right?" The customer was plainly angry.

"No. Not particularly. My guess is that if things go on much longer we'll have a situation on our hands that we can't control. We might have already reached that. If Ross isn't rational, and if he gets caught, then God alone knows what he might say. The fact that I'm not part of your grand design doesn't let me off the hook. I'm on the payroll. Christ, I *organized* this. The idea that he might not be rational is what worries me most. You asked me what I thought. I told you. I think he's having fun."

"Dear God." The customer took the replenished glass and sipped from it at once. "No chance of getting to him?"

"No."

"The wife."

"She'd be the last person to know where he is."

"We mustn't . . . He can't be allowed to just go on killing people at whim."

"That worries you?"

"Of course it—"

"*That* worries you?" The supplier paused for an answer, but didn't get one. "Because as I understood it, killing people at whim was the whole fucking idea."

"Not this. Not open-endedly."

"Ah, yes, that's it. The notion of order. Dead people—fine. Innocent dead people—okay. A whole batch of innocent dead people. But not more than we want. Not so many that things get out of hand. Well, that's what's happened, it seems. You don't have a hand on the brake. He's out of control."

The customer looked at his glass. It was empty again. "Yes," he said.

The supplier took the glass and poured more scotch. "Yes. And what I'm telling you is that I'm worried about that as well. In the same way that you're worried. For the reason I gave you a moment ago. Out of control means vulnerable. It means much more likely to be caught. It means do anything; *say* anything. If things had gone as planned, Ross would be back home by now, finished, paid-off, and silent. We can't count on that any longer. Can't count on *silent*. You're worried about your own skin, to say nothing of your reason for giving this commission in the first place. I couldn't give a fuck about your little scam, but I care a lot about me."

"There must be something."

"I can see that you'd hope there would be, yes. It's not just the money with you; it's not just your own involvement. I'll bet there are some exceptionally large fish swimming toward this net."

The customer didn't reply directly. He said, "Is there, or isn't there?"

The supplier finished his drink and set the glass aside. "I try not to do business with anyone unless I know things about them." He paused, smiling. "You'd be surprised to discover what I know about you. Well . . . Ross has a history like everyone else. There's something I know. One thing. It might help us. It might not."

Dusk was a good time. Dawn and dusk were best. As the light receded, flowing slowly like water to a weir, you could see points of brightness starting up amid the dark mass of the city. Street lamps, shopfronts, apartment windows, the lights of cars. By the time the day had emptied out over the western skyline, the city was aglow. It blazed with possibility.

The best time. Eric Ross stood by the window. He was eating a hamburger and drinking beer from the can. Now and then, he would remember food. Now and then, he would remember sleep. He needed both as a machine needs energy.

Himself, but not himself. He knew who he was, but not what he might become. A thing of shapes and images, not quite formed, not wholly changed. Not yet. But there were clues. He could see himself in his mind's eye, as if he were watching a fragment from a movie.

The sky dark, except where the city's luminous uprush lit the middle distance, pearl and the bilious pink of neon. He saw something float down from the hill, down from the vantage point, eyes fixed on the source of light, the killing ground, while the creatures that lived there grew under its eye, each of them unaware.

He heard the hiss and double drub of wings. He sighted along the beam of its eye.

16

J AMES COURT LOOKED Culley up and down like a contemptuous tailor. "I spoke to someone," he said. "A more senior officer, I think."

"I know you did. Now you're talking to me." As soon as it was said, Culley regretted it. *Don't let it show. You think he's an asshole. Okay. Don't let it show.* He tried to cover the mistake by adding, "We're having a difficult time."

Court wasn't very forgiving. "It's not going to get any easier if you take that tone."

"I'm sorry." *You son of a bitch.*

Court held Culley's eyes with a level look. Culley dropped his gaze. The deference was just enough. Court pressed a switch on his desk console and said, "No calls." He clipped a cigar, taking his time, then lit it with extravagant care. "What do you want?"

"We . . . Well, the first time around, we asked the essential questions. Not essential, usual. We're backtracking. There's little else to do."

"Backtracking how?"

"Going over the ground again."

"With different ideas?"

"With different questions."

"Why?"

"We're wondering if we missed something."

"Do you think you did?"

Culley tried to say something disarming. "Not really. It might be pointless. It's best to try."

"What do you hope to find?"

"I'm not sure. We don't even know if there's anything to be found." *But if there is, I hope it hurts, you bastard.*

"About Susan."

"No. I mean, not her specifically. We're looking again at every—"

Culley dropped the word for the sake of tact. Court wanted none of it. "Victim," he said.

"Yes."

"Go on."

"We know that Susan was connected to a number of organizations that many regard as subversive," Culley said. "Until now, we didn't think that too significant."

Court rolled the cigar between his lips. "Is it?"

"Probably not. But we've decided to take a closer look."

"What? She took a trip in a plane, reported back, and the Flat Earth society had her killed?"

Culley smiled. "Not quite." *Your daughter, you creep. This was your daughter that died.*

"Then what?"

"We just think it might prove useful to talk to a few of the people she associated with. Now, we know most of them. That is, we know the organizers, fundraisers, branch secretaries, movers, shakers . . . We know who they are. What we don't know is who she was particularly close to. Who might have known her mind on this topic or that. Look," Culley tried to sound like someone not wanting to waste an important man's time, "we're doing this with everyone, like I say. The first time around was routine; this is routine of a different kind. Anything you can tell me. Any name you can give me."

"Susan was—" Court's cigar was burning unevenly and he took a moment out to wet a fingertip and dab it on the lower side. "Do you have a daughter, Culley?"

"No."

"Fathers and daughters." He smiled humorlessly. "Well . . . Freud had a theory."

"So I gather." *You prick.*

"If I liked it, she hated it. Music, theater, politics; it made no matter. If I took it up, she put it down. I suppose I must have been doing something wrong. It was impossible to know whether she actually believed the things she said, or was saying them simply to be on the other side. I remember—when she was a little girl—"

Jesus, I don't need this.

"—I gave her something, a doll, I don't remember, I knew she wanted. She gave it back. Didn't smash it, sneer at it, complain about it. Nothing really aggressive—I could have understood that. No. She gave it back. Left it on my desk. It was the same later. All her opinions, her way of behaving, the drugs, hanging out with those dikes at Greenham Common, slipping things to the press. We never actually argued about them, exchanged opinions. I heard about them later. She left them on my desk."

"But you must have known some names. The people she knew. Someone special, perhaps."

"Will that help?"

"It would be useful to have some line on . . . how far her feelings took her."

Court started to laugh. He laid his cigar down in the ashtray as the laugh grew. He said, "You can't suppose she was serious enough about all that to—what?—rifle the safe?" He paused and his laughter died. "There have been twenty or more killings. What are you saying?"

"It's been suggested that the sniper was only after one person."

"Then why kill—?" Court paused a moment, then answered his own question. His voice was thick with incredulity. "Just to confuse the issue? He wanted one person and killed all the others as a blind?"

"It's a theory."

"He's still killing people."

"Perhaps it's not much of a theory." Culley shrugged. "We're trying it out."

Court shook his head. "Impossible."

"I'm sure you're right."

Court got up from his desk and walked to the door. Culley followed. He hadn't noticed before that Court was seriously overweight. He had the spraddle-legged waddle of a man whose thigh tops chafed.

Court opened the door. "She was seeing a man," he said, "had been for some time. Josh . . ." He shrugged.

"Surname?" Culley asked.

"No. I don't think I ever knew it." Court smiled. "Bit of detective work for you."

"Thanks," Culley said. *You fat scumbag.*

"No," Dawson said. "She shared a house with three other people. Two women, one man. The man's—" he riffled through the file, "Henry North. I didn't speak to anyone called Josh."

"Start by going back to the house," Culley told him. "Then check with me."

17

THE HOUSE STOOD in a leafy street in the southern suburbs. Henry North opened the door to Dawson's knock.

"Yes?" he asked, then peered more closely, seeming to recognize

Dawson. Behind him, one of the girls floated past, completely naked, on her way to the bathroom. She paused and looked toward the door with eyes fogged by sleep. One hand dropped to her groin but she didn't move; she seemed to be trying to puzzle out who the caller might be. Dawson looked at her while North looked at Dawson. Finally she turned and disappeared down a short flight of stairs.

North took Dawson to the kitchen and started some coffee. "Carol's not here," he said. "Sarah's around somewhere." As if he'd temporarily mislaid her. "I'm not sure we can tell you anything new."

"Someone called Josh," Dawson asked. "A guy Susan was seeing."

North yawned. Dawson felt as if he were the advance party for a dawn raid. It was eleven-fifteen in the morning.

North repeated the name. "Josh . . ."

Sarah appeared in the doorway. She was wearing warm-up pants and a Lynx T-shirt. She said, "Josh Reid?"

Yes," Dawson replied. How many men called Josh could there be?

Sarah collected some mugs from a cupboard and set them down close to the coffee maker; she looked impatiently at the level of coffee in the jug, as if the slowness of the process was a familiar annoyance.

"I wouldn't have said she was *seeing* him."

"What then?"

"Well, they lived together, on and off."

"I thought she lived here."

"On and off."

North was slicing bread to make toast, the mechanics of their everyday life going on around Dawson as he stood there. He felt strangely inactive, as if he ought to offer to help in some way; pour glasses of juice, perhaps.

"What does he do?"

North dropped the bread into the toaster, noticed that it didn't operate when he pressed the lever, and looked around vaguely for the reason. He snapped a switch on the wall socket. Sarah began to fill the mugs. Droplets of coffee sizzled on the hotplate. Dawson began to wonder whether he was really there.

"How do you mean?" North asked.

"What does he do for a living?"

Sarah smiled. "He's an actor."

"Would I know him?" Dawson asked.

"Possibly." She handed Dawson a coffee mug. "He's currently appearing in hamburger medium-rare, salad, no fries, and a glass of house red. Longest running show in town."

"And lives . . . ?" Dawson asked.

They gave him an address. He drank his coffee while they chatted to one another.

Culley went with Dawson to talk to Josh Reid. A small, battered house in a small battered terrace; the buildings appeared to be leaning on one another for support. An array of dark, dusty windows, like mirrors that had lost their silvering. Blistered and chipped paintwork. Reid opened the door to them before they could knock.

"I saw you from the window." He spoke in a light whisper as they stood in the hallway. Through the living room door, Culley could see a child asleep on a couch, an embroidered shawl covering all but one pale cheek and a cloud of blond hair. Apart from the couch, there was a wooden armchair and a small drop-leaf table. Nothing more. The carpet was dark with wear.

"Afternoon nap," Reid explained. "She's begun to be difficult about going to bed, so I let her sleep there." He looked around, as if uncertain about where to take them, then led the way into the bedroom. A cheap, pine bed; an old-fashioned rail-sided cot alongside.

"It's about Susan Court," Culley said. "I gather you knew her."

"Yes." Reid nodded.

"That you were having an affair—had been for some time."

"Yes."

Dawson added. "You lived together. Is that right?"

"Sort of," Reid said. "Sometimes. Other times, not."

They stood in a group in the middle of the tiny room, speaking in lowered tones, like conspirators.

"Why?" Culley asked.

Reid sighed. He sat down on a small bedside chair, leaving Culley and Dawson no other option than to sit on the bed, which they did, side by side, like travelers on a train.

Culley watched Reid. The man seemed sunk in his thoughts. He had a beard that had gotten slightly out of hand, growing a little longer on one side; he twisted the hairs into tiny Bluebeard curls; there was something in his face—a certain quality—that seemed ingrained, weathered in. Looking more closely, Culley saw that it was kindness.

"Well . . ." Reid spoke without lifting his head. "We met about four years ago. Four and a half. We were together for—oh—three years? Yes, about that. I mean, together most of the time. Susan kept a room in a house owned by a guy called Henry North. She was worried about giving over her independence; it was a token— you know? But mostly she was with me."

"Here?" Dawson asked.

"Here?" Reid spoke as if the notion offered a small puzzle. "No, not here. We had a flat, quite a big one, more central. Susan got an allowance from her father. She sold the place more than a year ago. Almost two years." It seemed that time scales were important to him.

Culley said, "She never lived here?"

"She used to come and see me. She might stay over. I wouldn't call it living here." Reid's eyes suddenly engaged Culley's. "I don't understand this. She's dead. The sniper—"

"It's become necessary to go back. To look at everything again. We didn't hear about you first time around."

"To look at what?"

"We don't know. Anything."

"She left you," Dawson said.

Reid smiled at the abruptness, and Culley saw it again—kindness, gentleness; and tiredness. "It depends what you mean."

"For someone else," Dawson persisted.

You don't have to play that role, Culley thought. We're not Mutt and Jeff.

The smile lingered on Reid's face. "Susan and I were still together in a sort of way. We saw each other less often. In one sense, it was a bit like being married."

"In what sense?" Dawson again.

"She was having an affair. Had been for about eighteen months." He said this directly to Dawson, his tone level and low, as if countering a challenge.

Dawson responded with, "You didn't mind?"

"Well, I moved out, came to live here in a rented house I can't really afford, Susan sold the flat, which seemed a bit more than a symbolic act, I continued to love her and miss her, I tried to understand what she felt and hoped it was something she'd eventually work through so that we could be together again. What does that tell you?"

"Did you know Susan's father?" Culley asked.

"No."

"Did Susan talk about him at all? About his business activities and so forth?"

Reid looked interested. "Why do you ask?"

Culley didn't respond. Eventually, Reid said, "All Susan ever said about her father was that he was a grade-A shit who'd ignored her for most of her life and thought money was a good substitute for love. I've never met him."

"I have," said Culley. He didn't qualify the remark.

Reid laughed softly. He said, "Is that it? I don't enjoy talking about Susan much. I'm still in love with her."

The baldness of the remark made Culley start. He said, "Yes, I think that's it."

When they returned to the hallway, the child was standing by the living room door, looking as if she might be about to cry. Reid picked her up and she put her face into the hollow of his shoulder, both arms fast about his neck.

Culley opened the front door, then paused to look back at Reid, who turned, seeming to be taking the child protectively out of Culley's vision rather than offering a good-bye.

"You'll want to know who."

Culley nodded. "Yes."

"Yorke. Alex Yorke. He's in the book: Dawes Road."

"And what's her name?" The child squirmed closer to Reid. It seemed to Culley that she was retreating from the sound of his voice.

Reid stroked her hair reflexively. "Daisy," he said.

Dawson nosed the car out into the traffic and came to a halt almost immediately.

"It would be a treat to get into third gear in this fucking town," he said. Then, "I don't understand. *Did* he mind? About the other boyfriend—Yorke?"

"What do you think?"

"But he didn't do anything."

"Didn't do what?"

"I don't know. Kick the bastard's head off."

"That's what you'd do, is it?"

"Well, something like it, I expect."

Culley wondered whether he was hearing the tail end of some

old resentment. Almost to his own surprise, he heard himself ask, "And would that have helped?"

"Wouldn't have helped him much," Dawson said, "but it might have put me in a more relaxed frame of mind."

Something else in Reid's face, beside the sadness and the kindness. Culley thought back, wanting to identify it. He heard Reid's voice: *I tried to understand what she felt* . . . He saw the tatty rooms, the junk-shop furniture. . . . *hoped it was something she'd eventually work through, so that we could be together again.*

Strength was the other thing Culley had seen. The sort of strength that allows loss and confusion and remains constant.

"And the kid," Dawson said. "That would be his and Susan Court's, would it?"

"This traffic's not going to move," Culley observed. "You'd better break a few rules." Dawson flicked on the headlights and swung out into the path of the oncoming cars.

After a moment, Culley said, "Yes. Of course."

Helen watched Culley's face while he told her about Josh Reid and the child. She was suppressing a mild anger.

"No one knew? That Susan Court had a daughter?"

"No, it's not that. I'm sure her father doesn't know—James Court; but others must have. The people at the house, for example. Just—no one thought to mention it. As if the child wasn't very important."

"Except to Reid, what'shisname . . ."

"Josh. Josh Reid."

"None of which is relevant."

"That's right. We'll see the other guy, Yorke. He looks more promising. Reid was useful for that; nothing more."

"But you liked him."

"Yes, I did. She was seeing Yorke, you know, for a long time, sleeping with the guy, and Reid didn't . . . I suppose he simply didn't feel he could prevent it. Or should. Or had any right to. He looked after the child, Daisy, they live in this crappy house with matchwood furniture, he works at some hamburger place, and waits for Susan Court to come home. Not weak." Culley half-raised a hand as if Helen might have been about to challenge his judgment in this. "Not weak, but not bluffing either—not pretending he'd never really wanted her, hated her, was better on his own.

He looked so good with the kid. I mean, he looked as if he would cope without having to pretend that everything was fine."

Helen's anger stirred. She said, "I'm not sure what lesson I'm supposed to be finding in all this. Is it Robin Culley, newly sensitive, newly observant of human foible? Is it some sort of reference to your own noble persistence in trying to restore our marriage? Or are you saying I should have given you a child?"

Culley was taken aback. "Nothing like that. Something I hadn't seen before. Or if I'd seen it, I hadn't taken it in. He was—"

"Because my most enduring memory of you is late nights, or very early mornings, smelling of bars and gutters, still high from whatever dangerous moment you'd recently enjoyed. You liked it. I sort of assume you still do. Dark places, dark motives. The nursery is a new hang-out for you. I'm having trouble picturing it."

Culley felt the anger, but had little idea what he might do about it. He said, "I'm sorry," knowing that it was a foolish response.

Helen half-smiled. She said, "Promising in what way—Yorke?"

"It seems likely that he was the radical charge in Susan Court's battery. Workers' Revolutionary Party, helped run a hand-out sheet called *Arise*; that sort of thing." Culley wondered why she'd decided to let him off the hook. If that's what had just happened. "He fits your theory better than anyone we've come up with so far."

"My theory," Helen said. "Is that what it is?"

"Mine too."

"For that, thanks." She went to the fridge and rummaged around. "Cheese, eggs, pasta. It's the rhythm of our lives at the moment, isn't it? Deciding whether to eat in or out."

"I don't mind."

"Neither do I. What would you like to do?"

"What I would like to do," he told her, "is lick you until you scream."

Helen closed the fridge door. She said, "It's not that easy."

"Yes it is," Culley told her. "I've done it before. It's a cinch."

18

Two men had met in a London flat: customer and supplier. Later, they had spoken again, this time on the telephone. The supplier had a number of names and no one who dealt with him knew, or cared to know, which was the real one. The customer called him Francis: a first name, a last name, a man's, a woman's; it allowed the kind of vagueness the supplier liked.

"Will he do it? What do you think?"

"I don't know," Francis said. "I'll ask."

"Isn't that risky?"

"Yes."

"So should we—?"

"You want Ross stopped; it's the only possibility."

"All right."

"We haven't talked about a fee."

There was a silence on the line that Francis waited out with complete confidence. Finally: "You don't think of this as your problem?"

"If he gets caught—yes. Until then, he can leave London a ghost town for all I care."

"He was your choice."

"You asked for a particular service. I supplied it. You paid me. Things didn't quite go to plan—which has proved annoying for you, and you're now asking for a second service; for which you'll pay me."

"How much?"

"The same fee as for Ross."

"That's outrageous."

It was Francis's turn to be silent. He gazed at the view from his living room window: a quiet square, plane trees, early-morning shoppers.

"When will you go?" The customer's voice was businesslike now, trying to mask the defeat.

"We're agreed on the money?"

"Yes."

"Today."

You could smell it before you pulled into the yard—a hot, sour stench, heavy on the air. It stung the roof of Francis's mouth as he got out of the car. Fifty yards away, behind the house, was a series of corrugated Nissen huts; one of the doors was open. As Francis approached, there came a noise to accompany the smell —solid bodies thumping against the tin walls, then a cacophony of squeals and snorts.

Inside the hut, a lumbering saddleback boar was trotting along the aisle between two rows of pens, nosing the bars and grunting rhythmically. A man dressed in dungarees and a filthy khaki shirt was walking behind the beast, herding it toward the back wall. Francis stood just inside the door. The man sensed his presence at once and turned sharply.

Francis smiled. The man said, "What in hell do you want?" then, without waiting for an answer, turned his attention back to the boar, which had begun to slam its shoulder into one of the pens. He kicked it away from the bars, then continued to boot it as it shambled deeper into the hut. He got alongside the creature to open a gate on the backmost pen, cracked a toecap into the fat flank, and heaved the gate closed as the boar ran in. The sow was waiting there like an auction-block bride.

"It's been a while," Francis said.

The man leaned on the topmost rung of the pigpen, making it clear that Francis would have to approach. Farther in, the smell was thicker, rank with ammonia; the air seemed less breathable.

"What do you want?"

"Talk about old times?"

"Go on, then."

"And about the news. You watch the news, do you?"

Francis saw a light flicker in the man's eyes, like recognition, like pleasure. "It's Eric."

Francis nodded. "Yes. It is."

"Why?"

"No. That's not your affair."

The sow rattled the bars as the boar nosed her around the pen. From time to time, it made cumbersome leaps, trying to mount. The man said, "Tell me about it."

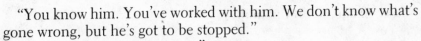

"You know him. You've worked with him. We don't know what's gone wrong, but he's got to be stopped."

"I haven't seen Eric in years."

"You were close." Francis wondered if he'd pushed too hard. The man's face stiffened; something closed down behind his eyes.

After a moment, he said, "It was never my job."

"We know that." Francis nodded. "A bit of freelance, though, a couple of times before Eric went pro; a couple of times after." He put a hand to his cheek and dabbed off a tear; the ammoniac fetor was crackling in his sinuses.

"You say he's got to be stopped."

There was a question in the remark that Francis chose to avoid. He said, "Someone who can get to him. So it must be someone who knows him well." Again, that shutter in the eyes. Francis wondered whether he ought to mention money, then decided it was too soon. No, play on the other thing—the thing they weren't quite mentioning. "You know there's no one else can do this."

The boar gave a double hop, then lurched onto the sow's back. She screeched while his rump heaved, her snout rammed between the bars of the pen.

Martin Jackson watched the mating for a short while, the boar's bulk shoving, the sow bearing him, as if he were seeing that savage, ludicrous event for the first time. Then he looked up, raising his voice so as to be heard over the sow's din. He said, "What's the money?"

Eric.

A low, scudding cloudbank was coming off the western horizon, purple with unshed rain. Jackson took his Land Rover off the track and juddered over fifteen yards of moorland grass.

Eric. Not far from here. It was . . .

After the chill of excitement, the ungovernable strangeness of the moment, they had waited for retribution, certain it would come. No point in lying; no point in running. But it hadn't come. They had completed their training, done their time, including a tour in Germany, left the army, and nothing had happened. It was a bond between them, closer than the killing itself.

Eric. Not far from here. It was so strange. And I knew . . .

Jackson crossed a stone bridge and began to climb. The cloudbank spread, seeming to soak up the light. When he thought back to those years in the army, and the year immediately afterward, it seemed to Jackson that he and Ross had scarcely been out of one another's company. Then everything had changed.

Now Jackson lived a solitary existence. Twice a week, he shot on the range of a gun club in a nearby town—turned up, shot, left. He farmed his pigs with the help of a man from the village. They said to each other only what was necessary.

Eric. Not far from here. It was so strange. And I knew we were bound, whatever happened, bound to one another. I thought . . .

He came to the rise that led to Bethel Tor. The backdrop of sky was a dull gleam, like pewter, and the great rock reared against it, a black slab.

I thought you must feel the same. Surely you knew. Not that I wanted . . .

He reached the base of the tor and stood alongside it. A wind plucked his hair and stung a tear from his eye.

Not that I wanted you to be my lover. Not really. Not necessarily. We didn't even have to say . . . But then I did. I told you. I said: I love you. And then you went away.

Jackson lowered himself to the ground. He looked out across the darkening moor, its becks and mires, its hills and bony ridges of granite.

I love you.

And then you went away.

19

CULLEY HAD NEVER HEARD Susan Court speak, but it was clear from what was being said that the voice was hers.

" . . . some fax messages. And then I got lucky. He'd recorded a telephone conversation—a call he'd taken at home. I found the

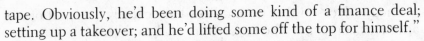

tape. Obviously, he'd been doing some kind of a finance deal; setting up a takeover; and he'd lifted some off the top for himself."

"How?"

Another voice. Alex Yorke, of course.

"Bought the right shares before the takeover bid was made."

"Insider dealing."

"Right. But better still—he'd used the profits to fund an arms deal. He doesn't usually do that; at least, it's not known that he does. All his business is strictly tabletop stuff. Of course, the contacts he's made—the circles he moves in—would make it possible to fund his own operation."

"And this one was under the table."

"Oh, yes. The guy he spoke to was American. They must have felt pretty safe, confident, you know, because they didn't bother to use much evasive language. It was a very straightforward deal. The American had used Father to set the financial wheels turning for the takeover; employed him, you might say; and he'd suggested the inside trade and how it might be made."

"How?"

"Through a shell company somewhere. They weren't specific about the route for the money. Then he'd sweetened the pot—"

"The American?"

"Yes, by coming up with the idea for the arms deal—and effectively trebling the amount Father would make in the process. The thing is—"

"Why was the deal clandestine?"

The two voices clashed, Susan's winning out. It was clear that she was eager to get to the high point of her story.

"—that, I'm telling you, that the whole business had to be a secret. Not just that the money came from insider dealing, but the weapons weren't coming from any official supplier or going to one of the usual customers."

There was a short silence. Culley imagined Susan's gleeful smile as she waited for Yorke to work it out.

"An American." He'd made the connection.

"Yes," said Susan.

"NorAid. The arms were going to the IRA."

A longer silence. Yorke would have been savoring the information; Susan looking at him, perhaps, with the smile still on her face.

"What will you do—now that you know all this?" It was Yorke asking the question. Culley reeled the tape back a little and listened to the question again. Puzzling—since it seemed that Yorke had been listening to information he'd specifically asked for. Shouldn't it have been Susan asking Yorke how he intended to use the knowledge? Then it came clear. Susan hadn't known how she was being used. She hated what her father did and made it her business to spy on him anyway; a daughter's revenge on a father who disappointed her. Yorke was playing the role of the wide-eyed confidante. It was pillow talk.

"I don't know." Susan gave a little laugh. "I ought to shop the bastard."

"But you won't."

"I'm not sure what to—"

"I mean, you haven't in the past."

"I've never come across anything like this before. A few shady deals, but—"

"Does it make a difference?"

"I suppose not."

"I mean, it depends how much you hate him."

"Hate him . . ." A pause. "Yes." Then: "You won't say any- thing? Won't tell anyone?"

"No."

"Because, I mean, I'm telling you because we're—"

"No. Don't worry."

A different kind of pause, while Yorke kissed her briefly, then more lengthily. The kisses were detectable in a breathiness on the tape. Culley listened to movements and small noises.

Susan's voice said, "No, there . . . Just there . . . Like that." Then she gasped.

Culley switched off the tape. Then he crossed the room and switched off the light. He sat in a rocking chair that faced the door.

Alex Yorke got back to his apartment a little more than an hour later. He closed the door before reaching for the light switch. The rocking chair creaked in the dark. He said, "Who's there?" and snapped the switch.

Culley smiled. He said, "If it reassures you at all, I'm not Drugs Squad and I'm not Special Branch. Okay?"

Yorke stayed close to the door. "But you're not the fucking Easter Bunny, either."

"That's true, I'm not."

"*Arise* is a registered newspaper; the publisher's name is under

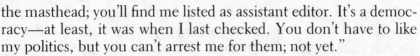

the masthead; you'll find me listed as assistant editor. It's a democracy—at least, it was when I last checked. You don't have to like my politics, but you can't arrest me for them; not yet."

Culley shook his head. "Not Special Branch. I told you."

"Okay. What?"

"Susan Court."

"Susan?" Yorke looked puzzled. "Susan's dead. She was one of—"

"Well, I know that," Culley said. "How long had you two been lovers?"

Yorke moved away from the door and went into the kitchen. He rooted around in the fridge, came up with a beer, and went back to Culley. "What's the problem?" he asked.

Culley looked toward a sideboard where the cassette player stood. Yorke followed his gaze. He said, "You've got a warrant, I suppose?"

Culley's smile was almost a grimace. "When was the tape made?" Yorke made a move and Culley added, "No. Leave it where it is."

"About six months ago."

"Was it?" Culley's near-smile came again. "I don't recall any press coverage of James Court's share dealings; I don't recall any banner headlines about arms for Sinn Fein, for that matter." Yorke sipped his beer. "I'd've thought that *Arise* would have made something of a meal of all that—top financier in shares scandal; weapons mogul arms IRA; that sort of thing."

Culley waited. Yorke took another swallow of beer and glanced again toward the cassette player, but said nothing.

"Well, listen," Culley's tone was low and unhurried, "one of several things can happen here. You can tell me the things I need to know and I can go away. Or I can charge you—withholding information, conspiracy, being an accomplice, possession of heroin, indecent exposure: anything that comes to mind, really." He paused. "Murder, perhaps; Susan was killed, after all."

Yorke looked up swiftly. Before he could speak, Culley continued, "On the other hand, I could take that beer can, ram it up your ass, and kick it out through your teeth. We call that resisting arrest." He looked at Yorke appraisingly. "On the whole, I think I'd prefer the latter."

"Susan was killed by a maniac. Nothing to do with the tapes."

Tapes; plural. "How many are there?" Culley asked.

"Lots. Nothing worth hearing." Yorke nodded toward the sideboard. "Apart from that one."

"Tell me about it."

"In bed. She liked to talk in bed." Yorke laughed through a cough. "Very convenient. I knew when to put the tape on, I could start it while she was in the bathroom, she didn't wander off while it was recording, and the machine could be underneath and out of sight."

"Where are the others?"

"Some I wiped. There are half a dozen about the place—I could find them. They wouldn't interest you."

"Then why did you keep them?" As soon as he'd asked the question, Culley knew the answer. Susan Court's voice came back to him: *No, there . . . just there . . . . like that.*

Yorke saw the recognition in Culley's eyes. He said, "It was careless of me to leave that one in the recorder. Still, I hadn't thought I was a big enough fish for this sort of attention."

"You're not," Culley assured him. Then: "Have you used it?"

"Yes and no."

"Meaning?"

"Court knows that the tape exists. He knows what's on it. He doesn't know who's got it."

"Why?" Culley asked. "You never had any intention of exposing Court—that would have happened at once if you'd intended it. The only cause you were interested in was your own. So much for the radical conscience. You were going to blackmail him. What stopped you?"

"I thought it would be useful to lay hands on the original tape— the conversation between Court and the American."

"And the idea was that Susan would get it for you."

"Yes."

"But she didn't want to."

"She wasn't . . . convinced." All at once, Yorke seemed alarmed. "Her death had nothing to do with this." He could see the possibilities: a need to kill someone; a spate of snipings; a convenient cover. "She wouldn't have shopped me; and she never gave me the tape. If she had, I'd've used it."

"I believe you," Culley said. Then: "Destroy it. Now."

Yorke walked to the cassette and flipped out the tape. He unspooled it, ripped it from the plastic, then rolled it in his palms before dropping it into an ashtray. He lit a book match and let it fall among the tangle. "The others?" He was eager to do the right thing.

Culley shook his head. "I wouldn't want to spoil your fun. It's no business of mine to worry about how sick you are." He got up. "Listen," he said, "I don't need you now. But if there comes a time when I do, I'll have you then. A trade-off, perhaps; a time when we need to bump-up the arrest statistics . . . Don't call James Court again. Don't try to use what you know. Don't sell it; don't offer it in return for a favor. Understand? In the meantime, keep looking over your shoulder."

"The tape's destroyed," Yorke said. "Court would never testify. What can you use against me?"

"Anything," Culley told him. "Anything I damn well like."

Helen Blake laughed. She poured Mike Dawson a scotch and water, and when she handed it to him, the laugh was still there. "Why on earth ask me where he is? I rarely knew the answer to that when we were married."

"He's been spending a lot of time around here. I thought he might have told—"

"It's a relative notion: a lot of time."

"More time than at his own place."

"Less time than elsewhere."

"Yes . . ." Dawson shrugged. "He's got one or two things on his mind just at the moment."

"Don't be arch with me, Mike. I know what's going on. I watch the television, I read the papers. I see people being frightened just because they're on the streets."

Dawson nodded, as if to say: *Well then* . . .

"I also have a memory. I remember that if it's not one thing, it's another."

"Give him a chance, Helen."

"You came here half-expecting to find him, right?"

"Yes."

"That's me giving him a chance. Don't push." There was an edgy pause. Finally, Helen said, "Someone wants him?"

"Protheroe."

"Do you know why?"

"We started with one murder: our patch. Suddenly it was all over the place. We're a task force, now. Uniform, plain clothes, specialist advisers, researchers. If we reconstituted the paperwork, we'd have a fucking rain forest. Robin's nominally in charge of a large slice of the investigation. I think Protheroe would like to get the occasional report."

"And Robin's being a bit eccentric."

"Nothing new in that. This is different. Basically, I don't think Protheroe believes his theory. Your theory. All the killings just to mask one killing. Robin's avoiding a confrontation."

"What do you think?"

Dawson paused, then shook his head. "It's a nifty theory. You have to remember that there are a lot of dead people. It looks like a madman. So it probably is." He swallowed the last of his drink. "I ought to go. If Robin gets back, or calls in . . ."

"I'll tell him," Helen said. "I know my role: secretary, housewife, mother."

"He's talking about remarriage, is he? And kids?" Dawson made it sound like a pincer movement.

"I was speaking figuratively. The war isn't over yet. It's a little early to be thinking about the terms of surrender."

"Speaking figuratively," Dawson said.

"That's what you think."

If Culley had been asked to guess a description of James Court's house, he would have been almost right. Fashionable north London, six bedrooms, an acre of garden, a surveillance system, electronic gates, a road-to-house intercom.

Court's voice sounded inappropriately loud in the quiet street. "It's after midnight. What in God's name do you want?"

"A talk."

"Call my secretary, Culley. Go away."

"I'm afraid it's rather urgent."

"Go away."

"Not possible."

Culley was beside his car, facing the intercom grille fixed to one of the pillars that supported the gates. The intercom issued a tiny electronic hiss, but nothing more of Court's voice. Then it went dead. Culley leaned on the bell push until the hiss returned. He said, "I want to talk about a donation you made to Sinn Fein. I can hold my end of the conversation from here, if you'd like me to."

When he was inside the house, Culley noticed the characteristic he wouldn't have guessed at. He'd imagined expensive good taste —big sofas, neutral carpeting, antiques, safe pictures chosen for their investment potential. The place was chrome and glass, tiles and white paint, bare, functional. It looked like a laboratory.

Court had decided to bluff. He said, "I don't know what you're talking about. What's more, you *know* that I don't. I can't imagine what it is you want."

As if he were telling the story to someone else, Culley gave him a full account of what he'd heard on the tape. He ended by saying, "Susan found the recording of your conversation with the American. She gave it to the person who contacted you. I expect he asked you for money. If he didn't, he was getting ready to. I wonder why you didn't phone your lawyer before I ever got to the front door."

They were in Court's drawing room. Four steel and leather chairs, floor lights that resembled test-tube supports. Culley wouldn't have been surprised to see a rat maze in the corner.

Court said, "There's no evidence for this."

"There's the tape of Susan's voice."

"An agitator, a troublemaker. It wouldn't be difficult to show that she wished me ill. Susan's activities must have been well known to the police."

There was a long pause. Eventually, Culley said, "She was your daughter. Wasn't she?"

Court smiled. "Was that an attempt to shame me, Culley? Was that supposed to cut? Are you trying to hint that blood is thicker than water?" Culley watched him; his finger ends were tingling. "Well, I suppose it might be. Thicker than water—perhaps. But then water's not much of a substance, is it? Surely there are more testing comparisons to be made." The smile disappeared. "Thicker than money? No. Thicker than jealousy? No. Thicker than love, lust, power, pain, need, greed, ambition, possessions? No. Thicker than ideology? No." He paused, offering a debater's courtesy. Culley was silent. "I can't remember having cared for Susan. I suspect I never did."

"You're being foolish." Culley spoke like a man biting his lip. "The American's findable. The people you dealt the guns to are findable. You imagine we don't know who they are? Apart from the fact that you sold weapons to a terrorist organization, you dealt shares on the inside. At the first whiff of something like this, you'd hear nothing but the sound of running feet. Business friends, golfing partners, members of your fucking club, whoever's on the board of your companies, anyone you've made a phone call to or had a confidential chat with, anyone who's asked for help or given it. Every friend you've ever relied on in government would have trouble remembering your name. So bearing all that in mind, perhaps you'd like to stop talking shit."

"If you were going to use this," Court observed, "we'd be having a different sort of conversation."

"No," Culley said. "If I were going to use this *now* . . ."

Court was wearing a light robe over a pair of pale blue pajamas. He pulled the knot on the belt, then retied it, tighter, as if the gesture afforded him some feeling of protection. "Go on," he said.

"A trust fund," said Culley. "To be set up in the name of Daisy Reid, administered through a lawyer named by me. He'll have the details, but you won't get them. Just pay the money—five thousand a month, maturing in fifteen years."

"If I don't—"

"Then I'll be talking to the fraud squad and to Special Branch. They can take it from there."

"You're blackmailing me." Court sounded almost indignant.

"I'm not asking you for a penny." Culley moved close to Court, who fought the desire to flinch. It was like watching someone push at an invisible turnstile. "I'll make regular checks on the payments."

"Who?" Court asked. Culley walked to the door. "Who? Your girlfriend? Your daughter?"

"She's nothing to do with me."

"Who then?"

"No one you know," Culley said. "No one you'll ever know."

20

Eric Ross took the scope from the windowsill and looked down at his killing ground. He rolled the disk over segments of the city, the cross hairs neatly quartering his domain.

"Bustle, bustle," he said; and laughed. He was imagining them as they scurried to and fro like rats, like rabbits when farmers burned the stubble off their fields. He saw the daft circles they made as a wind lifted the flames and turned them; he saw their hysterical galloping back and forth, and saw the cherry-red line crackling across the stumps of corn, towing its apron of smoke.

A field of fire. Yes.

And over the field, his vast, dark presence; shadow of a bird, shadow of a man; his laser eye, wings to soar, wings for the whip-lash drop; a speck in the sun, or a broad, black, noiseless shape skimming the flametop, watching the little creatures go to and fro.

It was dawn, a time he liked well.

He found a place to kill from and set down the leather case. He took the gun components from the protective foam interior.

Night workers were making their ways home. People on early shift were heading purposefully to work. Bustle, bustle.

Just one—since the place he'd found wasn't as secure as some. He would have to be fast, getting away.

He assembled the gun. It took no time at all; ten seconds to have it ready, scope in place, the stock up to his shoulder. Less time than that to break it down.

A man was running for one of the early-morning buses. A couple went by on bicycles, less hindered than usual because the roads weren't busy, the woman riding with one hand resting on the man's shoulder. Three girls came into the line of fire, each wearing a student nurse's uniform, walking quickly, but gossiping as they went, and laughing, their heads constantly turning to whichever of them took up the conversation.

Bustle, bustle. Ross laughed. Just a chuckle at first, but then it grew, and the images in the scope jostled with the shaking of his shoulder. He lowered the gun and got control of himself, then raised it again, but the laughter returned: a grimace, a flutter, and then a great stream of bubbles inside, floating up, jouncing his chest, until tears blurred the figures in the scope. He dropped the gun from his shoulder again and bent over as the laughter wracked him, all the more powerful for being silent, for being trapped inside.

His face was a rictus. He bounced with mirth, one arm folded across his belly, the other dangling the gun. He roared, he bellowed, he shouted with laughter, and never made a sound. He braced the top of his head against a section of partly demolished brickwork, and heaved with laughter, his face slick with tears, his limbs weak with the effort.

Eventually, he came back to himself. He turned and leaned his back on the wall, gasping. He was taken with little squalls of mirth that subsided, each more quickly than the last. Finally, he wiped his face and brought the gun back to his shoulder.

Bustle, bustle.

A hiccup of laughter, a steadying pause. Then he fired.

Culley came awake in the instant before the phone rang. He said, "Sorry," and snatched up the receiver. As he was bringing it to his ear, he remembered that he was in his own apartment, alone.

It took him five minutes to dress and leave the house. Even so, Mike Dawson was there before him.

"You live south of the river," Culley said.

"Yeah. I don't always sleep south of the river."

They went behind the canvases and looked down. It's like a scene from a play, Culley thought, and in each performance a different extra takes the victim's part. He said, "Who's this?"

The name meant nothing and it never would. Another performance, another stiff. One more for the body count.

They went to the place where Ross had stood, picking their way across a rubble of brick, concrete, and roofing girders. A road circled the site—a waste lot that had once contained shops, pubs, and a post office. On one side was a deserted truck park. The demolition was about two-thirds complete, allowing both access and cover.

Culley stumbled on a half-brick and Dawson caught his arm. "Susan Court was nothing, then?"

"Nothing."

"You saw this guy Yorke?"

"Yes." Culley made a duck-quack motion with fingers and thumb. "I don't see him storming the barricades."

"Champagne socialist," Dawson suggested.

"Well . . . spritzer, more like." He changed the subject. "Where was she going?"

"On her way to work—local hospital, only one street away."

"On her own?"

"Yes. Three of her friends—also nurses—had taken the same route a few minutes before. They'd all gotten off the bus together; this one had gone into a truckers' café for cigarettes and a con-

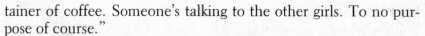

tainer of coffee. Someone's talking to the other girls. To no purpose of course."

"Anything different?" Culley asked.

"No. Easy target; center shot; no one saw a thing." Dawson paused by a jagged section of wall some nine feet high. A window space, devoid of frame, gave directly onto the road. They could see the canvas screens, the white tapes, three uniformed men trying to keep traffic moving. "What do you think?"

"Looks right." Culley turned and stared across the site. A crane with a sledge-block attached stood in the center; outside its scope, there were single walls, doors that opened onto nothing, ragged billboards. A bathroom had been laid open like a film set. The sun was up now, and strong; he could see a quiver of exhaust gases in the air.

"What?" Dawson asked.

Culley shook his head. "Can you smell anything?"

Dawson shrugged. "Brick dust; a whiff of carbon monoxide. I don't know. Smell what?"

No, it wasn't a smell. What was it? Culley moved around in the small space close to the window. "I expect that's it," he said. "Gasoline vapor."

It was hot and muscular, not a smell but something in the air. Culley thought of a gym after hours, a boxing ring when the bout had finished and the audience gone. He thought of a cage after the creature had flown. It was the fierce residue of energy and anger, once confined, but now free.

It reminded Culley of something he couldn't place.

The other end of day: an hour past dusk. The canvas was down and the tapes gone. The scene-of-crime team had done what they could, which wasn't much.

"Have you tried dusting a brick wall for prints?" one of them had asked Dawson earlier. "This bastard leaves fuck-nothing. I'm not hoping for a shell casing, you know, but if he'd just get a fucking nosebleed or something, I'd be a happy man."

Cars traveled the road around the site, a stream of red and white lights. The demolition workers hadn't been in that day.

Martin Jackson was standing where Culley had stood. He moved as Culley had moved, pacing the little platform of cement below the window space. He sensed what Culley had sensed. He looked out at the street, past the blur of headlights, and saw people going back and forth, moving swiftly and apprehensively, sometimes casting glances toward the hiding place.

Bustle, bustle.

Jackson sniffed the air like an animal taking a spoor. He smiled. The hairs lifted slightly on the nape of his neck and a rush of tingling spread on his scalp, then flooded his face so that he blushed in the darkness.

"Eric," he said.

"It was always the same," Helen said. She stood by the foot of the bed and unbuttoned her blouse.

Culley lounged naked on the coverlet. He turned to reach the two glasses of wine that stood on a bedside table; he'd brought them with him from the dinner table. Helen had waited for five minutes, not at all knowing why, then followed him into the bedroom.

She tossed the blouse onto a chair, took the glass Culley was offering, sipped, set it down, then unzipped her skirt and let it drop. "No matter what happened, I'd always fall for this."

"Which means . . . ?"

"Which means it doesn't mean much."

"I never thought that screwing you would get you back."

"Not a pretty word." Helen unsnapped her bra, shook it off, and took another swallow of wine.

"Why?" Culley asked. "Would you always fall for this?"

"You know how to fuck me. You always did."

Culley sighed. "Years of arduous practice." He grinned. "An exception to the rule.

"What rule?"

"Familiarity breeds contempt."

"I hope this sort of familiarity isn't going to breed anything." She was naked now, and kneeling on the bed still holding her wine. Culley took the glass from her and bit, gently, just under her breast, on the flat of her stomach, on the crease of her hip. She licked his face while he stroked her thighs apart. Presently, he heard the breath whistle in her throat, a gasp, a tiny groan.

She whispered, "Yes, there . . . just there . . . like that."

Dark places. A disembodied voice, a dead girl's voice. *There, just there, like that.*

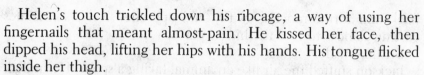

Helen's touch trickled down his ribcage, a way of using her fingernails that meant almost-pain. He kissed her face, then dipped his head, lifting her hips with his hands. His tongue flicked inside her thigh.

There, just there. He couldn't tell whether Helen had spoken or not, but her legs forked. Dark places.

He felt her shake, a tremor that came from the root. What was it she had said? *There's a darkness you like. There's a taste you like. There's a smell.*

Helen's fingers were in his hair. She drew him the length of her body, and he glided into her as she kissed his mouth. He thought of the derelict site and the broken wall. He thought of the window gap with its view of the canvas screen. There had been that heat, that fierceness like a scorchmark.

He knew, now, what it reminded him of. It reminded him of himself.

21

IT WAS SATURDAY MORNING and suburbia was busying itself with the tasks it likes so much. You could hear the chug of lawnmowers; hoses snaked out to cars parked at the roadside; bonfire smoke snagged in the branches of fruit trees. A terrifying place; a wilderness of venetian blinds and vegetable plots, of smiles and nodding heads.

When Angie Ross opened the front door, she was facing the sun. She lifted a hand to shade her eyes and Martin Jackson's face appeared on the backdrop of light, as if he were looking at her from the sun's center. He said, "Angie . . ." and she stood aside to let him in, lost for words, then followed him to the kitchen, as if he were showing her the way.

He sat on a stool by the breakfast bar while she made coffee. "It's been a long time," he said. "Years."

"Eric's not here." Angie took her time fetching cups and saucers. Jackson had always unnerved her. She glanced at the red, uneven features, the fair hair dusted with gray. He sat very still, his large hands resting in his lap, one atop the other.

"I know."

Angie paused, the coffee pot suspended over a cup. "Do you?"

"Where are the kids?" Jackson asked. "It's two now, isn't it?"

"Swimming," Angie said. "A neighbor . . ." She filled the cup and handed it to him. "If you know that—"

"I had a phone call," Jackson told her. "Yesterday. From Eric. It seemed that he wanted to talk to me. Then he hung up. About half an hour later, he phoned again. He sounded very distressed."

Angie sat down. She had filled a cup for herself, but made no attempt to drink. She asked, "What did he say?"

"Almost nothing." Jackson watched as she began to believe the lie. He knew he'd convince her; he was offering all the best ingredients of a successful untruth—it was possible without being obvious, surprising without being mysterious. Most potently, it was something she wanted to hear.

"He didn't . . ." Angie looked for something more or less neutral. "He didn't say what he wanted?"

"Not directly. I mean, it was clear that he wanted to talk, but we didn't really get down to what was bothering him. He mentioned old times, the army, you know, places we'd been to. The first call was really brief—just 'Hello, it's Eric,' not much more than that. I asked a couple of questions he wouldn't answer, then he said, 'I'll have to go.' The second call was longer." He drank some of his coffee.

Angie's hands were trembling slightly; she laced her fingers. "I haven't heard from him for, well, it must be three or four days, but then often . . . I mean, when he's on a trip, he doesn't phone every day. He didn't say what he wanted?"

Jackson smiled. "You asked me that. He didn't, no."

Angie wasn't sure what she was supposed to know. Eric and this man had been close. At one time, when she and Eric first met, Jackson had been a part of their life. She was aware of a past neither of them had spoken of much—at least, not while she'd been there.

At first, Jackson had seemed more or less at ease with her. But as her relationship with Eric deepened, he'd grown wary, sometimes openly hostile. There were things unspoken between the men. There were things the men never spoke of to Angie; and she had known instinctively that Eric's job was something she and he would never openly discuss. A web of silence. But caught in that web were jots of evidence that Angie quite simply lived with every day.

He'd had a separate telephone line installed; she lived with that. She knew that Eric's absences coincided with certain newspaper reports; she lived with that. She knew the gun was there; she lived with that.

She never queried it; it existed alongside their domestic contentment. She lived as a soldier's wife might. Or a hangman's.

To Jackson, she said, "He sounded distressed?"

"Very. He wasn't making a lot of sense. But he did say he wanted to talk. To *see* me and talk. I thought you might know where he is."

"No." A few seconds elapsed, then Angie shook her head as if to emphasize the denial.

"No." Jackson seemed to pause for thought. "Okay, well, maybe I could look around. Does he have a room he uses, somewhere he keeps—"

"The spare bedroom, but—"

"Because there might be something in there that—"

"I'm not sure I should—"

Their words ran over each other and they stopped. Jackson said, "You must be worried. Aren't you?"

Angie shrugged. "No, I—"

The silence between them was as bottomless as a dropped heartbeat. Angie made a tiny, delicate gesture, her hand moving upward and outward as if she might gather his words from the air and muffle them.

Eventually, Jackson said, "Aren't you?"

"At the top of the stairs," Angie told him. "It's the second door on the left. It's locked. Eric's got the key."

Jackson smiled at her. He said, "I won't take long."

The second phone line was connected to the room. There was a small desk, a lined pad, a tea mug holding a pencil and two pens, a stack of train and airline schedules, and a few pieces of personal clutter that could have been in any room in the house. The desk drawers were empty. On a shelf was a pebble that had been polished by running water; it was ovoid, a piece of granite about big enough to hold in a clenched fist; a seam of quartz halved it on the diagonal. Underneath it was a map of London. Jackson picked up the pebble and held it until the stone warmed. Then he slipped it into his pocket. A talisman.

When he unfolded the map he saw it was completely unmarked.

Later, he phoned Francis. "I'm in London," he said. "I've started."

Francis sounded remote, as if he were eating or reading. He said, "And?"

"I've seen his wife. Nothing there." Jackson was in a small hotel close to the city center. He had the map spread out before him on the bed.

"I wondered whether I ought to organize a tap on her phone."

Jackson laughed. "Don't bother. He's gone from there—if you see what I mean." His eye roved over the diagrams of streets and parks. "I'm just checking in. I'll call if there's anything to report."

"Listen," Francis's tone sharpened; he'd remembered something he had to say. "Ross is the most important thing here. But there's something else. You're not the only person looking . . ."

"Culley," Jackson offered. "Is that the name?"

The killer was faceless and nameless. Denied that focus, the media had made Culley's face and name signatures to their stories.

"Culley, yes; but anyone—anyone who's trying to track him down. It's crucial to find him. It's also crucial to stop someone else finding him first."

"I understand."

"We don't have long."

"I understand that too."

Jackson put the phone down, swung around onto the bed, and drew his feet up until he was sitting cross-legged. He stared down at the map. Lying beside it was a sheet of colored adhesive markers and a handwritten list that noted the location of each of Ross's killings. He spent ten minutes attaching markers to the map, then sat back to look at the result. It appeared entirely random. In truth he'd expected it would.

He took a mapping pen and wrote onto the markers the dates when the killings had occurred. This showed him nothing except that Ross had been skillful in the way he had chosen to combine places with times. Random again.

He ran his eye down the list, looking at the column in which he'd noted the time of day for each killing. Almost random; there seemed to be a preference for early morning. It wasn't much.

He looked again at the scatter of markers, hoping that some system of lines might appear, some focal point. There was nothing. Finally, he peeled the markers off the map, leaving it blank once more.

Eric, he thought. Eric . . . I know what's happened. Of course I do. Kill one, kill three, kill nine. Is that where you should have stopped? Did they think you would? Perhaps they did. But how could they understand?

Kill one. It's a job. Or maybe it's a grudge. Business or hatred, there's something that stays the same—it's just *that* person; just about him. You know the name, you know the purpose: to kill one person and then go home.

You plan it for minimum trouble, minimum risk. You look at the problem; you think it through; you find a way. Maybe there's a slight fizz of excitement when the day arrives. Everything's a little brighter, a little louder. When you get to the spot you've picked—while you wait—you might notice the lick of pulse in your wrist is a little faster, a little harder. Of course. You might have time to savor the moment, while you watch him approach, while you pick your shot; but then it's all movement, whatever route you've chosen, whatever method for getting clear.

Then, when it's over, you won't think of it much. The fizz, the pulse beat, the moment slightly delayed . . . yes, that was good, but it's all part of the job. And the job consists of being efficient, being careful, being precise. If you're good you'll get more. You'll remember not to be too greedy, to leave good intervals between them. To pace yourself, doing enough to pay for a comfortable life and little enough to stay invisible. Angie, the kids, the mortgage; nice holidays, nice car.

This is different, isn't it? I know what's happened. Kill one, kill three, kill nine, isn't the same. A fizz, okay; a faster pulse, okay. But somewhere, something happened. Where? Was it five? Was it seven? What was the crucial number when nothing was the same? When you felt the fever, felt lightheaded, your hands trembling, your eyes hot?

I know what's happened. You were doing the job. Everything was fine. Number . . . what? You looked along the sights, just like before, just like the other times.

And what you saw there took your breath away.

114

22

No ONE KNEW WHAT TO DO. There were daily statements by senior police officers, by the Home Secretary, by the Prime Minister. Everything they said meant, "There's nothing we can say."

Television specials were mounted in which psychiatrists offered theories that meant, "We know certain things that underline how little we know."

Advice was given about how people might behave. It added up to, "Don't go out. Apart from that, there's nothing we can tell you to make you safe."

Robin Culley was interviewed for the fiftieth time. Among the things he said was, "Someone knows who he is."

Angie Ross lay in bed and watched a spangle of light flicker and fuse on the wall as a breeze moved the curtain. It was just past dawn and she believed she hadn't slept: not that night, nor the previous night, nor the night before that. The truth was that she would doze now and then—ten minutes here, twenty there; but her dreams were so vivid and so close to her conscious fears that she might as well have been awake.

She thought, It can't go on. Then: Why would it stop? Then: How might it stop? If I told them . . . She banished the idea, and in the next moment brought it back. What use would that be? What would they have? A name. He's not here, and I don't know where he's gone. How would his name help them? In any case, they've got a name for him already. They've got several. Beast. Maniac. Fiend.

She was suddenly aware of the absence in her bed. Of the absence in her life. And knew that it would never be otherwise. She thought it, then said it outloud: a whisper that broke up in tears. "He won't come back. Eric can never come back."

Five days had passed since Martin Jackson had arrived in London. In that time, there had been two more killings. He had nothing to say, but he phoned Francis anyway. It was early—a countryman's time to wake.

"Is there anything you need?" Francis asked. "Just ask."

"Luck," Jackson told him. "A mistake."

Helen Blake watched Culley as he slept. She thought, It's too tough. All this going on . . . it's lousy timing. And apart from that, who knows if it can work? Old patterns, old ways, old resentments still there to fuel the disagreements. It's like being in a house where you used to live, but you can't quite remember its danger points. Forget to duck—*whack*; your head hits a lintel. Miscount the stairs in the dark—*crunch*; you're on your ass in the cellar.

Did I stop loving him? Not sure. Don't know. Hard to say. Sometimes. Yes, sometimes I certainly did. Then I'd start again. It was all motion, always moving . . . so I suppose that must mean I didn't stop; not really.

I couldn't cope with his life, that's what it was. Not the shit hours, the danger, the uncertainties. No; I couldn't stay close to whatever it was in him that liked it so much. Not liked it; liked it *so much*. Something dark in him. Something that liked dark places. Now here he is saying, "Have me back. I've changed."

She moved the pillow she was leaning against, and when she turned back Culley's eyes were open and looking directly at her.

"Were you watching me asleep?" he asked. "Because that's definitely cheating."

"I need some kind of advantage."

He sat up, twisting the heels of his hands into his eye sockets, and looked blearily at Helen. She said, "I'll make some coffee."

When she leaned forward to get out of bed, Culley reached under her arms, taking a breast in either hand. He said, "Let's get married so we can stop fucking."

"A terrific offer."

She made the coffee and brought it back to bed—a compromise. Culley was lying with his hands beneath his head, gazing at the ceiling. "There's got to be something," he said. "Christ knows . . ."

"For instance?"

Culley and Jackson didn't know one another, but they knew the same thing. "He's got to make a mistake," Culley said, "or else we get lucky."

Both happened. The luck came through Helen.

23

JAY HAMMOND HAD BEEN Ross's sixth victim: the tennis player, taking time off for a game with a business contact. They had stood at one set all, but Hammond held two service breaks in the third. It wasn't necessary for him to throw the game in order to please the other man—his particular business was a seller's market.

He'd been feeling good that day: finding the sweet spot time after time, the ball coming off the racquet head with no sense of effort. The game had stood at thirty-love when he tossed the ball up to serve and the man at the back of the opposite court had watched him hop and stumble, then fall, the racquet leaving his hand on the upswing and curving away. His legs had buckled and knocked, a comic effect, and he'd gone down too soon for his partner to see the ugly roundel that had begun to form on the white tennis shirt.

Everything had been very still. The ball had bounced on the court, then dribbled away.

Hammond had been a rich man. His lifestyle had reflected it—his cars, his clothes, the restaurants he chose to eat in. But most of all, it was evidenced by his house.

You turned off a main road into a broad driveway. There were ornate, wrought-iron gates fifteen feet high, maybe twenty; they were usually open. Winged lions, sculpted in stone, crouched on the two pillars at either side of the entrance.

A two- or three-minute walk would bring you to the house. It was Georgian, a perfect balance of elegant windows, discreet pillars and pediments. The brick was a warm, russet color and shaggy with ivy on the west facade.

Inside were elegant hallways and high-ceilinged rooms. The furniture was almost all antique of the period, though on one wall, at a corridor's end, a Louis Quinze tapestry hung above an eighteenth-century pew. The paintings were usually English or French, some oils, but watercolors for the most part—country scenes, portraits, and one curious canvas of a lady dressed in a ball gown and holding a dead hare by the hind legs. It was a curious lapse in carefully balanced good taste.

Nicola Hammond walked rapidly along a corridor, her heels making a rapid staccato on the polished boards. She passed the lady and the hare with an indifference borne of familiarity. A casual glance would have made it seem that her expression was stiff with anger. She was angry, for sure, but a closer look would have revealed a heaviness in the mouth, a darkness under her eyes: the face of someone who had cried a good deal recently, and had some crying yet to do.

Gunter Schmidt strode behind her, tall, white-haired, elegant. He seemed exasperated, though well in control. Previously, she had known Schmidt only slightly—as a business contact of Jay's; since Jay's death, he had rarely left her side: guardian, or guard.

Nicola spoke over her shoulder—"I'm a prisoner in my own goddamn home"—her voice made uneven by emotion.

"Nonsense." Schmidt smiled patiently. Although she couldn't see the gesture, he waved a hand as if to demonstrate the extent of her freedom. "We can go anywhere you like."

"Exactly. *We* can go."

"It was agreed—"

"Not by me," Nicola said sharply. Then, as if to herself, "Not by me."

She opened a door into a large, sunny drawing room, crossed its breadth, sat on a sofa, got up immediately to look for a cigarette, found a pack on a low table by the window, then sat down on a chair. As soon as Schmidt settled, she rose again and walked to and fro in the room pecking at her cigarette.

"I've given you an assurance . . ."

"Yes, Nicola." Schmidt's tone was both apologetic and mildly patronizing. "But we feel you are upset. You might perhaps change your mind."

"Like having a jailer," she said.

"Surely not."

"Like having a ball and chain."

She went back to the window, crushed her cigarette, and took another from the pack. "By day, it's you—eating with me, walking with me, waiting in the hallway while I have a shit."

"Nicola . . ."

"By night, it's that fat idiot taking the night shift, Goldman, sitting on a chair in the hallway with his flask of coffee and a plastic tub of sandwiches. *Christ.*"

"Would it be a good idea, perhaps, if you went away some-where?" Schmidt modified the offer at once. "If we went away. A holiday."

Nicola looked at him steadily for a few seconds. "Don't patron-ize me, you bastard."

Schmidt gave a wry smile; he shrugged. "Look, Nicola, you know what's going on. I understand your distress. I understand your need for—" he hesitated, finding a way around the word *revenge*—"well, to have things straight. But we don't live in that kind of a world. When Jay died, it was necessary to conserve, to protect."

"When Jay died." The words turned her lip—something of a sneer, something of sorrow. "He was murdered; isn't that what you all think?"

"Yes. You know we do."

"A maniac," she said, "but a maniac with a purpose."

"It was unwise to have told you. That should not have hap-pened."

"Oh, really? He was my husband."

"He was my associate in business. There are some things that we simply have to . . . let go."

Nicola started another cigarette. She sat on the chair by the window and gazed out at the wide lawns edged by chestnut trees. After a while, Schmidt asked, "Is there anything you would like to do today? Anything in particular?"

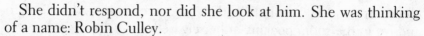

She didn't respond, nor did she look at him. She was thinking of a name: Robin Culley.

She was thinking of a way.

Nicola Hammond had always been aware that her husband was a criminal. It hadn't bothered her in the slightest. She liked their life together, and her conscience had never been troubled by the knowledge of where their wealth came from. It wasn't as if Jay might storm into banks with a shotgun or ram an armored truck. He was a dealer; his business was a civilized one, and legitimate for the most part. Now and then, he was able to perform a special service for one of his clients and there was a little secrecy involved. Something might be in Jay's hands for a short while—a certain item—then it would be gone. Or, more likely, Jay would simply match a customer to such an item and negotiate a price.

Nicola and Jay were a rare example of people who had met in their early twenties, fallen in love, married, stayed in love, stayed happy. Their marriage was nothing to Schmidt, nothing to Jay's other close business associates. They felt no grief and experienced no real sense of loss. In Nicola, those feelings were overwhelming; and alongside them was a fierce desire to see Jay's murderers punished. Not so much the man who had killed him, though it would have pleased her to know that man was dead. No, the people who had ordered Jay's death—they were the ones who had to be punished.

She didn't know their names; she wouldn't have recognized their faces; but she knew they existed. And someone would be able to find them; someone would be able to take Jay's name as a starting point and make a journey that would lead to those other names. Robin Culley would be able to do that.

Nicola sighed, trying for the right combination of sadness and surrender. "It would be nice to go for a walk," she said. "I suppose there's still a world out there." She turned to Schmidt and pressed a smile onto her mouth. "Is it okay—to go for a walk?"

Schmidt nodded and smiled back at her. "Yes," he said, "why not. I would like that too."

She would make it up as she went along—like a story told to a child at bedtime; like a clever lie that relies as much on the truth as on deception.

A chauffeur, someone she'd never seen before, brought the car to the front door. Nicola and Schmidt sat in the back. When Schmidt tapped the chauffeur's arm, the man pressed a button that raised a glass panel at his back. He didn't start the engine.

"There are certain conditions," Schmidt said. "We will walk for an hour or so. Is that agreeable? This man will wait for us in the car. Should we meet other people, you will stay clear of them. Please empty your pockets."

Nicola laughed. "What do you expect to find?"

"Paper, maybe, and a pen."

She was wearing a linen jacket, underneath that a blouse and blue jeans. Schmidt looked through the few things she brought out. There was a lipstick, which he didn't hand back. He leaned forward and slipped a hand into Nicola's jacket pockets, then gave her a brief look of apology. She slid forward on the seat while he patted the front and back pockets of her jeans.

"I'm sorry," he said, then tapped the glass panel. The car moved off.

A couple of little feints to begin with.

They drove through a town. At one point, when they were balked by traffic, Nicola touched the door, close to the handle and shifted in her seat. She felt Schmidt's corresponding move, his hand dropping onto her forearm. She pushed on the door as if for support, turning toward him and settling into her seat again as if that had always been her intention.

They stopped at a red light. In the front seats of the car next to them, two men were talking business, the driver taking his hands from the wheel now and then to amplify whatever point he was making. In the back a woman was looking out of the open window, her chin propped on the heel of her hand.

Nicola looked directly ahead, but pressed the button to bring her window down. Schmidt's eyes went to the sound. Nicola's face, at the open window, was no more than three feet from the other woman's. She turned from Schmidt and said, "My husband . . ." then immediately turned back, as if unaware of the other car, making it seem that her remark had always been intended for Schmidt.

Their voices clashed, his sharp with alarm, hers even and conversational.

"*Nicola.*"

"My husband was never a particular friend of yours, was he?"

Schmidt took a second to recover, then the concern went out of his face. The cars drew away, a breeze from the open window lifting Nicola's hair. He said, "We didn't see a great deal of one another, it's true; but I was fond of Jay."

"Yes," Nicola said. "Most people were."

For the rest of the drive, she chatted about Jay, about how they had met, the things they had done together. It seemed to Schmidt that even though the recollections made her sad, talking about them at all was the beginning of a means to recovery. Once or twice, she knuckled a tear. On one occasion, she asked his opinion and he was glad to give it.

"It's not possible, is it, to start again?"

"But of course it is. Eventually. You will discover a time for that."

"Just here," she said, "tell him to stop just here."

Schmidt tapped on the glass and the chauffeur ran the nearside wheels onto a broad stretch of grass fifty feet from the fringe of a beechwood.

A couple of feints, and now a couple more.

They walked through a dapple of sunlight that shifted as the breeze shifted the leaves. Overhead, a sound like distant surf. Nicola had taken them off the path and into a dense part of the wood. Three times she went one side of a tree when Schmidt went the other, emerging again without breaking her conversation. On the fourth occasion, she paused leaving Schmidt to walk on alone.

She heard his voice, then heard it stop. He backtracked rapidly. She was close to the tree's bole, crouching down to examine some-thing.

"Just there." Nicola pointed, then glanced up, smiling. "A wild orchid." She saw the tension leave his shoulders as he hunkered down to look.

Halfway around the walk, they came to a chalk escarpment that sloped away from a ridge, falling about thirty feet to a small clear-ing. Nicola paraded along its edge like a tightrope walker.

Schmidt was answering a question she had put to him. "It's simple: we can't win this time. To do anything at all would be to risk exposure. It's business. There are no rules." Nicola listened as she walked the grass lip. He said, "There will be other—"

Suddenly she was gone, off balance and tilting down the slope, running with windmill arms, sliding, running again, a plume of white chalk dust under her heels. She came off the slope at an uncontrollable pace that took her across the clearing and into the trees.

Schmidt went after her, falling twice before getting down. As he started across the grass, Nicola was emerging from the treeline.

"I missed my footing." She examined her hands, white with chalk, as if looking for the source of some small pain, then gave up on that and began to dust herself down.

Schmidt looked up the scarp. "We can find a way from down here?" he asked.

"Not really. We turn in the opposite direction to meet the path. It's not so bad." Nicola took a run at the slope and gained a third of it before dropping nearly to all fours to grab at little ridges and tufts of grass. Schmidt labored behind her; she could hear his grunts of effort.

When she reached the top, she turned and looked down. Schmidt was watching her, but still climbing. She crouched and put out a hand. "I'm sorry," she said. "Stupid of me. Are you all right?"

He nodded, reassured, and searched for a foothold. Nicola stayed put, her arm still outstretched. When he was in reach, Schmidt grasped her hand.

She stood up, drawing him with her, and for a moment he was upright, his feet on the slope, his head just above the rim.

Nicola braced herself and kicked out. At the same time, she wrenched her hand away. Her toecap took him under the chin, close to the throat. She didn't wait to judge the effect of that. Before he had disappeared, she was yards away, going at a dead run.

Schmidt went backward off his heels, dropping his full length on the slope, head and shoulders slamming into the chalk. His body leaped like a salmon, airborne, as he turned and crashed down again, then rolled off the scarp and onto the clearing.

Something had gone in his larynx. The sound of his breath as it sawed and whistled in his throat mingled with the rush and whicker of wind among the trees.

He couldn't move. His chest heaved atrociously. He lay on his back and looked up at the leaf canopy as it stirred and turned, sifting the afternoon sunlight.

24

IT RAINED THAT EVENING, a steady fall that kept people off the streets.

Two men walked through the downpour, their heads pulled into their coat collars. One of them wore a hat that dripped water from the brim. The men were professionals—costly, but efficient. The task they had been given was part of a broader pattern of events, none of which they were required to know about. They didn't want to know. They had never heard the name Hugo Kemp. They knew nothing about paintings or about art theft. It wasn't their speciality. To each, his own.

They went to a door and knocked. A woman opened the door, peering into the rain, and they muscled through. When she opened her mouth to yell, a hand caught her face, pinching into the angle of the jaw so hard that the cry died in her throat. Although she was silent, the grip didn't loosen.

All three stood in the hallway, the woman backed up to the wall, a finger and thumb goring her cheeks. The blood slipped from her face and she began to faint. It seemed that a dark halo enclosed the men's faces and her head filled with a sound of the sea. Her hands slapped the wall, like someone drumming a loose rhythm on a tom-tom.

They took her into the living room and put her down on a sofa. One sat next to her, the other stood close by. She looked at them dumbly.

The man sitting with her on the sofa said, "Are the kids in bed?" He had a lisp. The word *kids* ended with a tiny hiss and the tip of his tongue flicked out between his teeth.

The woman nodded. The man who was standing left the room. She looked after him in alarm. "Where's he gone?"

"He's just looking in on them. Making sure they're asleep. Don't worry." The man's tongue came back to his lip and he made a series of little whispered sounds, *huss, huss, huss*; his laugh. "Don't worry. He's very good with kids."

The woman half-rose and the man took her arm, pulling her back down. He slapped her, swiftly and casually, his hand coming back to cover her mouth in case she might cry out. He said, "No. We stay here." His tongue left a bead of spittle behind.

"What do you want?"

He didn't answer. He was looking toward the door. The other man returned and nodded. He looked around for the phone, found it, and took it to the woman, laying it in her lap.

She dialed the number they gave her.

A voice said, "Anne?" It was her husband's voice.

The two men watched her reaction and registered it as the right one. That was as far as their understanding went. Secrecy depends on ignorance. Just as they had never heard of Hugo Kemp, so the men had never heard of Anne Pope. Even now they didn't know it was her name, or that she was speaking to her husband, or that he was about to play his part in the theft of a painting. Their only concern was that when Anne heard her husband's voice she should say the things she was supposed to say, feel the things she was supposed to feel.

Terrified, of course she was terrified; Michael Pope had expected that. But when the moment came, when he heard her, talking in a fear-ridden whisper, it wrenched at him.

Seconds after he'd broken the connection, the phone rang again. A voice said, "All right?"

"They won't hurt her?" Pope asked.

"Of course not."

"They won't hurt the children?"

"Not her, not the children; don't worry."

"She sounded so scared."

"Yes, well, she would. That's the whole idea." A laugh, offering reassurance. "Let's get on with it."

Pope climbed a flight of stairs to the main part of the house. In the hallway, close to the door that led to the family's rooms, was a small, wall-mounted console. He went to it and opened the hinged flap to reveal a series of numbered buttons, zero to ten, like a telephone dial unit.

. . .

The people who were running Michael Pope hadn't heard the name Kemp, either. Like the two men who waited with Pope's wife, they were doing a job—working under instructions. Their job was to organize the theft, make it foolproof at any cost, then get the merchandise to its initial destination. They were professionals, too; they had gone to great trouble to make sure that Pope understood his role completely.

"We'll do it like this," they'd told him. "Two men will go to your home. You'll get a phone call to say that unless you follow instructions your wife and children will be killed. Your wife will be frightened, but nothing will happen to her, of course. And because she'll believe it all, other people will believe her. That's very important. You say the house will be empty . . ."

"For a month. They cruise. Fly to Brittany, take the boat down to Nice, go up and down the coast, then the Adriatic or other parts of the Med. The Aegean." Pope had laughed. "It's a fucking dull life."

"Okay. After you hear from your wife, you'll hear from us. Use the cellular phone; let the caller know as soon as you've switched off the alarms. How long will we have?"

"When the alarms go off in the house, they'll go on in Central Station. The response time can be as short as ninety seconds."

"Don't worry. The men who'll come in know what they're looking for. Someone will give you an injection."

"What?"

"You'll be unconscious when the police arrive. It's the best way —best for you. What would you be doing otherwise? Chasing the guys down the street? Screaming 'Help' like some hysterical girl? Phoning a description of the vehicle? Also, it looks good. You've been threatened, you've been doped, you're groggy. You won't have to act; you won't have to worry about the expression on your face when the squad car turns up."

Pope had thought this through. It seemed right. He said, "What about the money?"

"A little at a time. Open an account somewhere in a false name and let us have the account number. We'll make payments each month; a grand here, two grand there. You'll have it all inside two years. The only crucial thing is—don't tell anyone. Don't get boastful; don't drop hints to your best friend over a bottle of scotch."

"Are you serious?"

"People do."

"Not me."

"Your wife will believe it, the police will believe it. You kill the alarm, then go to sleep for ten minutes. That's it. It's money for nothing, and danger-free as long as you keep shut."

Pope had smiled and shaken his head. Tell someone, he'd thought. Christ, I don't want to know about it myself.

"We'll need a sketch layout of the house; floorplan."

"Sure."

"And the precise position of the paintings."

"Yes."

"Fine. That's fine. It's all you have to do."

Pope ran it in his head. An image leaped up of his house, of the front door opening, of the men going in. He said, "What about Anne?"

"Who?"

"My wife."

"She'll be fine. We phone as soon as we're clear and the guys who're with her just walk out. Good-bye. She'll phone the police, but by that time, who cares?"

"They won't hurt her?"

"Don't worry."

"The kids . . ."

"Don't worry."

Still holding the phone, Pope opened the casing of the console. He punched in a five-digit code, then said, "Tell me when."

There was a pause on the line of no more than thirty seconds. A voice said, "Now." Pope pressed *Enter*, and the code registered. He went to the door and opened it.

They came past him at a run, three of them, two heading straight for the room that Pope had indicated on the floorplan. The third held back. Pope had already removed his jacket and begun to roll back his sleeve. The man hit him, left hand, back-handed; he was wearing a weighted glove. Pope felt the vertebrae in his neck pop. Everything clouded. He'd bitten his tongue when the blow landed, and a splash of blood looped onto his chin.

"Sorry." The man was tapping the barrel of a syringe. "It looks better—you know?" He gave the injection. In the same moment, the others came past. Each was carrying a taped package, foam-wrapped.

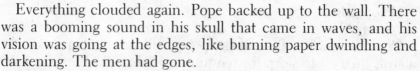

Everything clouded again. Pope backed up to the wall. There was a booming sound in his skull that came in waves, and his vision was going at the edges, like burning paper dwindling and darkening. The men had gone.

He slid down the wall and sat with a bump. He was aware of shadows amid the gloom, then the darkness poured over him. Five seconds later he was dead.

The man with the lisp said, "It'll put you out for ten minutes. No more. Time for us to get clear."

Anne shook her head. The man standing behind her grasped her left wrist and tucked the arm up behind her back; his other hand went into her hair, drawing her backward.

"It's nothing; I promise." A bubble of saliva lingered on his teeth. He massaged the crook of her elbow to raise a vein and slipped the needle in.

After a moment, her eyes fogged. The second man released her and went into the hall to collect two coats and a hat. The man with the lisp joined him. It was still raining. They stepped out, dressed for the weather.

The children hadn't wakened, so they'd let the children live.

25

THE END OF THE DAY should bring good food, good wine, good conversation, and, for perfect symmetry, good news.

Hugo Kemp took a mouthful of poached salmon and chewed slowly to get the flavor. He cleansed his palate with a sip of iced water, then flooded it with the crisp, light taste of Veuve Clicquot.

An Indian wearing a starched white coat and a black bow tie stepped forward and refilled his glass. The man had enjoyed a blip of peyote earlier in the day, and there was a mild, dreamy look on his face, a look of effortless tolerance; but his hand was steady.

Kemp said, "He was one of the true originals. There are few, really. Each in his manner, of course, and greatness is originality enough. But there are some who appear to stand apart from their contemporaries in a particular way. It has to do with a lack of influence. They tend away from the school mentality. Look at the Impressionists—all painting with the same palette. But some . . . Rembrandt, El Greco, Picasso. Cezanne." He glanced sideways and his plate was removed from the table. A cheese platter was brought.

"Cezanne . . . He felt the work of others, of course; no one creates in a vacuum. Veronese, Corot, Delacroix. From them he took a notion of proportion and of color mass. But he was his own man."

Nina turned the fragments of food on her plate with all the delicacy of an archaeologist lifting a shard onto a trowel. The tines of her fork tapped the china, drawing a clear note.

"He was single-minded, but broad-minded too—open to other disciplines. He knew Zola well. They would read poetry together, people like Hugo and Lamartine. Cezanne liked it for its fierce romanticism. I can't believe he would have taken much of its meaning. 'A vision born of solitude'—that's what one critic said of his work."

She let the champagne touch her mouth, then opened it slightly so that the clean coldness flushed the fatness of her lower lip and spilled from her teeth to her tongue. She imagined it as a tiny surge welling over a dam and splashing into a parched valley. Her mouth was very dry.

"It's said he was a boorish man—moody, quarrelsome. He lost friends. Called Zola vile when they fell out, and never spoke to him again. He said, 'Isolation is all I'm good for.' He had a Catholic faith—strong to the point of bigotry. 'I don't want anyone to get their hooks in me,' that's what he said. He moved around a lot, but his heart lay in Aix-en-Provence. He lived to paint. You can see his own contradictions in some of the landscapes—rich, placid greens, hot ochers."

Nina broke a piece of fish into damp flakes. The Indian emerged from his soft, stoned world for a moment and took her plate away. He had to ease the fork from her fingers. The expression on his

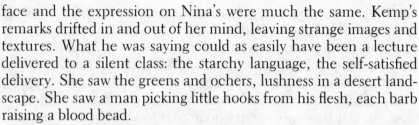

face and the expression on Nina's were much the same. Kemp's remarks drifted in and out of her mind, leaving strange images and textures. What he was saying could as easily have been a lecture delivered to a silent class: the starchy language, the self-satisfied delivery. She saw the greens and ochers, lushness in a desert landscape. She saw a man picking little hooks from his flesh, each barb raising a blood bead.

"He was working one day, painting from nature, and got caught in a rainstorm. He collapsed. God knows how long he lay there. Someone driving a laundry cart found him. He died a week later." Kemp reached for the cheese; in the same moment, the Indian stepped forward with a claret decanter.

Nina got up and smiled a smile that was meant for no one. She said, "I'm tired."

During the time he'd been talking, Kemp had scarcely once taken his eyes from Nina's face. He said, "Yes; you look tired."

"Perhaps I'll go to bed." She walked the length of the table and kissed her father. He watched her approach and watched her as she went toward the door. Henry Glinwood came into the room. He and Nina passed without a glance.

Glinwood sat in a chair halfway along the dining table. He said, "They're on their way."

Kemp smiled and lifted his claret glass. Good food, good wine, good conversation. Good news.

26

Y OU RUN AN INTERSECTION, looking neither left nor right but simply slapping the gas and driving across. The intersection is on your route home, and you do it every day, and nothing ever happens.

Whenever you take a trip to the sea, you like to swim. You find a place to dive from, because diving is something you do particularly well—a ledge on a cliff, a boat pier. Of course it's dangerous; there could be rocks or a killer current. It's always the same—each time you dive, you find clear, calm water.

You know it's neither judgment nor luck. It's meant to be that way. You're invulnerable.

Eric Ross sauntered through the park. Like everyone else, he was wearing weekend clothes: jeans and a light jacket. He was carrying a small backpack by one of its straps. People strolled past without giving him a second look—couples hand in hand, families with strollers, groups of friends looking for a good spot to picnic. Three young men in cutoffs had colonized a triangular space and were flipping a Frisbee. Ross watched as it shuttled between them, going from hand to hand across thirty feet of air.

Maybe they all felt okay because no one had been shot in a park. Maybe, like Ross, they felt invulnerable, that it couldn't, wouldn't happen to them. Maybe it was nothing more than the statistical impossibility of everyone staying home all of the time.

As he passed them, Ross stifled an impulse to laugh. Pick and choose, he thought. It seemed so odd to think that they didn't know. Animals would have known, would have caught his scent, or have seen him suddenly among them, and they'd have turned and fled as a herd will turn from a predator. But no; they wandered by him, offering themselves like gifts—pick, choose; pick, choose.

He found a place in sight of one of the park's two lakes where a small plantation of young trees had been fenced off for protection. It was thick with bracken and fern. He hopped in and unzipped the backpack, taking out only the scope, which he pointed back toward the lakeside. A man on horseback was circling the water, the reins slack in his hands to let his mount go at an idle walk.

Ross assembled the gun and found the rider again, swinging the cross hairs past the Frisbee players, a man with a child on his shoulders, a woman throwing a stick into the water for her dog to chase and fetch. For a moment, he took the scope back to the child perched on his father's shoulders, then again to the horseman, who was coming directly toward the gun.

The woman threw her stick and the dog raced past to the water, going almost under the forelegs of the horse. It shied; then, as the rider gathered the reins, reared and skittered backward on its hind legs.

That was the moment when Ross fired. He saw the horse rise in the same fraction of a second that the recoil jabbed his cheek.

The horse screamed as the bullet scored its neck, and it seemed to leap with its hindlegs, making the rear a mighty buck that shipped the rider off and into the shallows of the lake. Ross fished around with the scope, looking frantically for his target, but nothing would stay still. The rider had managed to keep a hold on one rein and the horse was masking him—hopping and kicking out in an effort to break free. People were in the water, helping the fallen man; others were trying to calm the horse; everyone was moving and milling. The shot had been clearly audible and the activity by the water was energized by panic.

Ross knew he had already waited too long, but he continued to look through the scope, hoping for a clean shot at his chosen mark. The man refused to come clear; he stood on the far side of the horse, soothing the animal and examining the fresh wound on its neck.

Now. Go now. Ross actually said the words out loud, even as he took the cross hairs to and fro over the scene by the lakeside. *Go now.*

A furious anger lay in him. *Not this. Not like this. Not fail. Not lose control. They die at my touch. They die at my whim. They must.* He broke the gun down and stowed it in the backpack, slipped the spent cartridge case into his pocket, then jumped back over the fence. A man was watching him from no more than ten feet away, standing still but looking backward, as if his attention had been drawn to Ross's sudden appearance.

For a moment, they merely stared at one another; then Ross began to walk away. The man came after him. He said, "Hey . . ."

Ross continued to walk. A couple of men rounded the plantation, going at a run toward the lake. The man said, "Hey . . ." The others glanced toward him, but didn't stop.

It was just a matter of time, Ross could see that. He turned and walked toward his pursuer, smiling, his eyebrows raised. He asked, "What's the problem?" and in the same moment, struck at the man stiff-armed, a karate blow. It should have come as a complete surprise, but the man swayed, taking Ross's fist on his shoulder. He was young and fit, and had been half-expecting an attack. As Ross followed in, the man swung, catching Ross solidly on the side of the face; he was wearing a ring that opened a deep gash along the cheekbone.

Ross ducked under a second punch and the man grabbed him. They wrestled, grunting, Ross hampered by the backpack. The man kicked out sharply and connected just under the knee. A weakening pain raced from the joint to Ross's hip and he staggered slightly.

The man stepped back in order to measure a punch. Ross levered himself up, going against the pain, going fast, making his hand stiff from wrist to fingertip. He slammed the straight edge into his opponent's face, taking him between top lip and nostrils. The man fell to his knees. His eyes turned up so that only the whites were left and he made an ugly sound deep in his throat, then he went forward, full-face onto the ground.

Ross turned and ran from the park. When he saw or heard other people, he slowed to a walk until they were past, then he ran again. He had chosen a place close to one of the gates on the western side, always knowing that his time for escape was limited. Now there was no time at all. They could close the gates and have him bottled up.

Not like this. Not fail. He was sobbing with effort and anger. *Wrong. Wrong. Wrong.* He made for a line of scrub between two gates and waited until the street outside was fairly clear, then climbed the railings and dropped down. A few heads turned toward him—passers-by who didn't yet know what had happened in the park. He walked quickly, getting three streets clear, then hailed a cab.

People had seen him in the park. They were able to give a description.

Others had seen him as he jumped down from the railings. They were able to give a description.

The cab driver had dropped him a couple of streets from the rented apartment. He was able to give a description.

The descriptions varied widely. Some had him with a mustache, others clean-shaven. Some put him at average height, others said he was a tall man. He had brown hair, fairly short; he had dark hair worn long; he was dressed in a green jacket with jeans, a beige jacket with black trousers, a T-shirt, a polo shirt, sneakers, deck shoes. But there was enough that married to provide a series of relatively accurate characteristics.

It seemed certain that the dead man in the park had attacked the killer and had left his mark—many people mentioned a cut and a badly bloodstained face. For the police, it was a hell of a lot better than damn-all.

And they had other leads now. A district, for one thing. It was possible, of course, that their man had taken his taxi to a part of London far from the place he was staying in. On the other hand, he'd been flustered. For the first time, he'd made a mistake. Maybe he wasn't thinking straight. It was worth a try.

There was another thing. Walking from the taxi to his apartment, Ross had felt the sting and throb in his face for the first time. He'd put his hand to the place, amazed to see it come away bloody. He felt even more exposed, as if the wound were shouting his identity. He took a handkerchief from his pocket to hold against his cheek. He was hurrying, he was distressed and angry. *Not like this. Wrong. Wrong.*

The spent cartridge came out with the handkerchief and dropped onto the roadside verge.

Billy Knowle held a chicken and mayonnaise sandwich in his mouth in order to leave both hands free for the report. Finally, he put the folder down on his desk, bit a mouthful from the sandwich, and followed it with a gulp of lukewarm coffee.

"Yeah, it's probably from his gun. Anyway, it's a three-oh-eight." He took another bite. "I'd proceed on that basis if I were you."

Mike Dawson smiled. "We already have."

Culley ordered a house-to-house in the area. He tried to keep it quiet, but there were people in the neighborhood who were all too eager to be a part of the excitement. Some of them were approached by the press and TV news reporters. Had they been given the time, they'd've talked their faces off.

A day, thought Martin Jackson. A day, if I'm lucky. Longer than that and he'll be gone. He's got to hole up. He's angry and he's puzzled. He probably isn't the only man in London with a cut on his face, but it'll feel that way to him. It's Sunday night. He'll hole up and move again tomorrow, after dark.

A man on a journey, who suddenly loses himself. A man with a mission, who suddenly loses his faith. Where do you go when there's nowhere to go?

Go home.

27

IN OCTOBER 1987 the edginess that had been afflicting stock market dealings in London, New York, and Tokyo grew steadily until it was a full-fledged panic. The smart money had moved some time earlier, becoming cash or commodities, anything that could survive the flash fire of a market crash.

Other investors perished; or, at the very least, watched helplessly as their assets, like trees in the path of a firestorm, wilted, singed, then were consumed. On October 17th, over fifty billion pounds was wiped off share prices worldwide.

Not everyone was ruined, though many were badly burned. Some, for example, lost a couple of million, but had three or four other millions to spare. It's reasonable to think that a two million bite from a fortune of several million is a bearable loss. For the multimillionaire, though, it doesn't work like that. It doesn't feel like that.

Bernard Warner had lost that sort of a sum from that sort of a fortune. A number of his friends had been affected in a similar way; one or two had, in their terms, been wiped out—left with a million or less. All of them had lost faith in the money market. They would reinvest when things picked up, of course. But they wouldn't be risking everything.

Six weeks after the crash, Warner had called a meeting of a dozen of his friends. He had a proposition to make. It involved an investment cartel in a commodity that always held its value, no matter what might happen in world affairs, no matter what the state of third world debt, no matter who was at war with whom. Money had proved itself flimsy in the face of those imponderables. Fine art, Warner contended, would not.

Each of the men at the meeting was powerful in his own way. And, in part, their power came from an understanding that they were not as other men. They were among those few who controlled or owned the bulk of the country's wealth and influence. It was plain to them that they were an elite. They firmly believed that people should be given rules to abide by to ensure that society ran on an even basis; they didn't believe that the rules applied to them. Warner, in particular, believed this. He had been a member of Parliament for more than two decades. He helped to make laws, though it never really occurred to him that he should be governed by them.

When he hinted that some of their dealings might be—well— *confidential*, no one at the meeting asked questions. A mugger might go to prison for lifting a few pounds from his victim—and so he should. It simply wasn't the same thing as an investment proposal from a friend. If a few petty rules were bent, then so be it. These were the descendants of the great families, the few buccaneers left in a drab world. In any event, it wasn't necessary to know how Warner organized matters.

A fund was established, the money salted away in carefully disguised accounts abroad. As long as the money grew, everyone was satisfied. And the money did grow. Many of the transactions were legitimate. Warner went into the fine art buisness, using his friends and his influence to match buyer to purchase. He didn't often actually handle a painting, but that mattered little to him. Art was neither here nor there; money was the issue.

There was competition, of course. One of Warner's principal opponents was a dealer called Jay Hammond; not least because Hammond was also happy to deal on the wrong side of the law.

There were times, too, when Warner was obliged to involve himself with people he'd sooner not have known. One such person was the man who called himself Francis. Their relationship had put Warner in the uncomfortable position of being a customer.

"Well," Francis said, "he made a mistake. That's what we were hoping for."

"It makes a difference?" Warner asked. "In what way?"

"He'll probably go to ground. I just spoke to Jackson. He's hopeful."

"Jackson knows where to find him?"

"It's possible."

"Before the police find him?"

"Jackson has the advantage; the police don't know who he is."

"Let me know as soon as there's any news."

"Sure."

"Francis . . ."

"Yes?"

"Before the police find him. You understand?"

Francis's shrug came over the line. "They're no closer than they ever were."

Warner broke the connection and redialed. He said, "Sir Edward Latimer. It's Bernard Warner."

A phone rang and was lifted. Warner heard Latimer say, "That's all for now. I'll call you back in." A pause, then: "Bernard . . ."

"Checking in," Warner said. "What's going on?"

"I can't take these calls here." Latimer's tone dropped to a near-whisper.

"If I make them," Warner told him, "you'll take them. What's going on?"

Latimer sighed. After a moment, he said, "They found the cartridge case—"

"Jesus Christ, I know that."

"They've started a house-to-house."

"And?"

"No. The man had gone. They expected that."

"They're sure?"

"Pretty sure. Nothing's for certain, is it? They're checking places that are empty, or seem to be empty. It's a long process in a big area. No local sightings, at any rate."

Warner paused for thought. "He could still be there—simply not answering the door, or in a place they haven't checked as yet."

"He could be. They don't think so. The man's no fool. He made a mess of things in the park, but it's the first time he's got it wrong. He might be mad, but he's also methodical. The obvious move would be to get out of the district."

"And that's what they think?"

"Yes . . . Bernard, I'll have to go. I can't—"

"Is Robin Culley still heading up the task force?"

Another sigh. "Yes."

"You're still getting his reports."

"Yes; from time to time. His methods are a trifle eccentric."

"Bring him to heel."

"Not possible. I'd need a reason. I can't just—"

Warner's tone grew sharp. "He's dangerous—thinking as he does."

"I can't be seen to hinder things without cause. Don't worry. He's no further forward."

"He's got a theory. It's a correct theory."

"Culley doesn't know that." Latimer's voice had grown louder; he dropped it again. "Bernard . . . this has got to stop. I can't give you any more."

"You can," Warner said. "You will." He allowed a silence, not for Latimer's response, but to underline the lack of it. "Keep me informed about what Culley does. I want to know his thinking."

He paused again. Latimer's voice came on an indrawn breath. "All right, Bernard."

Warner heard him well enough. He said, "What?"

"All right."

"What would you like?" Angie asked. "Something to eat?" Ross didn't reply. She went to the fridge and fetched some cheese and a chicken leg. She put bread on the table. When the kettle boiled, she made two cups of instant coffee. He ate the food and drank the coffee.

She said, "We missed you." Then, riskily, "It's wonderful to have you back."

Ross shook his head. "I can't stay." He went to the glass door that led to the garden and looked out. It was dark, but he knew there was nothing to recognize.

It was two A.M. Angie hadn't been asleep. She'd heard him at the glass door—a double knock, very light. He must have come across the low fences that separated the row of back gardens.

"You'll be okay here with us," she said. "Me and the kids. Or we could go away. Sell up and go away. What would you like?"

Ross peered out at the garden. The faint glow from a street light showed him the outline of a hedge, neat flower beds, a black oblong of lawn. Closer to his eye was a reflection of the kitchen, which seemed to hover in the darkness, a silent capsule, a moment from a time warp. Angie was there, wearing a robe, hair touseled, her lips moving soundlessly.

"We can talk about it in the morning. Shall we go to bed, now? What would you like?"

A place you try to find after a long absence . . . Roads look familiar, landmarks seem to point the way. "This is it," you say, "I'm sure this is the place." But it isn't right—it doesn't recognize you.

"You look tired. Eric . . ."

Not tiredness. Anger. He wanted to go back and find that man, the horse rider, the man he'd chosen to die. *Wrong*. He put a hand to his cheek and saw Angie's reflected image float up and drift toward him from the garden.

"Let me see."

He sat on a kitchen chair while she peeled back the plaster he'd stuck over the wound. A puffy bruise divided by a clean slit rimmed with blood. She fetched antiseptic and some cotton wool, then bent toward him and dabbed at the place, a pose that brought their heads close together. When she spoke, her breath fell on him and his eyelids fluttered.

"We could go away for a bit—a break; a couple of weeks perhaps. Or you could just stay here and rest. What would you like?"

The anger surged and dropped like an errant tide. There was nothing here that belonged to him. He thought of his vantage point and the view through the scope; he thought of the way the cross hairs quartered the scene, seeming to draw a victim onto the crux, dead center. He heard the rush of wings.

Angie led him through the living room. Table, chairs, sofa, television. And upstairs. Carpet, banister rail, laundry basket on the landing. And into the bedroom. Dressing table, mirror, books, and a clock radio on the bedside stand. He undressed and got into bed, switching off the lamp.

"Eric . . ." Her breath on his face again.

He gathered her under the hips as if he were lifting laundry, before she was ready, spending no time on her at all. She whispered, "Wait," and he was inside her, abrasive, moving without the need of an answering rhythm. In the light from the partly opened curtains, she could see his head above hers, his neck stretched, his eyes open and staring at the wall above the headboard. She put a hand on his shoulder, to slow him, to make him think, and he tightened his grip on her haunches, dragging her into the quickening thump of his hips.

He came—she felt the moment in pain and sadness—but he continued to move, banging at her, clutching just that part of her that he needed, as if he'd felt nothing, as if he didn't know when to stop. His head was still up; his eyes were still fixed on the wall.

The same dream—Eric walking through a throng and pausing, now and then, to touch someone on the shoulder. Angie saw herself in the crowd. She hurried toward her husband, pushing others aside. There was nothing of recognition in his face as he passed her by.

She woke and found herself alone in the bed; a door closed and she identified the sound. She thought: I should have told him. But it might not have mattered. I want him back. Perhaps it doesn't matter.

Ross stood in the doorway of the bedroom. He asked, "Who's been here? Who went into my room?"

"In your room?" She felt foolish as soon as the words were out.

"Who's been in there?" Ross advanced on the bed. "*Angie.*"

It didn't sound like her name. She said, "Martin Jackson was here."

While he dressed, she cried, her face in her hands to stifle the sound in case she woke their children.

Eric . . . Not in the house. Not with her there. Not in one of the rooms you've lived in together. Our moment—it has to be our moment. I want to see you and I want you to see me. We don't have to talk, no, but we need a moment for ourselves. It's been so long.

I said, "I love you." And then you went away.

Let's think this through. Let's put our heads together. She'll tell you I called. She won't want to, but she'll have to. It depends when you find the pebble gone, and the map. You'll probably leave the way you came—over the gardens. How do I know that? Because I've been watching the front of your house long enough to know. I'm sure you're inside by now and I didn't see you, so it must have been over the gardens to the back door. Make sense? Okay.

Which is your car? You don't want to tell me? All right, that's fair enough. Right now, you're probably making guesses of your own and, listen, I'm not giving you any help with those.

I checked the cars earlier. I was looking for something fast and reliable, but not ostentatious. A suburban road, suburban life-styles and salaries. You know how important it is not to look exceptional. In the road to the left, two candidates; in the road to the right, two more. Seems like even odds. But one of them—in the road to the right—is a better candidate than the others. It's empty of books, umbrellas, maintenance manuals, coats, maps, all the usual detritus. I think that's your car, Eric.

All right. Now we've worried at this, what have we got? Your car is parked in the road off to the right. The thing is, we *both* know that; after all, we worked this out together. So you'll think: Martin knows where my car is. And he knows I know he knows. What are my options? Isn't that what you're thinking?

If I go to the car, he'll be waiting. Or—

He'll assume that I won't go to the car because he'll be waiting, so I'll go to the left, and that's where he'll be waiting.

Eric . . . Does that sound right? Perhaps I'm a thought ahead. Or one behind. How badly do you need the car? Pretty badly, I guess we're agreed on that.

So—there's our choice. Do we try the double-bluff, or not?

Jackson went to the road that bordered the gardens on the left. He waited for three quarters of an hour, until the mottled gray of false-dawn had given way to a pink-and-pearl flush above the silent rooftops, then left, walking between the rows of drawn curtains and smiling at his wrong choice.

28

BEFORE NICOLA HAMMOND HAD GONE for her walk with Gunter Schmidt, she had taken all the money in her wallet and lined her bra with it. She had guessed it would look better—more disarming

—not to be carrying a bag; as if she expected to be out only for a short time. Her cache amounted to just over a hundred pounds. She was living in a bed-and-breakfast place for thirty-five pounds a night, and paying each day—it wasn't the kind of hotel where you settled the bill as you left. She'd been there two days and was running out of money. Running out of time.

Protheroe and Latimer weren't the only people who had trouble tracking Culley down. Nicola had phoned a dozen times, without luck. It wasn't permitted to take incoming calls on the pay phone in the hallway of the hotel. In any case, she couldn't have held a conversation there.

Dawson passed the messages on. "She doesn't say who she is; she doesn't leave a number. She's phoned several times over the past couple of days."

Culley shrugged. "She'll get me eventually, I suppose. What do you think?"

"Who knows," Dawson said. "Could be a nut. On the other hand—"

"She won't talk to you?"

"No. She asks when she's likely to find you in."

"Ah."

"And she's not the only one."

"No?"

"Helen phoned a few times. As did Protheroe. Same question."

"What did you say?"

"How deep is the ocean," Dawson said. "How high is the sky."

The obvious route is often the last to be taken. Nicola Hammond looked in the phone book. There were listings for Culley a florist, Culley a bookseller, and Culley's, a restaurant; there were seven listings for other Culleys, three of them Culley, R. And there was a listing for Culley, Robin. She got an answering machine and was pretty certain that she recognized his voice from the times he'd given a TV reporter a few words at the scene of a crime.

"I'm not here to take your call. Leave a message, or try me on . . ." Then a number.

Nicola dialed and got Helen Blake. She said, "I've been trying to reach Robin Culley."

"Stand in line," Helen told her. Then her voice took on a tone of mild suspicion. "Who are you?"

"I need to talk to him. I've called his office; he's never there."

"That's right. Well, I'm not sure I can be much help."

"Are you his girlfriend?" Nicola asked.

"In a manner of speaking."

There was a pause. "Perhaps I could speak to you."

"Go ahead." Helen sounded intrigued.

"Not on the phone. Where do you live?"

Helen had been with Culley long enough to recognize a red light. "No," she said, "but I could come to you if you like."

They met in the lobby, which was little more than a hallway graced by a couple of wooden armchairs. Nicola led the way to her room. "There isn't much," she said. "I've got some scotch." Helen shook her head. They sat on the bed together.

"Jay Hammond," Nicola said. Helen raised her eyebrows and shrugged slightly. "My husband. He was killed by the sniper. He was a fine art dealer; paintings mostly, occasionally china. There were occasions," she chose her words with care, "when his deals were confidential."

"The paintings were stolen," Helen offered.

"He didn't—"

"Cut them out of the frames himself; no, I'm sure you're right. A customer approached him, he arranged the theft, someone else took the risk, someone else again arranged for transport, your husband paid them, of course, but he collected the fee from the buyer." Nicola looked at her, but said nothing. Helen smiled. "I work for a gallery," she said. "Cork Street."

"Jay was arranging a sale. I don't know who the buyer was. He never told me those things. But I do know that he was threatened."

"Why?"

"Someone else wanted the merchandise."

"A buyer?"

"No. A dealer—a supplier."

"What happened."

"They tried to buy him off. In fact, they offered him a very large amount of money. Jay was annoyed, I think. He said no. They told him that unless he backed out of the deal, they'd kill him."

"Did he?"

"No."

"And the sniper killed him."

"Yes."

Helen was hearing her own theory given circumstance and flesh. She asked, "What are you saying?"

"There's a man called Gunter Schmidt. One of Jay's associates. You said a moment ago that there'd be someone to organize transport. That's Schmidt. Jay had told me a certain amount—about the offers of money if he left the deal clear for someone else. He made light of it. Joked about how much they might pay. He didn't tell me about the death threat. Schmidt did that."

"Why?"

"After Jay was killed, the police called. They didn't expect . . . I mean, it was a routine call. But Schmidt was edgy. I was very upset. I think he was frightened that I might unwittingly say too much—that if I knew everything, I'd be more likely to guard my tongue; be part of the conspiracy."

"If you knew everything . . ."

"Schmidt—and one or two of his people—think they know about the sniper. They think it was a means of killing Jay without making Jay's death stand out. That way, it would seem like someone gone mad—everyone would be looking at the sniper, no one would be looking for a motive. If he'd killed only Jay, it would have been easy to make connections."

"It's a theory," Helen said. "What makes it believable?"

"Someone told Schmidt."

"Someone . . ."

"Yes. I don't know who. If I did, I'd tell you. He got a call on the day of Jay's death. Just: You've seen what happened to Hammond. It could happen to you. Call off the deal. That sort of thing."

"What did Schmidt do?"

"Called off the deal." She paused. "Whoever killed Jay, whoever ordered him to do it—I want them caught. I don't care about much else."

"But Schmidt does."

"Yes. That's why I'm here. They wouldn't . . . it was a bit like house arrest, really. I managed to get away."

"What will you do?"

Nicola shrugged. "Can you lend me some money?" she asked.

Helen looked around the room. "What have you got?"

"What I'm wearing."

"Yes." They sat in silence for a few seconds. Helen said, "I think we'd better go."

. . .

Schmidt had been able to hear the chauffeur crashing around in the woods. He'd tried to call the man's name, but it had emerged as a slurred gasp. Ellut. *Ellut.*

It had been an hour before Elliott had grown concerned. It was a further hour before he found Schmidt. It was a full day later before Schmidt had been able to form a coherent sentence, though his words still came in a low, wracked whisper. He was able to write, though. Elliott and Goldman were given instructions.

Get her back, Schmidt had written. *Need to know what she's said —who she's said it to. Maybe she hasn't yet. She'll hide. Think it over perhaps. She's implicated too.*

Elliott said, "She'll talk to the police if she talks at all—who else?"

Police, but only once—only one man. Talk to this person, talk to that. No good. Then he'd written, *Culley.*

They'd staked out Culley's flat for half a day and most of the night. Then they'd gone in for a look. The tape on his answering machine had said, " . . . leave a message or try me on . . ." They'd taken this information back.

Schmidt had made a phone call. His voice sounded like chains being dragged through gravel. He asked two questions and put the phone down.

If you know people who know people, you can find almost any information you want. Schmidt had phoned a dealer, the dealer asked his wife, a business journalist, who asked a colleague on the news desk. He asked a policeman who owed him a favor that he wanted no one to know about. The phone calls had doglegged back. It had taken two hours.

"Helen Blake," Schmidt had said. "Ex-wife. Uses maiden name." He'd been sparing with words: it hurt to talk. "Possible. Try that." He'd given the address.

Helen said, "I don't know what will happen."

"To me?"

"Yes."

Nicola smiled. "I'll talk to your husband about me . . ." She seemed oddly lighthearted, a woman suddenly overtaken by good humor.

Helen wondered if she was seeing the first moment of a gathering hysteria. She took her eyes off the road briefly and glanced at Nicola. A calm face, bright eyes. She said, "I wouldn't count on—"

Nicola's laugh cut her short. "There'll be a deal. There's always a deal."

Helen pulled into a ground-level parking lot. From there, a quiet back street led to the rear entrance of her apartment block. She and Nicola walked past the delivery doors of a bakery and a Chinese restaurant. A kitchen worker appeared, dumped two black garbage sacks, then disappeared.

Elliott moved the car along the street, staying a few yards back from Goldman, who was twenty feet behind Helen and Nicola, his pace increasing as the distance narrowed, timing it nicely. Car and pursuer would coincide before the women noticed that they were being tracked. It was Helen who broke the rhythm of things; she delved in her bag, searching for her house keys, and when she didn't find them, stopped to search more carefully.

Goldman was no more than two paces back. When Helen paused, he cannoned into her and she turned, offering a startled apology that turned into a cry of alarm as Goldman shoved her to one side. Nicola had stopped also. When she saw Goldman, her voice rose above Helen's. She turned to run, but Goldman was on her, grabbing her arms, her shoulders, fending off the wild blows that she aimed at his face. The car was alongside. Elliott pushed the passenger door open with a foot as Goldman wrestled Nicola to the curb side. At one end of the street, a man turned toward the noise and began to walk slowly back; then he paused.

Goldman's push had sent Helen backward over a low wall, hips and legs one side, torso on the other. Her face struck concrete, dazing her, and a fierce humming started up in her ears. When she put her hand out, trying to rise, she skittled a row of bottles. Nicola's voice was coming and going like a tricky radio signal; she could feel a stinging dampness where her calves had dragged over the rough brickwork atop the wall.

The man was still a spectator, walking slowly toward the action now, but without having made any kind of a decision. Nicola had stopped trying to hit Goldman; she was wrenching her body sideways each time he grabbed her, turning away from him, away from the car, using her full weight against his and losing the contest moment by moment. Goldman had his arms around her, trapping her at the elbows, his hands clasped across her breasts. He kicked at her legs, tried to lift her, kicked at her legs again. When the man saw this, he began to walk more quickly, then to run, as if triggered by some vulnerability in Nicola that he hadn't found before.

Helen had scrambled back over the wall. She crossed to the curb, looking for an opening, a bottle in her right hand. Elliott was half-in, half-out of the car, trying to work out where he would be most use. Gripping Nicola's shirt, Goldman pulled her in and punched her, missing her face, but taking her on the body. Her feet went; she scrambled and sat down, dragging him with her so that his body stooped in a low bow like some subservient courtier.

Helen swung the bottle, clubbing Goldman at the base of the skull. He dropped to one knee and stayed there. Nicola tottered backward on heels and hands. She stood up and Helen went to her. The man was standing just behind them, still watching. All three looked at Goldman, then at Elliott getting out of the car.

The man said, "What's going on?" He was speaking to the women, but looking at Goldman who was kneeling, head lowered.

Elliott got a shoulder under Goldman's arm, the other around his waist, and they shambled to the car. He opened the rear door and folded Goldman onto the seat; his legs trailed into the road and Elliott tucked them up on the seat. His eyes flicked to the man from time to time, making sure he came no nearer. As the car moved off, the man strode into the road as if his intention to confront Elliott had simply been mistimed. Helen and Nicola were moving along the street. He went after them.

"What was that?"

"It's okay," Helen said. "Thanks for helping."

"Is she all right?"

Nicola was crying softly, held in the crook of Helen's arm, her shirt wide open. "She'll be fine."

The man seemed reluctant to leave. He stared at Nicola in silence, his eyes everywhere.

Helen watched him until he rounded the corner, then walked Nicola the ten or so yards along the street that took them to the entrance to her building.

When they were inside, Nicola said, "I feel sick." She tried a smile, then her mouth turned down and she hiccoughed; her cheeks belled.

Helen took her to the bathroom and held her hair back while she gagged and spat. "It won't come," she said, and sat back on her haunches. Helen left her trying while she made a phone call.

A room had been set aside for the investigation. A bank of phones, paperwork cascading over a long table, two computers programmed to look for patterns, similarities, oddities. There were twenty or so people in the room. The law of averages had made one of them Robin Culley. Someone held a phone up as he walked past.

"Who?" Culley asked.

"A woman."

He made a guess. "Protheroe's secretary."

"No."

He took the call and listened for a while. Finally, he said, "Yes." Then, "Now. Of course, now."

When he let himself into Helen's flat, Nicola Hammond was alone in the living room, naked to the waist, her back to the door. She was standing close to an alcove filled with bookshelves, reading the titles like any visitor might. She turned to Culley's arrival, making no move to cover herself. A large bruise colored the upper slope of one breast; dark imprints striped her arms close to the shoulder where Goldman had gripped her.

Helen came in, carrying a shirt. Nicola took it and turned her back while she put it on. She said, "There's got to be give and take in this." Her voice was a little too loud—an attempt to cover her shakiness.

"No deals," Culley told her.

"I want something; you want something. There ought to be leeway in that."

Helen felt as if she were hearing Nicola for the first time. She went through to the kitchen to fetch the coffee she'd put on earlier. Cups, saucers, a small jug of milk; she made herself busy while they talked business. A go-between, somebody's secretary. A flash of anger rattled the cups.

"All right," Culley was saying, "tell me. What do you get?"

"I get to be anonymous."

"What do I get?"

"You get Schmidt."

When Culley looked blank, she said, "Jay's partner. The one who—"

"Yes." Culley remembered. "And the men who came here . . . ?"

"Elliott drove the car. And Goldman."

"Will they be with Schmidt?" Culley was still ordering the information she'd given him, and the few things Helen had said on the phone.

"Bound to be. They're his minders."

Helen came in with a tray. Nicola dropped her arms and the shirt cuffs fell over her knuckles; it was a full size too big. She rolled them onto her forearms. Culley said, "Are you all right?"

Helen half-turned and tipped her toes to show him the grazes on her calves. "Otherwise, fine."

"I could simply arrest you." Culley's attention switched.

"Arrest Schmidt."

"Not without you. How do I charge him? What with? He didn't kill your husband."

"He knows who did."

"Does he?"

"Well . . . he knows who ordered it."

"A different thing."

"I still won't be involved."

Helen poured coffee but left them to take it from the tray. Culley held his cup like a truck driver, hand wrapped around, handle outermost. "It's not just me," he pointed out. "There are people I report to."

"Don't report." To Helen, she said, "I don't suppose you smoke?"

"Not anymore. I've got some though." She went to a drawer and came back with her tough-it-out pack, unopened, and some matches.

Nicola lit a cigarette and waited.

"I could lie," Culley pointed out. Nicola smoked, still waiting. He said, "All right."

She gave him an address in Highgate. "They'll want to leave the country, but they'll have to go there first—records of sales, addresses, phone numbers. They held me at my house, but this is where Schmidt lives when he's in London. Jay liked to keep a distance."

Culley put down his cup and left the room. The women heard the front door close.

Helen took the coffee cups into the kitchen. A little quake of delayed shock nudged her—breathlessness and a desire to sleep.

Nicola was examining her bruise, her fingertips stroking the place and moving only in one direction, as if she might draw the pain down and away. When Helen came back, she closed the shirt and buttoned it.

"You said you might lend me some money. Is it possible?"

"How much?"

"Enough to get me home. A taxi. They'll be gone from there."

"What will you do?"

"Spend the night. Go away tomorrow."

Helen fetched her bag and gave Nicola all the money she was carrying. "Go where?"

Nicola smiled, as if she were catching Helen out in some childishly transparent ruse. "I can't tell you," she said, "because not even I know that."

The house was in a terrace backed by garages. Culley checked the garage cul-de-sac. Each house had its own wrought-iron gate hung in a brick arch. A green BMW with the trunk ajar stood outside the rear entrance of the fourth house; a man was loading boxes and files. Sandy-haired, broad across the shoulders; Elliott, from Nicola's description. He pulled the trunk down and slammed it. Big hands; a longish reach. Goldman emerged from the wrought-iron gateway with a briefcase in either hand. He tossed them onto the back seat and went to the passenger side of the car. Elliott got in, arching in his seat to fish in his pocket for keys.

Culley went back to the street, passed the front of the house, then turned and retraced his steps in time to see the car pull out of the cul-de-sac and move away from him.

A solid front door with a narrow fan of glass in the transom; two elegant sashcord windows flanking it. I hope I've got this right, Culley thought. I hope she was telling the truth.

He stood off from the left-hand window and kicked the big bottom pane, pulling his foot back before it interrupted the fall of glass, then kicked again to clear the residue. He rolled through the space, snapping a shard of glass that sliced his jacket and put a nick in his shoulder. A door into the hallway, a door beyond that, and Schmidt going for the French window that let onto the patio.

Culley said, "Don't bother," but Schmidt had stopped anyway.

"Who?" His voice was rocks in a churn.

"Move away from the door." Culley took a captain's chair that was standing by a wall and placed it just back from center in the room. "Sit there." Culley stood behind him as if he were proctoring an exam. "There isn't much time for this."

Schmidt began to turn his head and received a light slap. He faced front. "Who?" he asked. "I stopped the deal."

"Deal?" Culley was tempting him.

Suddenly, Schmidt's shoulders tightened. He remembered a face on the television screen; a voice saying, ". . . at this stage. We're following a number of inquiries and hope . . ." He'd been too frightened to make the connection immediately.

"A name," said Culley.

"Name." The word was spoken as if it were part of a mystery too arcane to be rapidly solved.

Culley yanked the man's head back by his hair and cuffed him lightly across the throat. Schmidt gagged and jerked against Culley's grip. His mouth opened and pulled air in like drafts of water. Culley waited for the spasm to pass, and loosened his hold a fraction. Schmidt hunched his shoulders and gobbled like a turkey. Culley stretched the man's neck and cuffed it again.

"A name," he said. "I can see you're having trouble talking at present, so I'll give you a lead. You can do the rest. I don't think you know who shot Jay Hammond, but I'm sure you know who paid for the job to be done. I know about the deal on the paintings. I know about the warning. I know that Hammond told them to fuck off. I know that you know who Hammond was talking to. That's the name I want. It's not difficult. It's just a word."

Schmidt's chest was crowning with effort, like an asthmatic in a sawmill. Culley pulled on the man's hair as if it were a bell rope, backhanded him across the throat again, then clamped his hand over Schmidt's mouth.

"One or two syllables," he suggested. "Three at the most, I suspect. It's not much to ask." A crimson flush going purple spread onto Schmidt's forehead. His body bucked off the chair with such violence that his knee joints popped.

"The name."

"Kemp." He gulped the syllable, taking it down with a swallow of air.

"Again," Culley said.

A door slammed and footfalls hammered the hallway floor. Culley moved away from Schmidt. He felt the wide gaze of the French windows at his back and the awareness put his timing out. When the door opened, he was too far into the jamb to confront Elliott directly and his kick came off the wood, catching an arm and missing the ribs entirely.

Elliott backpedaled fast, then circled to Culley's left. He didn't spare Schmidt a glance; his eyes held Culley's, waiting for the glint that betrays sudden movement. Coming through the door off-balance, taking the deflected kick—he'd absorbed that. He looked competent; engrossed.

The other, Goldman, would soon arrive on the patio. Culley's shoulders tightened, but he didn't glance back. He feinted left, drawing a punch and slipping it, then played the bluff and went in fast, going left again. Elliott saw the move at the last minute. He went back on his heels, but couldn't clear the punch entirely. Culley felt a tooth cut into his fist. When he stepped forward to use the other hand, something cracked into the small of his back, and he stumbled. Schmidt had kicked him.

Elliott hit him on the rise, misjudging the blow slightly. Culley heard a small detonation in his face, like a damp stick breaking. He took another head punch before ducking under Elliott's arm and turning so that they passed one another, Culley clubbing with laced fingers. He broke the nose. Blood hosed over Elliott's chin and he backed off, looking for a moment's pause. Over Elliott's shoulder, Culley could see Goldman wrenching at the handle on the French windows. Schmidt started toward them, intending to throw the lock.

Culley went straight for Elliott, then sidestepped at the last minute, almost a leap backward. Schmidt suddenly found himself in the space between them, his hand outstretched for the lock. Culley swung at him, coming up on his toes for the blow. His fist went into Schmidt's throat like a hammer into dough. Schmidt took a short step backward, then his legs went as if someone had pulled a string. He unraveled. His face smashed a pane low down in the French window and went through, stippling Goldman's shoes with blood.

Elliott stepped forward a pace, then stopped. To get to Culley, he would have had to step over Schmidt. Outside, Goldman was looking down at Schmidt as if he were standing on a cliff's edge and peering at the drop. Elliott palmed blood off his face and coughed.

Culley moved to the door, his eyes on Elliott. He was watching through the door-space as he backed down the hallway. They stood still, the man in the room and the man on the patio, looking down at Schmidt.

Culley opened the front door and turned back. The men were in the same position, but now they were looking at each other.

Early evening, a rhomboid of sunlight mellowing on the wall, Brahms's violin concerto ripening toward its second movement, the pungent crispness of gin as it swamped her tongue. Helen amused herself with the pretense that she always lived this way.

When Culley arrived, she was smoking a forbidden cigarette. He poured himself a gin, sipped it, then added ice and tonic water as an afterthought. His left eye had half-closed over a tight, blue bruise. Across the cheekbone was a thin line, strangely bloodless, where the skin had split. Elliott's other score had put a graze on Culley's forehead, close to the hairline.

Helen looked at him. She laughed outloud, but there was a downturn to her mouth. "Yes," she said, "that looks familiar."

I must have killed him, Culley thought. He must be dead.

Helen went into the bathroom and came back with antiseptic and cotton wool. "It's my day for this sort of activity. Nurse Blake soothes another patient; to care is to serve." Her own legs were dappled with the pale primrose of iodine. "Did that hurt?"

"I think my cheekbone's cracked."

"Oh." Her hand withdrew, then came back, gentler than before. "It just heals up, given time."

"Do you have to do anything?"

"Smile a bit less often."

Dusk swarmed in the room, a galaxy of dark particles. The window framed a deep blue square of sky. When a breeze shifted the curtain, she could see a plump line of jet trail and the flexing brilliance of a rising planet.

Culley's hands settled on her. He was browsing, going slowly, while she watched the planet's pulse-light, imagining the fierce arcs of fire crackling in blackness. Absentmindedly, she opened to him and his touch brought her head around.

She said, "I'm lazy."

"It doesn't matter."

"I'm a bit drunk."

"It's all right."

"Do that. Just keep doing that."

She drifted for a time, warm, letting the feeling build, her hips

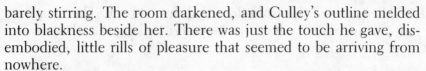

barely stirring. The room darkened, and Culley's outline melded
into blackness beside her. There was just the touch he gave, disembodied, little rills of pleasure that seemed to be arriving from
nowhere.

The sensation sharpened and she gave it more attention. Her
breathing became a tiny sound, a mew, and her hips rose from the
bed.

Are you there? Are you there in the dark? So still that all she
could count on was her own heat, her own response; so still that
she was alone with the moment, her own delight, the sound of her
own voice crying out.

Are you there in the dark?

She said, "What happened this afternoon? Did you get what you
wanted?"

"I got a name. I'll have to confirm it."

"A dealer? The person who threatened Jay Hammond?"

"I'm not sure."

"What happened?"

"Somebody hit me. I hit him back."

She put out a hand and felt him wince as she found his injured
eye. "You're a dangerous bastard," she said, and dropped her fingertips to his mouth to see if he might smile.

Do I want you? she thought. And if I do, what for? What's wrong
with my life without you? Is there anything wrong? I bet I could
find what all the others have; I bet I could track it down. Evening,
music, a drink, and someone coming home on the six-eighteen. A
meal, a chat, a cozy fuck sometimes. Next day, the same again.
What have you got that I might want? Is it something I shouldn't
have? You're dangerous. People can smell it on you.

He kissed her, but she couldn't see him. Are you there in the
dark? Are you there?

She swung up and straddled him, moving fast, one hand flat on
his stomach, the other under the fork of her legs, gripping him
while she sat. Back bowed, she plunged, pulling her own knees to
spread them, feeling the dig of her heels each time she dropped.

Are you there?

Her eyes were open in the darkness, but she could only see
herself.

29

CULLEY LOOKED AROUND at the bare walls and smiled. The cream paint was beginning to yellow; a couple of crusty, filling-station mugs stood on top of a metal filing cabinet. The Art and Antiques squad had enjoyed a checkered history. Once disbanded, then opened up again with two officers, it now consisted of eight men and all of them overworked.

Paul Binyon followed Culley's gaze around the bleak room. "What did you expect? A sprinkling of post-fucking-Impressionists?" He was a little older than Culley, a beefy man in an out-of-date suit. Even when he'd just shaved, you could see how his beard would look if he grew it.

"Something like that," Culley said. "I've never been down here before."

"Don't tell me your man's been taking pot shots at a Rembrandt."

"It's just something we found. Odd, probably nothing to it, but worth a look."

Binyon didn't ask. He said, "What do you want to know?"

"When paintings get stolen, where do they go?"

"Easy," Binyon said. "America."

"That simple?"

"Pretty much."

"Why?"

"Well, I expect there are at least two answers to that. One's in the realm of psychology, the other's a more practical issue." Binyon sounded like a man settling into his subject. He leaned back in his chair and laced his fingers over his paunch.

"Try the practical."

"They've got a fuck of a lot of money. No one else can afford to buy stolen gear, really. Well, a few. One or two things end up in Holland or Tokyo. The paintings can sometimes be offered at knock-down prices, given what they're valued at. It's the organization that takes cash."

"What about the psychology?"

"Oh, I don't know. They like to own things, don't they—Americans? I mean, they own the fucking world, more or less."

"What about shifting the stuff?" Culley asked. "Getting it out of the country."

"Not too difficult. Again, it all comes down to money. Speed's important. Something stolen in Europe will get to its destination within a couple of days. The idea is to get it under lock and key, fast. From Britain—you'd probably smuggle it to France, put it through a maze, you know, take it south, country roads; that's half a day with two drivers. Then private jet."

"What about customs checks?"

"What about them? Dogs can take you directly to a few kilos of heroin welded into the chassis, but they're not too good at sniffing out a Renoir. Same with a customs officer. Sixth sense for smack; wouldn't know a Poussin if it moved in next door and fucked his daughter. Do you want coffee?"

Culley glanced at the mugs on the filing cabinet. "No thanks."

"Me neither." Binyon took a hunting flask from his jacket pocket and poured a couple of inches into a Styrofoam cup.

Culley shook his head to the flask. "How does it work?"

"Demand. Supply. No one pops into a gallery and nicks a couple of old masters on spec. It can be an insurance scam, of course; some owner who needs money more than he needs the family heirloom. Or sometimes it's a kind of ransom—send money or we'll play tic-tac-toe on your Leonardo cartoon. Often, it's a custom job. A painting by Brueghel the elder was lifted from the Courtauld a few years back. No ransom asked for. Never heard of again. Obviously, they had a market for it. Stolen to order."

"I remember."

"Yes, you would. We've got a reported-stolen list a mile long, but the media only cares about the sexy stuff. Van Gogh's pretty much top of the list. Poor sod. Spends his life trading paintings for a glass of wine and a fuck; a hundred years later, some toffee-nosed clown at Sotheby's is knocking them out for upward of eight million. What can I help you with *exactly*?"

"Has anything gone recently? I mean, stuff worth mentioning."

"Recently—this year?"

"Recently—this month."

Binyon looked at Culley with renewed interest. He said, "If there's anything here for me, I want it. I have enough trouble with the Serious Crimes squad pissing in my pot."

"I promise," Culley said. "Whatever I get."

Binyon swallowed his drink, his eyes on Culley, and poured himself another. "Two canvases by Paul Cezanne."

"Worth . . . ?"

"Not eight million; not a piece of piss either. Well over half a million. But that doesn't matter. Someone wanted them, someone else had them."

"Who?"

"A guy called Throwleigh. Part of a very nice private collection."

"How did they go?"

"Well, that's a bit confusing. The security guard died, so did his wife. He was on-site, she was at home. You'd have to suspect that they were holding the wife to ransom so that her husband would give them access."

"Did he?"

"Must have. The security system was flawless. Heat-sensing passive infrared detectors with a fifty-foot range. You don't want to lock your pictures away in a vault, so you make a vault of the room they're in. The sensors cover everything, wall to ceiling; they're amazingly sensitive. The body heat from a bird would trigger them. You switch them off with a button code. If you've got more than one guard, each will have his own code. He never tells anyone what it is. So you know who disarmed the system. The whole thing is connected to Central Station. If someone punches in the wrong code more than three times, the alarm sounds automatically. Foolproof."

"Why would they have killed the guard and the wife—if they'd got what they wanted?"

"Who knows? ID, probably. Descriptions. How does all this relate to your sniper?"

"When I find out," Culley assured him, "you'll be the first to know. I will have some of that."

Binyon topped up and pushed the cup over to Culley, then took a swig from the neck of the flask. He said, "Here's mud in your eye," and laughed. "What happened there?"

"I fell going upstairs," Culley said. Binyon laughed again. "Where are they, do we know?"

"The Cezannes? America, for sure."

"Who'd want them?"

"I can think of a few names. Our problem is we can't get at the buyers. We're here, they're there; that's one drawback. Another is that they don't shove the gear up on their dining room walls; you

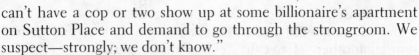

can't have a cop or two show up at some billionaire's apartment on Sutton Place and demand to go through the strongroom. We suspect—strongly; we don't know."

"Who would you go to?" Culley asked. "If you could."

"O'Connell," Binyon offered. "Ashe, Morton, Kemp—"

"Who?"

"Hugo Kemp." Binyon looked steadily at Culley. "You've heard the name before."

"It rings a bell."

"Does it?" Binyon seemed thoughtful. "Yes," he said, "Kemp would be a reasonable bet."

Culley arrived at commuter hour. Helen stared at him, as if he'd read her mind. He dumped a bag of groceries on the table.

"Lobster bisque—not homemade, though it has the virtue of being imported. Lamb chops, salad, cheese, fruit. More than enough for two, so the limitations of your fridge needn't worry us for once. If I told you what the wine cost, you wouldn't dare drink it."

"Are you being a husband?" she asked. "Because you're making a fuck-awful job of it."

"You like lamb chops—I remember."

"And I remember you being a husband. I'm not fooled." She picked up the wine and examined the label. "Very nice."

Culley took the bottle from her and went to find a corkscrew. He said, "Why do people collect paintings?"

Not fooled; not fooled. In the dark she had hammered at him as if she were driving a spike. Into myself, she thought. Into myself. She remembered well the way things had been. Love into symbols of loss; passion into lust and regret; sad alchemy.

What was exciting about Culley? A sense of violence, a sense of danger. His civilized behavior was something he'd learned to do. But that was an affair, wasn't it? That made him the perfect fling. The beast by candlelight; the trip to bed where all the things you wouldn't do, haven't done, are things he'll make you do, and things you'll want; and then the beast's departure, out on his own, still smelling your smell but looking for fresh tracks.

I was married to that. Sometimes he faked his role, and sometimes not. Sometimes he'd come back, bringing a stink of the badlands. Sometimes he'd bring lamb chops, salad, and wine.

"Well," she said, "let's see. You can buy them as a hedge against inflation, or as a straightforward investment. If you're the truckers' union or whoever, they can underpin your pension fund. You can buy them to sell later on at profit. They can beef up your status if you're a society hostess. They're useful for bribing diplomats and other types who'd be embarrassed by a sudden influx of cash. You can dish them out to visiting dignitaries at the end of a state visit. There are those who like to hang them on the wall and look at them, but generally speaking that's taken to be pretty eccentric behavior."

A seamless delivery. Culley looked at her curiously. "Have I upset you in some way?"

"Yes. You walk in here with a bagful of goodies and that preposterously expensive bottle of wine, looking like shit wouldn't stick to your shoe, and want me to pretend that we're married, we're happy, and that it's always happened like this. I'm amazed that you didn't bring me a bunch of fucking flowers."

"Tried to. Couldn't find any. Should this wine breathe?"

"What?" He tilted the bottle to pour, and she said, "Yes, of course it should, you barbarian."

He set the wine aside. "I thought so."

"Why do you want to know?"

"I'm looking for someone who collects. Not the investor or the salesman. The customer. He's at the end of the route. I find him and start walking back. Somewhere along the way, I'll come across the man who organized Jay Hammond's death; then, further on, the man who killed him. It's good to know something about the man. This one collects paintings. You work in a gallery; I thought you might have an opinion. If we wait until I've made the salad and grilled the chops, will the wine be ready?"

Helen nodded and followed him into the kitchen. "Which paintings?"

"Any paintings."

"We're not talking about any paintings. Are we?"

"Two Cezannes."

"Oh, yes." She thought for a moment, then said, "Well, well . . ."

Culley paused, knife in one hand, lettuce in the other. "What?"

"Nothing, except they made a bit of a stir; their disappearance did. Maurice Throwleigh owned them. Unpleasant bastard, but a good customer for some. Seriously rich. He bought a Michael

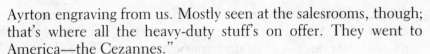

Ayrton engraving from us. Mostly seen at the salesrooms, though; that's where all the heavy-duty stuff's on offer. They went to America—the Cezannes."

"How do you know?"

"That sort of work always does. I mean, ninety percent of stolen pictures end up there." Culley nodded as if to confirm the fact, and Helen gave a small start. "You knew that already. You've talked to someone already."

"Art and Antiques squad. A guy called Binyon. Very handy with a hip flask, but didn't look as if he could tell a Renoir from a Renault. Appearances can be deceptive."

"Then why ask me?"

"Money—that's easy to understand. Most villains take money, or whatever converts to money. This guy—whoever he is—he's *paying*. And when he gets the painting, that's the end. That's what he wants. A picture salted away in some fireproof vault. He can't display it, not really; he can't boast about it. He can take it out and look at it. I want to know about that."

"Do you know who he is?" Helen asked. "Do you know his name?"

"A name's not much. That doesn't tell me who he is."

She poured the last of the wine, distributing it evenly between their glasses. "How long will you be gone?" The question was out before she could bite it back.

"Gone where?"

"Please." She held up a hand. "Why would you want to know about someone you're never going to meet?"

"A week, I expect. That's about as long as anyone gets. You're assuming they'll let me go."

"Who will you ask? Protheroe? Latimer?"

"Both. Simultaneously."

"What reason will you give?"

"Nicola Hammond. Not all of it. But some."

"You said you wouldn't."

"I lied." He drank his wine. "She's clear by now. Someone else can chase her, if Protheroe wants that."

Helen lifted the knuckle of lamb bone from her plate and grazed on it. She'd tried to hold onto the anger she'd felt earlier, but it had slipped away from her, dissolving with the wine. His betrayal of Nicola Hammond ought to have annoyed her—not for Nicola's sake, but because she was reminded of risks she'd taken; of risks she might have to take. It didn't annoy her though. She had been amused by the easy way he'd said, "I lied."

"That was it, then?" she asked. "The Cezannes. That's why Hammond was killed. And all the others."

Culley raised his eyebrows and shook his head—meaning, That's what I'd like to find out.

"One was a landscape," she said. "A view of Aix-en-Provence— mountains and cypresses. The other was a still life, part of a series painted during a prolonged stay in Paris. He didn't like Paris much." She nibbled a few more flakes of meat and dropped the bone back onto her plate. "I suppose it's got something to do with possession. Wouldn't that be it?"

He nuzzled her. He drew finger patterns on her thighs, and she opened her legs because she wanted to.

Not fooled, she thought, not fooled.

"Why possession?" he wondered. "You take a painting out of its vault and look at it. It's yours and no one else's . . . That sort of thing?"

"I don't know. Ask a shrink."

His hands were growing idle, his mind elsewhere.

You bastard, Helen thought. You're already on the plane, already there. You think I care? You think I've lived like a nun since we split up?

She ducked her head and nipped the skin on his chest.

Do you think I-want-you-back is a game with only one set of rules? Do you think the whole thing is fueled by your needs, your ambition, your effort, your lust?

Her hair dragged across his belly. She bit softly just below his hip and watched him stir.

Oh, no. It's my rules, too. Don't take me to bed, then make me wait. For my share. For your pleasure.

She wetted her lips.

I'll make you understand, she thought. I'll lick you into shape.

He wondered what made her laugh.

Protheroe lifted his mustache with a forefinger, as if getting air to his mouth. He said, "I've spoken to Ted Latimer." He liked the familiarity; it made him feel one of the clan.

"Thanks." The word didn't fool either of them, but Culley thought it was a reasonable indulgence.

"I gather you've spoken to him as well."

"I thought it best."

"Where is . . ." Protheroe turned the corner of Culley's report to find the name. ". . . Nicola Hammond?"

"I don't know." Culley shrugged, palms up, the whole business. It felt like bad acting and he made a mental note. "It was a phone call, as I said in my—"

"Logged?"

"She called me at home. I'm in the book." He shrugged again and thought, Enough.

"The name she gave you—"

"Schmidt."

"Yes."

"Well, that was *all* she gave me. Art and Antiques are looking at her husband's business. She's gone."

"You like this theory, don't you. Mass murder to get one."

"I'm telling you what she told me. After Hammond was killed, they got a phone call—you'll get what he got unless you pull the deal. Why would she make that up? How could she? It has to be true."

Protheroe looked at the report again, selecting a name. "Kemp is speculation."

"Kemp is a lead. What did Latimer say?"

Protheroe sighed aggressively. "We've talked to the Police Department in Tucson," he said. "You can talk to them as well. They don't mind that, it seems. They've pointed out that there's no guarantee they'll talk back."

"Why?"

"They've heard what Binyon's heard. It's clear they're not impressed. It's all rumor, so far as they're concerned. It seems that Kemp is an important man. Not too many people see him, but his checks arrive when the local schools and hospitals are in need."

"Who's my contact?"

Protheroe lifted a memo from his desk, glanced, then lowered it. "Beck."

"It was Beck you spoke to when you called?"

"Among others."

"How long can I have?"

"Talk to Beck before you make any plans. Call him."

"If I go, how long can I have?"

"A week—tops." Protheroe tossed the memo across the desk. "Talk to Beck. Then talk to me."

There was a noise on the line like the sound of a clarinetist practicing in a far room. Culley tried to make a tune of it. There was a lilt that reminded him of Ella Fitzgerald.

   . . . had we thought a bit of the end of it . . .

Beck sounded as if his mind was on other business. Checking the week's break-ins; adding up the traffic violations. "Forget it, Culley. There's nothing here for you."

"Have you spoken to Kemp?"

"Sure. He's a wealthy man; he collects pictures. They're all legit. He's got the . . ." He broke off. Culley imagined him looking at his notes. ". . . provenances. That right? Provenances?"

"You spoke to Kemp."

"His . . . this guy who works for Kemp. Henry Glinwood."

"What's he? A lawyer?"

"Yeah. Something like that."

"But not Kemp?"

"I've checked. Listen, don't come out here. Don't spend the time. We'd have to say we can't help. I've spoken—you know— everyone. FBI—those guys."

"Do you know Kemp?"

"Sure. He's a nice guy."

"I'm told he's a bit of a recluse."

"Well, he likes his privacy. He's entitled."

"What did the FBI say?"

"They think he's a nice guy too."

"You know about—"

"I know you've lost some paintings. So what? There's nothing that connects Kemp. There's nothing. You can't hassle a guy like that without . . . I mean, you need to have something."

"Okay," Culley said.

"I'm sorry."

"It's okay."

"Sorry to lose you the trip. It's a good time of year for Arizona."

"Some other time."

"Nice talking to you, Culley."

   . . . one of those bells that now and then ring . . .

. . .

Latimer had gone to his study to take the call.

"Is this better?" asked Bernard Warner.

"Better than what?"

"Than calling you at the office."

"Marginally." A voice laden with distaste.

Warner said, "You don't have to like me, Latimer. It's not important that you should. Just stay in line; that'll be enough."

"You expect too much."

"Do I? Let's talk about what you *expect*. I've read your speeches. I've seen them reported in the papers and on TV. They seem to be full of references to lofty things. The moral high ground. Cities on a hill. Standards that ought to be raised. Pinnacles of achievement. But what I know about you isn't really very uplifting, is it? I know about things you like to do and the people you like to do them with. And you *expect* me to keep that confidential. You *expect* me to keep that a secret. From your wife, your children, relatives, superiors—the world at large, in fact." Warner paused, but not long enough to invite a response. He said, "Culley wants to go to Arizona."

"Yes."

"What's the response?"

"I don't think he'll get much of a welcome."

"Does he know that?"

"I imagine so. They gave me a contact name for him—just a brush-off. They really don't want to know." Latimer hesitated, then said, "Neither do I."

"I tell you enough; no more. What you find out through Culley is your problem."

"Yours too. I'm not the only one to know. He reports to a man called Protheroe, not directly to me. And there's his sergeant— Dawson. Culley talks to him, I expect."

"It's becoming a problem." Warner paused.

"What do you—"

"Shut up," Warner said. Another pause. "What will Culley do?"

"He wants to go. He'll try to persuade me that he should. Lie about the response in Arizona."

"Can he do that, and expect to get away with it?"

"He's a fairly senior officer. We don't ride herd. We read the reports and make judgments based on that."

"Let him go."

"I could. It wouldn't be for—"

"He's becoming a real nuisance. Let him go."

30

Francis gave himself a drink and raised the bottle questioningly. Martin Jackson shook his head. "You missed him."

"Yes," Jackson agreed. "I was close."

"Close isn't good enough."

"I know that." There was a light frost of anger in Jackson's tone.

"Do you know where he is now?"

Jackson was standing by a window, a little to one side, looking absently down into the street. "I know where he'll go."

"Where?"

"Not an address. A district."

"Can you find him?"

Jackson spoke softly, still looking out of the window, his head turned from the other man.

"What?" Francis strained to hear.

Jackson raised his voice a notch. His tone was oddly gentle. "I think we'll find each other."

"There's someone else."

"Oh, yes?" Jackson was either not surprised or not concerned.

"Culley. Robin Culley. He's heading up the task force from west central."

"A policeman. We spoke of him before."

"Yes."

"Is this a contract?" Jackson asked.

"He's going to America for a short while. When he gets back . . ."

"All right." Jackson smiled; he still had his back to the room.

"But it's Ross—you know that. He's the priority."

"Oh, yes," Jackson said. "He's the priority. I understand that."

The investigation control room was full of cold technology; silent phones, blank screens. Mike Dawson was sitting at a dead computer, strumming the keyboard and offering a toothy smile to an invisible audience. He only knew one word in three of the lyric he'd chosen.

"I give up," Culley said. "You'll have to tell me."

"Elton John." Dawson came down the scale and finished with a bass boom, index finger down heavily, thumb extended. He walked over to Culley and stood close. "That's coming along nicely."

The bruise was a dull, greenish sickle of shadow just under the cheekbone and then a comma of purple on the side of the nose, as if Culley had been wearing ill-fitting glasses.

"It earned me a name—Kemp. Do you really need to know how?"

Dawson grimaced. "No one expects you to go by the book; it's not your speed."

"They're giving me a week. They seem to think it's a waste of time."

"It probably is. Kemp's a bit of a long shot, isn't he?"

"He came to me from a very reliable source."

"The Hammond woman."

"Indirectly, yes. I'll fax Protheroe, if I have to. I'd like to think I can call you at home if there's something I need."

Dawson laughed and slowly shook his head. "For God's sake, Robin; of course. What did you think—I'd hang up?"

"I thought you might be a little pissed-off with me, yes."

"It'll pass." Dawson sat down in front of the computer and strummed the keys, a rapid clatter. He looked at Culley, eyebrows raised.

" 'These Foolish Things,' " Culley guessed.

Dawson sighed. "It's Beethoven's first piano concerto. Couldn't you tell?"

"Are we talking about someone in particular," Stuart Kelso asked, "or collectors of paintings in general?"

"Why?"

"Because it's not much to go on, is it? I mean, lots of people collect paintings. I wouldn't suppose that a cross section of their neuroses would give similar patterns."

"I think this guy's a bit of a hermit."

"Doesn't care much for his fellow man."

"So it seems."

"Shuts himself away from the world."

"Yes."

"Sounds like a sensitive and likable fellow."

They had arranged to meet at a pub in Soho, not far from Helen's flat. Culley had the feeling that Kelso would be better value after hours and off police premises.

"Collectors," Kelso said. "Collectors in general . . . Anal types, perhaps, selfish, single-minded. Probably obsessive, which can be interesting or dangerous or indescribably boring; sometimes all three. The obsession can be a projection—the paintings or whatever stand for something else."

"Like what?"

"Self-esteem, perhaps. A love object." He waggled his glass to indicate a quote. "Obsessional neuroses relate to a repressed sexual act performed with pleasure during childhood."

"Who's that?"

"Freud, obsessive old bastard. What did he know? Your man might have tendencies toward ruthlessness, like to be in control of people and situations, make his own rules, be good at taking but not so good at giving. I'm making this up as I go along, really. It could be that he's a very poor loser."

"Doesn't sound to me as if you made it up," Culley said.

Kelso finished his drink and extended his hand for Culley's glass. "My turn," he said. Then, "I collect snuffboxes, myself."

The streets were busier than at midday. A juggler was entertaining a theater line, turning an orange, a book, and a saucepan in an incongruous circle.

Helen had said, "Let's go out to eat. You'll have to get back, won't you, to pack a case?"

That's right," Culley agreed.

She had made a reservation at a restaurant next door to the pub where Culley had met Kelso. They sat looking at menus; Helen said, "What do you want?"

"Minestrone," he said, "calf's liver, sautéed potatoes, broccoli."

"That's terrifically funny."

"You."

"I know; you've told me that. I'm asking about the terms."

"It sounds as if you want me to have a contract drawn up for signature by the parties of the first part."

Helen said, "It takes a lot of faith."

"Well, you have to *want* it, yes." He paused. "Do you?"

"I think so. I'm not sure."

"You're not sure that you want to be with me, but you're here with me to say it."

"I'd thought of that." She smiled and looked away.

"There's a time limit on this, you know."

"Is there?" She was startled, then annoyed. "Limited offer, is that it?"

"Not like that. Just . . . everything has its time. What lasts forever?"

The waiter arrived. "Minestrone," Helen said, "calf's liver, sautéed potatoes, broccoli."

A pleasure boat was moving upriver, ropes of colored lights strung on poles from prow to stern. Figures were moving about on deck. As the craft came closer, Helen could see that they were dancing. Gusts of music eddied across the water.

Culley stood by the door. He said, "Are you coming to bed?"

She waited for the boat to pass.

31

MARTIN JACKSON SAT AMONG the people waiting by the arrivals gate and read a journal he'd picked up at the newsstand. He'd found an article on shoreline fishing and was engrossed in it. There was a rather stagy photograph of the man who'd written the article casting on a shingle beach; in a companion photo, he'd set up a three-rod line and was gazing mistily over the breakers. His equipment was state-of-the-art, though, and he knew how to write about sea-angling.

When Culley passed, Jackson gave him a count of ten, then followed him toward the departures gate. He liked the look of the man—about Jackson's own build, a lean, slightly sallow face. His walk was nicely balanced, arms swinging loosely. The faint bruise under one eye was oddly exciting.

Someone, Culley thought. Who? As he reached the departures area, he swung his walk-on bag from right hand to left and took his boarding card from a hip pocket. A uniformed official checked it and handed it back.

He turned, just before going airside. There were faces at the barrier, people craning for a last look.

Jackson smiled briefly and raised a hand. *Yes, it's me. Have a good trip. See you when you get back.*

Other passengers were lining up at the checkpoint, most of them looking back as if that glimpse was all they could carry with them to their destinations. They passed through the barrier, waving, jostling Culley as they went.

Jackson turned and walked away. He could have been smiling at anyone.

THREE

→

32

No SMILE, no welcoming handshake, no policeman called
Beck. You don't announce yourself when you know you're not
wanted. Culley went to his hotel and checked in. He'd neither
eaten nor slept on the plane—his method for defeating jet lag. He
ordered a sandwich and a bourbon with a beer chaser from room
service and sat by the window while he ate.

The hotel was a hollow square with a courtyard at the center. A
fountain lipped water over five circular tiers into a marble bowl.
Birds ducked from the rim, sluicing their backs, then riffled their
feathers like a pack of cards. Everything in the sun was old gold;
everything that lay in the shade was blue.

He stuffed a wedge of sandwich into his mouth, went to the
bedside cabinet, brought the local directory back to the window.
He ran through the listings and picked out Carl Mathers because
he liked the brusque tone of the ad: Inquiries. Daily rate.

Helen's number was busy. He put the phone down, intending
to call again, and stretched out on the bed with the last swallow of
his bourbon. When he woke, the room was blue and white—
moonlight and a glow from the courtyard. Too late to call.

He opened his window and listened to the hiss and trickle of the
fountain. In a room across the courtyard, a noiseless television
shed stabs of light, as if a vast spotlight were being played around
the walls. His body was humming with fatigue and he shivered
slightly, though the evening was heavy with heat. He stripped
his clothes off, peeled back the sheet, and climbed into bed.

There was music, soft, a slow rhythm, coming from some other room.

He thought: Tomorrow, I'll . . . And: What the hell am I . . . ? And: That tune is called . . .

And then he was asleep.

He met Carl Mathers in a diner on Congress Street. A skinny man who looked as if he didn't sleep nights. Almost the first thing Mathers said was, "You're asking for something you can't get."

"Then why are you here?" Culley asked him.

"I didn't say you shouldn't ask. I said you can't get it. If you want to pay my rates, I'll try for you. Just don't complain when it doesn't work out."

"Is Kemp that well protected?"

Mathers twitched a cigarette out of a pack in his shirt pocket. He laughed. "How much do you know?"

"Pretend I don't know anything."

Mathers lit the cigarette and immediately plucked it from his mouth, a busy gesture. "He's got a small ranch, not far, forty miles maybe, but desert. He grows roses out there, an acre, maybe more, front of the house and back."

"In the desert?"

"Yeah. Roses. Beyond the roses, a fence. Between the fence and the roses, people with guns."

"Are they guarding the roses?"

Mathers twitched the cigarette from his lips again and laughed. A rumble started, deep in his lung, like an old engine turning over. "What's your interest in Kemp?"

"Do you need to know?"

A waitress brought coffee, and a plate-sized Danish for Mathers; raisins under icing, the whole thing under a bright glaze. He lifted it with both hands to take a bite, glancing wistfully at his cigarette in the ashtray. "It might help."

Culley slid his warrant card across the table. Mathers licked the thumb and forefinger of his right hand and opened the little wallet, then pushed it back. "You're not working with the locals. Why's that?"

"They didn't seem able to help."

"Who did you talk to?"

"Someone called Beck."

Mathers smiled around a fresh bite of Danish. "Tyler Beck."

"You know him."

"Well, I know them all. Tyler and I go back a few years. Good guy. Big guy. He works out, you know, skis up at Mount Lemmon, plays a lot of handball and tennis. What did he say?"

"Just that they couldn't help."

"So you're here on the fly."

"I suppose so."

Mathers was halfway through the Danish and his needs had switched. He dropped the pastry onto his plate, crushed the burning cigarette into the ashtray, and lit another. "I can't believe Hugo Kemp put his head that far above the trench."

"No, not really. Some paintings were stolen in London. Kemp might have them. I mean, they might have been stolen for him."

"No kidding." Culley waited, not sure whether Mathers was being wry or was genuinely intrigued. "Well, he's rich as hell; I'd heard he was an art lover. You're here for the paintings? For Kemp? Both?"

"No. There were two buyers for the paintings. Someone was killed to leave things open for Kemp. I just need some information."

"From Kemp?"

"From someone; possibly Kemp."

"You're asking me to work around the police department here."

"Not really. They didn't say no."

"They didn't say yes, either." Mathers finished his cigarette and started the second half of the Danish. "Are you paying for this?"

"Well, I get some expenses; I'll be making up the difference."

Mathers twisted his head to pull off the bite he'd taken; he chewed for a while. The waitress freshened their coffee.

"Whatever you want, you want it pretty badly."

"Just information."

"How long?"

"About a week."

"A week. Yeah, I guess you can afford me for that long. There's someone we could talk to. A guy called Gerry Cattini—used to work for Kemp."

"How closely?" Mathers shrugged. "I mean, did he work *for* Kemp, or *with* Kemp?"

"Oh, right. No, for him. Used to walk the line with a rifle. But he'll say what he knows. Claims Kemp had him beaten up."

"Did he?"

Mathers delved for a fresh cigarette. "Someone did. Gerry

worked for me, just for a while—days I could afford help. I smuggled his booze into the hospital. They'd stomped all over him. He lost the sight of an eye. Told Tyler Beck he'd been hit by a truck. Looked like that, too."

"What else can we do?"

"What would you like to do?" Mathers was amused.

"I'd like to get a listening device into Kemp's home."

"Yeah." The rumbling in Mathers's chest was gravelly and deep. "Sure. No problem." It became a coughing fit. He dragged a handkerchief from his pocket and put it to his mouth; dark sediment lifting in a subterranean cavern. He folded the handkerchief carefully, keeping it in his hand ready for another attack. "I'll rush right out there and shoot a cable mike through one of the windows." He coughed twice more, but pushed the impulse back.

"It would help a lot," Culley said.

Mathers smiled. He restored the handkerchief to his pocket. "You said you were here for just a week?" Culley nodded. "That's good."

Three makeshift stalls had been set up at the entrance to a shopping mall. They were draped in blankets, ocher and blue. Necklaces, pendants, bracelets, rings; silver and turquoise glittered in the white light. Three rows of tiny figures circled a Navajo basket, holding hands forever in the weave; black squares for heads, so that they seemed to be facing inward to preserve the sanctity of the dance.

Mathers stepped around a semicircle of tourists. "Tomorrow, we'll drive out there. Early morning would be best." He looked back to make sure Culley was still with him. "Really early?"

"Okay."

"I'll pick you up. You tell me what Gerry Cattini said; okay?"

"You're not staying?"

"A couple of things to do. I'll make the essential introductions. Essential meaning I introduce Gerry to a few friendly drinks. Don't worry; he won't get so loaded he doesn't make sense. He's forgotten how that works."

Culley's time clock was nagging him to eat. When they got to the bar he ordered a sandwich and took a bowl of tortilla chips to the table. Gerry Cattini arrived as soon as they'd sat down. To Mathers, he said, "This the guy?" then, without waiting for a response, looked at Culley and said, "You're looking to hassle Kemp."

The dead eye was shuttered under a black patch held by a cord that went under one ear then reappeared, coming out of the hairline and down across the forehead. A seam of indentation ran beneath it. The good eye was green as a cat's.

"I need some help," Culley said. "I'd be grateful for what you can give me."

Cattini ducked his head, smiling at Culley's accent. He said, "You sound like Sean Connery."

"I don't. He's Scottish."

"You sound like him to me."

Mathers had gone to the bar. He came back with a clutch of drinks.

"Not for me." Culley shook his head.

"That's right," said Mathers. He lined three glasses up at Cattini's elbow, keeping one back for himself.

Music welled in the bar, a samba with many guitars. Cattini got up and walked over to the barman, who was wiping glasses. As he started back to the table, the music stopped briefly, then returned, a gentle country number. The singer's voice was just audible.

Mathers was leaving; his glass was empty. To Culley, he said. "Tomorrow morning. Start paying me then."

Cattini looked over his shoulder and lifted a hand as Mathers went to the door. "Carl's a good man," he said. "You couldn't do better." He sipped from the first glass. "Seen me through some things."

"You worked for Kemp," Culley said. "Is that right?" He thought Cattini must be in his mid-thirties, though it was difficult to say for sure. Whiskey had made him heavy in the torso and puffed up his face so that the true features were blurred, as if permanently in shadow. A patchy stubble blotted his cheeks and chin. Culley used his imagination to refine what he saw, and a handsome man stepped out of the half-light.

"Yeah, I worked for him."

"Tell me about him."

"What do you need?"

Culley smiled. "All I can get."

"Know thine enemy." The green eye flashed at Culley, then settled on the next drink.

Was that showy, Culley wondered, or is he brighter than I think? He said, "Something like that."

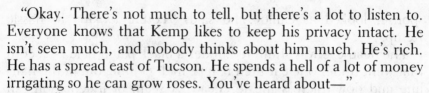

"Okay. There's not much to tell, but there's a lot to listen to. Everyone knows that Kemp likes to keep his privacy intact. He isn't seen much, and nobody thinks about him much. He's rich. He has a spread east of Tucson. He spends a hell of a lot of money irrigating so he can grow roses. You've heard about—"

"Yes."

"Okay. Well, that's all right; I suppose people figure he can spend his money on whatever. Rich people are like that, right? He comes into the city now and then. He gives money to local charities. It's known that guys with guns patrol his land, but so what? It's not illegal. Who needs prowlers? Some kid wanting roses for his girl; some Indian looking for jug money."

"What are they really guarding?"

"He collects pictures."

"How do you know that?"

"Don't kid me. Everyone knows that. One of the best private collections in the country. People bid for him at auctions, a guy called Henry Glinwood mostly—'an anonymous buyer'—but his reputation goes before him."

"He could install a security system."

"Yeah. It's not just the paintings. He's keeping the world away."

"There are things in there—paintings—that he'd sooner no one saw?"

"Maybe. Maybe." Cattini looked at the one full glass left on the table. He said, "You're gonna have to buy me a drink."

Culley half-rose, but Cattini put out a hand to stop him, and glanced back at the barman, who lifted a bottle and dug a highball glass into an ice container.

"What happened with you?"

As if the question reminded him it was there, Cattini eased the eye patch. The cord rolled a little and found a new position. A red weal lay across the lines of his forehead like a strawberry mark. "Paintings aren't the only thing he keeps out there. He's got a daughter. Nina. If I told you she was a little flaky, you wouldn't be getting the half of it. Most of the time, she seems to be asleep— that's when she's walking around the place."

"Drugs?" Culley guessed.

"Yeah, she takes, I mean not smack or anything, things to keep her level. But that's not it."

"What, then?"

The barman arrived with Culley's sandwich and three drinks on a tray. He set the drinks down on Cattini's side of the table and left the sandwich and the tab with Culley.

"They come in threes," said Cattini. "Three's my lucky number." His sips were getting bigger. "You know the stories about the princess in the tower? Locked up. She looks out every day for a knight who'll ride by, so she can unbraid her hair. He climbs up, rescues her, they ride off together. That's it; except Nina stopped looking for any knight a long time ago."

"Why?" asked Culley.

"Check it out," Cattini told him. "If you come up with an answer, let me know." His hand went to the patch again. He put a finger underneath and massaged the socket slowly. "I liked Nina. Can't tell you why." He laughed. "Perhaps I come from a long line of knights and no one ever told me. We used to talk—nothing important, you know, just this and that. She likes to read. Sometimes I'd fetch a shopping list into one of the city bookstores. I had an Indian wristband she liked, got it from one of the reservation workshops, leather with turquoise beads. I gave it to her. She's a nice girl. I don't know what I thought."

He took a drink. "She started to get, like, fixed on me. She started looking for me. One day, she came out to the perimeter fence; another, she came into the kitchen when they were making me some food. I didn't mind. I guess I'd've fucked her, given the chance. One of the other guys asked me about her. We were just talking, you know, how she'd got a thing for me. He asked me if I'd screwed her. I said, no, but if she came out to the perimeter fence again, that'd be the time. It was all locker-room talk.

"That night, they took me out into the desert and beat me. I don't know if I was supposed to live or not. I don't think they cared one way or the other. I caught a boot heel in the eye; apart from other places." There was a drink left; he turned to the barman.

"You told Tyler Beck you'd been hit by a truck."

Cattini laughed. "Yeah. I was alive. I wanted to stay that way. Kemp could buy Tucson. I don't know why he hasn't. Tyler was okay about it. He stopped by the hospital on his way to a tennis match."

"Does Nina come into the city?" The barman collected the empties. He set down three drinks and a new tab.

"I wouldn't think about that."

"Does she?"

"No."

"Does Kemp go away?"

"Business trips; yeah, sometimes."

"When he does, who's Nina's minder?"

"Her what?"

"Looks after her; stays close."

"An Indian—Ira Sanchez.

"Can I get to him?"

"Oh, shit, I don't know what you're looking for, but I'm damn sure I know what you'll find." The good eye, the green eye, scanned Culley's face. A dab of bruising, yellow now, on the upper slope of the cheek, a nevus of purple on the nose.

"See here," he said, and his fingertip brushed Culley's eyelash. Then, "See here," as he flipped up the patch like a lid.

Crumpled flesh, sunken and dark as fig fruit; at its center, a black hole, a tunnel-mouth to the place where dreams are stored.

Culley came back from the bar. He'd paid the tab and organized another round for Cattini. He said, "If I think of anything else, can I find you here?"

"Maybe." Cattini lifted his drink. "Through Carl is better."

"Or if you think of anything else . . ."

"Sure. Through Carl."

Culley nodded. He said, "Thanks."

"Ira Sanchez likes going to the fights," Cattini said. He took a good third of the whiskey; ice rattled against his mouth. "You'll find him there if you look."

"Boxing?" Culley asked.

"Not exactly, no." The barman was standing behind Culley with a tray. Cattini said, "Lots of luck."

33

First light was pearl, a thin, almost transparent shell on the underside of the sky. Then a buttery glow leaking from horizon to horizon, flooding the mesas and outcrop rock of the high desert.

A snake paid its length out of a crevice, seeming endless because its coils were out of sight in the niche. It hung two thirds of the way down a nine-foot drop and kept coming, then paused.

Shadows tightened to a hard outline as the light sharpened—saguaro, scrub trees. Something moved in the brush and the snake dropped its length between two rocks.

When Carl Mathers's car pulled up in view of the rose garden, just a few golden trails were left on the hard blue, a threadbare tapestry. The desert was alive, but you couldn't tell how or where.

They got out of the car. Culley looked at the roses—a red flood. He said, "It's ridiculous."

"Yeah, well, kind of *extravagant*," Mathers said. "Monuments, you know? Man's vanity." His cigarette burned his finger and he dropped it under a boot heel. "Like the Pharaohs. Who needs a tomb with a fucking *door*, for Chrissake?"

"Where's the fence?"

"All sides. Tough to pick out from here. Electrified." A thought struck him. "You weren't thinking of—"

Culley shook his head. "Just curious."

"What do you need," Mathers asked, "and for how long?"

"Some sort of monitoring system. And for as long as possible."

"Yeah . . . Well, I can't let you listen to what's being said in the entire house without having access to the entire house. I might get you a couple of rooms—but then again, at some point I have to be in the rooms to do that."

Mathers opened the driver's door and fished around in the glove compartment. He came up with a pair of binoculars and handed them to Culley. "So if you can come up with a way of going down there, past the guards, up to the house, into a room or two, and being left alone for a couple of minutes while I secure the devices —okay, you've got what you want."

Culley leveled the glasses and the acreage of roses leapt toward him, fat blooms, close enough to pick. A man wandered into the disk, then out. Culley tracked left and found him again, startled by the way the image was drawn to stand before him, as if his voice must be heard, as if the man must see as clearly as he was seen— Levi's, Stetson, a loose shirt; a rifle cradled in one arm.

Beyond the perimeter, the house. A rocking chair on the verandah.

"What are the options?" Culley handed the glasses back to Mathers.

"I could wait for dark, bypass the current in the fence, climb over, sneak up to the house, stick a bug on one of the windows, and hope they wouldn't see it."

"Could you?"

"No. Or there's a laser device—you bounce a beam off a window; the window vibrates, acts like a diaphragm in a radio speaker. The sound comes back up the laser beam to a modulator. Costs a year's salary. CIA might lend you one—or some big company that's recently completed a successful takeover and doesn't need it anymore."

"What else?"

"I could send in a fake mailing shot. Kind of thing that advertises a new electronics package. Free gift of a calculator enclosed. Mike's inside the calculator. Takes time. You have to get letterheads printed, make it look good, have a fake box number. Has to be authentic—something that Kemp would expect to receive. Then you have to allow that Kemp probably doesn't open his own mail. Someone else might keep the calculator, give it away, throw it away. Seen all you need to see?" Mathers asked. "I'd guess I'm not the only guy around here with a pair of field glasses."

Culley got into the car. Mathers spun the wheel with the heel of his hand and they bounced back onto the approach road.

"There's no sure way unless we get into the house?" Culley asked.

"You, me, someone," Mathers said. "Except it's not going to be me. Hi, there," he was trying the role for size, "your telephone's been reported out of order. Maybe I could come in and check it out while you wait in another room."

"The telephone's a good method." Culley was calling on a brief training in surveillance techniques.

"The best. On-site, undetectable, reliable." Mathers let go the wheel to get a cigarette from his shirt with one hand and press the dashboard lighter with the other.

"Gerry Cattini mentioned a man called Ira Sanchez."

"Yeah?" Mathers lodged the cigarette in his mouth and closed one eye against the smoke.

"Works for Kemp."

"Well, I know Ira. Don't know him well. He's a bright guy. Seemed to go back and forth between the reservation and the city for a while looking for the right place to be. I guess it was neither. Or both. He wound up at Kemp's place a couple of years ago. Foreman, I guess. Looks after the guys with guns."

"And the daughter sometimes."

Mathers took a long sideways look at Culley. "That so?"

"Cattini said something about Sanchez liking the fights. Is that right? Fights?"

"That's right."

A silence grew. Mathers held the butt of his cigarette in a pinched grip, drawing smoke through his finger ends.

"You could point him out to me," Culley said.

"Sure. I could do that."

The pit was nothing more elaborate than a series of planks chocked up to make an erratic knee-high circle. The handlers stood on one side, each holding his bird in a double grip, one arm underneath for support, the fingers of the other hand loosely grasping the crop. There was a lot of noise; people were getting bets down on the first pair. The birds were silent and still.

They had driven to the edge of the city, into the brittle mauve of dusk, lights starting up in buildings everywhere as if some vast signal beacon were slowly igniting.

Mathers had pointed from behind the windshield. "That's Sanchez." A stocky man, too much weight below the barrel chest, but power there, too. His hair was tied back at the nape of his neck.

Someone collected five dollars from Culley and he walked into a roofless space. Carbide lamps hissed on the walls; a few had been mounted on poles close to the plank circle. Their glow bleached everything it touched and threw deep shadows beyond the circumference of the pit.

Two handlers stepped in and stood either side of a scratched line. They held the stags by their waists and headed them, bird to bird. A dun and a barred blue, both trimmed for the pit, combs and wattles scissored off. Their necks stretched as they tried for a beak hold. The handlers thrust them at each other, withdrew them, thrust again. Both cocks were wearing full-drop American gaffs, curved steel, an inch and a half long.

The handlers stepped back and released. The cocks went straight in, spring-loaded, their neck and saddle hackles up, trying short jabs to breast and neck.

Culley worked his way around the circle. Ira Sanchez was looking at the birds; then he glanced up to where a man was taking bets on the far side. He nodded and the bookie nodded back, his eyes everywhere as he scanned the other faces, looking for takers amid the din.

"Ira Sanchez?"

The blue was a flyer, wings trimmed to prevent him from going too high in the action; he got up in a sudden whirr of fury, looking for a brain blow, but gaffing the dun bird in the breast. The judge was midway around the circle, looking down the scratch line, a gray-haired man in a torn suit jacket and a homburg. He called a handle and the owners clambered over the planks.

Sanchez didn't take his eyes from the pit. "Dangerous to bet a flyer," he said. "Gets too much height, he can be gaffed coming down. Blue's gonna win, though. Great wingwork. I saw you looking at me."

"I wondered if we could talk."

"You Canadian?"

"British."

"That right?" The handlers were setting their birds again. Sanchez caught the bookie's eye. "You should get something down on this. Odds have narrowed some, but people don't like a flyer."

The racket grew, ringsiders calling their favorite, arguing, laughing, laying bets. Culley was having trouble hearing Sanchez. "How do I do that?"

Without turning, Sanchez put out a hand. Culley gave him a ten dollar bill. The bookie's head bobbed.

The dun stag stayed back, sidestepping like a boxer. The blue rose on stubby wings, twisting acrobatically to slip the blow. The gaff raked one wing and the birds circled, necks stretched toward each other, then engaged at the same time, heels clubbing. Their eyes were stark with fury. The blue stood off for a moment, and the judge called another handle. Angry shouts came from the pitside. The dun's handler plucked a tail feather and held the down at the quill end against a neck wound to stanch the blood.

"See?" Sanchez grinned. "Your money's safe."

"Can we talk?"

"It better be good. There's a naked heel fight after this. I've got the inside track." He glanced across to where a fat woman in a braid shirt stood waiting, a big, slate-colored stag tucked up beside her breast.

"Leave a bet."

"That's not it. Naked heel's a long fight. That's a slow starter. I could double up on the first hit and get better odds."

"Take the risk," Culley said, "and I'll double your bet for you."

"Fifty," Sanchez told him. "Be your winnings on the *gallo fino* there."

The dun strutted a circle, long-necked, long-backed, his eye mad with delight. He went in fast, jabbing one-legged, and made a hit. The blue-barred stag twisted away from the steel and found height, dipping like a lapwing, and dropping for a head shot. The dun cock went down as the blue followed through, landing full-flush and kneading the gaffs on the dun's heart as if he were working a treadle.

Sanchez collected the winnings, pushed half the roll into his shirt, and gave the other half back. He spoke into the bookie's ear, while the man stared at the ground, as if that might aid his concentration. Then he glanced at the fat woman carrying the naked-heeler.

Outside, the sky was dusky-black and the air as warm as wool. A shooting star fell toward the city's crown of lights. Sanchez walked a way off, then sat cross-legged on a piece of rough ground. There were buildings with no one in them, walls gone, roofs on the slide.

"I'm taking a risk here, too," Culley said. "Longer odds; bigger stake."

"I figured you might be."

"You work for a man called Hugo Kemp."

Sanchez reached into his shirt pocket and drew out a fat paper cylinder, stroking its length with pursed fingers to smooth the kinks. "That's right, I do."

He put the joint in his mouth and brought both hands up to his face, palming a Zippo. The thick flame wavered in the breeze, rimming his lips, his nostrils, and his eye sockets with shadow.

"I'd like it if you'd work for me. Just a short while."

Sanchez laughed on an indrawn breath, and held the laugh down for a count of three. "You're right. About the odds." The words arrived on a long feather of smoke.

"Am I wasting my time?" Culley asked.

"Could be."

"He collects paintings. Sometimes he collects the paintings I want."

Culley was improvising now. He'd decided to tell Sanchez that something had come into the market, something both he and Kemp would want. A little espionage would go a long way—that sort of thing. He'd made the assumption that Sanchez wouldn't know one way or the other. He was on bunkhouse duties.

Sanchez said, "You want the Degas."

There was nothing revealing about Culley's pause—the surprise was genuine, as if Sanchez had come straight to a point that Culley had intended to arrive at slowly. "The Degas; yes."

"I'm not your man. You should be talking to Henry Glinwood. Except that Glinwood wouldn't do what you're asking me to do. He's Kemp's man."

"Is he?"

"Body and soul."

"Are you?"

Sanchez cupped the coal of the joint and took a long toke. Smoke purled out of his nostrils, taken this way and that by the breeze. "It won't help you. I don't get to hear about that stuff."

"You know about the Degas."

"We go horseback riding in the desert sometimes. He talks to me. Well—" Sanchez gave a brief laugh, "he talks to himself. I'm around while he does it. But I don't know about the deals, you know? Who from, when, how much."

We've got this far, Culley thought, so I'm going to assume that you're for sale. He said, "That's not what I'm asking for." Sanchez cocked his head—a parody of listening; he drew on the joint and held his breath. "I want to get a bug in there. I want you to take it in for me."

"How would I do that?"

"Should I tell you?"

"If it's what you're here for."

From the rectangle of hard, white light fifty feet away came a hubbub of shouts and catcalls. Through the open doorway Culley could see activity near the pit, and shadows jostling on the walls. It was all gamble now; all risk.

"Check on the types of phone in the main room and in Kemp's bedroom. Let me know what they are. You go in with two identical phones; you take the existing ones out."

"That's it? Switch two phones?"

"Pretty much."

Sanchez nodded thoughtfully. "Now let's hear what you do."

"I give you a third of the buy price of the Degas."

"What?"

Culley plucked a sum from the air. "A hundred thousand dollars; maybe a little more."

"A third of the third up front."

"Not possible," Culley said.

Sanchez uncrossed his legs and looked toward the pit. "I could be making a week's pay in there."

"I'm not the buyer," Culley told him, "I work for the buyer. He doesn't know I'm doing this. I don't think he'd mind much, but I'd sooner not try him out. Apart from that, it's my action, not his. I get a commission on the sale, understand? If I take this out from under Kemp's nose and present it to my buyer, I'm first choice when he needs an agent again. Kemp's often in the market. These bugs you're planting don't wear out. I'll be able to tap into him any time. That's worth a lot to me. I can't pay you until I've bought the piece and sold it on. I'll be giving you my commission; it's worth that much. I've told you that it gives me a terrific edge in any sale where Kemp's a bidder. We could talk about a proportion of that for you—each time I take him out of some piece of action, you stand to gain. I can't pay you until I've been paid. But if this works, if I hear something I can use and it works, then we both make money—you now, me later." Culley had no idea whether what he was saying was taking effect; Sanchez's face was turned to the light, his cheek deeply shadowed. "You're a gambler. This is low risk, high reward."

"Low risk for you." Sanchez hadn't turned his head.

"You can't do it? Two phones in, two out?"

"It's possible."

"You don't have to stay there. Just the bugs." Culley laughed. "Take another job, move away. I'll keep the money coming. Think about it—I'm relying on your silence. If I screw up, any time, you make an anonymous call to Kemp telling him what to look for. All my advantage gone. Christ, you could do it anytime. I'm in your hands."

There was a full minute's silence. Sanchez got up and they

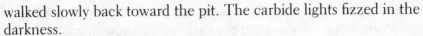

walked slowly back toward the pit. The carbide lights fizzed in the darkness.

"I said, 'Is that it?' You said, 'Pretty much.' "

"I want to meet the daughter. Nina. When Kemp's away, you look after her, am I right?"

Sanchez took a step nearer to Culley, as if they should lower their voices. His breath was sweet with dope. For the first time, he sounded alarmed. "What do you need her for? She's crazy."

"Just to talk. She'll know what's in the house. Give me a better idea of what he's doing—how much he's spending, what he's spending it on."

"Too close. You're talking about getting too close."

"For a few days. Then I'm gone." When Sanchez didn't respond, Culley added, "We're not talking about a payoff, here. It's income for life."

"Where do I find you?" At no time had Sanchez asked for a name. Culley gave him Carl Mathers's office address. In the snow-light and pitch-dark planes from the ruined door, the man's Indian features stood in hard relief; cheekbones and square jaw, strong nose, broad upper lip.

A series of whoops came from around the pit, followed by a shout and a gabble of voices. Sanchez half-turned, then looked at Culley full-face. "Okay." He put out a hand. When Culley did the same, he found himself holding a cold roach.

"Peace pipe," Sanchez said.

It was the seventh handle, and the fat woman's stag was still eager. As she bent to the set, holding the bird's waist and wheezing slightly, her big breasts tumbled into her shirtfront. The heads of the two cocks banged at one another and their legs churned the air. Ira Sanchez offered a bet and the bookie took it on the nod.

This time of year, Kemp liked to take his ride around eight in the morning, before the sun had gained height. Three times a week, Ira would saddle a couple of quarter horses and they'd walk between the banked roses, listening to the *zip, zip, zip,* as water from fifty sprinklers fell among the blooms. They'd lope out to a mesa two miles away and walk back.

Kemp would talk about the land as if he knew how to live there.

"Ratany plant," he'd say, dismounting to peer at the tiny magenta petals. He'd tell how sandhill cranes migrated to Sulphur Springs Valley each fall, or deliver a short lecture on the vast dance circles and power rings in the *tierra del muerto*. One time, he patiently informed Ira about the Navajo code talkers.

Ira would nod, neck-reining his horse away to smile. It wasn't a fond smile. It meant, *Fuck you*.

A job's a job, Ira thought. Time to move on.

He thought, *Anglos*. They want to own everything. They want to own each other.

The slate-colored bird had weight and pit-craft on his side. He slashed at his opponent's head, wearing him down.

The office air-conditioning chugged like a two-stroke engine. A scarf of smoke rolled in a cold shaft of sunlight. Carl Mathers sat at his desk, a telephone on his lap, a small screwdriver in one hand.

"He called in first thing. Gave me the model name, number, colors. Just that. Be here to collect them in an hour. What in hell did you offer him?"

Culley perched on the arm of a battered sofa and watched Mathers at work. "A new life."

"Will he get it?"

"Who ever does?" Culley asked.

"A philosopher," Mathers observed. The phone separated in his hand and he tweezered a one-inch-diameter circuit board from the top of his desk. "There you go."

"What happens?"

"Kemp uses this phone like any other phone. Well, it's the same as any other phone. People can call him—no different. Except this gismo is just for you. An encoding device. You know when you bleep in to your messages from somewhere else? Like that. You dial; you bleep in; same thing. The phone won't ring because there's a two-second delay to get you into the device. You can use any phone with a direct line facility—your hotel will have one; nine, then the number, whatever. If Kemp's making a phone call, you'll hear both sides of the conversation. You'll also hear anything that's said in the room, anytime, whether the phone's in use or not. Just dial and listen, okay? I hope that Indian believed whatever you told him."

"He gave us the details of the phones."

"He did."

"He's calling to collect them."

"He is."

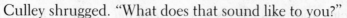

Culley shrugged. "What does that sound like to you?"

Mathers smiled. He put a cigarette in his mouth and waited to light it until he'd reassembled the phone. "Poker player called Slim Preston—won the Crazy Horse Saloon game a few times. Used to say, 'Not all trappers wear fur hats.' "

"Is there a way I can record what I hear?"

"Sure. Easiest thing for you would be a hand-held recorder with a suction plug for the earpiece of the phone. That's another thirty dollars you owe me."

"Do you always keep it this cold in here?"

Culley's throat was dry and itchy by the time Ira Sanchez arrived. The Indian stood in the doorway, a duffel bag looped over one shoulder, and looked at the two phones on the desk. Then he came forward and scooped them into the bag. He behaved as if Mathers wasn't there.

"The main room and the bedroom," Culley reminded him.

"I'm not due back for a while," Sanchez said. "They'll be in by this evening. Make it eight o'clock." He paused. "I need to know where to get you."

"There's a fight tomorrow evening?" Culley asked. "I'll see you there."

"No," Sanchez said. "Where I can find you."

"Here," Culley said. Sanchez shifted the duffel bag back to his shoulder. He waited. Culley gave his name and the name of his hotel.

Sanchez nodded. "Fine. We can meet at the fight; that's okay with me."

As he left, Mathers wafted a hand—"Bye, Ira." To Culley, he said, "Well, I'd've wanted to know that too, I guess."

"He didn't speak to you."

"He's not doing business with me."

Culley's teeth ached slightly along the line of the gum; he imagined he could feel the air trickling through his lungs like snow-melt in a delta. He wanted to be outside, but most of all he wanted a hunter's advantage, another look.

"Can we drive out there again?"

"To Kemp's place?"

"Within view."

Mathers lifted a shoulder. "What else is there to see? You've seen it. Christ, you'll be inside the fucking place—good as."

"I know that. I just want to take a look."

Mathers stood up and checked his pockets for car keys and cigarettes. He switched on an answering machine. "Why not," he said, "I'm charging you by the day."

34

A GIRL WAS SUNBATHING ON A LOUNGER in the courtyard outside Culley's window. Lithe, dark-haired, her waist deeply curved like a cello. She was wearing a turquoise string-and-patch bikini bottom and had a technique, when she moved onto her back, of cupping the discarded bra to her breasts and nipping its sides with her upper arms as she turned, in order to cover herself. It was late in the day and she was taking the last of the sun. She had moved across the courtyard, flagstone by flagstone, to cheat the shadow; now she was boxed in to the last corner of light. The fountain made a noise like Chinese chimes.

Mathers arrived with a hand-sized tape cassette machine and a sucker cup for the telephone.

"This jacked into the recorder," he said, "and this on the earpiece of the phone." He checked a card on Culley's bedside table. "Yeah, dial nine, then dial out."

While Culley examined the equipment, Mathers took his chair by the window. The girl had about six feet of sunlight left. She turned onto her front, dropped the bra alongside, and put her cheek on folded hands. Mathers lit a cigarette. "They gave you a room with a terrific view."

"Especially for tourists and sightseers," Culley agreed.

"Always sexier," Mathers mused. "Whole ass in view apart from that scrap of cloth there; bare back, so you know she's got a bare front, but all you get's just a promise of something you never see. They know how to do it all right." His eyes were fixed on the hint of plumpness under the girl's armpit.

"Give her a try," Culley suggested. "Maybe she's waiting for someone to show her the town."

Mathers sighed. "Time was," he said. "This one's waiting for a guy to come back from some big-shit business deal. He'll be thirty-five, work-out pectorals, concertina of credit cards, stretch limo, company jet. I hate the bastard."

"He might be lousy in bed," Culley offered.

Mathers laughed. "Think she cares? What time are you going to try Kemp?"

"In a couple of hours. Sanchez said eight o'clock. I'll give him some leeway."

"You need me for anything else now? You've got the bug; you've got Sanchez. I guess I could sign off."

"I'm not sure how secure that makes me feel," Culley said. "I'd still like to be able to call on you."

"I'll put you on retainer rates. Half the daily fee. I might not always be there exactly when you want me, but I'll check in from time to time. Leave a message if there's a problem. I have to spend some time with my kid tomorrow, but I'll be in and out."

"You're married." Culley hadn't pictured Mathers in the role—throwing a football to some kid with braces on his teeth, wearing a Snoopy apron at the barbecue, sleeping easily alongside the same woman each night.

"Used to be. Seven years, all told."

"What happened?"

"I was a cop when we married. She didn't like the life. You know how it is."

Culley stifled an urge to laugh. He said, "Irregular hours, late nights," but didn't offer anything of his own situation because he wanted to hear more about Carl's.

"Yeah, that . . . The people you mix with—friends and enemies; the fact that it's often tough to tell them apart. But mostly the loneliness, I guess."

"The kid's how old?"

"Ten." It seemed that Mathers had closed the conversation down. Then he said, "I quit the Department, trying to save the marriage. First two cases I took were missing persons. It's not unusual—kids from the northern cities growing a racial conscience along with their back teeth, inventing something called

Real America, hanging around the reservations looking for the spirits of someone's goddamn ancestors. Third case—straightforward fuck 'n' duck. Guy screws his friend's wife; the guy doesn't know it, but he's got the clap. The wife doesn't know it, so she passes it on to her husband. Pretty soon they all know it."

Mathers chuckled. The chuckle grew into a full-fledged laugh. "Jesus Christ, you never know what you're going to wake up with. Anyway, the wife had a real cute idea. She accused her husband of fucking around and retained me to prove it. Maybe he had been, I don't know. Before I could dig much out, the guy arrived at my house. I wasn't there, but my wife and the kid were. He was drunk and he was angry. Looking at it, I can't blame him for that. Broke a few windows and scared everyone shitless until Tyler Beck turned up and cooled him off. Did more damage to my marriage than he did to my house. She left a couple of days later, with the kid."

Mathers had smoked five cigarettes since his arrival. He lit the sixth and spoke a fluctuating stream of smoke. "Dumb thing is, she lives with Tyler now. Go figure it out."

The girl in the courtyard was on her back when she lost the sun entirely. She sat up and reached blindly for the clasp of the bra, and just for a moment her breasts swung into view. She ran a finger down either side of the bikini bottom, smoothing it over her rump, then walked the breadth of the courtyard, heading for some double glass doors. Her skin was a pale coffee color. Her narrow waist swayed and her hips lifted and dropped with each step.

Mathers shook his head. "I'd better go," he said. "I'm beginning to hate my life."

Culley dialed and was patched-in to a conversation straight away. Thank you, Ira Sanchez, he thought. Someone else in search of a new life. It took him no more than a few seconds of the exchange to decide which voice was Kemp's. He was talking to a man with a sharp nasal accent. Culley imagined a suit to go with the voice— well-cut, expensive, unobtrusive.

". . . can be viewed, of course. I should warn you, there are others who have the piece in mind."

Kemp's tone was slower, deeper. "Three days' time?"

"Would be fine." The man gave an address in Manhattan, then the name of his gallery, checking that Kemp had the details right.

"Three o'clock," Kemp suggested.

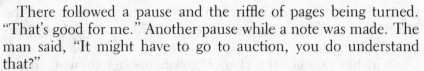

There followed a pause and the riffle of pages being turned. "That's good for me." Another pause while a note was made. The man said, "It might have to go to auction, you do understand that?"

"You have a reserve price."

"Of course."

"We'll talk about that, Mr. Bryant. Most of all, I want to see the sketch."

"I understand. Three o'clock on Friday, then."

There came a rattle as the phone was hung up. Kemp's voice was no less clear than during the phone conversation.

"I'll go to New York on Wednesday. There are other things to be taken care of."

"Back on Friday evening?" Henry Glinwood, Culley guessed. A light voice that dropped rhythmically on the syllables.

"Yes."

"He didn't mention a price?"

"No. But then he wouldn't. I've had dealings with Bryant before. He made the mistake of letting me in on the ground floor when he was offering a Pissarro. I guaranteed a starting price so long as I got last refusal—he was auctioning the piece. Other bidders found out that I could top their bids, and no one came to the party. I bought the painting for my first offer."

"It was you who let the others know," Glinwood said.

Kemp's laugh was unadulterated delight. "He suspected—couldn't prove it, of course."

"So he doesn't like you too much."

"He doesn't have to. He likes my money; that's good enough."

There was a pause, the sound of glass on glass. Kemp said, "Don't put ice in that." Then, "That's fine, Henry."

"Friday," Glinwood said. He suggested a flight time and Kemp agreed to it. "I've some documents for you to sign. Share transfers."

"Tomorrow."

The sound of a glass being set down on a table, then a door closing. Alone, Kemp gave a tiny groan followed by a breathy laugh. The sounds said, I need Glinwood, and he bores me. Footsteps on a wood floor; then silence as the feet stepped onto a rug. And into the silence, sinuous and pin-clear, the first few notes of a flute concerto.

.   .   .   .

Culley put the phone down, then dialed Mike Dawson's number. Dawson answered on the fourteenth ring. He sounded as if he were underwater.

"Please," Culley said, "don't ask me if I know what time it is."

"I'm sure you know exactly what time it is, you bastard."

"Are you alone?"

There was a pause; Dawson was angry or amused, perhaps both. "I'm a personable fellow," he said. "I've still got all my hair and most of my teeth. It doesn't follow that my life is a marathon of remorseless screwing."

"Rumor has it differently."

Dawson laughed. "What's happening?"

"That's what I was going to ask."

"Easy. Nothing. Hold on."

A rumple of bedclothes, then silence. Culley gazed out of his window. A cloistered walkway bordered the courtyard on three sides, arches supported by white pillars, on each pillar a lamp. Water belled from the crown of the fountain, a perfect, circular fall, and plashed from shelf to shelf, translucent in the lamplight. Dawson came back to the phone two or three minutes later.

"What was that?" Culley asked.

"You woke me up. I had to go for a piss. Nothing—" Dawson picked up his earlier remark. "No more killings. No more leads. But that doesn't mean no more hassle. The general opinion seems to be that since the bastard's decided to stop shooting people, he can remain anonymous, stay at large, enjoy life and freedom, and laugh up his sleeve at an incompetent police force until he decides the time has come for a little more high-velocity fun."

"Whose general opinion?"

"Papers, TV, the rest."

"Protheroe?"

"Well, who do you think they got the idea from? When interviewed, he sort of wavers between apology and regret. It's fucking pathetic. Meanwhile, we're working fifteen-hour days and getting nowhere. There's nowhere to get. They've reduced the Task Force by more than half."

"The idea is that he's stopped for good."

"For the moment."

"Yes, that's what I mean. Stopped."

"What about you?"

"Not sure," Culley said. "Too soon to tell."

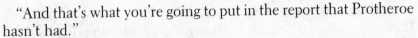

"And that's what you're going to put in the report that Protheroe hasn't had."

"He's mentioned that."

"Oh, yes. He's mentioned it. He tried your hotel; you're not there."

"Too expensive," Culley said. "A burden on the taxpayers."

Dawson laughed. He said, "You're not popular."

"Nothing's changed," Culley agreed. "Good night, Mike."

Dawson's reply came from a distance; he was holding the phone away from his mouth. "Say good night to Robin."

"Good night, Robin." The girl's voice was fruity with sleep, muffled, the syllables blurred like lipstick on a kissed mouth.

Culley dialed Helen's number. It was busy. He tried again ten minutes later with the same result.

He dialed Kemp and got silence, punctuated by the sounds of sleep.

He tried Helen again. The phone rang, but no one picked it up.

35

THE JUDGE IN HIS HOMBURG and tatty jacket; the fat woman cradling her stag; the bookie like an automaton, nodding, turning, nodding again. Culley felt as if he had come back to the auditorium after the play's first interval. Knife-blade shadows from the lamps; the blue-barred cock, spurred and trimmed, eager to go on stage.

Ira Sanchez waited until the handlers stepped in, then intercepted the bookie's gaze. Culley handed him a twenty dollar bill. "Ten for you," he said, "and ten for me."

The blue's handler was a skinny man in a straw Stetson and the kind of fancy shirt rodeo cowboys wear. The double cuffs flopped onto his wrists and the fringing showed bald patches. He headed his bird to a red-black opponent and both cocks pecked like rock drills.

"He'll fight over three days, if he lasts," Ira said.

"We're still betting the blue?"

"Sure—wingwork, staying power too. Something else. See that rose comb and rose wattles? Means there's Black Game blood in him somewhere. Killing machines, Black Game birds. They'd go naked heel against a locomotive. Everything function the way it should?"

"Works perfectly," Culley told him.

"Get what you wanted?"

"Some of it."

The judge dropped a handkerchief and the birds were released. They circled, pointing at one another like arrows. The clamor around the pit silenced Culley and Sanchez.

It was like waking in a strange room before the memory arrives of how you got there. A sudden puzzlement and the onset of panic. One moment, everything made sense; the next, nothing seemed recognizable. The ringsiders, yelling and elbowing for position; the singing hiss of carbide; the two stags tumbling and stabbing in the pit. Culley felt as if he had been bludgeoned by shadow. He couldn't remember the name of the man beside him.

He turned with one hand lifted, like someone under a blindfold, while shouts and catcalls lapped at his ears. With his back to the pit, he was hemmed in by faces. He turned again; Sanchez was craning forward, fixed on the fight, his face expressionless. Culley spoke, though he had no idea of what he'd said, and the noise was too great for him to hear it. There was a coldness in his stomach, as if his blood were puddling there, and his head hissed like the lamps, blind-white, empty of thought.

Then it all came back, focus and a sense of place, as if the images had suddenly rushed to reassemble with a *whoosh* of slipstream. He shuddered. Recollection brought him the sound of Helen's phone ringing endlessly. The blue thrashed his wings and went feet-first at the red-black cock, needlepoint spurs ripping tufts of feather from under the crop.

During the handle, Ira said, "This mother could stop a rhino." He looked across the pit, but the man's eyes were switched off; the book was closed.

The skinny guy in the fringed shirt had rolled his sleeves up. When he held the blue out for the set, his forearms were ropes of vein beneath old leather. The bird's neck hackles were up like a sword guard. He leaned over the scratch line and clubbed with his beak.

At the release, both birds climbed in a hectic clatter of wings, heel to heel, as if they were walking up either side of an invisible wall. The blue rolled back to strike, legs hammering, the drop gaffs coming up bloody. The ringsiders howled and crowed.

An answering scream came from the blue stag. He pitched the other bird to the floor of the pit in a welter of feathers, and crashed down on the upturned heart-lung area, spurs raking. A handle was called, but neither of the owners hurried to get into the pit. The blue hacked at his opponent for a moment, then flapped down and circled the pit, stiff-legged with hate. Eventually, the red-black's handler stepped in and hauled the carcass out by a wing.

Outside, Sanchez fanned their winnings like a deck of cards. A chipped rectangle of white light fell from the doorway.

A man jostled Ira's back, angry and eager to leave. "Fuckin' flyers. How come he beat the fuckin' weight?" He stepped through the wall of darkness that bordered the pit and was lost.

Some homemade wicker and lath boxes stood to one side of the door. The handler of the blue-barred stag was kneeling down to crate his bird, tightening thongs on the front flap. Wings crashed against the bars as he straightened up. The man laughed, then said something in Spanish, softly, as if to a child.

Ira walked off, towing Culley into the darkness. He said, "How long—before you pay me?"

"As soon as I know I've bought the sketch. Could be less than a week."

"Out in the desert," said Ira, "there's a whole series of intaglios. They're like gigantic drawings on the desert floor, very old. A hunter with his spear, the sun overhead, under his feet some wavy lines for water and below that the fish he's after. There are others. The stones are like jet if they stand undisturbed; scrape them away and you make lines. That's how the drawings were made. Sacred sites, you know? A year or so back, some kids with trail bikes rode all over one of them. Tire marks'll stay there a thousand years."

"Why would they do that?"

"People don't like to see what they can't own." A new jeep was parked just off the road. "I'm baby-sitting from tomorrow," Ira said. "He must be going to look at the Degas."

"I know," said Culley. "Yes, he is."

Ira unlocked the jeep. "Company car," he said. "Let's go for a beer."

They sat in a booth under dim red lighting and listened to a strings version of Beatles hits. Everything in the bar seemed very still, as if the drinkers there were expending just enough energy to get glass to lip. A tall, blond girl in jeans as tight as a bandage took their order and was back almost at once.

"How do we do this?" Culley asked.

"She never goes out, you know? She never goes anywhere."

"Never?"

Sanchez shook his head and mouthed foam off his beer. "Hardly ever."

"So sometimes."

"I guess so. Listen, I've told you about her. She's weird."

"Tell me more."

"She doesn't talk much, she sleeps a lot of the day, she—I don't know—drifts about. She's like smoke among trees; half the time you're not sure whether she's there at all."

"Depressed," Culley suggested.

"Yeah, maybe. One time I did bring her into the city, we got to the highway and she said, 'It's such a long way to go.' I said something about it was just a few miles. She said, 'No, it takes half your life to make a step or two.' Something like that. I mean, she talks like she's on some other planet."

"Is there a mother?"

Sanchez shrugged. "Story is she died when Nina was young. No one knows."

Culley drank half his beer in three swallows. "Who sits in that rocking chair outside the house?"

Sanchez looked up suddenly, one eyebrow cocked. "Carl Mathers take you out there?" Culley nodded. "Yeah, that's Nina's chair. Sometimes she reads, but not often. Only time she looks up is if Kemp happens by. Then it's like something has her full attention."

"In what way?"

"I can't figure out whether it's a snake watching a rabbit, or a rabbit watching a snake."

"She hates him?"

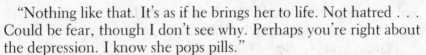

"Nothing like that. It's as if he brings her to life. Not hatred . . . Could be fear, though I don't see why. Perhaps you're right about the depression. I know she pops pills."

"Will you try?" Culley asked. "There isn't a hell of a lot of time."

Ira reached into his shirt pocket and took out a thinly rolled handmade and the Zippo. A scroll of smoke, heavy with the smell of dope, drifted across the table. "I'll call you."

"We could be talking a few extra percentage points on the first deal."

Ira nodded and took money out of his shirt to settle the check.

"If memory serves me right," Culley said, "I won some of that."

Two bills went down on the table, the rest back into Sanchez's pocket. "On account," he said, and smiled.

People still strung about with cameras were strolling past St. Augustine Cathedral or filing into restaurants on East Broadway. Culley had taken a cab from the bar; Sanchez had stayed on to drink. Culley worried about the man, but realized that there was little he could do. Sanchez had to be taken on trust. The dangers were obvious—that Kemp had been told about the bugs and would use them to draw Culley on. Disinformation is a subtler trick than any other; but if there was a way of being safe, Culley hadn't the time to find it.

He collected his key from the hotel desk and arranged for a plane ticket that would take him in and out of New York on the same day. In his room, he opened the window onto the courtyard and poured himself a drink before lifting the phone.

Silence. A rustle of papers. A brief cough, like a note of disapproval.

Culley lay on the bed, his back propped by pillows, and sipped his drink. He listened to the jots of sound like a daylight predator hunting in darkness.

A small, repetitive tap, like moths butting a lampshade, or someone's fingernail ticking on a tabletop while he made a decision. The rasp of a chair, pushed back. A drawer opening and closing.

Then silence again. And behind the silence, faint singings and sighings, an electronic warp and weft, nothing more than the sound of an open phone line, though it seemed to come from some deep and airless place, some massive, black trough that Culley had unwittingly tapped.

He listened as the sounds from the room and the sounds from the other dark place orchestrated themselves and became slow, melancholy music.

Someone entered the room but didn't speak. Culley closed his eyes, as if that might help.

"How long will you be gone?" Nina.

She must have brought Kemp a drink, or something to eat, because there followed a slight clatter as a plate or cup was set down on a table, and Kemp said, "Thank you," and then, "Until Friday evening."

"I hate it when you go away." Her voice was a dry, soft sound, like sand blown over rock.

"I know. It isn't for long. Henry will be here. And Ira Sanchez will get you anything you might need." Kemp was distracted. Culley imagined him still looking down at his papers, reaching absentmindedly for the sandwich she'd brought him.

"Henry doesn't know I exist."

"He's there if you want him."

"And he's got cold eyes, like a fish."

"He's just a servant," Kemp said, "like the rest. Ask him for whatever you want."

A sudden landslide of fury. "I don't want to talk to him, he's got fish eyes." Her soft tone followed almost immediately. "I had a dream this afternoon. I didn't feel well, so I went to sleep and I dreamed that creature again."

Kemp said, "It's just a dream. You like it too much."

"It's a wolverine." Nina spoke as if she hadn't heard her father. "But you wouldn't recognize it as that because it's longer, much longer, as if it needed an extra set of feet, the same as a wolverine but not, some other thing, some hybrid. So long it flows over the ground, over rocks by the place it's coming from, some sort of cave. It has red fur, bushy fur, and a sharp face and neat ears. Its mouth never quite closes, so you can always see the fangs. When it stops and sniffs the air, the fangs chatter, then it goes on, flowing, close to the ground. It scampers and its back undulates as it moves, as it crosses some obstacle. You can't see it," she said, "in—"

There was tension in Kemp's voice now. "There's no such creature."

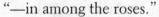

"—in among the roses."

Kemp's boot heels sounded on the wood floor, then were deadened by the rug. A silence. Kemp said, "I still have work to do."

Nina started low, but increased in fury. "I shall get Ira Sanchez to take me into the city, and find a job and find an apartment and that's the last you'll see of me. I'll go away—somewhere, Los Angeles—and live there, and that's the last you'll ever see of me."

"Go," Kemp said. "Why don't you?"

Light, swift footfalls and the door banging shut.

Silence. And behind the silence, whisperings. The open phone line—nothing more than that; like hearing the weather, like hearing shiftings in space. But Culley strained to listen, as if something crucial was being said, as if the whisperers might be talking of him.

He waited for five more minutes, occupying the silence and the whispers that lay between himself and Hugo Kemp. Then he dialed Helen's number.

She said, "I can't come to the phone at the moment, but if you leave a message, I'll call you back." He found himself holding on while the tape turned, but he didn't speak.

He woke in a sweat. Dream images tugged, then let go. The wall opposite the window showed pasty squares, black-barred, from the courtyard glow. Culley lay still for a few moments, then dialed Kemp's number.

Silence and music. Silence and whisperings.

A door opened and closed. Linen crumpled. Then Nina's voice. "I heard you come to bed."

"I thought you were asleep."

"I couldn't. I tried. I tried to be asleep." Both Kemp and Culley waited on Nina's contrition, one set of eyes on the penitent face, one ear at the grille.

"I'm sorry," she said.

"You know there are times when I have to go away."

"Yes." Culley imagined the word coming with a nod and lowered eyes. "But when you go away . . . everything holds its breath." She sounded thoughtful, as someone might who was anxious that the memory be accurate. "Sometimes I think I might die before you get back and never see you again."

"Do you? Do you think that?" Culley struggled to read Kemp's tone of voice—tense, but far from angry; something there that lay beyond curiosity. Then he had it. Delight.

Nina said, "Sometimes, if I open my window and lean out, I think I can hear something moving among the roses. Moving and stopping and moving again." She spoke carefully, like a child counting. After a pause, she said, "I expect it's the wind, though. Don't you?"

What happened next was difficult to decode. Culley heard Nina's voice, half sigh, half sob, and pictured Kemp in the act of holding his daughter, giving comfort and perhaps some small sign of remorse. Then came a moment that offered no image at all— something soft being torn—until Culley remembered the sound that Mike Dawson had made as he got out of bed, and got back in.

He listened as their voices mingled, whispers too low to be understood; abstract, lilting sounds that fell on the ear like music.

Except from time to time when their words came clear.

". . . love me like that, unless you . . ."

". . . find me. I'll never leave you."

". . . real, or just a dream. But when you . . ."

". . . nothing can change all that, unless you . . ."

And later, Kemp's voice, tight with need, saying, "Yes, like that." Then again, "Like that; just there."

And Nina's breath shortening, the quick, harsh crowing in her throat rising from some source that was pleasure or fear, or both.

And Culley listening, eyes closed, head bowed in the dark, as if he were a musician, note-perfect, testing a concert performance for its pace, its truth, its depth of feeling.

36

MARTIN JACKSON KICKED the last fat pink rump into the truck
and took a signed loading sheet from the driver. Together they
heaved up the tailgate and dropped the locking pins into place.
The panels of the truck shook and boomed as the pigs turned in
their pens. They snorted and screamed, as if they had just got
news of why they were there and where they were going.

Jackson decided that he'd delayed long enough. Three days, just
working the farm as usual, three nights of light sleep, all doors
unlocked, waiting for an arrival. There was no danger, he knew,
of a shot from cover while he hauled buckets of swill or sat by the
uncurtained window of his kitchen. That was for victims. Eric
would want to be there, to stand face to face. There was too much
between them for distant good-byes.

He saw the truck out of the farm gate, then went indoors. Now
that he'd harvested his pork, he could leave things to a foreman.
Staying put wasn't going to work. Eric knew where he was, but
wouldn't come down to meet him. He was beckoning with his
absence. He wanted to pick the terrain.

He was either living on the moor, Jackson decided, or walking
the moor each day, watching the farm from time to time, perhaps,
and waiting for Jackson to join him there so that the game could
begin.

Like a single combatant circling the arena. Like a champion
striding each morning before his army's tents, the sun flashing
from his breastplate as he called for opponents from the enemy
camp.

Jackson took a runner's backpack from a peg on the kitchen door
and packed into it the things he'd need. A waterproof poncho that
would stake out like a tent with the wearer as the tentpole, head
covered by a fitted hood. A silver, thermal body wrap; survival
rations; a compass. In the pouch pocket, a 9mm. Beretta handgun

and two spare clips: because they would be that close—to see one another's eyes, to hear one another's words.

The army had a term for it—the runs over hill country, the exercises in storm weather, the tests that found the limits of a man's endurance, then pushed him on beyond that; all the sickeners together, the entire course of make-or-break. It was called "beasting."

Jackson zipped the backpack. His walking boots were by the door, as if the first few steps to the threshold had already been taken.

Eric, he thought, this one is just for us. Our beasting.

He ate eggs and bacon, and some fruit, then sat in a wooden ladderback chair to wait for dusk. In the forefront of his mind was a view of the moor, its scarps and sunken valleys, quagmire and rock. Also there, was a face he only half-remembered, a young face that the years would have changed.

Eric.

And further back in his mind, another face. Culley in the airport café; Culley as he turned, just before going airside. Francis had given him the details of the flight that would bring the man back from the States. It was logged in his memory like a task that must take its place in the order of things.

Plenty of time, he thought. Everything in its time.

37

RAZOR, MIRROR, BANDAGE, antiseptic. And the little washes of blood joining like tributaries as they trickled from thigh to knee, from knee to shin, and then between her toes and off—drop by drop—a flux of sin that was shed onto carefully laid sheets of toweling paper.

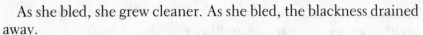

As she bled, she grew cleaner. As she bled, the blackness drained away.

In her rocking chair, she stared at the roses until it seemed she could see their scent rising like a brilliant mist, a curtain of color that seeped into the sky and leached the light. She slept for a while, and found her dream creature, its richly red fleece rippling down a hillside. When it paused to find direction, its teeth chattered.

She opened her eyes. Ira Sanchez was standing in front of her, blocking the sun. He said, "I have to go into the city. You want to stay here? Maybe you'd enjoy the trip."

Nina said, "Yes, all right," surprising them both.

She heard herself: "I'll get Ira Sanchez to take me into the city . . . that's the last you'll ever see of me." You don't have to want it to try it out; you don't have to buy it just because you've seen it in the window.

"Give me an hour," Sanchez said.

Culley woke to the telephone as if it were saying he'd been away too long. He picked it up, almost believing that he might hear the sounds of Kemp and Nina's lovemaking, their whispers, still stored in the earpiece.

Sanchez said, "I'm bringing her into town. You came out here with Mathers . . ."

"That's right."

"The intersection where the desert road meets the highway. You've got half an hour. Put the hood of your car up, okay? We know one another, but not well."

"Will she ask how?"

"That's your problem. Improvise."

Ira hung up abruptly, as if he feared interruption. Culley got into the shower and stood still, like a statue being hosed down in a public park. He tried to empty his mind, but it was a losing game. The whispers were there in the hiss of water; they rose with the steam billows, breathy and bed-warm, to fog the glass panels of the shower stall. Nina's voice, cresting; the gutturals that peaked in a series of muted yells: *Oh. Oh. Oh.* The telephone clapped to his ear.

When he saw her, it was like catching a glimpse of a famous criminal, or a movie star. She was sitting in the back of a big Mercedes, her face turned toward the incident at the roadside. He was the incident.

Sanchez took the Merc a yard or two past, then swung in. Culley walked to the front passenger window as it hummed open.

"Robin . . ." Ira was in-role; he'd probably rehearsed it.

"I don't know what's wrong," Culley said. "Stalled, and I couldn't get it started after that. Can you give me a ride into the city? The rental company can take over."

There was no way out of joining Ira in the front. He hung his forearms over the back of the seat to be introduced to Nina.

"Nina Kemp, Robin Culley," said Ira. "Robin and I met—oh, two or three years back. I was working as a wrangler up at Wickenberg; Robin was holidaying at the ranch. He called me when he got to Tucson, this trip. We had a few beers." He said it rapidly, doing Culley's improvising for him.

"I'm just touring," Culley told Nina. "Seeing something of the countryside. At least, I was until my car gave up the ghost." He felt as if he and Ira were two characters in a play, giving each other details of the plot so that the audience could get the drift of things.

Nina didn't seem to need their subterfuge. Culley wasn't even sure she'd heard it. She looked at him as if he were a puzzle to be solved, then turned her face to the window. There was a full minute's silence in the car. Without looking back, she said, "How far have you come?"

"From England," Culley told her. "I'm English."

"Why did you make the trip?"

"I like America. I enjoy coming here."

"You had to leave your home." She said it as though Culley had perrformed some act of thoughtless abandonment.

"Well, yes. You have to do that to go anywhere."

"What?" Her head came around quickly, as if she had just heard, in a foreign place, someone speaking the language of her own country.

"Getting somewhere," Culley repeated. "The first act is leaving."

He talked about the landscape, about deserts, about Britain's rainfall. He talked about the unreliability of cars. He talked about traveling as if it were something anyone could do. Sanchez drove in silence. Nina listened. At one point, she lifted her left leg onto

207

the seat, holding it close to the ankle, where her loose pants over-lapped her shoe, and for a moment Culley thought she was going to tuck both legs up—the pose of a child fixed by the storyteller's art.

He talked about other places he'd visited—France, Italy, Spain—making a comparison of cities and countryside and people. She shifted the leg slightly, and Culley misread her wince for a half-smile.

When they came into the city, she asked, "What are you going to do?"

"Now?"

"Yes."

"Call the car-rental company, do some sightseeing . . . I'm not sure. I was planning to drive to Flagstaff, but there's only half the day left."

"Can I come with you?"

"If you'd like to, sure."

Ira said, "Where shall I pick you up?"

"The bookstore," Nina said, and they set a time.

She was tall; when Culley took her arm to steer her across the street, his hand rose to the level of his own elbow. She allowed the touch, but didn't cooperate with it.

He faked a call to the car company. While Nina waited, he dialed Helen's number. The answering machine was on. When he glanced around, Nina was standing ten paces away, arms folded, head down, with the look of someone who has given up on an overdue train.

For a while, they followed the tourists—La Placita, the Man-ning house, the walled city of the Old Pueblo. Nina was his guide, though she didn't talk about the city—she simply stopped when there was something to see, then moved off when he'd had enough time to look. Finally, she led him into a park and found a place to sit.

She was wearing a long-sleeved shirt, cuffs buttoned; the baggy pants tapered at the ankle. On one wrist, over the shirt cuff, was a leather and turquoise bracelet. Her hair was dark and heavy, cut in a bob that shrouded her face whenever she bent her head. It semed to Culley that he was looking at her through a veil of dusk. It was clear that she was beautiful, but you couldn't quite see how.

He was reminded of portraits of long-dead women in municipal galleries, their features blurred by cracked varnish.

"Where did you go," she asked, "when you went to France?"

"The last time?" Culley thought back. "Close to a place called Figeac. It's in the south." Sitting in a café in the square with local kids playing pinball, Helen picking their route for a drive to the Pyrenees next day. A thunderstorm had pushed them inside. Fat raindrops swept past the open window and hissed on the cobbles.

"Will you take me there?"

The suddenness of it defeated him. He said, "If you want to go," then laughed to point up the joke.

Her expression didn't change. She sat cross-legged on the grass, left leg uppermost, and peered at his face. "It sounds like a place I've always wanted to go to." Culley stayed silent. Her voice was soft, but she seemed suddenly alert. "I could find a job, and an apartment, and that would be the last you'd see of me."

Culley leapt, like a man who hears a voice in the dark. Nina was looking at her hands, waiting for a response.

Eventually, Culley spoke. "You could go there," he said, "if you wanted to."

When Ira arrived at the bookstore, Nina was showing Culley a book on Arizona, color plates of cities and the desert, of plants and animals, the Grand Canyon's ruby and russet moonscape.

Ira led Culley outside. "How did it go?"

"I need more time," Culley said. "I'm going to New York tomorrow. After that, I'll need to see her again."

"It's a risk."

"Not much of one. She likes me. What could anyone say? She'd met your friend from England and wanted to spend some time showing him around."

"Do you know how fucking *normal* that sounds?"

"Well—fine."

"No," Ira said. "That's the problem."

"It takes time. I can't say, 'Hi, it's good to meet you. What paintings is your father likely to have his eye on in the near future?' She's talking; it'll come."

"You've fixed this—to see her again?"

"Day after tomorrow. We're meeting at my hotel; you drive her there."

Ira grinned, but there was no mirth in it. "Pay a good price for that Degas," he said. "I'm earning my third."

Nina came out of the bookstore carrying a parcel. The book they'd been looking at. She gave it to Culley.

"Not tomorrow," she said, "but the day after." A child's method of calculating.

"That's right."

Sanchez pointed to the Mercedes, parked across the street, and started to walk away.

Nina turned to Culley, almost his height, their eyes almost level, their mouths. She put a hand on his shoulder and leaned in. Culley thought she was about to kiss him good-bye. He angled his cheek, but then felt her lips touch his ear.

She whispered, "I hate it when you go away."

38

THEY CAME IN THROUGH cloudbank, losing altitude until the colossal stalagmites of Manhattan bristled into view, seeming to sway as the plane banked, as if they were being viewed through a fish-eye lens.

Culley had waited until the last minute to have his conversation with Bryant. The Degas sketch had offered itself by accident—a perfect device for drawing Ira Sanchez on. Perfect, too, as a means of meeting Hugo Kemp. Culley wanted to be close to him, close enough to touch. It would be like seeing, but not being seen; like the camera lens that captures its subject's soul.

"I don't know the name." It had been Bryant's first response.

"I'm acting for a client."

"Am I permitted to know his name?"

"Or her name," Culley had said. "I'm afraid not. At a later stage, perhaps. If it appears that we might be going to be successful—at that point, of course."

"And you would like to see the piece tomorrow. That's terribly short notice." A primness in the tone, mincing the vowels; Culley had shifted the phone and grimaced with distaste.

"I'm in New York for that day. Then Chicago. I could fly back, I suppose, though I'd sooner not."

Bryant's voice had presented pursed lips. "It depends how anxious you are to acquire the sketch, I guess."

A mistake. Culley had tried for a note of eagerness, tempered by confidence. "There's no doubt of our enthusiasm, Mr. Bryant. Tomorrow would help my schedule; it's nothing more than that."

Bryant had fixed the appointment at four o'clock, an hour after Kemp's. Culley arrived at three-fifteen.

"It's somewhat embarrassing; another client . . ." Bryant wore his dark suit and striped shirt like someone under lock and key.

"I'm sorry," Culley said. He spread his hands like a beggar. "It's clearly my fault. And now I'm short of time. I thought we said three o'clock."

"If the other client doesn't object," Bryant said. He walked away. At the far end of the gallery were doors that let onto offices, and between them another door with a small microphone grille mounted alongside. A security guard was sitting on a chair nearby. Bryant spoke into the grille, his hand ready to push the door.

Culley wandered around the exhibition—big, brutal abstracts, the paint laid on in heavy blocks and clotted whorls that stood off the canvas in jagged bas-relief. Dull reds and greens, blacks and muddy pinks. They looked like aerial photographs of a battlefield.

"The other gentleman doesn't object." Bryant had appeared at Culley's side.

I'll bet, thought Culley. *Know thine enemy.* Kemp would be both angry and curious. More curious than angry at the moment. Bryant spoke into the grille, and the door buzzed open.

She was dancing on water, or else she was dancing on air—a faint dusting of blue pastel at her feet. Back slightly bent, her arms extended and lowered, left leg forward, the long, soft skirt falling back from the litheness of her calf. Her face was turned away; there was just the curve of her cheek, a single stroke; but had you passed her in the street you'd have known her at once. The lines were laid down with such sureness, such fluency, that you could feel the movement that resided in her limbs—arrested briefly, but on the brink of release. She was all light, all grace, all moments that stun the eye.

Kemp turned from her, his arm extended stiffly. "I gather we might be in competition."

His handshake was dry and testingly strong. Culley smiled inwardly at the assumption. Weak handshake, no balls. He stood back and looked at the sketch until Kemp's impatience spilled over.

"Bryant tells me you're not here for yourself."

"A client."

The Degas had been propped on an easel and placed in the center of the room, an unashamed request for attention; this is what's on offer, nothing else, just this. If you care what it costs, don't look. Kemp's eyes were drawn back to it.

A slender man, average height, gray-brown hair touseled slightly as if by the wind. There was a tightness about him; balked energy, perhaps. A lean face, just the first hint of slackness under the eyes and by the jawline. He looked like a one-time athlete, but no team man; a middle-distance runner, someone who would go up against the clock.

Bryant said, "We're asking for offers within the next two weeks."

"That's fine," Culley said. "I'll call my client tomorrow. And I'll be back in England well before your deadline. How will you work the auction?"

"Two rounds of bidding; three if any of the interested parties are within—oh—three to five thousand dollars of each other. In that case, we'll take a best-offer round."

"Sudden death," Culley said.

Bryant winced. "Yes, in effect."

"And the provenance . . ."

"The piece has been attested-to by several curators. There's no doubt that it's a Degas. I'll let you have copies of the documentation, of course."

"What do you think?"

It was clear that Culley's remark had been addressed to Kemp. He was startled by it. "Think?" he asked. His gaze went back to the sketch and he paused while Culley waited for him to sum up the inexpressible. "Perfect," he said.

Culley felt as if he'd scored a rack of points. He took a couple of paces closer to the sketch. The dancer held her pose; music was stalled behind her, waiting to break.

"Yes," he said, "I think we can raise the cash for this little hoofer."

New York was surly; irritated by itself. There was rain in the air and the crosstown traffic was backed up everywhere. Culley walked up Second Avenue, away from the gallery, then headed west. On Thirty-fourth Street, construction workers bellowed at each other over a generator that was as loud and rapid as a Bofors gun. If people had walked any faster, they'd have broken into a trot. The beggars were having a bad day.

He found a diner and ordered coffee. *Know thine enemy.* He'd needed to see Kemp, to give the voice a face, to confront him. At some point, the confrontation would be of a different order; but for now it was enough to have some measure of the man.

Culley remembered when—seven, eight years before—he'd been told about a new face on his patch. A call from Glasgow, a detective sergeant on the line letting him know that a hard man had moved south. He gave the impression that a large proportion of Glasgow's hospital beds were occupied by people who had upset the man in some way or another. Gone to places where they shouldn't have been seen. Said things that proved unwise. Laughed at a bad moment. Wore the wrong faces.

Culley had arranged it so that he was drinking in a certain pub on an evening when the hard-case was sure to show up. He'd waited for half an hour before that happened. Then he came in, a weasel of a man in a business suit, his hair flicked up in a quiff. He ordered a drink and sat by himself at a table. From time to time, people would come into the pub, consult him, go away again. Light blue eyes that never looked anywhere but at the table in front of him. Narrow shoulders; a thin, raddled face. All deceptive. Culley knew that he was looking at a dangerous man. He leaked evil and violence; it would stand out in his sweat, rank, like the tenements he grew up in. But Culley saw something else there, a special quality. It was undirected hatred, a hatred that was too intense, too general, to worry about *who*, or *why*, or *whether*. It meant that he wouldn't know when to stop, or want to.

A couple of months later, Culley had to go looking for that man. He'd been glad of those few moments in the pub when he'd simply watched, gauging the depth of hatred.

Kemp didn't have that quality. The Scot had been a man with scar tissue behind the eyes. Kemp was more dangerous, Culley saw that. Kemp bought and sold people like the Scot. He used them as keys to unlock doors. Kemp had what he wanted not because he fought for it, but because, deep down, he knew he already owned it. In the world, there were people, and then were people like Hugo Kemp.

A girl in a red checked dress paused alongside him and Culley accepted a refill. It was important to get the timing right. He drank the coffee slowly, then went out into the crush and flagged down a cab.

The girl at the desk smiled as she took his ticket. He said, "I wonder if Mr. Hugo Kemp has checked in yet."

She tapped the computer. "Yes, Mr. Kemp has been allocated a seat."

"Could you sit me next to him? We're colleagues. We have to talk. I'm a little late getting here."

She smiled again when she handed Culley his boarding card.

"What do you want?" Kemp asked.

Culley fastened his seat belt and looked around. The Club compartment was half-empty. "To talk."

"How did you know I'd be on this plane?"

"I know that you live in Tucson. Near Tucson? At any rate, it wasn't difficult. They checked the passenger lists for me; found you at the first attempt."

"Before you arrived in New York."

"Of course."

"Bryant didn't tell me your name."

"Davis," Culley said.

Kemp fell silent for a while. Culley didn't push. He watched the thin rain make broken lines on the window.

"You've gone to a lot of trouble," Kemp observed. He was intrigued; a touch worried, perhaps. He could have moved to another seat.

214

"I'm well paid for it."

"By your client."

"My client; yes."

They taxied out to a runway and joined the line for take-off. Away from the airport buildings, the rain seemed grayer and fiercer. They lifted off and banked along the East River, looking for their airway. The city was humped in the rain, its cloud-high pillars seeming deserted, like megaliths from a dead era.

"Why Tucson?" Culley asked.

"What?" Kemp had the window seat. He'd been peering out, perhaps trying to avoid Culley until he felt ready.

"Why not New York?"

Kemp grimaced. "New York is a hostage to Mammon. When the world ends, we'll simply hand it over like a bad debt."

"That doesn't tell me why Tucson."

There was a look on Kemp's face that said, Whatever you want, you're not going to get it. If it's something I've got, you can't have it; if it's something I want, it's mine already. Since it was impossible for him to lose, he could afford to play. He said, "I like the desert."

"I can't remember," Culley said, "whether I've ever been to a desert. What's so special?"

"You know about T. E. Lawrence? Lawrence of Arabia?" Culley nodded. "He was asked the same question. He said, 'It's clean.' "

"That simple?"

Kemp added another virtue. "No people."

"None?"

"Few enough." Kemp was amused by Culley's probings. He asked, "And you—where are you from?"

"Britain," Culley said. He plucked a name from the air. "Town called Lyme Regis." Not from the air, he realized—Helen's birthplace.

"Many people there?"

"You have to go on a waiting list to get ill."

Kemp laughed. "And what do you want of me, Mr. Davis?"

"I want you not to buy the Degas."

The laugh picked up again, and grew. Through his mirth, Kemp said, "Go fuck yourself, you son of a bitch." He made it sound quite friendly, because he kept laughing.

. . .

215

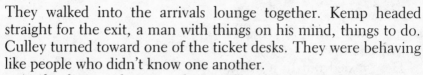

They walked into the arrivals lounge together. Kemp headed straight for the exit, a man with things on his mind, things to do. Culley turned toward one of the ticket desks. They were behaving like people who didn't know one another.

As the distance between them widened, Kemp said, "What will you do?"

"Get the next plane back, I suppose."

Kemp raised a hand. "Good trip," he said.

Culley watched as the exit doors opened and closed. Kemp had the air of a man who didn't need to look back.

39

IT DIDN'T REALLY HAVE A NAME because there was no place for it in the list of rooms most houses contain. The door had a microphone grille alongside it, just like the door in the New York gallery. There were two locks that required keys, and one combination time lock that only Kemp could override.

It ran the length and breadth of the house apart from the vault space at one end. The lighting was organized for the paintings that hung on the two long walls and on the wall opposite the vault.

Kemp paused in front of a small Gauguin, the rough prime colors, the sense of fleshiness and heat. An art critic might have pointed out the triangular composition, the way perspective was distorted to present landscape and figures with equal weight, the draftsman's art in making line dominate color. Kemp knew about those things and valued the painting for the particularity they gave it. He also valued it because it was his. He possessed it.

To have something is not to possess it. Let's say you buy a book. You go to a kennel one day and come home with a dog. You fall in love and marry. Someone—you forget who—borrows the book never to return it. The dog dies. Your wife grows tired of your black moods and leaves you.

You didn't possess those things. You simply *had* them for a time. Possession doesn't understand *give* or *share*. It has no truck with *freedom*. In the vocabulary of possession, the word *relinquish* doesn't exist. The terms it understands are *property, seizure, command, hoard*. It understands *deceit* and *imprison; stealth* and *conceal*. It understands *eat*.

There's another word that's crucial to the notion of possession, a word that precedes it and inspires it. The word is *collect*. Collectors are not mere admirers, not fans. They want to envelop; they want to be fed. Collectors are cannibals.

Kemp moved to where the two Cezannes hung at the center of the short wall. His possessions, part of his collection, looked at only by him.

Henry Glinwood might be called to the room from time to time. Kemp would consult him on this purchase or that. Sometimes it was clear that they would be talking about a picture that wasn't for sale, but which nevertheless could become one of Kemp's possessions. Glinwood advised, drew a gigantic salary, and was never troubled by scruple. For years he had been a consultant to people who used art as an investment. He was a first-rate judge of the market and helped many investors to make a good return, without ever having the capital to prosper from his own knowledge. He knew a lot about art, but cared a lot about profit. Before long, at Kemp's rates of pay, he'd be able to go into business on his own.

If he was called to the room, Glinwood simply conducted the business in hand, then left. He knew better than to do anything as crass as make a tour of the paintings, or even glance at them. He tried to behave as if they weren't there.

Kemp walked around his collection. He loved each one of them. In Kemp's mind, love and possession were as closely bound as war and victory.

He never thought about loss. When he looked at his paintings, when he looked at his daughter, he saw possessions, and never thought about loss.

"You went into Tucson."

"Yes."

"Henry saw you heading off with Sanchez."

"Yes."

"What did you do?"

"Walked. Went to a bookstore. Sat in a park."

Behind their speech, slow music; a Beethoven string quartet, vibrant and melancholy. Nina was taking a circular path toward the armchair opposite to Kemp's. As she journeyed, she touched various objects lightly, making fingertip contact with a vase, a bowl of polished stones, a Mexican terra-cotta figurine. Each thing she touched she stared at intently before moving on, as if trying to work out what it was, or what it might become.

She asked, "How did it go in New York?"

"I saw the sketch. I shall buy it. Did you meet anyone?"

"Meet?"

"See anyone you know."

"I don't think I know anyone in Tucson. Do I? Not now."

Kemp lifted the decanter at his elbow and dribbled brandy into his glass. "Will you go again?"

"Yes, I might." She settled into the armchair. "I went to a park."

"You mentioned that."

"There were people going to and fro, walking, you know, on their way to do things. I watched them. They looked like . . . when the titles end and the movie starts and you see this shot of people in a park, and they all have lives; but then the camera moves in and you see just one person, or two perhaps, and you know it's their lives you'll be hearing about, not the lives of the others. And as the movie goes on, as the story moves on, and it's will they be happy? will they get married? will the adventure save them or destroy them?—you think about the lives of the other people in the park."

"Do you?"

"Yes."

Kemp could feel the new tension in her, an agitation. He read it correctly as restlessness, but didn't guess that it might have anything to do with choice. It was instinct, alone, that made him ask, "Did you miss me?"

She settled by his chair, her face lifted as a flower lifts toward the light. He told her about the Degas, and although she didn't listen carefully enough to make complete sense of what he was saying, his words tingled her scalp and brought a blush to the base of her throat; she recognized the passion and the power.

In her mind's eye, she saw the fluency of arm and calf, the way in which shapes were drawn on the air. She heard the music and saw the dancer leap, a moment suspended, the inch-by-inch return to earth, the drawn-out whisper as the flimsy material of her dress made corrugations along the arc of the spotlight. Wafting light, a half-dream, the way she felt each morning after the red and black pill, after the yellow and black pill. But Kemp could still sense something eager about her, eager or troubled.

In his room, he slipped her shirt away from her shoulders, he stepped her out of her baggy cotton pants; he stripped her and stroked her as if her agitation was something he might draw off like a childish fever. Only when he had found a calm in her did stroke become caress.

She turned to him, suddenly anxious, suddenly hot, hands everywhere, taking his hands, too, and drawing them on as if he were doing too little, as if he wasn't giving her enough.

They seemed to fight, hands, teeth, their limbs colliding, heads knocking, as Nina went under him like someone drowning. Her arms flailed and wrapped him; her legs forked and rose. He fell onto her, burying himself, burying them both. Nina shouted a brief string of separate words—a sentence broken by surprise and effort.

The last word was "hurt," though whether a plea or a warning, Culley wasn't able to tell.

40

THERE WAS HEAT IN THE ROOM before there was light, and light before noise. When Culley opened the door, Nina sidled in— furtive or sexy, he couldn't decide which. Either way, it looked absurd. While he answered the phone, she stood in a rhomboid of sunlight, one shoulder against the window shutter, and stared into the courtyard. Her gaze was so constant that you'd imagine something was going on in the sunlit space: mime theater, perhaps.

"This is Ira Sanchez; I'm calling from the lobby."

"Yes, well, that makes sense."

"You have to . . . I have to take her back in an hour."

"Why?"

"I have duties to perform out there, you know? I told her an hour. That seems to suit her fine."

"It does?"

The mime artists were finding invisible walls, juggling impossible objects, walking into incredible winds. Nina was smiling a quiet smile.

"Seems to. Kemp often disappears for a couple of hours at a time; she does her own thing. I guess he wouldn't miss her—like, an hour would be safe enough."

"Where?" Culley asked.

"I'll call the room from the lobby."

"That's fine."

"Be there."

If Culley was amused by Ira's caution, he didn't show it. He said, "Don't worry."

In the mime world it was someone's birthday. Gifts were being opened in an ecstatic silence. Nina's smile was stocked with anticipation. Culley took a couple of steps toward the window. "What can you see?"

She turned her head slowly. "The fountain. I was looking at the patterns. Come and see." Patterns of light on the water, patterns of water-shadow on the ground. He stood a pace back. The breeze from the window touched her, then touched him. She bore a faintly musty scent, rich, like spice.

She said, "Where do you come from?" In her mind's eye, she held pictures from the book she'd bought.

"London," he said.

"A city."

"That's right."

"Why live there?"

He improvised. "I don't. Not all the time."

"Sometimes Figeac . . ."

"Sometimes." He tried to think of somewhere that might sound likable and came up with the place he'd given her father. "I have a cottage near a town called Lyme Regis," he lied.

"I want to hear."

He told her about the high fields and the lanes, about the woodlands, about the harbor and its great, curving breakwater, so long that if you walked to its end you were almost out to sea. He told her its name, and she repeated it like an incantation: "The Cobb."

"How did you choose?" she asked.

For a moment, he couldn't think of anything that might help. He settled for: "It's near the ocean," then added rapidly, "How did you?"

"What?" There was a genuine puzzlement on her face; it was a more difficult question in his mouth than in hers.

"Choose to live where you live?"

"My father lives there." As if he were scenery or climate.

"You live with your father?" She nodded. "All the time?" he asked.

She nodded again. "Except . . . I might go away soon. It might be that I'll be going away."

"Somewhere nice?"

"Figeac." She laughed. "Lyme Regis, to walk along the Cobb." She looked up at him, and when his laughter didn't arrive to match hers, the smile grew lopsided and fell off her face.

Oh, yes, Culley thought. That's right. That's what I want. That's what I'd hoped for.

He knew where the slavishness came from, and could see how deep in her the impulse lay. Hugo Kemp's baby, his little girl, his teenager, his woman, his possession. But Culley could only guess at the desperation that allowed her to shift the need so strongly, and so fast.

He said, "Part of its length is made of cobblestones, but there's also an English phrase 'cobble together'; it means: build roughly. So it could be either—or both." He was remembering things Helen had told him as they'd walked out along its broad back. She had taken him, as lovers always do eventually, to the place of birth and old memories. Old joys, old fears. Helen had worn a dark blue mackintosh with caped shoulders—he saw it clearly; but as the memory grew, as he tempted Nina with the picture he was painting, he couldn't make Helen turn or show him her face. He walked behind her, a vapor of spray stringing beads on his eyelashes.

"You can get out so far that you forget the shore, but you never forget the sea, however calm a day it is. If there's a breeze the sea runs at the stone; you see lines of spray thrown over like wet ropes."

Nina looked as a child looks when it is caught up by some story. Helen strode on, face lowered, hair streaming away from her collar. A sky of thunderheads and wild light.

"When you reach the end, you stand with nothing in front of you but the sea. There's no noise, no sight to remind you of the land. Sometimes there's a sea mist and if you turn around, but keep your head up so as not to look where you've walked, you're out there alone, mid-ocean, on top of the water, like a moment from a dream."

Nina seemed scarcely to be breathing, her eyes fixed on Culley. Helen stood at the farthest tip, her feet on the overhang, hands in pockets, face to seaward. A wave clouted the base and rose like a shout. A glaze of foam hissed through the cobbles.

Culley asked, "Do you want to go out? Go for a walk?"

Nina had sat in the chair by the window to listen to him; Culley had lodged on the edge of the bed. She crossed the room, her face solemn, and passed him; for a moment, Culley thought she was heading for the phone. Then she backed up, all part of the same movement, and sat down on his lap, one arm around his neck, her face against his as she nuzzled and pecked. Her free hand grasped his and shifted both to her breast, clutching the fingers that clutched her. Her eyes were wide open, as if she had startled herself.

Her need, her strangeness, her vulnerability, her willingness, all hit Culley at once; a fist of lust. Her thighs across his thighs, her breast under his hand, her breath fanning his eyelids . . . The desire took him so strongly that he leaped, almost toppling them both onto the floor. Something to do with delicacy and its capacity for pain.

He stood up, forcing her to stand, and put an arm around her shoulders. "Let's go out," he said.

They walked past the corridor that flanked the courtyard and found a coffee shop. Nina chose a table by the window on the sunny side. They drank coffee and talked.

Nina asked, "How would we get there?"

"Drive from London to a port," Culley told her. "Caen, probably. Then south through countryside. No big roads. Brantôme. Rocamadour. Cahors. Heading toward the Alps."

"How long would it take?"

"A couple of days? No need to hurry."

"Figeac," she said.

Sunlight tangled in wisps of their hair, thin coronas that looked, from the distance, like halos. At one moment, Nina brought her head close to Culley's, as if to whisper or to kiss, and the circles of light bled into one another.

"Where would we stay?"

"There's a hotel just above the harbor. You can see everything from there. You can look out to where you walked; where you stood."

"How long would we stay?"

"Until we'd seen all the weather—sun, rain, mist . . ."

"The Cobb," she said.

He took her back to the room in time to catch Ira's call.

"It's room forty-six, right?"

"That's right."

"Listen, a few minutes after I hang up, I'll come knock at the door—take her back."

"Sure."

"She right there with you—you can't talk?"

"That's right. But you can."

"Culley, this is gonna have to be the last time. Kemp's getting edgy. She told him about the time when he was in New York, and I don't think he liked it. That's why she wanted to come in now—just for an hour—so he wouldn't know she'd been gone. If he asks and she lies and he finds out—I'm part of the lie, you know?"

"Would that happen?"

"That he asks?"

"No."

"That he finds out?"

"Yes."

"Sure, if he really wants to know. I mean, he puts someone on the case, Glinwood, whoever. She's not invisible. There're people who know who she is."

"Don't worry."

"What does that mean?"

"It's okay."

"Is that: It's okay, there's no problem, you're talking shit; or: It's okay, I agree, I won't see her again?"

"Yes," Culley said.

"Won't see her again."

"Yes."

"What's happening about the Degas?"

"I'll buy that."

"When?"

"Two days, or perhaps three." Nina's head came around and she looked concerned. What Culley had said sounded like a departure date, the end of something. He improvised. "Is that okay with you?"

"I guess," Sanchez said. "We can talk about the money? How I get it? When?"

"Any time you like," Culley said.

"I'll call you later. I gotta get back now."

Culley put down the phone. Nina said, "Two or three days?"

"Nothing," he said. "A colleague in London asking me what to do. I'm supposed to be on holiday, but you know how it is."

It was what she'd wanted to hear, so she forgot her fear at once. Nothing they'd said to each other had touched on the way in which most people define their lives. There had been no "What's your job? oh, really, and what does that involve? and where do you . . .? and how long have you. . .? and do you enjoy . . .?" No mention of the possibility of wife or children. As if, outside of her company, Culley didn't exist. Had never existed.

Culley opened the door to Ira's knock. "Coupla minutes, okay?" Sanchez pointed down the hallway. "I'll be in the jeep." His gaze flickered around the room: Culley, window, bed, telephone, Nina. She nodded and Sanchez left. Culley closed the door, just his fingers preventing it from shutting completely.

Nina put a hand to his cheek. She said, "Don't worry. I'll wait for you."

When the window shutters were drawn against the darkness, magnesium-white light barred the bedspread. Culley rewound the tape. Their voices spooled out in a cackle, a crackle, faster and faster until it sounded like the thin broken-backed whine of Morse: a message needling through the desert air.

He stopped and started. Nina said, ". . . lives of the other people in the park."

"Do you?"

"Yes."

"Did you miss me?"

Culley wound back. Kemp said, ". . . off with Sanchez."

"Yes."

"What did you do?"

"Walked. Went to a bookstore. Sat—"

He rewound again. Kemp said, ". . . Friday evening."

"I hate it when you go away."

"I know. It—"

Culley hit the fast-forward button, stopped, tried that.

". . . stops and sniffs the air, the fangs chatter, then—"

". . . no such—"

". . . last you'll see of me—"

". . . like that. Like that; just there."

Culley listened to the rest of it, the sounds she made, the crowing that rose in her throat, the rumplings, the creaks. Kemp's voice, urging her. Then he went to the end of the tape. Those gasps again, fierce breathing, little cries. Nina's voice saying, ". . . hurt . . ."

He sat on the bed, his face striped by light, and sent the tape backward and forward through voices and kisses and crowings.

". . . like that . . . like that . . . like that . . ."

He remembered Helen's voice.

Like that.

He remembered Susan Court's voice on the tapes he'd found in Alex Yorke's flat.

The room grew darker. The bars of light lay on his forehead, his eyes, his throat. He thumbed the button and the voices rolled like dice.

41

On Carl Mathers's desk was a photograph that hadn't been there before. Mathers had put it into a thin silver frame—a kid with blond hair standing on a rock and grinning a gappy grin. Behind him, a small rowing boat was moored to a tree; sunlight snaked between ripples on the water.

"They went up to Lake Powell for a few days," Mathers said. "Tyler, my wife, the kid. Seems they had a good time." He lifted the photo and set it down in a slightly changed position. "You don't like the hotel?"

"It's fine," Culley assured him. "I just need somewhere else to be."

"No one knows you're there."

"Ira Sanchez knows."

"He's working for you, isn't that right?"

"Some of the time." Culley paused. "At the moment."

"You expect that to change."

"Well . . . It's possible."

Mathers shook out a cigarette and tossed the pack onto his desk. "The money you've promised him . . ."

"There's that, yes."

"You've told him you won't see the Kemp girl again."

"That's right."

"Chrissake," Mathers said, "this sounds like a fuckin' TV quiz show." He spoke through an exhalation of smoke and it flickered like a cinema projection beam. "So you *are* going to see her again."

"Yes," said Culley, "I am."

"But Ira Sanchez isn't going to be fetching her to you, is he? And he isn't going to be taking her back." When Culley didn't respond, the guessing game was over. Mathers laughed and shook his head. He said, "I don't know what kidnap pulls in Britain. Here, it's ten to life."

"I'm not going to keep her," Culley said. "In any case, she's coming because she wants to."

"Yeah? I expect she believes that. Others might not."

"She's over twenty-one."

"She's a fuckin' *fruitcake*." There was a pause. Mathers knuckled his eye like a tired man. "Listen, you're getting in too deep. Your people might think there was a welcome here for you, but that's not so, is it? I'm no friend of Hugo Kemp. It's nothing to me if you want his phone tapped. If you find out what you want to know, that's just fine. If some time in the future, somehow, it ruffles his feathers—who cares? But that's not the same as walking up to his cage and shoving a stick through the goddamn bars."

"I need a place," Culley said. "A room, something . . ."

"Not through me," Mathers told him. As Culley was leaving, Mathers said, "Sorry." Then he said, "Lots of luck, okay?"

There was country music playing that said lonely nights, said ain't no use, said done me wrong. It said, he don't love me the way I love him. There were three empty glasses in front of Gerry Cattini.

Culley arrived at the table with three more. He was moving toward Cattini's good eye and without turning his head the man said, "The Lord keep you." As the glasses went down, one by one on the table, he laughed and amplified the remark. "The Lord keep you coming."

Culley decided not to fake—mostly because he didn't believe it would work. He said, "I'm here to ask you for something that Carl Mathers won't give me."

"That right?" Cattini sniffed his drink for fun, then downed a third of it in one gulp. "You like country music?"

"Sure," Culley said.

"No kidding?"

"I hate it. Whatever you want me to say."

"Yeah. It's crap. No question. Booze and cigarettes and love gone bad. Steel guitars, pick-up trucks. Guys with sideburns and napalm breath, girls with silver hair and tits like bombs. Thing I like about it—trash talent. Alchemy. Corn makes cash."

"A room," Culley said. "Somewhere low-profile. Just for a day or so."

The rest of the drink went down. "Carl Mathers is a man of great good sense."

"You're right. I still need the room."

"Don't tell me why."

Culley had brought a drink for himself, Jack Daniels on the rocks. He said, "I wasn't going to."

"Move out of the hotel you're at; move into another."

"Hotels are easy to check."

Cattini's good eye, green eye, was watering. He took another drink. "I know Carl's rates."

"You do?"

"Sure. So don't try to lie."

"I won't."

"Okay. A week's pay."

Culley pushed the Jack Daniels away and got up. Cattini said, "Okay, two-thirds of that."

Culley walked off a couple of paces. He paused and said, "Percentages . . . How long to find a place?"

"Three days."

"No." Culley walked out of sight, almost out of earshot. When he came back, the barman followed, bringing a triplet of drinks. "Two days' money," Culley said, "for a morning's work." He revised his opinion. "For a phone call."

Cattini laughed, head lowered. One eye was shuttered by the patch, the other in shadow. He sipped a new drink without lifting his chin, swiping at the whiskey with a sideways pull. Then he put the glass down and heaved himself out of his seat like a cripple pushing against the wheels of his chair. The phone was left of the bar. When he came back, Cattini said, "Two days' pay for me; the rental's extra."

"Where do I go?"

"I'll take you there. Plenty of time."

It was four-thirty. The bar existed in constant twilight. A red, vaporish glow came off the wall lamps, and long scrolls of smoke unwound in damp thermals. Toward the back of the room, in booths and corners, were pockets of deep dusk.

Time enough, Culley thought. Not plenty of time, but time enough.

You can look at a painting, give it all your attention, but fail to notice something obvious: a shadow that's more energetic than the object it falls from, a wrong color used for emphasis, a shape in a cloud. One day, you'll be thinking about the painting and the realization will come.

For several days, Kemp had been thinking about the Degas.

Whatever he'd been doing, her shape had played on his back brain like a ghostly projection. Beneath the downy skirt, a dancer's corded muscle; behind every leap and turn, stretched sinew and scorching lungs. What he loved was the marriage of grace and power; of delicacy and pain.

He wanted to own it. *Own* it. Sometimes, when he thought about the sketch, he saw himself in the vault room at Bryant's gallery, the easel set up to display the piece, Bryant fussing about in the background. In the picture that Kemp painted in his mind, there was another figure. Kemp would pay him little attention, an onlooker, someone watching that passage in the painting where the real tension lay—the confrontation between Kemp and his ambition.

Now, though, he stopped his eye to look at the interloper. Suddenly, it was important; suddenly, the figure had become mysterious. Like a watcher in the corner of some medieval canvas, put there by the painter to represent famine or loss. A specter at the feast.

Kemp made a phone call.

"No," Bryant said. "An offer, of course, from yourself. In all, four. But nothing from Mr. Davis. However, there's still time."

Kemp's second call was to England. "This guy Culley you said I'd hear from. I haven't heard from him."

"He's out there." The answering voice was heavy with sleep.

"What does he look like?"

"Not sure what you mean."

"Describe him to me," Kemp said.

It was the phone call that Culley would have most wanted to hear. It was the call he'd tapped into Kemp's phone for. While the conversation was in progress, Culley was looking around a cramped one-bedroom apartment near the Barrio Historico. Two or three used dishes lay in the sink. There was bread on a cutting board, overripe fruit in a glass bowl, clothes in the closets.

"Let me know when you leave," Cattini said. "I'll tell the guy he can move back in."

Culley found some bed linen in a cupboard. He said, "It's not yours, is it Gerry? Do you live here?"

Cattini yipped with laughter. "Jesus . . . You should see where I live. You don't want to know about that."

"And the guy who lives here. Where will he go?"

"Yeah." The laughter shrank to a slow grin. "Yeah, he'll be staying with me."

He turned off the highway. There was a full moon, stark and heavy in a clear sky, and he was able to drive the small roads using only sidelights. He found Nina where she had said she would be, at the junction between the back road and the ribbon of paving that led to the rose field. She was sitting on a small suitcase like an immigrant.

Culley cut the engine and walked to where she was sitting.

"Up there." He followed her gaze. She was looking at the mesa.

Everything touched by moonlight was washed white; the shadows were blue.

"Like a wolverine," she said. "You only see it at night. It comes down, down off the mesa. You can hear it among the roses."

Culley said, "Don't worry—"

Nina's words lay over his. "Don't worry. We're okay here. We're safe here."

She got up and walked away from the road, slipping into shadow —bathed blue—then emerged into the moonlight as a backlit negative with smudges for eyes.

Culley caught up with her. "Nina . . . we ought to go."

She smiled and shook her head. "No one's looking for me. I'm in my room. No one goes there."

The moon's light made craters; acres of bright dust, magenta lakes. She walked and he followed, past white rocks with blue shadows, through a cathedral of marbled saguaro, Culley and Nina, their feet in the white dust, their own blue outlines rippling behind them.

Finally she stopped and looked at him, seeming to signal that she'd found the point where they could start back, and their embrace was the result of one person arriving, the other returning.

Nina's face, when she lifted it to Culley's, was halved, blue-white, like Harlequin's mask.

In the apartment, she lifted her face to him again as she lay beside him, waiting to be touched.

Culley stroked her cheek, her shoulder, and felt the thump of lust he'd felt before, like a soft explosion in the small of his back. As if that tremor had reached her too, she parted her legs at once and pulled at his upper arms, a pleasure machine, a geisha, wanting nothing for herself.

He emptied himself in her, then held her until her eyes closed. After ten minutes, her breathing deepened; a tiny thread of moisture dampened the corner of her mouth. Culley eased himself off the bed and got dressed. She lay half on her back, limbs anyhow, as if she had tumbled there. On her forearms, on her calves, on the curve of her upper thighs, the cross-hatched scars glistened like a pale web.

He telephoned from a nearby bar: anonymous music, anonymous voices. Kemp sounded calm but alert, a man opening a business negotiation. "What do you want?" he asked.

"Nothing," Culley said. "I'm calling to let you know. Nina and I are in love. We're going away together. She didn't want to be the one to tell you."

"She's there with you?"

"I just slipped out to make this call."

"Perhaps you could ask her to contact me. Before you . . . go away."

"I don't think she wants to talk to you. I'm pretty sure she doesn't."

"When will you go?"

"Oh, very soon."

"I wonder whether there's something I might do to prevent that." A pause. Kemp added, "Is there?"

"I don't know."

"Could we talk about that?"

"It's possible."

Another pause. Kemp said, "How did you and Nina meet, Mr. Davis?"

Culley said, "We haven't known each other long, but . . . you know how these things can be. You know how Nina is."

"It is Mr. Davis, isn't it?"

"We could meet tomorrow morning, if you like," Culley told him. "Somewhere fairly public would be ideal."

Kemp mentioned a gallery. They fixed a time. Culley broke the connection and dialed Helen Blake's number. "I'm not here at the moment, but . . ."

He waited, then said, "I'm out of money. Can you organize something?" He gave the name and address of a bank. "I'll be leaving here in two or three days." It was all he said.

When he got back, Nina was sitting on the bed, her knees drawn

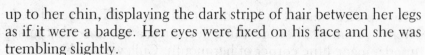

up to her chin, displaying the dark stripe of hair between her legs as if it were a badge. Her eyes were fixed on his face and she was trembling slightly.

"Don't go away," she said. He knelt on the bed and circled her with his arms—her shins, her bowed back. "When you go away, everything holds its breath."

42

Henry Glinwood stood stiffly, almost to attention, as if the room was being swept for bombs. A man wearing headphones was going to and fro, watching the LCD register on a spectrum analyzer. After a second circuit, he slung the headphones around his neck and went out.

Kemp looked at Glinwood and smiled. "Don't worry, Henry. I believe you. That's why we're having the place swept. There's something . . . He's too close, too well-organized. He knew how to find me in New York; knew what time I'd be there." Kemp paused. "No one else knows that Nina's gone?"

"No one," Glinwood told him.

"It must stay that way." They didn't mention her again.

After a few minutes, the operative returned. He said, "I just wanted to check that long window again. Lot of glass area there. It's clean though." He jerked a thumb. "Amazing, the roses; never seen anything like that." He stowed his equipment in a custom-built case lined with foam. "You've got two," he said. "One in the phone right here, one in the phone in the master bedroom. What I've done—I've unplugged those phones, so effectively you're clean."

"Just those two," Kemp said.

"Right. All the other phones, they're working normally. You can use them. No one's tapped in. You want me to bill you?"

Kemp smiled. "You'd sooner have cash?"

"That'd be good."

Kemp motioned to Glinwood, who left the room. "Someone was listening in," Kemp asked, "to calls I made in here and in my bedroom."

"Yeah, that . . . Also, they could hear you."

"Using the phone."

"Yeah, no—they *could* hear that, sure. But what the bugs are— they're infinity devices. Phone bugs and area bugs. Anyone who was dialing in to the device would have heard anything said in here, or said in the bedroom, whether you were using the phone or not."

Glinwood came back with the cash. He said, "It's important that —"

The operative cut him off. "We're discreet. Wouldn't stay in business if we shared our secrets." He took the money without counting it, then handed Glinwood a card. "If you need us again. Good idea to have regular checks, y'know?" He picked up his case. "Tremendous," he said. "The roses? Tremendous."

Anything said in here. Anything said in the bedroom.

Kemp looked at his watch. To Glinwood, he said, "I'll give you fifteen minutes; then I'll follow."

Culley sat with Nina over juice and coffee. She had opened her small suitcase and taken from it new clothes for the new day. White pants, a shirt smocked with brocade; she wore the leather and turquoise bracelet. She smiled into his eyes. The index finger of her right hand dabbed at the capsules, red and black, yellow and black, pushing them back and forth.

Culley touched her hand to make it still. "What are they for?"

"They take the edge off." It sounded like something a doctor had once said. She picked them up by pursing her fingertips around them, and dropped them into her saucer. "Maybe later."

"I have to go out for a while," Culley said. "Not long. An hour, perhaps."

"It's strange . . ." Nina's eyes were on his face; she didn't blink. "You just have to take the risk—that's all it is. You think that life's one thing, you know?—one pattern. The hours go past, you do the things you're expecting to do. You walk—your feet go in the direction you're expecting to take. But you can break the pattern in a minute. Sometimes I see things clearly, sometimes not. It's like going in and out of a dream, and you don't know which is dream and which is waking. Perhaps it doesn't matter. You think that what you've got must be everything you need. But it's not because . . ."

Her eyes were too painful to look at and too intense to avoid. "Because . . ." Culley prompted.

"Because you didn't know what else there was to want."

"What do you want, Nina?"

"To go away with you. To go away."

Kemp and Culley stood shoulder to shoulder, like two connoisseurs, both cynical, who'd been asked to judge a work of dubious origin. Kemp glanced sideways a moment, then back to the painting. "Your client must be very eager to acquire the Degas."

"I don't want the Degas. You can have it."

They were looking at a large canvas of a cowboy riding at a gallop across a plain littered with barrel cactus. The brim of his Stetson was folded back by the wind and a quirt trailed from his wrist. "Well," Kemp said, "I'm intrigued, of course. How is Nina?"

"She's fine."

"A young woman in love," Kemp observed.

"That's right."

"Crazy about you."

"That's the way it seems."

Kemp laughed softly. "If I give you what you want," he said, "and in exchange you return my daughter to me, be sure you make the transition smooth. Leave me a gap, and I'll have you killed."

Henry Glinwood traveled around the room with a small group of tourists, then left.

"It's good of you to be frank," Culley said. "I appreciate it."

Kemp took a few paces sideways to the next canvas. A stagecoach robbery: shocked faces looked out from a lamplit interior; outside, two men stood in ankle-deep snow, their rifle muzzles showing polyps of flame. The driver was falling among the horses' hooves.

"If not the Degas, what?"

"Sometimes works come onto the market, though they're not spoken of openly," Culley said. "Only a certain number of collectors are likely to be told that such works are available. Most recently, two paintings by Cezanne." He paused. "My client is

anxious to be among those who are told—to have the opportunity
to bid, perhaps. To let dealers know about his particular enthusi-
asms. It occurred to me that you might be able to supply some
names. Who found the Cezannes, for example."

Kemp nodded slowly. Finally, he said, "Well, well . . . Yes . . .
Do you want to continue with Davis, a client, all that bullshit, or
what?" His gaze had switched from the painting to the floor, as if
he'd discovered some rich mosaic there. Kemp said, "Robin Culley,"—the tone of someone who has just spotted a friend in a
crowd.

Culley's head snapped around for an instant—he couldn't prevent it—and he saw the thoughtful look on the other man's face.

"I can't be touched," Kemp said. "I'm fireproof."

"I know. I don't want you."

"What's more, you don't want Nina. Does she know that?"

"Nina isn't in any danger," Culley said.

Kemp's control slipped for an instant. He seemed to grind his
teeth. His voice was low and staccato with fury, the barely audible
words seeming to erupt from his clenched mouth like a swallow of
water that hits the windpipe. "I want her back. I want her back
untouched. I promise you if you've touched her I'll break your
fucking spine, you bastard. Get her *back to me*." He folded his
arms on his chest and lowered his head, breathing deeply. When
he looked up, he found Culley's eyes, level and hard, and he knew
what Culley knew.

Anything said in here. Anything said . . .

"Did you know about Jay Hammond?" Culley asked.

"Who?"

"A lot of people were killed. Hammond was one of them. He
wasn't a particularly honest man, but that doesn't make it legal.
He wanted the Cezannes for someone else. That's why he died. In
fact, that's why all the other people died."

Kemp shrugged. "I was offered the paintings, I said yes. You're
telling me there were two dealers for two customers. One of each
lost out. That's not any business of mine."

"How does it work?" Culley asked.

"It's pretty much the same no matter where the offer comes
from: Britain, Italy, France . . . Whoever sets up the deal collects
the money once the merchandise is delivered. Nothing complicated: a transaction that has a number of temporary homes. You
can launder it through half a dozen accounts—John Doe, numbered, whatever."

"A name," Culley said.

"Your side of this?"

"You give me the name. I run a check on it. When I hear that it's valuable to me, I'll bring Nina back. Tomorrow morning would be a safe bet."

"I don't like the deal."

"Who cares?"

Kemp went crabwise to the next painting. Bright water, men on horseback with trinkets in their hands, men pulling a travois laden with furs. Soldiers and Indians, gathered by a creek to trade.

"A guy called Porter," he said. "Ralph Porter. It's also the name of a gallery."

Culley went through the exhibition rooms, walking slowly. Out on the street, he took his time, pausing to look into windows. He bought a newspaper and walked a couple of blocks until he found a bar. He went in and stood close to the door. Two people came in soon after him: Henry Glinwood and a tall man in a workshirt, his hair drawn back in a ponytail. Culley stared at both of them, making his interest plain. The man in the workshirt gave Culley a hard look. Glinwood walked past, going to the far end of the room, his eyes lowered.

Culley left the bar at once and hopped a bus. He hadn't spotted Glinwood; he hadn't known whether he was being followed or not. What had happened in the bar was standard technique. He went to the place he'd phoned Kemp from on the previous evening and made a collect call to Mike Dawson.

"Did I wake you up?" he asked.

"Of course. Now let me do the same for you. You're in shit to the shoulders. Protheroe has spoken to the locals. It seems you weren't wanted. In fact, they don't know you're there." Dawson corrected himself. "Didn't."

"Tell Protheroe I'm on the way home."

"Are you?"

"More or less. Check a name for me. Ralph Porter. I want to know that he exists. I want to know that a gallery of the same name exists. I want to know that he's a candidate. I'll call you in four hours, okay?"

"What's the weather like with you?"

"Fuck off."

"It's raining here," Dawson said.

236

Culley walked three blocks to a bank. He was told that no one had organized a cash transfer in his favor.

The room had a leather armchair and an old, spring-interior sofa covered in blankets. Nina had chosen the sofa to wait out Culley's absence. Her feet were tucked under one haunch; her cheek lay on an arm of the sofa and her eyes were closed.

As Culley crossed the room, she said, "I'm not asleep." The capsules were gone from the saucer. "You were longer than I thought you'd be."

"I'm sorry," he said. "Things to arrange."

"Plane tickets."

"That's right."

"To France, or to England?"

For some reason he found it more difficult to lie when presented with a choice. Nina opened her eyes and looked at him, but didn't raise her head. "England," he said; then, as if to disguise his hesitation, "France afterward."

He made two cups of herb tea and took them into the living room. Nina held her cup two-handed, keeping the rim close to her lips like someone drinking broth after a cold journey. Watching her closely, he said, "I spoke to your father."

Her eyes were blank windows in a dark room. "What did he say?"

"He wants you to go back—I think that was the gist of it."

"Why did you speak to him?"

"I felt that I should."

"What did you tell him?"

"That we're going away together."

"I love him," she said, "but I don't want to go back there. I used to think it would be impossible to leave. I couldn't see a way of doing that. I guess I didn't want to; for a long time, I simply didn't want to. Then I got so tired, you know? Everything was so complicated." She put the cup down carefully and leaned back on the sofa, closing her eyes.

She seemed to doze for a few minutes. Culley watched her. There was a bruised look about her mouth and a heaviness around the eyes, the result of too much sleep. He wondered about the glisten of scar tissue that he'd seen on her arms and legs.

Her eyes opened with a violent suddenness, settled on him, and softened. She said, "A man went to see a doctor. He had become badly depressed. You know—he was . . . felt terrible all the time; blackness and despair. This is a story." Culley nodded. "He told the doctor how he felt. The doctor said, 'There's a circus in town. I hear they've got a terrific clown—very funny, makes everyone laugh. Why don't you make a visit to the circus, watch the clown, he'll cheer you up.' The man said, 'I *am* the clown.' "

Culley waited a while. Eventually he asked, "Why did you tell me that?"

Nina shrugged. "It's the saddest story I ever heard."

Culley took a beer to the phone. Dawson said, "Do you know what a collect call from the States costs?"

"No idea," Culley said. "What have we got?"

"There is a Ralph Porter. There is a Ralph Porter Gallery. He does import and export paintings. He's the name on the shingle. Some of the money comes from sleeping partners, all rich, many influential."

"How influential?"

"Old money, new money, borrowed money, blue money. Not many partners, but the right ones."

"It'll do," Culley said. "Tell Protheroe I'll start back some time tomorrow. That ought to hold him."

"I doubt that," Dawson said. "What's the weather like there?"

"Screw you," Culley said.

"It's still raining here."

Culley's plane left at twelve-thirty the next day; until then, there was little to do but spend his time with Nina. Like a husband, his plans for abandonment already made, seeing out Christmas. Like a delayed traveler finding intimacy with some stranger at the depot.

On his way back from phoning Dawson, he picked up some food, a sinister housewifery in the way he bought just enough for two meals. Nina stood close to him while he made them a late lunch. At one point, she organized it so that her hip nudged his and he put an arm around her waist, loosely, then took it back to hold tomatoes while he sliced them.

Something in the gesture disturbed her; perhaps she detected a coolness. His need of her had gone and with it most of his passionate interest in her; most of the lust.

She walked out of the kitchen and sat on the sofa. "When do we go?"

"Tomorrow," he said. "In the evening. I'll have to pick up the tickets around noon." That small detail made things real to her and she believed him again. They would go because they both wanted to. The future would be the two of them together; the past would become a foreign country.

A luminous sky, the mountains sharpening to silhouette. Six men were walking toward a jeep outside Kemp's house. Ira Sanchez walked on a tether, swaying slightly to hold his balance. His hands were tied behind his back and the tether was around his throat. Henry Glinwood opened the rear door of the jeep.

"Let me see Kemp." Sanchez cracked his knee on the bodywork as he turned. Glinwood looked at him, but didn't respond. "At least let me talk to him." Ira's mind raced with possibilities. ". . . didn't know she was . . ." ". . . asked me to take her. She never said . . ." ". . . told me she needed to go to the bookstore, so . . ."

The other four men loaded Ira into the back like a wheatsack. One of them went to the driver's side and joined Glinwood in the front.

"Just because I *drove* her?" Ira said.

Glinwood glanced back. "Forget it, Sanchez. You were seen with them both. A desk clerk at his hotel says you took her there and collected her from there. You knew him. Someone wanted phones with ears in the place. Who? Culley. We know that and we know why. Someone put them there. Who? That's right. You."

Glinwood slapped the driver's arm and they started toward the gate.

"Why can't I talk to Kemp?"

"He doesn't want to talk to you. I'll do that. I'll be letting him know what you said, okay? Now shut up."

"You've got this wrong, you know that?"

"Shut up."

The driver slowed, waiting for the man on the gate to swing it open for them.

"Let me *talk* to him." Droplets of saliva showered from Sanchez's mouth.

Glinwood turned in his seat and spoke to one of the men in the back of the jeep. "Just keep him quiet, all right? Tread on his fucking face."

A powdery sky, plum-blue; mountains smudged by twilight. Nina thought through the stories, scene by scene. Fact or fiction?

She rose from the sofa and quickly stripped, a pale column in the room's murk. Then she walked into the bedroom. Culley followed her. It was as if she imagined she might test Culley's truthfulness on herself: a thermometer, waiting for passion's fever; a tuning fork, waiting for the right note.

He drizzled his fingertips over her lips and throat, over her tight breasts, upward from the ridges of scar tissue that webbed her thighs.

". . . *you forget the shore, but you never forget the sea* . . ."

She didn't believe a word of it. When Culley hoisted himself up, she pushed him onto his back, then crawled on top, forcing him inside. She covered him, and lay still, stunned by sorrow. Minutes passed; he simply bore her weight. Her eyes glistened in the half-light; his form merged with hers. They were motionless but at the same time tense and alert—like reptiles who seem to mate without movement.

". . . *you stand with nothing in front of you but the sea* . . ."

Of course it was true; she believed as a disciple believes. Culley felt the tension go and turned her onto her back, her arms and legs wide, like someone in the moment of falling.

She spoke, a near-yell, *won't hurt* or *don't hurt; can't hurt* or *doesn't hurt*.

He plowed her and didn't listen.

The mountains just shadows; sky the deep blue of moonrise. The headlights of the jeep lit trunks of saguaro, scrub, and rocks; a dark hummock at the point where the beams focused. Glinwood put out a toecap and the hummock changed shape.

"Pick him up." Ira had toppled onto one side. Two of the men picked him up and held him out to Glinwood, a bloody gift. "Let's see what we've got," Glinwood said. "He promised you money once he'd bought the Degas. Well, that's shit. Never mind, you weren't to know. It was good enough for you. You staged the meeting with Nina. You helped with the other meetings. You planted the bugs." He paused. There was something suddenly empty about the half-collapsed form before him and Glinwood was struck by the possibility that he was talking to an unconscious man.

"Turn him to the light."

Ira's eyes swiveled in the glare. His face was covered by a sheen of blood, slick as paint, and a deep vee of discoloration ran from the neck of his shirt to the waistband.

"Okay," said Glinwood, reassured, "you knew where he was, you don't know where he is now. Or what his plans are. He didn't tell you." There was a long silence. No one moved. Glinwood's head was poked forward—the slight duck and stretch of the hard-of-hearing. Sanchez hung between the two men like a wounded comrade. Finally, Glinwood said, "That's the part we've having trouble with."

Sanchez made a sound in his throat like a *flub* of mud in a sulfur spring.

"We think he must have told you something. And we'd like to know what it was."

The wet sound again. "No-nng." *Nothing.*

Glinwood smiled and shook his head. "That's tough to believe, Ira—y'know?"

"Stu-uh. Ah doh-oh." *It's the truth. I don't know.*

"Just a place, an address. Just something about what he plans to do."

Sanchez moved his head to one side, like someone refusing food. Glinwood stepped back. The remaining two men came forward, appearing out of the penumbra cast by the headlight beams. The men holding Sanchez hefted him slightly, shifting his weight, to make him ready.

"Hit him low," Glinwood said. "I can hardly tell what he's saying, his teeth stove in like that."

He knelt up behind her because that was the way to go deepest. Nina knew that; and she knew what he wanted—to touch her so deeply that no one would ever supplant him. She wanted that too. Her face in the pillow, her back sloping toward him, the low, seismic shock inside her as he delved again and again, hands gripping her haunches.

All the pretty pictures were real: seascape, parkland, dusty side roads. All the intentions were real: a cab ride, a plane circling to land, a new life. All the words were real: England, France, tomorrow. Nina-Robin. Robin-Nina. A fierceness made her hands clench and she felt the orgasm lance her, and he didn't stop.

Like something numb, like something you don't even own; no feeling, no chance of any feeling, but he labored on her because he had to, like an ox yoked to a wheel.

He pulled her back by the hips each time he lunged, *slap, slap, slap,* kneeling up behind her so that she wouldn't see his face.

The moon was up; the mountains had returned as distant shadows. The lights of the jeep weren't needed, now.

They had draped Sanchez over the hood like something spread out to dry. You could hear his breathing from a long way off. Glinwood was sure that Sanchez had told the truth; he wished it were not so, but that wouldn't change matters. Of course, he'd also said a few things that weren't true, but that was to be expected. They weren't lies of cunning and deception, they were lies that really meant: *Say anything to make it stop, invent anything to make it stop, agree to anything to make it stop.*

To himself, Glinwood said, *Shit.* To the four men, he said, "We'd better get back."

They climbed into the jeep, Glinwood next to the driver. When the engine fired, Ira Sanchez turned his head slowly toward the windshield; it was all the effort he could make. The driver swung the wheel, making a rough U-turn, then shifted up a gear. They bounced over rocks, Sanchez's body clattering like a marionette.

Glinwood noticed that Ira was looking directly at him. His face was dark, like a crater of the moon, but his eyes had a strange opaque light. The two men stared at one another; then the jeep hit a deep rut and Sanchez rose off the hood, rearing up and heading directly for the windshield. Glinwood jerked back in his seat, and in the next instant Sanchez was gone, snatched away like smoke in a slipstream.

Nina slept deeply, as if exhausted from having made the very journey she was making in her dream.

Culley lay wide-eyed beside her. A soft double knock at the door had him out of bed and half-dressed in a few seconds. He went through the living room without switching on any lights.

The knock was repeated. A voice said, "Gerry Cattini." Culley opened the door. Cattini raised his hands in apology. "I'm sorry," he said.

Culley made an angry gesture that meant, *speak quietly*. "Sorry —what?"

"There's someone wants to see you. You'd better come. I didn't say where you were, y'know. At least I wouldn't say that." Cattini shook his head—a man disappointed. He handed Culley a sealed envelope, then peered into the darkened apartment like a curious salesman.

Culley was reading the note. "You can take me here?"

"You gotta car?" Culley nodded. "Okay, I'll show you where it is."

Culley shut the door in Cattini's face. He went back to the bedroom and finished dressing in the dark, each movement delicate and cautious.

He thought it must be about nine o'clock; nine-thirty, perhaps. Early enough, though Nina's sleep seemed fathomless. Her slow, even breathing filled the room—as deep as peace, or narcosis.

The courts were a great patch of brilliance in the middle of the park. Floodlights on each corner threw a hard, examining light. Culley watched as a woman in a sweat suit swayed back, lofted her arm, and hit a power serve. The ball fired down a narrow trajectory and four shadows raced toward the point of impact. When they converged, the ball cannoned off the line. A perfect ace.

Tyler Beck sat alongside Culley, ankle on knee, tapping the sole of a tennis shoe with the head of his racquet. He was wearing a pale blue, long-sleeved sweater above tennis shorts. Culley thought he would be about six-four and close to two-hundred pounds. Like Culley, he was watching the play. He said, "I recall that we talked on the phone. It seems you decided to come anyway."

"I thought it might be useful," Culley told him.

"That right? Listen, I talked with Carl Mathers. He told me one or two things I'd as soon not have heard."

"How did you know Mathers was the man to talk to?"

"We had a call."

"From Hugo Kemp?"

"Whoever I speak to, that's my damn business."

"From Henry Glinwood, perhaps."

"Jesus Christ." Beck whacked the racquet head off his shoe as if

243

he were driving a nail. "You ain't here to talk to me, you're here to goddamn listen."

The game on the nearest court was a mixed doubles. The players took their positions for service, forward and back, spokes of shadow radiating from their feet. With the ball in play, they ran and swerved, making the shadows spin and tangle. Culley listened.

"The things you've done here you've done without cooperation, without authorization, without telling us you were here, what for, just going ahead, doing—you know—bugging places, committing what might well be a federal offense, like—is that girl with you right now?—I mean, *Jesus Christ*, Culley, I ought to break your fuckin' ass." He paused, but his mouth was still working, as if he were getting ready to mention the worst thing of all. "I mean, where the Christless *fuck* do you think you *are?*"

Culley looked straight out at the mixed doubles. "I've annoyed you," he said.

Beck gave a shout that turned heads on the court. "You're real close, man. You're so fuckin' close, I can't tell you. You're one step away from it. Just keep talking—I'll be taking your teeth out through your asshole."

"What's my next move?" Culley asked.

"I was hoping you'd want to know that." Beck waited while a close point was played. The game went to deuce. "Go home. Go back to England."

"Tomorrow noon," Culley said, "I'll be gone."

"No good." Beck shook his head. "Go now. Right now. That's all the chance you've got."

"You mean, all you're giving me."

"Who gives a fuck? It's what you're gonna do."

Culley looked down at the ground, at a point some three feet in front of him. He seemed to be thinking. His breathing was quiet and slow. Beck watched the game; he believed that Culley was taking a couple of moments to adjust; and, hell, that was okay because every man had his pride. The truth was that Culley was arguing himself out of tearing Tyler Beck's head off and shoving it up his ass. An arm flew up; four shadow racquets swooped.

Culley said, "Some of this you got from Mathers. I don't know what allows you to control him. Cancel his license, threaten to give him a bad time forever . . . I guess he knows what you can do. After all, you're fucking his son's mother." Beck half-turned, but Culley went on talking, keeping control that way.

"But you can't have started with Mathers unless Mathers came to you, and I don't believe he did. So you got it from Kemp. That doesn't mean Kemp pays you, or tells you what to do. It just means that you're wary of Kemp. More often than not, you'll do as he asks. Okay." Culley had his eye on the racquet head as it thumped against Tyler Beck's tennis shoe. "Hugo Kemp is a scumbag. He's very rich, and he's a scumbag." Anyone could have heard the invitation in Culley's voice. "He's a very rich scumbag. And you protect him by seeing nothing, hearing nothing, most of all saying nothing. That's okay. He's pretty sure you'll do it. Why is he sure? Easy. He thinks you're an asswipe. Let me tell you something, Tyler, before I go. He's right. That's why you do it. You're an asswipe."

Culley continued to sit beside Beck for a while. He sat silently and still. On court, the match ended. Sixteen shadows trotted to the net for a crossover handshake.

Culley got up and walked away without looking back. He went to the hotel and collected his bag, then checked out. He took his car to the airport and left it in the parking lot with a note inside telling the rental company to contact Tyler Beck. At the information desk he discovered that he could get a flight to St. Louis early next morning and make his connection for London there.

He bought some coffee and went to a waiting area where he sat with his feet propped up on his bag. The airport was like most others: bright, functional, and unkind. Some were bright, inadequate, and unkind. Now and then, his eyelids drooped and closed. Each time he opened them, he half-expected to see Tyler Beck standing in front of him.

He spotted a magazine on one of the other seats, so he got up and fetched it. He flipped through a few of the articles without reading more than a sentence or two, then laid it aside.

He phoned Helen's number and she told him she wasn't there. "If you would like to leave a message . . ."

He watched a clock face as the minute hand ate its way around in little two-minute bites.

Finally, he slept, his container of coffee cold and untouched on the seat next to him.

When Nina woke, half an hour before dawn, Culley was in the kitchen. Unable to sleep, he'd decided to get up and make himself coffee. Nina turned onto her belly and spread her limbs over the bed, making the shape of someone running. Tomorrow was now today. The past was a foreign country. A musky smell from low in the bed filled her nostrils and she felt a flicker of lust dance between her hips, like flame in a copper bowl.

She heard a *chink* from the kitchen as he set out the coffee cup. No, tea. She was sure it would be tea. He would guess that she was still sleeping, so wouldn't bring her any. In a moment, she would go into the kitchen and share some tea with him, then take him back to bed.

She dozed for a while. She half-remembered a dream about rivers, or else it was the sea. She and Culley had stood on some vantage point and looked down at breakers or white water over rapids. She had retained only that image, but it made her feel good. As she dozed, she re-entered the dream and found she was able to look down on the stretch of water as if her eyes were binoculars. She picked out a raft, and focused on the two people aboard. Herself and Culley, laughing, ducking spray, steering the rickety craft neatly between rocks.

For about an hour, Ira Sanchez had lain where he fell. He had meandered in and out of consciousness, his thoughts sometimes wild, sometimes eerily practical. The pain would lap at him in the same moment that he came around. Seconds later, it would surge like black water flooding a conduit.

He'd thought, I shall flow. This tide will carry me to the horizon. I can be carried off, and leave the pain behind.

His face was mashed agony. Ribs cracked, one broken entirely; a cold feeling in his chest like winter rain. Between his legs, where they had liked to kick him, a great root of pain, a white-hot growth center that sent fire branches tunneling upward toward his eyes.

He'd thought, They broke my balls. They actually broke my balls.

He hadn't known where he was. If it had been light, he wouldn't have been able to pick out landmarks, because his eyes were pouches filled with blood. He'd spent ten minutes getting onto his elbows and knees; then he'd begun to crawl.

He'd crawled for half an hour and covered forty yards. Then he'd died. After a short while, little creatures had appeared. They'd scampered over him, excited and tentative at first; then they'd grown still and concentrated; nothing had moved but their heads.

Now the sun was up, low in the eastern sky, and other scavengers arrived to continue the transformation of Ira Sanchez.

Not in the kitchen. And no teacup had been set out or used. She went back to the bedroom and saw that his clothes were missing. He'd gone out for the tickets. Or else it was too early for that. He'd gone out for a walk. Or else there was no sense in that. He'd gone out for some reason she couldn't quite think of. Or else there was no such reason. He'd be back very soon. Or else he would never be back.

Nina sat down to wait. There was a fist of ice under her heart.

Culley used the men's room to freshen up. From a dispenser, he bought a toothbrush impregnated with toothpaste. Gargle, spit; he felt better. A tingle of spearmint along his gums.

Back in the waiting area, he made three phone calls.

Mike Dawson said, "So effectively, tomorrow morning."

"Yes; but I get in late this evening."

"Is that a new flight?"

"No. It's the flight I'd always planned to take."

"Shall I meet you?"

"Not necessary," Culley said. "Just let Protheroe know."

Carl Mathers said, "I'm sorry, Culley. I can't afford to have Tyler fuck me around. It's my living, y'know?"

"Don't worry," Culley said, "it didn't make a hell of a lot of difference. I'm mailing you some money. It's for Gerry Cattini—two days' rental."

"I'll see he gets it. Listen, Culley, I'm sorry. Okay?"

Helen Blake said, ". . . if you'd like to leave a message . . ."

Nina put her clothes on like someone who had only just learned how to do that. Buttons went to the wrong buttonhole on her shirt; she twice found a right shoe with her left foot. From her suitcase she took a single item. From her purse she took enough for a cab ride.

Leaving everything else behind, she went to the front door of the apartment. A moment or two later, she stepped out into the brightening day.

. . .

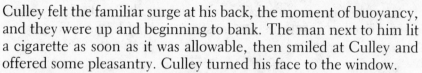

Culley felt the familiar surge at his back, the moment of buoyancy, and they were up and beginning to bank. The man next to him lit a cigarette as soon as it was allowable, then smiled at Culley and offered some pleasantry. Culley turned his face to the window.

The desert was ocher and red going forever, here and there smudged with green. The sun cartwheeled on the window. He looked down as the landscape heated up. A warp of haze made all the distances flow. Apart from that illusion, nothing moved.

The cab set her down at the junction where Culley had stood, looking forlorn, the hood of his rented car raised. She walked to within sight of the house, using the vantage point that Culley had used, and kept low to the horizon, as he had done.

The roses swam up. They shimmied like dancers. They all wore hysterical red smiles.

Nina had walked for two hours. In her hand was the mirror she had taken from her suitcase. Just ahead—filling her vision—was the mesa.

She climbed to a small shelf—not high, but it took her ten minutes with the sun full on the rock face. It wasn't the cave, but she could see the cave—a dark oval cleft on an unapproachable ledge thirty feet farther up. She thought she could smell the creature's sleep-heat, a gamey reek.

She tapped the mirror against the lip of rock in front of her and it broke along a slightly curving line. The half she held was a downturned scimitar; sunlight scoured the cutting edge.

When you go away . . .

She drew the mirror edge over her upturned wrist, then changed hands and drew it over the other, quickly, before the first hand lost its strength. She cut deeply. The flesh sprang open: two little mouths suddenly shouting anger and pain.

The mirror fell down the rock face, a necklace of light, unstrung. Her wrists hopped like little hydrants, squirting blood, and she could see the badness pouring out of her.

She was as light as chaff. All her senses were lit like filaments.

. . . everything holds its breath.

248

FOUR

43

THE BEST TIME WAS early afternoon. If a house was empty at that time, then the likelihood was that everyone was out for the day. A child might get back from school at four o'clock, but you could be gone before then.

The house Eric Ross had chosen this time stood on its own, the last in a short row of middle-class, middle-range houses. It would be poorly protected and would yield enough. Twice before he had come off the moor to steal. He would take money if he had to, but food was even more useful; it meant he wouldn't have to go from the house to a shop. One one occasion, he had taken a cold meal that had been set on a table to await someone's homecoming.

He felt low. He felt lowly. Like some predator forced in from the wild to take what he could of the roadside offal: crash victims glued to the pavement, their pelts slimed with oil. He was no longer sure why he was doing this—what it was *for*. He remembered that he had come here to meet Martin, and knew that the meeting had to be on his own terms. He wasn't ready for that. He'd lost something. A way of seeing the world. A bird's-eye view. Freedom and power. Sometimes he would argue with himself about how he might restore those things. The arguments were fierce. They made him grind his teeth and shout. They brought pain to his chest and to his eyes.

This one was easy. An open fanlight at the back of the house. He crouched on the sill, eased the main window, then closed it when he was inside. He carried a grimy burlap bag that he'd taken from another house. He filled it with food from cupboards and fridge, then found a plastic store bag and half-filled that.

He toted the bags upstairs and found the main bedroom. He opened the closets and went quickly through the pockets of every garment. He came up with eight pounds. He took a couple of shirts, a sweater, three T-shirts, some socks, and stuffed them into the plastic bag. He closed the closets and went to the door and someone came into the house.

A woman, from her footfalls. There was nowhere to go. Ross stood blind side of the bedroom door, clutching his bulging bags like any laden housewife. He listened for doors closing, wanting to read their position in the house. They didn't slam. The woman came directly upstairs. When she walked into the bedroom, she was pulling a sweater over her head, so she didn't have a hand free to close the door. It saved her life. That, and the telephone.

She walked to the bedside and answered it. The door was two-thirds back on the jamb; Ross was only just covered. She sat on the bed to talk, her back to the doorway. Her voice was low. It had the fluid rhythm of someone offering reassurances.

"Next week . . . . Yes, I told you that. Ten days. Yes. Yes, of course we can. No, he'll be in— That's right. Of course I do. Of *course*. Look, I can't talk now. Don't worry. I'm going to tell— Yes. Everything will be fine. Everything will be all right." Her tone was soft with cajolery, a fluctuating note played on a breathy flute.

She put down the phone. Ross tried to imagine what her silence meant. If she went to the closet, she might notice the missing things. If she undressed to change her clothes, she might close the door—as people will, even though they're alone.

He hoped she might close the door. He imagined it swinging back, her seeing him, standing face to face, the moment of silence before she could speak or move—the moment in which he would step forward and enfold her. Take her under his wing.

And he suddenly saw what he wanted; he knew how he might become himself again.

A door slammed and a man called out. The woman left the bedroom. Ross waited until he heard the swell of their voices fade from the hallway. A door closed. He went downstairs, bags in one hand to leave the other free. They were in a room off the hallway. The man was laughing.

". . . star hotels everywhere. Ten days of high life."

"And business." The woman's voice was light, encouraging.

"Well, yes; little enough. The rest of the time's our own."

"I'm looking forward to it," she said. "It's so long since we've had any time to talk."

Ross went out by the front door, leaving it slightly ajar. He walked through the town. No one saw him because no one wanted to. His rough clothes, his ten-day beard, and his crammed bags signaled him as a tramp, one of the almost-invisible. In towns and villages he was a drab shape in the corner of the eye. When he stepped onto the moor, he disappeared entirely.

Francis was rolling a chess pawn between the balls of his thumb and second finger. The pieces and board were entirely ornamental. He said, "You weren't there. To meet him."

"No." Martin Jackson stood at his kitchen window, the phone tucked into his chin. In the yard, Jackson's foreman was herding a pair of saddlebacks toward an isolation pen. "It wasn't necessary. He came back on time?"

"Oh yes. On time. And bringing a problem."

"He got what he went for."

"Yes."

"Oh, dear." Jackson sounded amused. "You're telling me he's become a priority."

"He has. Which is why we're disappointed that you weren't there when—"

"To do what?" Jackson demanded. "Blow his head off in the middle of the arrivals hall?"

"We're anxious about Culley. We're anxious about Ross."

"I know. Don't worry."

"It's been better than a week—I'm talking about Ross."

"Yes."

"You can't even be sure he's down there."

"Yes I can," Jackson said. "He's here."

"And Culley's in London."

"Not for long."

"What?"

"I said, 'Not for Long.' "

"What do you mean?"

In the last moment of the penning, one of the pigs ducked out, running between the gate and the foreman's arm and finding refuge in a forest of nettles. The foreman waded in, waist-high, flashing his stick. It made Jackson laugh.

"What?" Francis asked.

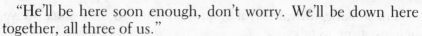

"He'll be here soon enough, don't worry. We'll be down here together, all three of us."

"You can guarantee that?" Francis asked.

The pig galloped out of the nettlebed, upending the foreman. Jackson gave a shout of laughter. "Yes," he said. "Make sure he stays on the investigating team and I can guarantee that."

Ross wasn't the only one replenishing supplies. Jackson had come back to pick up food, to fill his flask, to cram paraffin-soaked firelighters into a plastic screw-top bottle. It was his third trip back; his house had become a staging post.

Twice he'd had Ross in view. Once crossing a stone bridge, early in the morning in hazy sunlight; Jackson had been a valley away. The second time, Jackson had seen a form lift from the skyline amid a haze of windblown rain and descend the far side of a hill as if it were taking a staircase directly into the earth. The sightings were only momentary, but there was no doubt in Jackson's mind. It was Eric; and Jackson knew him as a hunter knows prey.

Ross was holed up on the fringe of a small fir plantation on the western side of the moor. He'd been there a day, and he'd risk it for that night. There would be a time when he'd want to meet Martin, but not yet. He didn't feel strong. He didn't feel in possession of himself.

His daytime foragings had equipped him with a waterproof sleeping bag. He had that, extra clothing, food, and the means to make a fire. He also had the gun.

44

LATIMER'S OFFICE WAS WHOLLY untypical of the man: high-tech brutalism. Glass-topped table, steel and leather chairs, chalk-white venetian blinds. A floor lamp swung in from one corner like the jib of a crane.

Lionel Protheroe had just asked the question "Why?" in a voice loud with surprise. Latimer passed a hand backward over his head, the action of a man smoothing his hair, though the hand stayed a millimeter away from contact. It was a dapper little movement, a distraction, all for show: Latimer's hair was impeccable, razor-parted and slick as paint. He knew he could control Protheroe; even so, he wished the man would simply evaporate.

"If we suspend him, we'll have to say why. I don't want to do that. It's an embarrassment, but nothing dreadful has happened so far as we know. The Americans aren't proposing to make a fuss." He paused. "A reprimand, if you like. I leave that up to you."

"But give the liaison job to someone else. Take him off the investigation."

Latimer shrugged. "Why? Things are winding down, isn't that so? There's no reason to prevent him from filing a few loose ends."

"And the information he says he got from Hugo Kemp? I assume he'll want to go further with that. It fits his conspiracy theory. Is that allowable?"

Latimer shook his head, slowly. "No, I don't think that would be a good idea. The killings have stopped. It's agreed that we have a madman who's now gone to earth. Everyone hopes he'll stay there. Perhaps he will. So tell Culley to let that bit of information drop. If the Porter Gallery's bent, Art and Antiques can have a look."

Protheroe shrugged. "I can tell him. It doesn't mean he'll do as he's told." He hesitated. "It's not just a matter of what's politic— what's best left unsaid. Culley lied to me. He spent money on a trip to America that should have been disallowed. Would have been if he'd told the truth. He didn't report back once. It's not unusual in him, but it's an extreme example. He behaves as if he were a bloody civilian with police powers but no accountability. He knows he's done it; I know he's done it. You're telling me to let it go."

Latimer pushed a row of pens into parade order along his blotter. "Well, Lionel," he said, "it's not as if it came as any surprise to you, is it?"

Later, it was Latimer's turn to ask "Why?"

"If he's suspended, even if he's no longer concerned with the case, he's less vulnerable," Bernard Warner said, "less connected. I want to be able to move him around, push him back and forth. I want him where I can see him."

"The man Porter. Ralph Porter . . ."

"Yes?"

"Is there something—"

"You gave instructions that he drop that?"

"Yes. That's not to say he will. If I knew more about—"

"Just do as you're told, Edward. And everything will be fine. It's annoying that Culley should have had some success in the States. We assumed it would simply be a useful waste of his time. Useful to us. Keep him out of the way while other matters were attended to. Things didn't quite turn out that way, it's true. But if we just keep him close to the fire for a little longer, I can guarantee you that he'll get burned. After that, there'll just be a little more mopping-up to do. Then everyone can sleep at night."

They were sitting in the hush and chestnut glow of a club library. A servant brought them brandy.

Latimer said, "You have to understand that I can't—" He broke off, as if no more needed to be said. Warner looked at him steadily, asking for the rest of the sentence. Latimer tried to hold advantage but couldn't. "—continue to do this for you."

Warner cupped his brandy balloon and swilled the liquid around the bell of the glass. "Well, Edward . . ." He took a sip. He sounded like a disappointed uncle hearing of a poor school report. "I think you'll have to. Continue. Just for a while. If I didn't know that you pay rather young boys to suck your *cock*, Edward—if I wasn't aware of the fact that you manage to persuade them to make use of all sorts of unpleasant *equipment*—if I hadn't heard about your addiction to such things, Edward, then I suppose you might not have to do *anything* for me.

256

"And beyond that, Edward, there's the money you owe me. Not much of a sum to us, perhaps, though there *are* people who might view it as a small fortune. Just a loan between club members, Edward. Except that people in your position aren't supposed to do that, are they? Not *supposed* to be in debt, not *supposed* to like boys and pain and syringes, not *supposed* to have such secrets. But you have. So it looks as if you'll just have to—ah—*continue,* Edward, until I tell you it's all right to stop."

Latimer was trembling. Separating the words with great care, he said, "You have got to leave me alone."

Warner nodded over the rim of his glass. "Really, Edward, don't worry. When all this is over, you won't hear from me again." He sipped. "Almost certainly not."

Warner called Francis from the club. He said, "Soon."

"Sure." Francis was doing something, possibly to himself, possibly to someone else. A soft crackling like a gift being unwrapped.

"Listen," Warner said. "Soon. Do you understand?"

"I've spoken to him. Something's going to happen."

"What?"

"He didn't say. You've made sure that Culley won't get sacked?"

"Yes. Jesus Christ, is this some sort of fucking parlor game—it's a play, it's a book, four words, first word, listen—*what* is going to happen?"

It seemed that Francis must have unwrapped the parcel; the noise stopped. "I don't know," he said. His voice was without inflection, colorless. "It's a surprise."

Culley looked around the ops room. A couple of telephones, a dead VDU screen, a kettle. Dawson stood at his elbow. Culley said, "Why not run out and buy a bloodhound and a magnifying glass?"

"Reduced capability," Dawson observed. "Reorganization of priorities. Lots of people died, so there'll be a decent period of activity and a few more homilies. Give it three weeks to a month, then file it under unsolved crimes. I'm surprised to see you here."

Culley ambled down the room. On the far wall was a map with locations marked. Death sites. "Is anyone fielding this lot now?"

"Oh, yeah; now and then."

"What have you been doing?"

"Reporting to Protheroe."

"What the fuck have you had to report?"

"Computer analysis of eyewitness reports. Computer analysis of MO. Computer analysis of geographical data. Computer—"

"Have you seen Helen?"

Dawson looked wary. "No."

Culley sighed. "All right—have you *spoken* to Helen?"

"Briefly."

Culley wandered up to the map and looked at the lines of triangulation; proliferating connections, endless points of coincidence, a crux at every corner.

He said, "I tell you what . . . Let's not have one of those conversations where you witter on about what friends are for and ask me to respect a confidence, okay? That way I won't have to hit you to relieve the fucking boredom."

Dawson laughed—genuine mirth. He said, "You're a joke, Robin." He walked toward the door. "I've got a few things to do. Computer analysis of victim types—third scan."

Culley kept his eyes on the map. A wilderness of geometry, he thought. A tangle of angles. He picked out Helen's apartment block, just beyond the killing field.

Dawson paused at the door. "I called her. What else did you think? That she phoned me in tears? I asked if she'd heard from you. This was before you decided to report back. She said she hadn't. I've told you what I think." He went out, then reappeared immediately. "There are several files on your desk. The story so far. Boring as shit. Lots of luck."

Culley smiled. He wondered what Helen had really said. What Dawson had said. He went to his office and tossed the files from his desk to the top of a filing cabinet, then he dialed Helen's number.

". . . message, I'll get back to you."

He let the tape run on for a few seconds, though he didn't speak. As he was hanging up, Dawson appeared in the doorway.

"I asked you a question earlier."

"You did?"

"How is it that Protheroe isn't carrying your head around on a pike?"

Culley shrugged. "Maybe he's taken a liking to me on account of my talent and good looks." He frowned. "I'm not sure."

Dawson came into the room and closed the door. He opened the top drawer of Culley's desk and rooted around until he came up with a half-bottle of whiskey. He removed two Styrofoam cups from his jacket pocket and poured for them both. Culley raised his cup. "Good health," he said. Then, "To friendship."

"What's the brief?" Dawson asked.

"The brief is to arrest the crazy bastard who recently shot a large number of people in and around central London. The expectation —an altogether different thing—is that I'll wipe a few noses, kiss a few asses, and sign off gracefully. It seems that the general theory is that our mad-dog killer has decided to hang up his psychosis and retire from the wearying business of indiscriminate slaughter."

"You don't think that."

"I don't think it was indiscriminate slaughter in the first place, remember?"

"What about this Porter? The gallery?"

"Yes, well, there are fairly firm hints that we should leave him alone."

"How firm?"

"Pretty firm."

"Like orders."

"Yes."

"You're going to tell me that we're turning him over tomorrow."

"Not tomorrow. Quite soon. You could do some preliminary work on the associate directors. A trip to Companies House. You know the form."

Dawson raised his cup. "To friendship," he said. Then, "You could be wrong."

"It's possible," Culley said.

"You think so?"

"No."

Dawson tossed back the rest of his drink. "She's no good for you," he said. "You never listen to a fucking thing I say."

The windows were blank, curtains pulled back. Lights from the street streaked the glass like rainfall.

Culley pressed a few bells on the street door and was given an answering buzz. Helen's apartment was a different matter: two-cylinder Banhams and a deadlock. He sat down in the hallway to wait. Jet lag made him lightheaded and hot-eyed, like a Halloween pumpkin.

When he woke, Helen was leaning on the opposite wall, arms folded. She asked, "Drunk or lagged?"

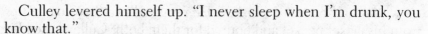

Culley levered himself up. "I never sleep when I'm drunk, you know that."

Inside, he poured himself a whiskey as if her question had given him the idea. She dumped her briefcase and decided it would be all right to kiss him hello. "You start," she said.

He laughed. "What's this? A face-slapping contest?"

"You've got a look in your eye that says it might be."

"Do you want a whiskey?" he asked. "It's yours."

"Might help to deaden the pain, I suppose." She held her face sideways, lofting the jaw, as if inviting a punch. He gave her the drink and kissed her upturned cheek, then sat on a dining chair that he'd turned away from the table. Helen went across the room to the sofa, as if to offer some sort of a hint—distance between them.

"When we were first married," she said, "I used to hate it when you went away."

Culley's arm shot out as if he were fending off a blow. Whiskey raced across the polished surface of the table. He stared at Helen, following her with his eyes as she went out to fetch some sheets of kitchen towel, then watching her back into the room. She mopped the table and gave him a fresh drink.

"I'm sorry . . . . Clumsy."

She shook her head. "It's okay. Maybe you're still half-asleep." She retreated to the sofa again. ". . . Then I didn't mind so much. Then I used to look forward to it." She regarded him in silence for a minute. "Do you remember Brett—the night he was recaptured?"

"I remember it happening," Culley said, "if that's what you mean."

"Yes, well, I wasn't there for that. I'm talking about afterward. You came back with Mike Dawson."

She drank all her whiskey and went to the table for more. Then she walked back over the space to the sofa. Back over the bridge. She left the bottle on the table—either absentmindedness or a reason to cross the bridge again.

"If I've got it right, you missed him at the address you'd been given, but only just. He hijacked a car—right?—at a traffic light. Threw the guy out and roared off down the M-40 with you and several others in pursuit. And he ran out of gas. Wasn't that it? Ran out of gas?"

Culley's lips curved into a grin. He couldn't help it. Whenever he thought about the incident, it made him laugh.

Brett had pulled onto the hard shoulder and gotten out to run, but there really wasn't anywhere to go. Along with five others, Culley had ringed the man. They'd all had their guns drawn. Brett's arms had hung at his sides; then he'd lifted them, fists cocked for a fight. All the coppers had laughed. They'd closed the circle, not hurrying, all of them laughing. The squad car light had spun, turning their faces blue-white, and they'd closed in like a noose, all laughing.

It was what Helen had remembered best. "You were still laughing when you got back," she said. "I remember thinking that I wanted you out of the house. You and Mike. You both drank a lot, but it seemed impossible for you to get drunk. Later, you woke me up and fucked me as if you were trying to wreck the bed. I didn't like any of it. I still don't." She shook her head. "You tell me things have changed. But when I think back, when I look at you —as if I were looking at a bunch of old snapshots—what I see is darkness. You know?" There were tears in her voice. "I see things that make me think of darkness. Tunnels. Alleys. Dank corners. And I think you must like it, you must like the darkness, the dark places, because otherwise what on earth are you doing there?"

Helen walked across from the sofa to where he sat on the other side of the bridge. She crouched down in front of him and took his hands. "I can't see any hope for us unless things change. But it'll take more than your promises. It'll take something I can see; something I can touch." She stood up. "Okay?"

He nodded. He knew that he ought to ask, "What? What will it take?" but he thought he'd guessed the answer and didn't want to hear it yet.

Helen opened the fridge and looked in—that old joke. She said, "There are a few small but significant disadvantages to living alone, of course."

"No food?"

"That's right."

"What else?"

"No sex."

With the window open, there was a faint, bitter tang of exhaust gas in the room; you could imagine it curling over the sill like a sea mist. In the street, a motorcycle left from a standing start as if sheet metal were being fed into a buzz saw. A chorus of male voices chanted in crescendo.

The light from the window was all the light they wanted. Near-dark. A murkiness. When she opened her mouth, saliva glistened on her teeth. The boss of his shoulder was chalk-white, then bright blue as neon pulsed on a peepshow across the street.

He asked her a question, and she whispered, "Yes. Do that."

After a while he heard her voice, as if it were coming from a way off, but growing louder. Little cries, gaining strength as the feeling pressed on her. Her hips rose and stayed still—tense and concentrated—until she shouted out and seemed to fall away from him.

His arms were around her at shoulder and hip, as if he had caught her in mid-flight, and her legs circled his waist to drag him down.

"What?" he asked. "What will it take?"

"Come out of it tomorrow." She lifted up on one elbow. It was too dark, now, to see his face, but she was looking at him nonetheless. "Tonight, if there's a way of doing that. Leave. Quit. Stop being a copper. Just . . . Whatever's in hand, whatever's on your desk, forget it. Don't go in. Stay here. Come out of it now."

"That's the way?"

"That's the way, yes."

A silence crept in, stealthy and cold. She sat straight, and backed up to the headboard, knees to her chin, arms locked around her knees, forehead onto her arms. He couldn't see her in the dark.

She said, "Go home, Robin."

He put a foolhardy amount of whiskey into a glass and took it to the windowseat that looked onto the river.

He could see that Helen was right. There was little else that could make things possible. Except coppering wasn't the problem. It simply gave the problem a particular place to exist. A stage, a script, a supporting cast. And sometimes—most dangerous of all —applause.

Not possible. Not possible this time. Not this one. Not *this*. There were things he needed to know. There were places he needed to visit. To be presented with a choice was bad enough. The fact that he seemed to have made it filled him with fury. A cargo boat went upriver, its stern lamp releasing elvers of light into the water. He drank half the whiskey at a swallow.

He thought about what Helen had said. About the dark places. He knew that she was close. And he also knew that because it was him, because it was *himself,* he would never find it so strange or wrong or dangerous. Like being able to stand on the edge of a drop, but finding it an unbearable thing to watch. Like committing adultery—someone else would be helplessly hurt by an incident that *you* knew didn't matter much.

There was more. Of course he wanted to make use of the information he'd forced out of Kemp; wanted to nail whoever had decided that all those people were expendable. And he wanted to find the sniper. Sure; that was what his job was about. But there were other things.

He wanted to know about how it was possible. He wanted to know about how it felt. He wanted to know about its taste and smell. He wanted to know about these things because he believed he might already have a pretty good idea about them; and he wanted to test the idea. He wanted to see how scary it would get.

Some people who knew Culley thought it had to do with rules. It was true that he did have a problem with rules. Other people constructed them, applied them, pronounced them good, fair, useful, whatever. And believed they could then punish you for not obeying them. It was a puzzle to Culley. *Whose* rules? Who *says* so? Shit, I've got rules of my *own.* Where were you when I invented *them?*

But it wasn't to do with rules. It was to do with love, hatred, fear, excitement, anger. All those things.

He watched boats pass downriver, little flames licking in their wakes.

He saw Nina Kemp's face. Her voice shivered his backbone.

Dawson said, "What the fuck's this about?" The last month of summer had come in with gray, wet billows, as if someone were emptying sackfuls of rain into the wind. He was huddled on the leeward side of a sodden pleasure boat that was tacking downriver. It was the view Culley had looked at for most of the night.

"A little outing," he said, "an excursion. I thought you'd like it. We're a seafaring nation, after all."

The last tourists of the season drifted from port to starboard with their cameras and focused through the shifting mist of rain. The sniper had kept visitors out of London; and even now only the brave or rash or duty-driven were there. They seemed listless, full of sleep—creatures ready for hibernation.

Culley was heavy-lidded, like them. He passed Dawson a liquor flask, keeping a hand extended for its return. The rain shuddered past in squalls. "You went to Companies House?"

Dawson dabbed his mouth with the back of his hand. "It's like reading a story with all the real information taken away. Once upon a time a beautiful princess was born. Her name was Blond-curls Holdings Ltd. And one day a White Knight . . . So she and her family made fifteen percent gross ever after. You get the bald details, but if microfiche could reveal what lies between the lines—"

"And as for the bald details?"

"The gallery's just called Ralph Porter, Limited. Six sharehold-ers. Porter's one of them, naturally. The others are all notables. You know that—I phoned it to you in Tucson."

"Where did it come from?"

"Fraud squad. They could run a spot check on the Royal Fam-ily. The interesting factor is that Porter has only fifteen percent of the shares. Three other directors have ten percent. Two others hold twenty-seven and a half percent each."

"Which looks organized."

"In theory, a combination of the other shareholders could get together with one of the twenty-seven-plus members in order to push some business through. Porter, say, and one ten-percenter, with one of the big guys. That would give them fifty-two and a half and a controlling vote. Or the three ten-percenters together with one twenty-seven-percenter against Porter and the other major shareholder. But it doesn't read that way, does it? What you see when you look at it is that two people have neatly divided a con-trolling share. You'd have to make them allies."

In order to give Dawson most of the shelter, Culley was leaning back toward the rail. The right shoulder of his raincoat was satu-rated, a dark triangle against the lighter, untouched material. He handed over the flask, and said, "Who?"

"Two women. Alison Travers. Marie Wallace."

"Mary?"

"No," Dawson said, "Marie."

"Who are they?"

"Haven't had time for that yet. As task forces go, many of us have already. Gone."

"Okay." The boat was completing a turn. Its engines slowed,

then churned into reverse for a moment as it sidled up to the dock. It was possible for passengers to alight upriver, do some sightseeing, and wait for a later boat.

Dawson started toward the ramp. "I'll get the bus back," he said. "You probably hadn't noticed, but there's a spot of rain in the wind."

45

WHO WERE THEY? Miss Bun, the baker's daughter. Mr. Chop, the butcher. Mrs. Wheat, the farmer's wife. Happy families. Master Hose, the fireman's son. Miss Fin, the fishmonger's daughter. Mrs. Wood, the carpenter's wife. *Happy* families.

Martin Jackson looked down from the battlements—a tower, just on the edge of the town, that had once stood on a private estate. Someone's folly; a fairy-tale turret, built on a whim by some indulgent father so that his daughter could be the princess Lonelyheart. The estate had gone broke and the town had bought the land. Part of it was now a parking lot. The tower had decayed, been restored, decayed again. Its door was boarded up.

He sat on the rampart, his legs stretched out, and peered down on the parking lot. Mr. Blackcap, the judge.

There was a strong, warm wind blowing. Clouds were going backward across the sky like the flow from a smokestack. He could hear the whipple and crack as the skirts of people's coats lifted and shook out, snappy as sails. Nothing in the wind apart from the smell of gorse and a thin tang of salt. It was exhilarating. Sea weather. Moor weather. Families got out of their cars, locked the doors, set off toward the center of town.

When he put the scope to his eye, he plunged toward them.

Their features were half-hidden by his angle of descent. He could see the plane of a cheek, a prominent nose, a mouth—as if he hovered directly above their heads. They spoke silently. He roamed among them with his brilliant eye. The cross hairs quartered their faces.

Who shall we have? Miss Bun. Who shall we have? Mrs. Wood. Shall we? Or Mr. Chop.

The girl had almost reached the parking lot entrance—a two-car gap in the low wall. He fired twice, taking her once in the lower back, then again a handspan higher, tearing the heart valves and shattering her breast. As the bullets hit her, she sprinted forward, both arms flung out, like someone coming full-pelt from a burning building. The impact took her into the road and into the path of a car. She body-surfed up the hood and over the roof.

He came back at once for the man. The first broke his shoulder and spun him around. Surprise and shock and pain threw his features haywire. His face was clear as day through the scope: clear and very close, as if he and his killer were eye to eye. The second took his throat out.

The tower had a spiral staircase made of stone for the magic prince to climb. He came down in a clatter, shedding dust and small pebbles over the lip of each stair. He ran with his back braced against the wall so that he could break the gun down as he went.

He put his shoulder to the door and shoved, shifting the battens that had been nailed across, then kicked it closed with his foot when he was outside. On one side was a minor road, separated from him by a head-high wall; on the other, a field that sloped up to become a low hill with a coppice of silver birch just below the crest. He made for the tree cover, walking briskly, the backpack that contained the dismantled gun swinging from one hand.

The wind ran clouds across the face of the sun. Massive, dusty beams of sunlight fell among the pale boles of the birches like ghost trees under a logger's ax. He stepped into cover and looked back. It was just possible to see the crowds and commotion. From far off, he could hear a siren. In time, someone would probably think of the tower. It wasn't an obvious thing to think because the gun and the scope were powerful and the tower was quite a way from the parking lot.

He set off through the trees, making for the brow of the hill. He was laughing under his breath, some joke that he'd just remembered. Some joke that he'd love to share.

Who knows? he thought. Tomorrow—who knows?—we might have a couple more. Mr. Silicon, the computer programmer. The invention made him laugh even more. Miss Capsule, the astronaut's daughter.

"Everything changed," Ross said, "and then it changed again. Not *back* again—a new difference. And you wanted . . ." He paused. "And it wasn't . . ." He paused again and shook his head as if trying to shake the thought free.

He was breaking camp. He plugged the fire pit, dropping its square of turf back like a lid. He rolled the sleeping bag.

"And it wasn't the same. No matter they died. No matter. It wasn't the same."

He clenched his teeth until the muscles at the points of his jaw bulged and ached. The argument with himself was always the same: *You made a mistake. You spoiled it all. There must be a way back. Find a way back.* That was one side. The other side was: *You made a mistake. You spoiled it all. It's too risky, now. Go away. You must go away forever.*

"Bury the food that's perished. Stow the rest in the backpack and one of the bags. Keep everything dry, especially clothes." His words boomed and shook, full of passion and anger, as if some clergyman were there, rehearsing a sermon to the trees.

"Untouchable. Couldn't be touched. No one could touch me. Always . . . Coming down from a cloud, from cloud cover. Under my eye. Their faces under my eye. The flame descending, a tongue of flame racing toward them as if I had stretched out my hand, as if I had released the fire, as if it sprang from my fingertips. And struck them."

He badgered himself while he closed the flap of the backpack and buckled the strap.

"It was different, then it changed. Not changed *back*. No. It changed *again*. Why did it? You know what to do. You know. You know what to do."

He stepped out of the cover of the pines and the wind struck him broadside. He staggered, then righted himself. The whole sky seemed to be streaming off the horizon and pouring over his head. His words were picked from his lips and carried off for whoever might finally hear them.

"Find a way back. You know what to do . . ."

He hiked into the wind, backpack hoisted on his shoulders, a bag of food in his left hand, in his right the case that held the gun.

Culley heard an hour and a half later. Protheroe told him. It was clear that Protheroe had other news that he wasn't happy about. He wiped a finger under the quills of his mustache and said, "They've asked for someone from the task force."

"No surprise," Culley said. "They'll want to know what they've got. We're the likeliest people to tell them." Without pausing, he said, "It's me. Is that right?"

"You're the obvious person." Protheroe pushed his chair back from the desk a little as if that was his best range. He said, "I'm going to tell you something that might not come as a complete surprise. I've never liked you much. Just lately, I've come to like you even less. I've been looking for a foolproof way of fucking you over. I don't care what it is as long as it works. More than anything, I'd like to see the day when you're an ex-copper. I know you've got a reputation for getting your hands dirty. I'm not impressed. I can see you're more intelligent than most. That just makes me suspicious. Let me tell you some of the things I really don't like about people—especially about coppers. I don't like tricky. I don't like hard to understand. I don't like *different*. Why? Because there's no need for it. None at all. You're different, Culley, but worse than that, you know you are; and worse than that, you like it. That annoys me, and it worries me. I'm looking for excuses—you understand? So go to Devon. Cooperate with the locals. Do what they want you to do. Have a quick look around. Report back. Okay? *Report back.* Just keep it in your mind that I'm looking for a way."

Culley nodded but didn't speak. He sat in his chair until Protheroe told him to go.

"What about Porter?" Dawson asked. "Hold up on that?"

"No." Culley shook his head. "What else is there to occupy you? Go and see him."

Dawson sighed. "I know you don't give a fuck. But this is my career, for what it's worth."

"I didn't say you had to nuke his gallery. Be subtle. If you ask the questions nicely, he'll probably come through for you."

268

"Why would a copper be asking about his business partners?"

"Don't be a copper," Culley suggested. "Be a potential customer. I don't know. Do what you have to do."

There was beer slop on the table and spillage from someone's lunch. On either side, fruit machines beeped like androids. A loop tape played featureless rock. Dawson said, "London pubs have become a fucking joke. Am I going to have your number?"

"Everyone'll have it," Culley said. "The locals have booked me into a hotel. The White Hart."

Dawson wandered off to fetch two large scotches and a beer chaser for himself. On his way back he glanced into the steam table and shuddered.

Culley was woozy with insomnia; the scotch went to his head. "You have to ask yourself what the fuck he's doing in Devonshire."

"You do," Dawson agreed. "What does that make it, copycat?"

"Ballistics have got the bullets. That ought to tell us something."

"What do you think?"

"See what tomorrow brings. Once he's started, he doesn't like to stop." Culley downed his drink and stood up. "Train to catch."

"You're going tonight?"

"I'm going now."

"I'd thought we might get something to eat—since you're not getting sex for dessert anymore."

Culley ignored the jibe. "Sorry." He gestured toward the steam table. "Why not get something here? Pub fare—simple but wholesome."

"Listen," Dawson said, "the things in there are kept dormant by the heat. If you take them out, they fight back."

46

CULLEY MADE A TOUR of the parking lot. He felt like an exhibit. On the three accessible sides, the space was ringed with watchers. If one or two people drifted away, others arrived to take their places. The police had long ago given up on the task of moving people on. The watchers were silent and serious. They stood around like the chorus from a Greek tragedy, sad eyes fixed on the amphitheater.

Screens had been rigged up to mask the principal blood splashes: the point of fall. Culley looked up and the tower fell into his eyeline. Chris Bullen was Culley's official guide—an officer of the same rank as Culley, though uniformed branch. Culley nodded into the distance. "He shot from there?"

"That's right." Bullen had taken his uniform cap off so that he wouldn't have to hold it on against the wind.

"What is it?"

"A folly. A local landowner's extravagance. Unsafe, now, so it's been boarded up for years. No one can decide whether to restore it or pull it down."

"Let's take a look."

The watchers solemnly parted to let the two men offstage. They went the short distance to the tower by car. Bullen led Culley around to the door, its splintered battens and smashed lock.

"Hold it back for me." Bullen yanked at the door, making a gap. Culley went through, then turned as Bullen started to follow. "Can I go on my own?"

"If you like." Bullen shrugged. "I've seen the view from up there." He turned away.

I know you're not a hick, Culley thought, and I'll be nice to you later. But I want to see for myself.

The staircase adjoined the wall, spiraling up the tower toward the crenellations. The wooden handrail was broken in places and some of the balusters had been kicked out; Culley walked close to the wall. The staircase ended at a trapdoor. It was made of untreated pine and had warped slightly, letting in a draft and spikes of light. Not the original. The hinges were shiny and the stop ropes new. Culley heaved it back and kept walking. All he could see was a pale blue sky and clouds jostling one another. Then the town came into view through the broken teeth of the battlements. They were three deep at the parking lot, like an audience gathered around a circus ring, not knowing that the clowns and the trapeze artists, the jugglers and the performing dogs, had all gone home.

Culley walked across the wooden flooring and sat on the rampart. He had to stretch his legs out in front of him—there was no room to kneel. When he stood up, he felt exposed; more than half his body was visible. And there was nothing on which to rest your gun arm. He sat down again, looking out toward the parking lot, and raised both arms, left hand supporting the gun, right elbow cocked to bring the butt up to his cheek and his index finger to the trigger. Sitting sideways like that, he could scan anything to his right. On his left hand side, both movement and vision were restricted. The restrictions had made the killer's choices for him. *These* people, not *those* people. It's an arbitrary business, Culley thought, being a victim.

He sat where the killer had sat, aiming an imaginary gun at the circled audience. Who? he thought. Suppose it were me. Who would I have? A woman in a red coat stood out. A tall man in a tweed hat. A girl wearing jeans and a big sweater with a bright, jazzy pattern. The woman in red began to walk away and he followed her with the gun. The wind touseled his hair.

Chris Bullen had walked a short way up the slope. He looked back and saw Culley's charade with the nonexistent gun. He wondered what it was for. It looked ridiculous, like the gesture people use to parody artists—the brush handle raised toward the sitter's face, one eye closed, a bent thumb judging proportions. As he watched Culley was thrust slightly backward.

A punch of recoil. *Bap.* The woman in the red coat died.

It doesn't matter, Culley thought. It doesn't matter who you choose. To be there, to be holding them in your sights, to be making the choice—that's what matters.

A cloud blocked the sun for a moment, then the wind pushed it on and light rushed down the hillside, washing the walls of the tower and sweeping on into the town. The watchers stood in a pool of sun, a vast spotlight, as if they were the stars of the show. Culley could see Chris Bullen waiting on the slope, pretending indifference.

It was time to go down, but he didn't want to. He could see how it would be easy to stay up there with the wind and the cloudwrack, with an imaginary gun and a perfect view of the victims.

"What's the verdict?" Bullen was doing his own driving: taking Culley back to the hotel.

"You've had the ballistics report."

"Not the same gun."

"No. Similar. . ."

"But no reason to switch," Bullen suggested.

"Who knows. We think the guy's a pro. We're fairly certain of it. It's not unreasonable to suppose that a pro would own more than one such weapon. Why change? Damage to the first gun. The notion that it might confuse us. Whim. Or, of course, it's someone else."

"Copycat."

"It's possible," Culley said. "One other difference."

"Two strikes per body," Bullen observed.

"Yes. In the case of the girl, the first shot might well have killed her eventually, but the second shot was better—more accurate. The man would have survived his shoulder wound. The killer definitely needed two hits to nail him."

"Not so in London," Bullen said.

"Not so in London."

"What are you saying?" Bullen asked. "That it's too early to tell?"

"Yes."

"How will that change? You don't seem to know much about the guy."

Culley was surprised not to be annoyed by the remark. "You're right," he said. "Given that he killed a lot of people on our patch, we know very little. In theory, he's more of a marksman than whoever shot from the tower. Though things change, don't they? Circumstances differ. It's a difficult shot from up there. And if it is the same guy, you'd have to allow that something's changed in him. He made one mistake, then disappeared. If he's reappeared here—why? And what's different about him now?" Culley was asking the questions of himself. "One thing seems the same: He knows how to organize an escape route. Apart from the instance in Richmond Park, no one ever saw the guy. That's pretty remarkable in a city."

"He'd have an even better chance down here," Bullen observed. He drove in silence for a while, then asked, "What does it feel like? Same guy, or not?"

Culley shook his head. "We'll have to wait."

"What will waiting bring?"

"This guy has a special characteristic," Culley said. "He likes it. He likes it a hell of a lot. If this is the same man, it won't be long before you've got a body count well into double figures."

In some organizations, secretaries are provided with punching bags that look like bosses. The bosses don't need punching bags that look like secretaries; they have secretaries. Protheroe's secretary said, "He's not here. But he told me that if you called in, I should ask you to call again in fifteen minutes."

"I won't be here in fifteen minutes," Culley said. "I'm reporting back. He asked me to do that."

"I know. And he wants to talk to you himself."

"Not possible," Culley said. "Sorry. Have you got your notebook and pencil handy?"

After ten seconds of dictation, she transferred the call to Mike Dawson. "Anything on Porter?" Culley asked.

"Give me a break."

"Okay—anything planned?"

"They're opening a new exhibition tomorrow. White wine and canapes, I expect. I thought I'd go along; pretend to be interested."

"Okay," Culley said. "There's a guy, Binyon, in Art and Antiques, if you feel you need any background."

"No thanks." Dawson sounded offended. "I used to have a girlfriend who'd been to art college. I can get by."

"What did she teach you?"

"Two eyes, two tits—old master. Four eyes, six tits—modern. What did you find?"

"Could be a home-grown crazy. He needed two tries to kill them . . ."

"You're not sure."

"It was a difficult angle. And that aside—both were very good shots. I mean, this man's good, whoever he is."

"Ballistics say it's not the same gun."

"That's right."

"And so. . . ?"

"And so it's probably not the same man. Still, I'll give it a couple of days; wait for the local reports. Eyewitness, house-to-house. See if anything rings a bell."

"What's the weather like down there?" Dawson asked. "It's raining here."

"Have a nice time at the gallery," Culley told him. "Try not to let on that you're stupid."

He dialed Helen's number and she answered on the third ring. He said, "I'm in Devon—"

"Terrific," she said. "Nice weather?" And hung up.

Out on the moor, the night was starry and loud with wind. In the town, awnings cracked and blown garbage tumbled down the main street. Orange light, an amalgam of all the shopfront neons, seemed to hang at rooftop level like a garish canopy.

Culley took a drink to the open window of his hotel room and stared down at the streets. It was past midnight. In London, there were always people on the street, there was always traffic, always movement. Here, the empty streets were like a film set.

A drunk appeared and played the part of a drunk. He tottered from one side of the pavement to the other; he put a steadying hand out to a wall that wasn't there; he fell heavily and seemed not to know what had happened.

A couple rounded a corner, arguing fiercely. Everything they said was clearly audible; the buildings were a sounding board. The woman broke away and strode on ahead, calling the man a bastard. He caught up with her and batted her in the face with the back of his hand. He walked off a few paces, then caught up with her again; hit her again.

A group of young men went past, laughing fit to bust, eating fast food from cartons. One of them stopped and pissed against a shop window.

By one o'clock the cabaret was over. Culley closed the window, having to pull hard to defeat the wind. The curtains collapsed against the glass.

There was enough light in the room to drink by. He lay on the bed and set the bottle down on the floor, within arm's reach. He thought of the tower—the airiness up there, clouds flying, the view of crowds circling the parking lot. He took a sip of scotch and felt the tiny, interior landslip that meant he had stopped being mellow and started to become drunk. He took a further sip as if to consolidate the position, then put the glass aside. His eyes closed, and he saw the tower as kaleidoscope—all its aspects coming under his eye at once, and magnified because he was close to sleep. The door with its smashed battens, the broken wood brighter than the rest. The staircase winding up to a rectangle of blue. The battlements capped with moss. He saw the view as the killer would have seen it. People coming and going in the parking lot, close enough to kill, too far away for it to matter.

A thought struck him: If he can see them, he can see me, too. A few seconds later he was asleep.

When he woke up, he was dying.

47

CULLEY COULD FEEL CONSCIOUSNESS slipping even as it returned. The violence had wakened him, now it was sending him under. He flung his hands up like someone losing his balance and struck a jaw or a nose. He tried to prize off whatever was choking him, but the man above him had the advantage of being able to bear down. Culley was struggling to rise and all the laws of physics were against it.

He heard a sound like a siren, swelling and falling, coming and going. He knew that if the sound faded completely, he would be dead. Something in his throat seemed to be slowly cracking, like a green branch, and lack of air had made a furnace of his chest. He fought using his body, turning and bucking. There was a sharp pain behind his eyeballs; his tongue popped from his mouth, involuntarily, a grotesque parody of defiance.

The man who was killing him made a featureless silhouette—a bulk of body, black sphere of a head, two arms held stiffly downward. Culley's panic and rage provided enough energy for a great heave of the torso, wrenching himself away, forcing the man to lurch in the direction of his twisting body in order to maintain his grip. As the body followed the arms, Culley drew his knees up to his chest, legs together, then straightened from the hips, launching his feet outward as hard and fast as he could. The impact made him quake. The hands scored his neck as they left it. Culley heard the rattling thump as his assailant hit the door. Then there was a pause that he didn't understand.

The next best move would have been to follow up the advantage. Culley was too weak for that. For a moment, everything was still. Then Culley rolled off the bed, almost falling to the floor when his feet made contact. Weak-legged, he tumbled over a small armchair, then grabbed its back for support and put it between himself and the other man. The door opened and the black outline sprang up in the frame of light, then was gone.

Culley rounded the chair and sat in it heavily. He stayed there for a full five minutes. When he got up to put the lights on, he felt something tapping at his chest like a dogtag: the garotte. He stood in front of the bathroom mirror and peeled it off, staring at the weal it had made—bright red and white pucker lines like the mouth of an old whore. The cord was supple and strong, a toggle whipped on at either end. Homemade; professional. His throat felt as if someone had pushed a branding iron down to the gullet.

He went back to the main room and snapped on the lights. The toppled chair, rumpled bedclothes, and half-empty scotch bottle made the place look as if people had recently left in search of a better party. Near the door, on the gray carpet, a splash of red advertised the party's obligatory brawl. Culley put on trousers and a T-shirt to feel less vulnerable, then squatted down by the little flub of blood. At its center something white glistened. Culley turned it with a fingertip and found a tooth, a whole canine, its point delicately even, its root bloody and stippled with fragments of flesh.

That's why he paused, Culley thought. I caught him in the face. He was stunned.

He collected the little trophy in a wad of tissue. Under other circumstances he would have turned it in to forensic for typing, but he didn't need Billy Knowles to tell him that there was nothing significant to be gotten from the tooth. He didn't need to be in possession of the few tiny items of information that might make finding his attacker easier, because it was plain enough that he was going to meet the man again.

He checked the door and found that the lock wasn't broken. A key was still in place on the corridor side—the key that hangs alongside the pigeonhole for your room in case you lose the one you got when you registered. Great security, Culley thought. He took the key out and double-locked the room, then took a slug of scotch straight from the bottle.

One or two questions, he thought. He put the bottleneck to his lips and tilted his head back. It hurt to swallow and it hurt not to. One or two questions . . . How did he know I was here?

He watched you until you came to the hotel.

All right—how did he know I was here *at all?* Here in Devon?

No answer.

Here's another. We're working backward to the more fundamental questions, okay? Why does he want to kill me?

You're dangerous to him.

Or to someone who's paying him.

Yes, that.

Okay—why?

Must be something to do with stolen paintings, wouldn't you say? Jay Hammond, Porter, Kemp . . .

Yes. I would. That's what I'd say. And here's another question.

I know what this question is.

You've guessed. How did Kemp know what he knew? By the time I met him in the gallery, he knew who I was. He called me by name.

The answer to that is: Someone, somewhere, knows more about you than you know about him. Now let me ask you a question. The guy who tried to kill you tonight . . . who is he?

Don't know.

The sniper?

No.

Who?

Culley asked the question of himself again. *Who?*

He had buttoned his shirt to the neck to hide the mark. It had faded a little, but he still looked like a man who had recently escaped lynching. They had set up a desk for him at a corner of an open-plan office; the view was a parking lot bordered on three sides by a line of cypresses, and beyond that low, damp meadows divided by a stream.

Chris Bullen dropped some files onto the desk. Culley hadn't heard him approach. Easy to ambush people in an open office. "Eyewitness," Bullen explained, "and house-to-house. And the first of the goon letters."

"Anything?" Culley asked.

Bullen became Mr. Witness, Mr. Interviewee. "I heard a bang —I saw her fall. I thought it was a car backfiring. I was locking my car. I didn't have my glasses on. He had dark, curly hair, big muscles, a sweat band around his head, was bare-chested and carried several hand grenades and a rapid-fire rifle." He paused for laughter, then said, "Are you okay?"

"I've caught a cold," Culley told him.

Bullen smiled. "We're all in danger of that." He started back to his own office. "Anything you need . . ."

Culley flipped through the reports. They all said the same thing. So did the letters.

. . . *woman, a sorse of evil and disese and Im glad I killed her, she was filth and she diserved to die . . .*

. . . *known it to be a place of sin, when more places to drink and gamble in exist than places of worship, no one should be surprised that . . .*

. . . *tell you about how I killed them. The gun is a single-shot Mauser given to me when I worked as an assassin for the CIA in . . .*

We're on the moor.

That was all it said. Culley looked at it. He remembered his last thought before sleeping the previous evening: Where are you living? It was a thought provoked by the doziness that comes when sleep is almost there. It merged two events and simplified them, proposing that this sniper and the London killer must be the same man. That he'd need to find somewhere to roost. But two men— couldn't that be it?

Culley looked at the note again. Capital letters, blue ballpoint pen, four words. It had all the casual plausibility of a note tacked to the door of an empty house. No point in sending it unless it meant what it said.

The card Dawson had picked up in the Porter Gallery had announced a new exhibition and noted the private viewing. Since it wasn't an invitation, it hadn't given a time. As Dawson understood it, these affairs happened between six and eight, so he split the difference.

There was a two-car space in a side street half a block from the gallery. Dawson drove past, intending to back in. A cream Porsche swerved and parked, leaving half a car's length either side. Dawson gave a bip on the horn, but the Porsche's engine died and the lights went out. He drove almost to the bottom of the street, found a parking place, and walked back. A tall, blond girl climbed out of the Porsche, throwing a fistful of cosmetics back into her shoulder bag. She swept her hair back with one hand and turned on her heel. Dawson watched the swing of her backside all the way to the gallery. She pushed the door open, and he paused so that it wouldn't spring back in his face.

Everyone had turned toward the center of the room, chatting, looking for faces they might recognize, or else being looked at. It seemed logical enough, since rooms full of people don't stand like a beleaguered military force, backs to the center, facing outward to repel the attack. Logical, but wrong, The paintings hung around the walls like plain girls at a dance.

Dawson collected a glass of wine and made a tour of the exhibition because he couldn't think of anything else to do. At the start of his second circuit, he knocked into the blonde. She was outrageously pretty: a fall of corn-colored hair, heavy on one side, smoky eyes, a tiny mole at the side of her upper lip.

Dawson said, "Do you know the painter?"

She looked at him a moment, as if she were having to translate the words slowly. "No." She lifted her hand. There was an unlit cigarette in it. While Dawson felt for a match, she put the cigarette back into the pack and the pack into her bag.

"Can I get you a glass of wine?" he asked.

She smiled; then the smile expanded to become a small laugh. "Look," she said, "piss off. All right?"

He went back to the bar—a trestle table covered by a white cloth. The office lay just behind it. A woman was straightening a stack of photostated price lists.

"Ralph Porter?"

"Over there." She nodded in the direction of a triangular conversation: two men, one of them in a suit so expensive that it would always look crumpled, and a leggy woman who, for some reason, was wearing a hat. Dawson stood close, making the triangle a lopsided cross.

He said, "Ralph Porter?"

Porter was the taller of the two men; he wore a suit of rather more conventional cut, though he'd brought a foppish touch to it by lodging a silk handkerchief in the sleeve of his jacket. The face was broad, fleshy around the jowls; he had thick, dark hair combed straight back and heavy eyebrows that looked like a child's representation of a bird. When he turned to look at Dawson, the bird made a lazy flap of its wings.

"I've been looking at number fourteen," Dawson said. " 'Water Meadow.' "

The couple who had been talking to Porter drifted off. Porter glanced toward the canvas Dawson had mentioned—an arrangement of blues, whites, greens, and blacks, the paint laid on in slabs thicker than putty. He said, "You like that piece?"

"Well, yes and no. In fact, I wanted a chance to talk to you for a moment." Dawson gave Porter an oblique view of his warrant card. "It won't take long. I want to ask you about a couple of your directors: Alison Travers; Marie Wallace."

Porter looked at Dawson steadily for a moment, then down at his own toecaps. The bird roosted on the bridge of his nose. Without raising his voice he said, "I'm going to show you to the door, now—see you out to the street. This is a private function and you're not invited. Later, I'll be having a word with your superiors." Porter's hands were in his pockets, his back slightly stooped —a very casual pose; the handkerchief trailed from his wrist. "You know you're not supposed to be here." The voice was thick with condescension.

Dawson followed Porter to the door. His hands were also in his pockets, fists bunched, nails digging white half moons in the fat of his palms. Porter opened the door as if he were putting a cat out for the night, his eyes and attention already elsewhere. The blond girl looked over from a circle of designer clothes, designer hair, designer accessories, to catch Dawson's eye. She fed him a little laugh that was pure delight, pure poison.

As he pulled out of the side street, Dawson snapped his lights on to full beam for a second, illuminating the front of the Porsche. Then he activated the radio and gave his call sign.

A man's voice copied in.

Dawson transmitted the name of the street, the area, the registration number and make of the Porsche. "It's causing an obstruction," he said. "Get it towed away as soon as possible. Within the next fifteen minutes: okay?"

The voice was clearly amused. "Friend of yours?"

"My bank manager," Dawson said.

"They're on their way."

When he got home, he telephoned Culley at the hotel.

"He knew who I was. Behaved as if he'd been half-expecting a visit."

"Then what?"

"Kicked me out of the place. Same set of circumstances elsewhere, I'd've nicked the guy for obstruction. He could tell that wasn't going to happen."

"Friends in high places."

"Sure. But something more positive. It was as if he knew I shouldn't be there. And knew that I knew that."

"Okay," Culley said.

"What do you want me to do?"

"Lay off, for the time being. I mean, don't go back there; don't make waves. If Protheroe hauls you in, say I told you to do it."

"I can look after myself."

Culley sighed. "I don't need a buddy. Make it my idea—an order —and only one of us gets his hand slapped."

"Are you okay?" Dawson asked.

"Sore throat. All right, otherwise. Listen—don't rattle Porter's cage anymore . . . but you can still run some discreet checks on the two major shareholders."

"Well, I can find their addresses, credit ratings, mortgage allowances, time payments, bank balances, and savings accounts. But that's not what we want to know, is it?"

"It doesn't tell us who they are, no; nor what their connection is with Porter. Take a look anyway."

As he dialed Helen's number, Culley chanted under his breath: "If you would like to leave a message . . ."

Helen's voice said, ". . . but if you would like to leave a message, I'll . . ."

Eric Ross came clear of the coppice and paused, looking down at the tower. It showed a sharp, dark outline against a sky made pale by the light of a half-moon. He was carrying only the gun case. His other possessions were lodged in a rock cleft on the west side of the moor.

He'd gone into the town for food, finding a small cache of money in the first house he burgled, then going to a supermarket. He had seen the newspaper placards and the headlines on his way back. The report told him about the dead people; it told him that the shots had come from the tower. It said that the police had refused to speculate on the possibility that London's sniper had moved south. The paper wasn't afflicted by that coyness. It was sure that the killings had been the work of the same man.

Ross had stood in the street, bags of shopping at his feet, and read the article slowly, twice, because it was difficult to absorb. He felt angry and cheated. He felt tearful and puzzled. He felt diminished. None of the things he felt made sense to him, but they burned.

He had walked to the parking lot, though his real interest didn't lie there. He had gone to the tower and glanced up toward its turrets, but knew he couldn't approach the folly or try to get inside during daylight hours. Now he returned, using the coppice for cover, then descending the slope at a sidling run that took him to the door.

It was late: the small hours; the road nearby was free of traffic. He stood in the dark, his back to the flint wall of the tower, and listened to the sounds of the night. After two or three minutes, he turned to the door and eased it outward.

Inside, the wind made little whickering echoes around the walls. Ross lit a match, sending a halo of light pulsing out to the crossbeams and the curve of the stairway, then held it aloft while he crossed to the stair and set his foot on the first tread—an explorer stepping onto a dark continent.

The view from the crenellations was heady. Either side and behind him, the edge of the country, fields and trees humped in the half-dark, a distant river showing a snail-slick of silver; in front of him the town.

He looked down at the parking lot, hedged by neon fog. It was empty. Beyond it, a glitter of streetlights, headlights, lights from windows and from doorways. He opened the case and took out the scope.

And, suddenly, there they were. The creatures he preyed on, the creatures he fed upon. Walking in the streets, looking into windows, going in and out of buildings: all their mysterious comings and goings. A great flush of excitement and heat welled in his chest and spread on his torso like a rash of lust. His scalp tightened and tingled and he felt the hairs of his head lift. There they were.

Had Martin felt like this? Had it been the same for him when he killed those people? Ross sat on the parapet in the only place possible to allow an effective shot at the parking lot. He had to stretch his legs out in front of him; the scope would only travel comfortably to the right. In his mind, Ross peopled the space, making them busy with parcels, shopping, coats, strollers . . . The night wind cooled the fever in his cheeks, and seemed to give him buoyancy. He closed his eyes and fell outward from the tower, a dark shape on the night sky, homing to the constellation of lights, thrilled by the clap and clatter of his own wings as he descended.

He wondered whether he'd slept: the dream had been so intense.

Martin, he thought, you drew me on. You knew you would. He swung his legs down and looked back toward the coppice. Suddenly, he felt very exposed up there on the battlements, a man-shape against the stern geometry of stone. He ducked down and assembled the gun before opening the trapdoor; then he lit a fistful of matches, holding them a moment to make the sulfur congeal, and threw the little flare down into the well of the tower. Nothing. He went down as Jackson had done, back braced to the wall. At the door, he paused to listen. Nothing again.

He emerged low, rolling left, away from the slope and into the cover afforded by the tower itself, then lay still. The gun case was a burden to him. He squatted and pulled his belt through two loops, threaded it through the handle of the case, then rebuckled it. When he got up into a crouch, it swung clumsily at his hip, but his hands were free. He went up the slope at a slow run, looking around all the time and making a wide angle across the grass toward the side of the coppice furthest from a direct route to the tower.

I'm right, aren't I, Martin?

A gust went through the trees, then died in the leaves, as if a room had fallen silent. The sudden hush reminded Ross of a bar close to the Wall in West Berlin, everyone quiet in the same moment and Martin Jackson walking forward. It was halfway through their tour of duty on the Rhine.

You could see that the girl was a hooker; all in all, she would have expected to take her chances, like the rest. Three French soldiers had picked her up; now they were tired of her. Too drunk, maybe, or else they'd already taken turns somewhere before getting to the bar. One minute they were all laughing, the next she was yelling. They hadn't paid her; or they hadn't paid her enough. The soldiers were still laughing. One of them flapped a hand at her, more dismissive than angry. She mistook it for a blow and fought back, glancing the heel of her hand across his brow.

The laughing stopped. The man she'd hit turned her by the shoulders and booted her toward the door, getting his heel hard into the small of her back. She fell into a table, scattering drinks. Her next move was to leave the bar. It was—but she didn't make it. Incredibly, stupidly, she went back and took a swing at the nearest soldier. He ducked, grabbed her by one arm, and slapped her hard across the face before tossing her to the next man, who did the same, then passed her on. That was when they started laughing again.

She went around and around the circle of three men, always in motion, slapped hard and handed on. Her face hooked sideways with each impact, her eyes banged shut. Her body was ungainly with speed and panic; spatters of blood sprang up on her blouse, on her arms, in her hair.

The bar was loud with voices—protest, alarm, excitement, whoops of encouragement. Jackson's shout had risen above all of them and the room had grown still as he walked forward. The soldiers paused to watch him come, the nearest of them holding the girl one-handed, as a child holds a rag doll.

Jackson had stood in front of them, unspeaking, a wry, almost apologetic smile on his face.

It seemed like yesterday, or else another person's life. On the edge of the coppice, Ross got down on his haunches to wait.

Jackson had seen Ross on the tower and had taken a wide circle that would bring him to a point just below the door. He had kept his eyes on the outline atop the tower all the time—or so it had seemed to him. One second he had the shape in view, the next it had gone. He'd stopped—both puzzled and worried. He was sure he couldn't have been seen or heard; but the figure had disappeared. He'd peered into the almost-dark; he'd bowed his head to listen; then he had continued down the slope, making for the precise spot on the blind side of the door where, at that moment, Ross was hitching his gun case to his belt.

When Ross gained the shelter of the trees, Jackson crouched as Ross had crouched, his feet where the other man's feet had been, as if nothing had changed. He straightened and moved a couple of paces around the tower. He gazed at the door. Above him, Ross had his eyes fixed on the battlements.

To stand face to face; no distant good-byes. Jackson eased in through the wedge of space where the door was yanked back, then went immediately left—away from the natural swivel of a right-handed man. With the trapdoor closed, the darkness was intense. Jackson went into a crouch. He was holding the Beretta in a double grip, arms extended, and playing the barrel around the invisible walls like a man spraying water from a hose.

He allowed the silence for two or three minutes, listening so hard that his own eardrums gave him back a sound of the sea, then he eased a lightweight flashlight from the flap of his camouflage jacket and set it on the floor, as far to his right as his reach would permit. The flashlight was small, but had a wide-angled beam. Jackson snapped it on and rolled left, one complete body-turn, then came up with the gun on full cock. He looked at bare walls. Then he looked up at the trapdoor.

The wind had shifted slightly and was coming off the moor. You could smell something like iodine. Furze and the granite-bedded brooks. Jackson walked once around the crenellations, like a sentry, then settled at the point where the town was in view. He was surprised and faintly disappointed.

Eric . . . Another night. Tomorrow, perhaps. But I'm sure you'll come. We'll meet. We'll have time for our good-byes.

He stood up and a hand slapped his shoulder, a comradely gesture. A word of greeting hummed off into the night.

Jackson scored his knees and the heels of his hands as he hit the flint-and-render base of the battlements. He worked his shoulder and felt nothing. When he put his hand there, the material was holed; he reached farther back and found the ragged exit tear. His fingers came away bloody from the scratch.

He rolled to the trapdoor, went down the stairs in a rush and straight through the door without losing momentum. The rifle's extended crack was shot and echo merging. A bullet went through the rotten wood of the door with a sound like a pebble flung into the undertow of a wave. Jackson looked toward the wall that bordered the road. The shots had been unmistakable. Soon enough, the road would be bright with headlights. He imagined Ross, under the brow of the hill, quartering the ground with his night-scope.

Keeping an angle that extended the line of Ross's fire, Jackson ran backward from the tower to the wall. It wasn't the best way out. The route to the moor had already been taken by Ross; blocked by Ross. He went over the wall like a jockey bent low to his mount, then headed away from the town and began to run. The banshee note of a siren whipped him on.

The sloping field was chalky with floodlighting; you almost expected the teams to run on amid yells and chants from the fans. Culley stood at the very top of a long shaft of shadow cast by the tower—a lone figure atop the ramparts. Chris Bullen slogged up the field to join him.

"Two shots, we think. Five reports came in, each of them the same. They're looking for the bullet that went through the door." A block of fierce light illuminated the door space and the interior of the tower. Men moved inside, almost invisible in the white glow, like foundry hands working close to the incandescence of a furnace.

"What do you make of it?" Culley asked.

Bullen moved to stand alongside. Both men looked downhill, their faces in darkness. "Someone with a high-powered rifle having a joke. Someone with a high-powered rifle wanting to know how it feels. Someone with a high-powered rifle intending to copycat, losing his nerve, and loosing off at the tower instead." He paused. "Or the man himself."

"Why?"

Bullen shook his head. "Fuck knows."

Or two men. One man shooting at the other. *We're on the moor.*

Culley prodded the night bell. A porter let him in and handed him his key. Culley glanced up at the pigeonhole to check that the spare was in place. It held an envelope that hadn't been there before.

The map was part of a foldout page torn from an old guidebook, the kind of volume a local library would keep in stock. It showed a section of the moor; a thick pencil had been used to emphasize the tightening, concentric rings of contour that culminated in a blind circle and the words "Bethel Tor." Culley glanced at it, then tossed it onto the bedside table while he fetched a scotch. It seemed a casual, dismissive action, but he was faking indifference even though alone—a performance without an audience.

He sat on the bed, scotch in one hand, the fragment of map in the other.

Kemp knew about me, he thought. Someone knew I'd be coming here: which hotel, which room. Porter knew about Mike Dawson. What do I know? Nothing. I know they are on the moor. With this map, I even know where on the moor they are likely to be. But I don't know who they are.

He finished his drink and set his alarm for four-thirty, then lay back, leaving the light on and the torn map propped up against the clock like a formal invitation.

48

THEY WERE CALLED CORPSE LIGHTS, the pale flames that ran on the marsh at night. Culley had stepped onto the moor in the hour before dawn. On all sides, little licks of fire had sprung up and died, now there, now gone, like tiny beacons in a fog.

His partial map had given him the access road and the approximate direction; he had made a mile or so before sunrise, now he was working off landmarks.

In the first dawn light, the moor was awesome. Endless bleakness. Granite outcrops, storm-scoured until they were worn down to a hard, heartless, irreducible core; becks running cold and brown to meet the shifting ground of the mire; hills like clenched fists. Under gale and downpour, under ice, under drought, the landscape had given all it had to give.

A wind came in from the northwest, seeming to swoop down

the escarpments and rush at head height across the cropped turf. Sheep turned their backs to it, their fleece thickening after the summer shearing. It was a cool day in late summer, but the moor made its own weather.

Culley was wearing jeans, sneakers, sweater, and a light anorak. He didn't know the moor, but he knew that it wasn't yet time for deaths from exposure. Those deaths would come soon enough— foolish humans, and animals who had nowhere else to go.

He topped a rise that put him in sight of a stone circle. The map showed the tor standing half a mile east of that, below the ridge of the next hill. As he started down, a lark went up from the turf under his feet, rising in a clean vertical as if hauled up on the plumb line of its own song. Another went up, its wedge-shaped breast cleaving the air like a prow. One by one, they spiraled through the air, muscular and hysterical, then drifted back to earth, one by one, silent, solemn, used-up.

Culley crossed the plateau, coming within sight of the great stone. The early-morning cloud was thinning, making the light sharper. Enough to see a buzzard turning slow circles over the far hilltop. Someone coming down from the crest in a crouching run. The shape of a man at the pinnacle of Bethel Tor.

Eric Ross saw the place in rain—himself standing in the wind-driven pour, listening for the stamp of boots and the hoarse bellow from the sergeant who ran on the flank. Martin was there, a quiet presence at his side. The squaddies ran past the tor. Ross stepped clear of cover and fired. He remembered how Halliday had levered himself onto his elbows to drag the dead weight of his legs, and how the squaddies had circled the body, staring down.

He remembered these things as he watched Jackson making an angled descent of the hillside, finding cover in folds of ground or in among the litter of granite that spread to the apron of ground beneath the tor. He knew that Jackson must have seen him, just as he'd been seen—unmissable, cross-legged on top of the stone. They were about five or six minutes apart. Ross swung his legs over the side and slid to a lip of rock on the blind side. The stone offered footholds more secure than a ladder. When his feet hit the rubble of scree at the rock's base, he loosened his grip and slid the rest of the way. The rifle was leaning nearby—he felt that secure. He picked it up without breaking his downward and outward slide, and started toward a cluster of earth mounds two hundred yards away.

. . .

Eric. Jackson was smiling as he ran. Up there like a flag on a pole. Like a tin cockerel to tell me which way the wind's blowing. This is better, isn't it? Oh, yes; better now that you've stopped avoiding me. The smile was marred by a gap on the left side, close to the front, where Culley's heel had taken out the canine. The cavity throbbed perpetually. Jackson dismissed it as he would a field wound.

He glanced up and saw that Ross had gone. No surprise; except that he'd expected the man to wait a little longer. He turned from the line of approach that was taking him down to the rock and sprinted hard toward open ground. The tor would still cover him, but he would emerge from its shelter some twenty yards beyond it and looking straight toward the earth mounds.

Culley knew that the one place he shouldn't be was between the two men. There was no chance to move across the open ground toward the tor without being stranded in clear view. He doubled back in order to get cover beyond the rising ground that had first put him in sight of the tor, then started to circle toward Ross's position. He wondered which of the two men had tried to kill him.

Running on the slope was difficult. Culley tried to miss the worst of the rough ground while still concentrating on the direction he was taking and trying to remain unseen. A line of pain had started up in his chest, reminding him that he hadn't taken much exercise lately. It was a nuisance now; it would stop him eventually. He made fifty yards and found a long fold in the terrain, even and smooth-topped like a burial mound. He ran to the point where it began to peter out—just at head height—and looked over into the bowl of the valley.

The tor stood on the lower part of the opposite slope, about a hundred and fifty yards to Culley's right. The earth mounds lay to the left. Culley looked back toward the tor and searched the ground, trying to find Jackson; nothing was moving, nothing out of place. Then he looked toward the mounds. Somewhere in there. Anywhere in there . . .

He went back down the slope, taking himself out of sight, and continued to run toward Eric Ross.

. . .

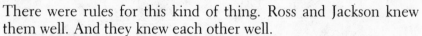

There were rules for this kind of thing. Ross and Jackson knew them well. And they knew each other well.

Come up on the flank—that was one rule. One man can't work a pincer movement, so the attack can only come from one side. But which side? Look at the terrain and see where the advantages lie. Then, when you've found them, wonder whether your enemy won't choose the less obvious side: the less advantageous. Then wonder whether he'll guess what you're thinking and, for that reason, come up on the other.

Don't break cover—that was another rule. If you keep out of sight, your enemy doesn't know whether you've stayed put, or *have* broken cover without being seen. So he'll be looking for you in more than one place; that'll split his concentration. But maybe he'll know that rule too and assume you won't have moved. So perhaps you should move.

Don't be drawn. Let the other guy make the moves—and the mistakes. Unless the move he makes involves getting behind you. In which case, the mistake was yours.

Keep moving, keep the advantage. Unless the move you make is directly into his sights.

Ross thought through the options. He put himself in Jackson's place—coming downhill, seeing Ross atop the tor one minute and gone the next. He would peel off, move back from the stone to give himself a view of the terrain beyond. A gamble, since Ross could have stayed blind side of the tor. But Jackson would have found cover to go to in case Ross had decided to snipe from there. He'd have bellied down behind a boulder and watched Ross disappearing in among the complex of mounds, too far and too fast for a shot.

Now he'd be deciding what to do. Gain ground, Ross was sure of that. Jackson would want to close the distance. It was in his nature to take the initiative. He would move forward, finding cover where he could, liking it more the nearer he got—until he was as close as you could get without being seen, as close as the other side of a door, beside the window, just around the corner, close enough to hear you breathing, close enough to touch.

And what would Jackson expect of him, of Ross? That he'd double bluff on the rule that said "don't break cover." Why? Because it was Ross's strongest inclination to do that. He had to force his mind beyond the point where the double bluff succeeded, taking his thinking into an area where everything was risk. Don't move equals move when you bluff. Bluff on move—don't move. Now go one further. *Move.*

Ross went to the edge of the mounds, keeping low. He would take a chance on getting below the slope, then move up to the long lip in the ground some fifty yards back. That way, Jackson would have to pass at right angles across Ross's line of fire; and he would be looking straight ahead.

At the edge of the mounds was fifteen yards of flat, open ground; then the slope. Ross knew there was no guessing whether or not he would be seen. It was the one moment of gamble. He gathered himself, hefted his rifle, then sprinted at the crouch over the cropped turf.

Jackson had already begun his move forward. He was belly-down behind a clump of boulders some fifty yards back from the mounds. He had trained a rifle about center of the area and was giving himself five minutes to look and listen before shifting position again. He hadn't seen Ross break cover.

Dry grasses fluttered like banners. The wind was a drone; it seemed to be finding crevices in the rock and using them like the lip of a flute—one sorrowful, fluctuating note, almost inaudible.

Then—suddenly—a row somewhere away to Jackson's left, as if someone had put up a game bird with a shout and a clap of the hands. He snapped around, getting into a half-crouch, and saw Ross standing head and shoulders above the little bank where the ground dipped.

Culley had seen Ross coming. He didn't count that much of an advantage; Ross was carrying a gun. While Jackson was looking directly toward the mounds, Culley was alongside the low ridge, pausing from time to time to take stock. The ridge was curved like a section of amphitheater, the curve becoming more acute as the ground grew shallower. Culley had realized that he would soon have to go at a crouch in order to remain unseen. He'd taken a breather, then followed the line of cover. Each step had taken him closer to the mounds. Then he'd seen Ross drop below the ridge, swiftly and silently, and begin to work his way forward on elbows and knees.

Culley had fallen back at once. There was a point where the

wall of the ridge bore a sharp, vertical rib, a line of erosion with a small hollow behind it. Culley had gotten into the niche, his back bent as if he were a pauper buried in an upright grave. He hadn't known what to do. He'd listened, trying to ignore the sound of the wind.

Ross's approach had sounded like the onset of rain, a rapid patter together with a sweeping noise that might have been his shoulder against the wall of the ridge. As he reached the niche, Culley stepped out of cover and kicked, trying for the gun. He half-connected and the weapon swung in Ross's hand. Ross shied from Culley's sudden appearance and, at the same time, instinctively grabbed at the rifle as it threatened to fly from his grasp.

Doing that, he straightened up. And Jackson saw him.

It was clear to Jackson that something was happening that he couldn't see. Ross was moving awkwardly, his gaze focused on a point below the level of the ridge. Then Culley came into view as well, lurching to one side with the momentum of his kick. Instinct made Jackson center his sights and fire. Ross's arm was lofted as he went after his gun. The bullet took him under the armpit, driving him backward and down. The second shot went through the fleshy part of his waist.

Culley lunged sideways. It seemed he was going for the man, to drag him back into cover. Instead, he hooked up the gun and looked over the ridge for a target. Ross curled and stretched like a worm, going inch by inch for the hollow where Culley had hidden.

With the ground at eye level, everything seemed to be in movement, grasses fluttering, furze bushes rocking slightly, even boulders stirring . . . Culley loosed off a shot, removing slivers of granite, and Jackson froze. Ross was tucked into the base of the ridge now, his head tilted back. He put out an arm, knocking Culley's leg, as if wanting to draw attention to himself. The color had gone from his face; even his lips were white. Culley could only guess at how much blood there might be beneath the man's waterproof anorak. He looked back toward the boulders, but saw no movement.

They made slow progress. Culley had sat behind Ross and hooked his feet under the man's arms. It meant his ankle was chafing on the wound, but no other method would work if they were to stay below the level of the ridge—both men sitting, Culley using his arms to heave backward and towing Ross, who was using his legs in the same way. They moved spasmodically, bodies linked but extended. Because Culley was using his arms, Ross cradled the gun. It didn't seem much of a risk; Culley was astonished that the man was still conscious.

Little by little, they covered the ground to the earth mounds, their knees rising in unison, then flexing as they levered with their heels, Culley's arms pulling backward over the gained ground. They looked like rowers in a two-man scull. Culley expected to see a face appear above them at any moment.

When they reached the flat ground between the slope and the mounds, Culley moved to be facing Ross, hunkered down. He pulled the man's arms around like a shawl, then straightened, bearing the load across his shoulders. They were in plain view. Culley raced across the open ground. The rifle in Ross's clasped hands knocked against Culley's midriff.

Jackson must have been looking for them elsewhere, because his shot came late and wild. Culley ducked at the sound, then stumbled, unshipping Ross behind the first of the mounds and going after him with the rapid, uncontrolled stagger of a man who has just stepped off a moving bus. He fell alongside Ross and reached for the gun. Ross was semiconscious, gripping the weapon reflexively. Culley had to yank it free. He rolled, going sideways of the mound for a look, and a bullet whickered past. He fired back, aiming at the boulders, not knowing whether he was likely to find a target still there or not. Then he hoisted Ross around his shoulders again, and began to jog back through the mounds, the rifle clutched in one hand. The earthworks would give him cover for a brief while; and at least he wouldn't be there if the other man moved in. He hoped that was what was happening. He needed time to find fresh cover.

Jackson came forward in a series of snaky runs. He was angry—principally with himself. The shots had been wholly reflexive. He knew Eric wasn't dead, though. Culley had been carrying him. Important to get close, to talk to Eric before he died. To see him die.

He went into the dunes at the same side as Culley and Ross had done, and began to run among them like a stoat in a warren.

. . .

A barbed-wire fetter tightened across Culley's chest. He could feel beads of sweat gathering along his collarbones like a damp yoke, then sluicing across his chest and belly. He was making for a dip in the ground that lay some one hundred yards beyond the mounds. Ross seemed to have passed out. As Culley had left cover, his pace had quickened, jouncing Ross, and the man had given a little shout of outrage and pain with each step. Now he was silent.

Culley needed that open space—the space he was now crossing. One of the rules said: Make your opponent come at you across terrain that offers no cover. It also said: Never cross such ground yourself. He knew he ought to be weaving as he ran, but the load was too great, the extra effort too taxing, and swerving too much of an invitation to stumble. Every moment, he expected the impact of a bullet. He felt as though he had a target tacked over his spine.

He didn't see the dip when he reached it. He stepped into thin air and came down heavily on the sole of his foot, knocking the breath from his lungs. He sat bolt upright, the bank to his back, and gulped at the air with a fish mouth; Ross lay where he had fallen, across Culley's knees. Still recovering, Culley rolled him off and lay full length on his belly to look back toward the mounds. No one.

Culley allowed a few seconds to look at Ross. His breathing was a series of brief, shuddering gasps and his eyes were partly open, showing a sickle of white. Because he'd been carried head downward, blood had run in rivulets from the neck of his waterproof, dark, glutinous tracks that meandered from his throat across his face and into his hair like a red web. When Culley looked down at himself he realized that what he'd mistaken for sweat beads had been drops of Ross's blood. His coat was patched with it; when he opened the coat, his sweater was saturated.

He got back to the bank in time to see Jackson starting out from the mounds. He watched the man make two little zigzag runs, each covering fifteen or twenty feet. Between runs, he dropped from sight. Disappeared completely.

Shit, Culley thought, this guy's good. He sighted on the point where he'd seen Jackson last. Before he'd had time to react and adjust his aim, a figure rose fifteen feet from the spot, made another run, and dropped. He was already halfway to Culley's position.

I've just run that terrain, Culley thought. There's no fucking cover out there. Where *are* you? He pulled left of the ground Jackson had vanished into, held his aim, and waited.

He had guessed about right, but Jackson's appearance was so abrupt, and his run so fast and mazy, that Culley's shot did nothing more than announce his presence. Jackson seemed to go down in the same instant as the shot was heard. He hadn't found the piece of ground he was making for, though; Culley could see an undulation that was neither rock nor turf. He fired, going just wide. Jackson did the only thing possible: he got up, putting himself in full view, and ran to the place he'd originally intended to reach. It was the last thing Culley had expected. He didn't even have time to get off a shot.

It was a case of when Culley would decide to run. No one could find cover on that ground forever—certainly not at close range. At some point, Jackson would have to stop. He couldn't expect Culley to miss if he made a rush to Culley's position from twenty or thirty yards away. It would be a stand-off. Except that Jackson would have put himself in a position where he couldn't move. So Culley —unless he decided on siege tactics—would have to be the person who did.

Beyond the bank, the land began to slope away, folding into a shallow valley. If he headed straight downhill, Culley would be able to stay off the skyline. But the hillside was entirely open; once Jackson got to the brow he would have a clear sight of anyone in the valley or on either slope. The other choice was to continue along the bank; it would afford a little protection for a while, and he might find more cover that way; but if he didn't he'd be in Jackson's sights whether the man moved or not.

Culley gathered Ross's wrists, hauled him upright, then ducked under the falling body and took its weight. He ran doubled for the first twenty steps, wanting his head well below the level of the slope. Then he straightened and quickened his pace, going crabwise to steady himself against the valleyside. His shoulder muscles, his leg muscles, the muscles in his back all shrieked against it. His chest was aflame.

There's a rule that says: If everything seems hopeless, make a stand. Put your back to something. Hold out. It says: Find the opposition's only weakness and use it.

Jackson knew that rule. In Culley's position, he would have gone for siege. It was the only thing to do. Jackson had to cross twenty yards of featureless ground—a perfect target; he had to do that or pull back. It was his only weakness. Culley's role was to stay put and hope that Jackson would give him a free shot. Jackson wasn't going to do that, of course. He was waiting for Culley to do something stupid—try to run, come straight at him, offer a deal.

Stay put: that was the rule. Jackson knew it; Culley didn't. By the time Jackson realized that a rule had been broken—by the time he made his final run to the dip in the ground, and looked down into the valley beyond—Culley was out of sight.

All he could hear was the sound of his own footfalls and the crash of his heartbeat. All he could feel was pain. Impossible to tell how far behind Jackson might be, impossible to know how far he had to go before reaching the road. Ross rode his shoulders like a carcass. A wheezy grunt came with every bounce. From time to time, they knocked heads.

There was a small conifer plantation to Culley's left—less than half a mile away. He made for that, wanting the protection the trees would provide. It wasn't clear to him how long he could keep moving; the fact that he was moving at all seemed miraculous. For the last fifteen minutes a voice in his brain had been telling him to stop. Recently, it had begun to scream.

When he crossed the treeline, it was still there—high and strident and louder than ever. He almost began to believe he was shrieking out loud. Then he heard it for what it was and turned to the sound.

Two of them—one wielding the bandsaw, one driving wedges. They had felled five trees; the sixth was toppling into the grid of trunks alongside. The trees were in die-straight lines up and across except where felling had laid broad avenues among the plantation. A small bulldozer had been used to clear the stumps. It was parked close by, its scoop blade canted up.

Culley appeared at the far end of a clearing as wide as a highway. Someone with nothing left; empty-eyed. He began to jog toward the men. They watched the tree fall and turned to the next. Then the man who was hitting wedges tapped his partner and pointed.

They came forward, each with his arms spread, like TV evangelists, and Culley unloaded Ross onto them. As he did so, everything cramped. Biceps, forearms, shoulders, back, legs. The rictus bent him over on himself, arms crossed, fingers splayed like broken straws; the pain was unspeakable.

The loggers took Culley and Ross out on the 'dozer blade, one man driving, one standing in the blade to steady the bodies.

49

IT WAS LIKE A LITANY, except that the responses didn't fall as they should.

Are you the sniper?
What's your name?
Who hired you?
All Ross would say was "Yes." He looked at the ceiling, his arms lying on top of the covers but aligned with his body, still as an effigy. His face was expressionless and his lips barely moved when he gave his answer—on each occasion to the first question only.

Are you the sniper?
"Yes."
What's your name?
Who hired you?
It seemed that he didn't blink, but that was just his stillness. The nurse said that his eyes hadn't closed all night.

Are you the—
"Yes."

Culley emerged from the gantries of steel and plastic tubing, drains, drips, monitors. Chris Bullen was peering in through the

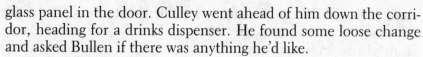

glass panel in the door. Culley went ahead of him down the corridor, heading for a drinks dispenser. He found some loose change and asked Bullen if there was anything he'd like.

"Coffee?"

"You're right to make it a question." He thumbed the money in. "I'll risk it, too."

"Still saying nothing," Bullen suggested.

"Still saying nothing he hasn't said before." Culley handed over a Styrofoam cup. "You can have a try if you like."

Bullen held up his free hand, palm outward. "All yours, until someone gives orders that say otherwise." He adopted a tone of official pomposity. "We have issued a communiqué."

Culley grinned. "I know someone who talks like that."

"Of course you do," Bullen said. "We all do."

"What does it say? The communiqué."

"That we've arrested the sniper. That he's confessed. That we're withholding his name at present."

"Mention me?"

"Not either of us specifically. The statement went out half an hour ago. The press is camped on the hospital forecourt."

Culley glanced back up the corridor to where a uniformed officer sat on a chair outside Ross's room. "What have we got for security?"

"Him, a man at the main door, surveillance front and back on a permanent basis, roving surveillance of the grounds." Bullen sipped his coffee, then looked at it in disbelief. "What did your lot say?"

Protheroe had sounded businesslike. "You got the bastard. Good." Then, "Who's this other man? What's his story?" Finally, he'd said, "Get him back here—back to London. We can work on him here."

"He can't be moved . . . Four days, maybe six." Culley had been working on the best prognosis.

"Back here," Protheroe's voice had been impatient with repetition. "As soon as possible."

Mike Dawson had said, "It's not really about him, is it? If you're right about Kemp and Porter and the rest."

It was and it wasn't. There were things Culley wanted to know for himself.

Bullen set his coffee down on top of the dispenser and followed Culley back toward the room. "Nothing on mug shots, nothing from his clothing. He's anonymous. The gun's right, of course."

"He'll have to be taken to London," Culley said, "as soon as he's fit to travel."

Bullen sounded slightly peevish. "He killed two of ours . . ."

"Statistics give him to us," Culley remarked. "They want him up there."

"Specialists?"

"Psychiatrists by the roomful, I expect."

"Oh—" Bullen raised his eyes, a man in search of the perfect response. In the end, he just said, "Yes. Psychiatrists." As if it were in some way connected, he added, "The bullet was lodged in the chest cavity. Broke a rib, missed the aorta by a hair. Missed everything else of note as well. The abdominal wound wasn't much. Mostly, he just lost a hell of a lot of blood."

Culley nodded and put a hand on the door. He'd spoken to the surgeon himself.

"Take a break," Bullen advised.

A day and a night waiting while Ross was operated on, while he recovered from the anesthetic, while tests were run, while consultants wagged their fingers under Culley's nose and made pompous remarks about how their commitment to the patient came before all else. As if, under their hands, Ross grew pure. As if their knives cut out the bad. As if the blood they fed into him might wash him clean.

Culley went into the room and took his place by the bed. Ross's head didn't move.

What's your name?

Who hired you?

Are you the sniper?

"Yes."

They gave him a certain length of time for each session. When he wasn't at the bedside, Culley slept on a couch in a small annex where people waited for bad news. If sleep wouldn't come, he drank coffee and fretted until they let him go back to the room.

A nurse went by and smiled at him. A celebrity. The man who . . .

He walked along the corridor to Ross's room. A different officer was on duty. They nodded at one another because rank didn't matter if no one else was there. Culley looked in on Ross as a parent looks in on a sleeping child. The light in the room was soft, enough to allow the nurses who checked from time to time to read the monitors and be sure that the drip needles were still properly attached. Ross's eyes glittered as he looked at the ceiling.

Culley went in and sat by the bed. He said, "You had a bullet in your chest, a flesh wound in your side. You're okay. You're going to be okay." Ross's breathing was even; it didn't change. "I don't know the moor. I expect you do. I don't. They tell me it was over three miles from the place where you were hit to the plantation where I got help. You don't remember that—a fir plantation. Two guys brought us out on a bulldozer—caterpillar tracks, a big scoop in front. Over three miles. Nearly four. I carried you. Do you remember?"

Ross might have been in a coma. He neither spoke nor moved. He breathed through his nose, his mouth a firm line.

"I carried you all that way," said Culley. "If I hadn't you would be dead. He would have killed you." A pause. "Whoever he is. Who is he?" Culley thought he saw a flicker in one eyelid, the slightest droop. "I saved your life," Culley said, "do I get anything for that?"

They kept silence for a time, side by side, one lying, one sitting, like analyst and analysand.

"Tell me about it. I know more than you think, but I still don't know enough. Jay Hammond, wasn't it? He was the mark. And the others to cover your tracks. But how did you start? How did you make your choices? Never mind the other man. Never mind who hired you to do it. Don't tell me about them, not now. Tell me about you. Tell me about killing those people."

The eyelid moved again, a shutter on the world.

"You wake up in the morning. It's a bright day. A dull day. It's raining. You know you're going to kill someone. More than one. Do you know how many? Do you think: men or women? Do you think: young or old? How do you choose? Someone who looks like your wife? Someone who looks like your father? Do you think: she's waking up, too; he's waking up? On the day of their deaths . . . You're cleaning your teeth? So are they. You're drinking coffee? So are they. Do you think how your hand is touching their lives already? As if you had tapped them on the shoulder. And still you don't know who they are. They don't know each other. They don't know you. They never will."

. . .

The hospital hummed around them. In every room, in every ward, people tiptoed toward health or slipped deeper into illness. In their waking hours, they thought about the tricks that bodies can play.

Culley felt a great weariness come over him; it might have been he, not Ross, who was recovering from surgery. In the moment that his eyes closed, Ross's closed too, and they dozed together for a while, old men on a park bench taking the last of the summer sun. Fifteen minutes passed, twenty . . . A doctor went past Ross's door at a flat-out run, his bleeper insistent as a goad. Culley opened his eyes. He didn't see Ross's head turn, but he knew that the other man had woken sooner and had been watching him.

"Tell me about it. Tell me how it feels. You've found a place—a clear route in and out; a good field of fire. Then you . . . what? Do you wait a while—do you enjoy the moment? Or is it too strong for that? Linger, or choose them fast and kill them? Which? Which are you—a gourmet, or a hungry man?"

A shadow moved on Ross's face, like a flake of ash stirred by an outward breath. Perhaps a smile.

"The excitement—where does it start? In your balls, in your belly? At the back of your throat, somewhere behind the eyes? Where? What's it like when you see them there—what do they look like? What are they doing? Hurrying or dawdling; waiting for someone, trying to keep an appointment . . .

"You look at them through the scope—is that right? Before you decide, before you know for sure. And it's just that moment in their lives, isn't it? Just that second, that tick of the clock. And everything's going to change; everything's going to end. In a second; in a tick. How does it feel? To be that powerful, that *conclusive?* Does it start in your balls, or somewhere behind the eyes? You look down on them, you see them, and you choose. Or perhaps they choose themselves."

It might have been that Ross's eyes, just for an instant, widened; the reflex of a cat's pupil in the dark. The shadow that had touched his lips ran on his brow. The bare bones of a frown.

"By being there, by choosing that place, that time; by looking the way they look, by choosing that coat or that shirt. Could it be that? Is it that? Although they can't know it, they've chosen themselves? And you look at them, and you say, 'All right. If that's what you want.'

"And afterwards—after it's over . . . Do you dream about it? Do you live it again? Do you go through it, moment by moment—the sighting, the choice, the instant before when nothing could be more normal, the instant afterward, when everything's changed? How do you see yourself? What are you? What do you become? Do you change too?

"Afterward . . . Is it sorrow, or joy? Excitement, still—or sadness? Do you think of what you've just done, or of what you might do? Is that it? Do you think of the next time? What's that like? Is it a plan, or a dream?"

Culley was dizzied by his own voice, by his own soft questioning. He had been leaning forward in his chair, like someone divulging a confidence, and his back ached.

"What do you become? Do you change too? Is it a plan, or a dream?"

The shadow was on Ross's lips again, a tremor, slighter than a moth's wing by candlelight.

"Why ask . . ."

Culley bent close to listen. A feather of breath. A whisper whispering.

". . . when you know?"

50

CULLEY MADE HIMSELF INVISIBLE to get through the press blockade. It was easy. You avoided the main entrance, you looked at the ground, you didn't wear a suit. He came back mid-morning. There was a new man outside Ross's room and Culley had to show his ID.

Ross didn't turn his head. Culley walked to the end of the bed and held up a notebook and a pen.

"In case you think of something."

He put them on the shelf of the bedside cabinet. Ross looked straight up. Someone had angled the blinds to halve the daylight. Culley said, "At the moment, it's just me. In a few days, you'll be able to travel—an ambulance ride to London. Then it'll be others. The county police know that they're going to lose you. I don't think they really mind. In the meantime, they've no objection to my sitting beside you in case you decide to say something. It saves them the trouble. In London, it'll be different. In London, you'll feel like some animal at the zoo—everyone clustered around to poke at you through the bars; everyone rattling your cage." He pressed the retractor button on top of the pen, then set it back down atop the notebook. "Think about it."

Faces bobbed in the door's transparent panel, big fish nudging the tank. The man watching the door gestured toward the room and Chris Bullen's head loomed as he peered in. Culley nodded in response. To Ross, he said, "Write me a letter. Dear Robin. Signed . . ." He paused, then joined Bullen in the corridor. They walked off together, Bullen leading the way.

Culley asked, "When did she turn up?"

"Five minutes ago." Bullen was heading for the annex where Culley had spent part of the night. "She was asking questions at reception."

Angie Ross sat in a small armchair, knees and ankles together, hands in her lap; she looked like an applicant. A policewoman sat on an upright chair slightly closer to the open archway that led to the corridor. When Culley and Bullen entered, Angie's head came up as if she expected to recognize one of them. She said, "Can I see him?"

Culley sat down at the end of the sofa closest to Angie's chair, "Who do you think he is?"

"His name's Eric Ross."

"He's your husband?"

"Yes."

"How do you know?"

"The reports—said you'd caught the sniper. That he was here."

"How do you know it's your husband?"

Angie looked at her hands. "Can I see him?"

They walked her past the glass door panel, once going away

303

from the annex, once on the way back, barely allowing her to pause: no more time than if she had stumbled slightly, or hesitated at a curbside. She sat down as she had before, arms and legs neat with dismay.

"You knew all the time." Culley's voice was level and low. Angie didn't reply.

He thought, Someone knows. Almost always—someone knows. He knew that Angie would feel vulnerable and wondered what it would do to offer something, rather than threaten. "Do you want to know how to help?" he asked. "How to help Eric to help us?"

A smile spread on Angie's face. She didn't look up, but the smile spread; she didn't know how to stop it. Finally, it was a great grin, stretching her lips, bunching her cheeks, making slits of her eyes. There was nothing merry about it.

Culley said, "There are things we need to know."

She sat among the drip supports and the bags of fluid and the monitor screens, in the chair Culley had used, her hand on her husband's hand. Ross had been propped up slightly on a bank of pillows. He and Angie might have been watching a movie together.

Culley stood back against the wall on the far side of the corridor and looked at them through the glass. From time to time, Angie spoke. There was no response. She was thin, underweight, her eyes smudged by tiredness, her lips ill-defined. Her hair was fine and lank, so that the tips of her ears pushed through. Culley wondered what she really looked like.

He joined Bullen in the annex and they drove back together. Culley asked, "Who knows?"

"About her? No one. I mean, you, me, the guy outside the room, the policewoman who sat with her before we got there."

"Give me until tonight," Culley said.

"How late tonight?"

"Tomorrow morning."

"Give you?"

"All right," Culley agreed, "give *her.*"

Bullen grimaced. "You really think she'll get something?"

"I think she stands a better chance than me."

"We've already run some checks—now that we've got his name. Someone might ask—"

"He could have given us that."

"Okay." Bullen nodded. 'Tomorrow morning, first thing." He said what Culley had thought earlier. "Someone always knows."

"Mostly. What did they tell us—the checks?"

"Not much. There are some fax sheets on your desk. I should think he's a pro, wouldn't you?"

"I don't imagine he took it up as a hobby."

"No." Bullen looked at the darkness around Culley's eyes and the thick dust of stubble on his cheeks, and decided to ignore his waspishness. "Even so, he's managed to stay anonymous. Small house in south London, nice garden—no one there, of course. The neighbors thought that the wife had taken the kids away for a short holiday. She must have told them that. So I suppose we can manage not to know about her for a bit longer. One of yours—Dawson, is that right?—"

"Yes."

"—asked a few people in the street. Without making a fuss, of course. As far as they're concerned, Ross is no different from the man next door."

"He *is* the man next door."

"Yes, I suppose so. I meant—"

"I know. But that's the point. They have wives, children, friends. They're just like anyone else."

"Except when they shoot people at random, yes."

"I don't mean Ross in particular. Any criminal—robber, killer, swindler, rapist, mugger. They all live somewhere. They all need somewhere to sleep at night, tables to eat at, bathtubs, television sets. For a small part of their lives—of their time—they kill, swindle, rob, whatever. It doesn't stop them getting married, having children, being normal."

"Normal?" Bullen tried the idea out and it failed him.

"Earlier, you said, 'Someone always knows.' The unspoken question was: Why don't they tell? I've wondered about that, too. I think it's because they can persuade themselves it isn't really there—the problem, the burden of knowledge. After all, how do they *know*? Do they see it? No. Are they told about it? Doubtful. Do they want to see it or know about it? Almost certainly not. A man goes out. Later, he comes home. Just like most men do. Only this man has killed, or robbed. But that's out there, wherever it happens, somewhere else. At home, it's not like that. Everything's normal."

"And Ross's wife?"

"I think things stopped being normal for her a while ago."

"He's mad. Is that what you mean? He's crazy?"

Culley looked out the window. After a while he said, "I don't know. I don't know what it means."

He phoned Helen at eight o'clock from his hotel room. A full orchestra was in mid-finale. There was a rattle as the phone went down onto a table. Culley hadn't heard it, but he imagined that she'd said, "Wait."

The music stopped and she came back. He said, "It's me. Was that Mozart?"

"Everything's Mozart to you. You're a peasant." She sounded slightly drunk. "Is it true—that you've got him?"

"Yes. I think so."

"Not sure?"

"He had a gun. It was the right gun."

"That all?"

"He confessed."

"You believe him?"

"Yes."

There was a silence between them—Helen's way of saying, What do you want?

"I need a favor."

This time he heard her. "Wait a minute." From a distance came little sounds that said, gin, glass, tonic. "You probably can't have it," she said. "I'm not sure why I'm allowing a conversation with you at all."

"There's a gallery: Porter's. Run by a man called—"

"Ralph Porter; yes."

"You know him?"

"Of him."

"He has a number of partners—investors, directors, whatever they're called."

"I expect he has."

"There are two I badly need to know about. Both women. Alison Travers; Marie Wallace."

"You're asking me as a friend—old times' sake?"

"For Christ's sake, Helen."

"As a chum, a pal, as one who bears no grudges?"

"Just this one. I've told you. I have to finish with this one. Then I'll do what you asked. Out—a new life. I want that. I want it with

306

you. Just this one." He waited. "I need to know who they are—those two women. You're in the business. If you ask the right people, someone will know."

"Robin, listen—"

"All you have to—"

"Fuck off, okay?"

"I'm just—"

"Fuck *right* off."

It was impossible that they hadn't moved. Her hand still on his, the wedge of pillows at his back, side by side, facing front, a king and queen waiting to receive courtiers. Culley looked through the transparent panel and Angie's head turned a fraction. He went to the annex to wait.

She arrived carrying two containers of tea and handed one to Culley, casually, seeming not to notice how she advertised her wifehood. He sat on the sofa, she in the chair—his place, her place. Angie hunched over her tea, elbows on knees, as if nursing a stomach ache.

"How long have I got with him?"

"A few hours. Tomorrow morning."

"What will happen?"

"I don't know."

"If he tells you things you want to know. Tells me."

"Nothing."

"It won't make a difference?"

Culley spread his hands. "How could it? He killed so many people. What do you want? Not eight life sentences but four?"

"Then why am I doing it?"

"Eric's taking the blame."

"What?"

"I'm not asking you to agree with me. I'm not asking you to say anything. Just listen. Your husband doesn't have the kind of job that most husbands have. You know that, but you and he don't talk about it. That's okay. I don't want to hear about the past. What I'm saying is—he's a freelance; people employ him. He didn't do what he did because the whim took him. Not at first. Someone asked him to do it. Do you see, Angie? It was someone else's idea. What's happening to him now—what's happening to you—is happening because of that. Because of someone else."

"And you want him."

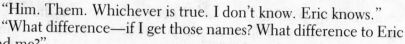

"Him. Them. Whichever is true. I don't know. Eric knows."

"What difference—if I get those names? What difference to Eric and me?"

Culley shook his head, slowly, as if the puzzle were too great for him to tackle. "You tell me." Then he said, "Someone's to blame. Why are you here? What brings you here? Think about it. Doesn't it seem that someone's to *blame?*"

The building clicked and tapped—small noises you hear only at night. There were footfalls, but no one came into view. Culley dozed on the couch, moving in and out of sleep, in and out of focus.

He was walking through a park with Helen; she was talking but the dream had switched the sound off.

On the top of Bethel Tor, Hugo Kemp was waving both arms above his head: a greeting or a warning.

But Angie Ross was real—ragged hair, and her perfume gone rank with sweat—standing beside him and holding a piece of paper torn from the pad.

51

WHEN ROSS THOUGHT OF THE MOOR he saw only one image: himself on top of the tor and Martin snaking down the hillside toward him. He rehearsed it again and again like a missed opportunity. Sometimes he knew that he wasn't seeing things—feeling things—as they really were. Dream fragments filled his mind. Dark angel, dark presence, man-bird. He couldn't share the dream, but he preferred it.

Martin descending the slope and himself on the pinnacle . . . There's another rule: Attack when you get the chance. He saw the soft, yellow flames of gorse between the clumps of granite strewn at random on the turf. It was vivid and close. He saw himself stand up, his outline clear of the rock. The vision's gift was flight. Wings stirred the air, ligature and tendon branching from his shoulders, the great tap root growing beside his heart.

He thought of the tor and because of that, thought of the tower. Not himself, but Martin, who picked them out to die. That night, he'd been angry. He had wanted to kill Martin for stealing his role, for playing the impostor. He remembered how the wind had touseled his hair as he stood on the battlements. He remembered other nights and other mornings—looking down at the city of lights from his vantage point on the hill; going out like a shadow, a throb of wings, the creatures beneath him, each asking to be chosen.

Angie had sat beside him, pen and pad in hand. He knew who wanted the name: Robin Culley, who had picked him up and brought him back. A waste of time. Staggered by another man's weight, soaked in another man's blood. Ross was neither grateful nor glad. He'd given Angie the name and she'd taken it away with her.

He tried to think back to the day of their marriage, to the births of the children, but all he could see were people he used to know and a man who used to be himself. He remembered the holiday, the home movie the kids liked to watch. While Angie pointed the camera, they ran on the beach, both with a hand lifted to clutch another's hand. Something loped between them. It was white and featureless, like a figure in negative.

Two lives, two people; how had that been possible? Neighbors, people he met, would say, "What do you do?" He'd offer the lie that seemed best for the circumstance: mining engineer, salesman, conference organizer, researcher—jobs that would require travel and come intermittently. But he would think, "I kill people for a living," as if he'd told the truth; and sometimes, after the other person had turned away, he would mutter it under his breath.

Life at home and life away; life indoors and life outside. He would come home having remembered to pick up a birthday present Angie had ordered for one of the kids, gift-wrapped package in one hand, gun case in the other. He would stow the gun case, lock the cupboard door, then put on a party hat and join the fun.

Two lives. When had that started? After the army. After the

moment at Bethel Tor when he'd stepped out of cover and shot Halliday in the spine. After the feeling he'd gotten from that: of power, of wholeness, and a tremendous sense of peace. Perhaps. Even before that? It was impossible to know. Childhood games and childhood stories; they were dreams as well.

Something came back to him, brilliantly clear. He was looking through a volume of illustrations—he couldn't recall quite when it had happened—pictures of people from stories and legends. Each illustration depicted some particular moment and the text was at the bottom of the page.

There was a spiral of bright beings, domed in light, ascending the heavens. A man and a woman were running through trees, a storm directly above their heads. A great tower rose in sections to the clouds. A figure tumbled from the sky, face up, as if some great hand had cast it down from the sun.

A text had accompanied the illustration; Ross remembered it and smiled. In the next moment, he saw Martin Jackson's face go past the transparent panel in the door, like the face of a famous person glimpsed in the street.

Culley had taken the paper and phoned Mike Dawson. Then he'd returned to Angie. He'd said, "It's time to make a proper statement, okay?"

She had nodded. They'd taken Culley's route out in order to avoid the press, leaving by a gate that led to the kitchen and service doors. Jackson had walked through the gate a few seconds after he'd seen them leave. It wasn't his first visit to the hospital, although on the other two occasions, he'd used the main entrance and arrived at a time when most visitors were there. He had been a visitor too: he'd carried a bunch of flowers as if slightly embarrassed by it and looked as if he knew where he was going.

It was obvious and that was why it was safe. No one knew who he was or what he looked like. On the first visit, he found the corridor that led to Ross's room. On the second, he walked a route from the service entrance to the end of that corridor. On the way out, he had seen Chris Bullen talking to the receptionist at the inquiries desk, but he'd missed seeing Angie Ross by a few seconds.

It would have worried him to see Angie, because she certainly did know who he was.

Jackson had watched outside the hospital for Culley and knew he used the service doors. He watched Culley's car rather than the man himself. He was waiting for the right opportunity. All things being equal, he would have preferred to make his move later in the day when visitors would be more plentiful; but when he saw Angie Ross with Culley he knew that there weren't any choices left to him.

It was a cool morning, so his light raincoat didn't seem out of place. He took an elevator to the fourth floor, then walked briskly to the annex just below the corridor outside Ross's room. He went in and removed his coat. Underneath he was wearing a blue surgeon's gown over a T-shirt. He took a blue skull cap from his pocket and pulled that on. The garments not only said "official," they said "authority." Most important, they said "normal." The policeman who sat outside Ross's door would have been passed by dozens of nurses, doctors, and surgeons every day. He wouldn't have challenged them any more than he would challenge Jackson. It would succeed because there was no defense against it.

The man outside the door glanced up as Jackson approached, then looked away as he came nearer. Jackson walked past. That was when Ross saw his face through the glass.

Just dawn—a pale gray light like the reflection of water on stone.

A nurse had checked on him ten minutes before; he'd pretended to be asleep. Now his eyes were open, but he wasn't looking at the door. He was facing straight ahead once more, like a bored passenger willing the end of his journey. After a moment, he reached for the pad and pen and wrote on the uppermost leaf, then pushed it to the back of the shelf.

You would think there was something left to do; you would think there was something left to say. Alive and then dead. What was it you couldn't quite think of? It's on the tip of your tongue. What was it, the task you meant to complete? You'll do it when you remember. Except that the word will never come, the task will never be completed.

A great tear welled in the corner of Ross's eye and rolled to his jawline. Suddenly, he regretted everything. Not the killings—that would have been remorse—his regret had to do with his own life. He had wanted to be something else; and even now, he didn't know what it was. Like a taste you've never tasted, a sight you've never seen.

There had been no noise, so Martin must have been clever with the man on the door. You walk past, and once you're past you might as well be in another country; then you turn back, quickly, before anything seems wrong. And there's the gun; and, very softly, you say, "On your feet . . ." He's too shocked to move for a moment, and you whisper, "Now. Do it *now*."

Martin smiled as he came into the room. He closed the door and made the step sideways that would take him out of view to anyone looking through the glass. He said, "Eric . . ."

The French soldiers had stopped hitting the woman, although it seemed that they hadn't really finished with her because the man who had slapped her last landed on her, almost absentmindedly, while looking at Jackson, and the man who'd received her held her arm tightly, though he was looking at Jackson too.

The room wasn't just silent; it was as though the noise had rushed away, carried on air, and they all stood in a vacuum. Jackson put out a hand and took the woman's arm. There was a moment's resistance from the soldier, then he let go. Together, they walked to the door of the bar, Jackson and the woman. He held the door open for her, and continued to stand in the doorway in order to watch her out of sight. You half expected him to raise a hand and wave her off. Then he went back to where Ross was standing at the bar and picked up the drink he'd left.

Later, better than two parts drunk, they had walked close to the Wall. Ross trailed his fingertips across the rough cement surface. Searchlights threw a halo around the springy scrolls of barbed wire along the top; it was a cold night and wisps of vapor floated among the steel thorns. There were slogans daubed the length of the Wall. Obscenities. Messages from the lovelorn.

Ross had taken a blow to the back of the neck and pitched forward into a pile of rubble and trash. When he'd come to, there was no one near. He walked twenty, maybe thirty yards, toward some buildings and an empty street. There had been a sound like someone hitting a carcass with a mallet. Ross had picked up his pace until he was maintaining a shambling run. He couldn't keep his balance that well and there was a shrill howl inside his skull. He came into the street and focused on a huddle of bodies by the doorway of the first house. One soldier was on the ground and lying still. The other two men were clubbing Jackson, trying to bring him down so they could get their boots to him.

Ross was still woozy but he covered the ground as fast as he could. Jackson's face was visible over their shoulders, raw and red. They were concentrating hard and hadn't heard Ross approach.

He stood off and kicked one of them in the back, going for the kidneys and finding the spot. The man dropped to one knee. Ross stooped and swung punches at the muddy outline of his own boot, leaning on the man's shoulder to steady himself and hitting the place four or five times. When the shoulder he was leaning on caved in, Ross fell on top of the man. For a short while they lay there, then Ross heaved himself up and started kicking the man again, walking around the prone body to pick his shots.

Jackson pulled him off and steered him away. The third soldier was halfway down the street, going at a lurching half-run. Some damage that he would only understand later made him veer to the left until finally he was stopped by a housefront. He went crabwise to his right so that he almost crossed the street, then began to trot, going off on the left diagonal again.

There was someone shouting on the east side of the Wall—a cry, silence, another cry; someone's name, perhaps. It seemed that the caller was expecting someone to answer from the west. After three more tries, the voice was quiet. Ross and Jackson walked back the way they had come, holding each other up as best they could. After a while, Jackson's arm slipped from around Ross's neck and he fell into a sitting position, his back to a parked car. A cackle of laughter rose from his throat, coming in fat bubbles of blood that burst over his lips.

Ross put out a hand and hauled Jackson back to his feet, but the momentum brought their bodies together in a stumbling embrace, both men holding on for fear of falling. Cheek to cheek and arms wrapped round, they stumbled in circles along the edge of the road like exhausted dancers. They came to rest alongside the window of a house. From inside they could hear a radio and voices talking over the broadcast. They were breathless and weak, still holding one another. Jackson's lips were drawn back in a broad and bloody grin, his teeth grouted with red.

He leaned forward and kissed Ross full on the mouth, then walked away. There was a bar nearby and he seemed to be making for the door. Ross followed, a line of dribble trickling from lip to chin. He could taste the salt.

Jackson smiled. He said, "Eric . . ."

It had always been in his mind that he'd want to talk; that there were things that had to be said. Such a long time ago . . .

I said: I love you. And then you went away.

Now the moment had arrived, and he couldn't find the words because there were no words. Nothing could make a difference, nothing could restore the past. A death might make it easier to bear.

He gave a quick glance at the door panel, then walked toward the bed. From his trouser pocket he took a handgun and gestured with it apologetically; he was showing Ross that the gun had no silencer.

Ross lifted his arms and reached back, wordlessly, grasping his pillow with both hands in order to draw it around his face. Jackson nodded, then smiled a brief thank you, showing the gap in his teeth.

You would think there was something left to do.

There was a moment when they looked at one another; then Ross pulled the pillow right around to cover his face. Jackson slipped the gun into the fold between Ross's hands. With foam to muffle it, the shot sounded like nothing more than a door being slammed or someone stacking equipment somewhere along the corridor. Jackson moved as soon as he'd fired, turning Ross onto his side and away from the glass panel, putting an unstained pillow beside his head. A few seconds after that, he was gone.

You would think there was something left to say.

52

THAT DAY, there were two views of the room.

Ross under the sheets, his body arranged tidily as if he slept, the pillows and linen on the upper part of the bed dark and sopping wet. On either side were drips, saline and pethodine, still adding themselves jot by jot to his thickening bloodstream. The blinds were closed and the dim light made the room shadowless.

Then there was the bed stripped to its bars and mattress and the room cleared of all equipment. The shutters were wide to the morning, the windows wide behind them, and there was a whiff of disinfectant in the air.

Culley had seen the first view, now he looked at the second. Only one thing remained untouched. He went to the bedside cabinet and reached to the back of the shelf to remove the notepad and pen. There was a ragged edge where Angie had torn off the first sheet. On the page that was now uppermost, Ross had written: Isaiah 14:12.

No one was interested in the lone madman theory now. Since Culley had brought Ross in, wounded, from the moor, everyone had been talking about a conspiracy, as if they had never really believed anything else. Protheroe had asked for a complete review of the case. He had also wondered out loud how Culley could have managed to lose a man who was both principal suspect and principal witness. It was clear that he was angry. The loss represented a procedural setback: a blow to his sense of order.

It wasn't quite like that for Culley; it wasn't like that for Angie Ross. They sat in an interview room, one either side of a small table, and Angie sipped the tea they had brought her. A police-woman, monitoring the tape, was crammed into a corner of the room like a reluctant chaperone.

Angie stared at the tabletop. She had spotted an area of rough-
ness, about the size of a postage stamp, where the varnish had
started to flake; when she set her tea down, she didn't draw her
hand back, but began to pick at the flaw with a fingernail.

"I could tell them he had a car crash," Angie said.

"Yes."

"I could tell them he had a fall."

"A fall?"

"That's what he . . . They think he is . . . A structural engineer.
A fall from a building."

"Yes."

"I don't suppose it matters much."

Culley glanced toward the policewoman. He said, "What did
you think he was?"

Angie almost smiled. "The same."

"We'll find a way of getting you back to London. After that,
you'll have to make your own way. You can take a holiday if you
let us know where you are. In any case, the best thing to do is not
answer the door or the phone unless you know who it is. Work out
a code with people you want to see or be in touch with. A phone
code is easy enough; a doorbell code has to be changed from time
to time, because they'll be watching and they'll work it out." He
meant the press; Angie was about to become a star—midnight
phone calls, deliveries of flowers, cash bids outside the window,
scum on the doorstep.

"I could sell the house, perhaps. Move away."

Culley didn't try to draw her back to other topics, he listened as
an old friend might. Angie was caught up in the practicalities of
the thing, a way of avoiding all else.

She said, "I lost him a while ago, really. Some while ago."

For the sake of appearance, Culley asked, "You didn't know
what he did? You don't know who hired him?" He delayed the final
question slightly. "You don't know who killed him?"

Angie looked at Culley's face as if searching among his features
for something to recognize. She said, "Who killed him?" as if the
question had suddenly occurred to her and she was eager to have
the answer.

The tape had been switched off and they sat in silence. The policewoman went to the door, then paused; Culley nodded her out.

Angie said, "I know what to do next, but I don't know how."

She was talking about going home. Her fingernail nicked shreds from the scab of varnish. "Everything seems so ordinary, doesn't it? Cars going by in the street, people shopping, kids on their way to school. I keep expecting things to be as they were, like a film played backward." The beach sequence reversed, the children appearing to dig their father up. Angie's face darkened with sorrow. "You don't expect days like this."

After a moment, Culley said, "Who killed him, Angie?"

"Martin Jackson," she said, and put a hand to her mouth like a shy girl who had spoken out of turn.

There was rain in London: fine, soft threads wafting in the wind, then settling to become a gray seepage that soaked in like stain. It blurred everything and seemed to muffle noise. When Dawson walked across the forecourt to the block of flats where Francis lived, he could hear his own footsteps but not the traffic on the street behind him.

The superintendent's cubicle was a home away from home. Dawson asked whether Francis was in.

"You can go up. Flat three-oh-three."

"I don't want to go up." Dawson showed his ID. "I want to know whether he's in."

"Who do you want to be?"

"No one. Tell him that a package has just been delivered."

The superintendent looked dubious, but he pushed a console button that started a faint beep amid a crackle of static. "He's not there."

"Okay," Dawson said, "*now* we can go up. I expect you've got a key."

The man didn't move. "Are you legal?"

"Go on," Dawson invited.

"Have you got a warrant?"

Dawson smiled. He'd been talking to the man through a double hatchway that opened onto the foyer of the building. Now he strolled around a small recess to the door and opened it. The superintendent said, "I'm responsible for security here."

On a shelf were a number of box files. Dawson lifted one down and began to riffle through it as he spoke. "I'm wondering what the fiddle is here." He glanced up at the superintendent inquiringly, then went back to the file. "Here in these flats . . . Because there's always a fiddle, isn't there. Maintenance, is it? Fittings?

Some useful arrangement with a company that supplies light bulbs and door handles, heating valves, radiators, that kind of thing? Then there are the jobbing builders when there's repair work to be done or an apartment has to be decorated. How do your bosses decide who'll get the job? Lowest tender, is it? Your recommendation?" Dawson closed the box file and took down another. "I wouldn't be the one to worry about such things—you know—but others might."

The superintendent said, "What do I tell—"

Dawson interrupted. "What I'm suggesting is that if you stop worrying about warrants and let me into Mr. Francis's flat, I won't have your records investigated. I won't have you turned over. If you make things difficult for me, I will. A deal, okay? It's not a strictly legal suggestion, but I'm offering it to you as a likable alternative to getting kicked shitless."

The superintendent handed Dawson the key. He said, "Do what you like. I'm not coming up with you."

Dawson bothered to rummage through a few likely hiding places —cupboards, desk drawers, a bureau. He wasn't looking for evidence because there wouldn't be any unless Francis was stupid. He was looking for a gun. There wasn't a gun either. He took down a book, gave himself a whiskey, and settled in an armchair.

When Francis came into the room he stood and stared at Dawson for a long time, then he said, "And so . . . ?"

"Eric Ross," Dawson said. "He killed a lot of people and he's told us that you asked him to do it."

"He's dead," Francis said. "You haven't got a witness."

"No, that's true," Dawson said. "But I don't think that's going to stop me arresting you on suspicion. If you're a broker—and I'm sure you are—I'll have you sooner or later. You'll find me when you step out of the door, when you eat in a restaurant, when you go to a movie. Understand?" He paused. "Who raised the commission? You hired Ross. Who hired you?"

Francis knew better than the superintendent. He asked, "What's the deal?" When Dawson didn't reply, he said, "There's got to be a deal. There always is."

The rain had grown more dense, washing the color out of everything, blurring the outlines of buildings. Dawson and Francis walked away from the apartment block to where Dawson's car was parked at the curbside. Inside were a driver and two other men. It had occurred to Dawson that Francis might not have been alone. He opened the back door and handed Francis in.

A man got out of the front passenger seat, vacating it for Dawson, and got into the back. He said, "Okay?"

"Sure," Dawson said, "he's fine. He wants to do a deal."

"Any chance of booting him around a cell for a while?"

"I don't think so," Dawson said. "He tells me that his solicitor's a very famous man. I expect he'll turn up pretty soon." The driver pulled out into the traffic. After a moment, Dawson said, "Of course, the famous man might be out of town for a couple of days."

Chris Bullen spent an hour with Angie, but the only voice on the tape was his. Afterward, he played back Culley's session. He said, "We know she knew. You said so yourself."

"Did I?" Culley shrugged. "Yes. I expect she knew. But she's not telling us that."

"I'm not doing very well," Bullen said. "And I'm not the only person who thinks that. I've got two dead citizens, a dead suspect, and a dead copper."

The man who'd been stationed outside Ross's door had been taken to a linen closet at the end of the corridor. Jackson had hit him several times with the gun, then gagged him in case he might regain consciousness. He had suffocated on the gag.

"We'll talk to her again in London," Culley observed. "You could do that too. Make a day of it; take your wife to a show."

Bullen laughed. He was holding a sheet from a yellow message pad. "A call came in from your office." He passed the slip of paper to Culley. "Someone called Protheroe?"

Culley reached out for a handshake, then gave the paper back. "Say I'd left."

Angie had also said "local" and she'd said "pigs." It was as much as she knew, but it was enough. She'd said, "It was years ago. He used to write letters. Eric went there once—I didn't go. After that, the letters stopped. We didn't see him again."

I love you. Then you . . .

Culley didn't expect him to be there, but he went anyway. From the sheds came sounds like engines shunting and there was a thin, sharp smell of methane, enough to ream your sinuses. A man was crossing the yard pushing a wheelbarrow. When he saw Culley, he lowered the legs of the barrow and waited to be approached.

They stood in the center of the yard and the man wagged his head rhythmically, like a horse looking over a stall. After each answer, he dipped his shoulders, reaching for the barrow, then straightened again when a new question was asked. Finally, Culley let him go.

The house was open and Culley went in to a smell of sacking and polish. In one room there was a stone-flagged floor and a wooden settle; in another a sofa, scatter rugs, an oak drop-leaf table. It had been occupied but not lived in. On the sideboard, a framed photograph of a dozen or so men in uniform. Jackson and Ross stood to one side, squinting slightly because they were looking toward the sun.

He took the call, even though he'd assumed it would be Protheroe. It was time to go back to London, anyway. With the phone tucked into his chin, he continued to shove clothes into his grip.

"Who they are, or what their connection is?" It was Helen.

"Is it the same thing?"

"More or less." Culley sat on the bed to listen. "They're both connected to a man called Bernard Warner. A member of Parliament. Extremely rich. He's an old friend of Ralph Porter's."

"How connected?"

"Alison Travers is his daughter. Marie Wallace is his mistress." Culley laughed. "Well, I'm sure that's what he would call her."

He laughed again. "I'm sure you're right."

"Will that do?"

"Oh, yes," he said, "that'll do." The line between them crackled slightly; distant energy. Culley hated silences during phone calls. He said, "Are you all right?"

The silence extended, then she said, "Look, I was drunk; okay?"

"Okay."

"I don't know what I want."

"Don't give up." He waited for a response. "Are you listening?"

"Yes."

"Don't give up on me."

"I don't know, Robin. *Jesus* Christ . . ."

320

"Listen—I'll do what you want."

"Will you?" she said. "What's that?"

He closed the grip, then remembered something he'd intended to do. The Gideon Bible was in a drawer along with a town guide and the room service menu.

Culley took it to the window where there was more light. The rain had traveled south, gathering force, and there was a wind behind it that rattled the glass. Ross had said, "Why ask . . .?"

Isaiah 14:12. *How art thou fallen from heaven, O Lucifer, son of the morning!*

53

THEY ARRIVED TOGETHER, two important men in large, impressive cars. The highway had been thick with weekenders, but Warner had allowed for that. Edward Latimer was a weekender himself; his house was less than four miles away. There was a small parking area, gravel over mud, and signposts that provided the symbols of a nature trail. Beechwoods covered two hilltops and formed a thick leaf canopy in the valley between. Latimer was dressed for a walk.

"Very nice." Warner looked above the trees to a dull sky with ragged hanks of gray clouds scudding on the underside. He judged there was rain in the air and took a heavy waterproof coat from the back seat of his car. As he shrugged into it, he said, "My place is in Wiltshire."

They walked for about five minutes. Latimer said, "It has to end now."

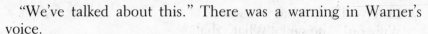

"We've talked about this." There was a warning in Warner's voice.

"I don't think that matters anymore."

"Well . . ." Warner tipped the collar of his coat and pushed his hands into his pockets. "You'll be able to judge that. All sorts of people are going to be hearing all sorts of things about you."

They had reached a point where the pathway narrowed toward a small pole-and-cage gate, and stood in single file to pass through. Warner spoke from behind, standing close. "Don't be foolish. It's just information; just an occasional report."

Latimer waited on the other side. "You think I'm just going to stop telling you things? No—you're in more trouble than that."

Warner nodded. "I wondered. He let the pole slam back to the gate. "Why am I hearing this?"

"A warning," Latimer said. "I don't need you to blame. I shall have to name you; but if you know a way out, take it."

"Why now?" Warner asked.

"Things have changed," Latimer said, "haven't they? Eric Ross was murdered in the hospital. We were looking for a sniper; we found him. Now we're looking for something else. I told you what was in Culley's reports—Kemp, the Cezannes, now the Porter Gallery." He stopped a moment to look at Warner. "How long do you imagine you've got, anyway? Whatever I do or say isn't going to make that much of a difference."

"Anything you say will finish me off," Warner said, "Culley might not get there." He wondered where Culley was at that moment; where Jackson was.

The leaf canopy grew heavier as they went down the hill; the light thickened. Each tree had a knee-high brush of saplings that bowed and sprang as the men passed.

"It's easy," Latimer was saying, "because I'm sick of it. I can't imagine . . ." He broke off as if the remark might prove pointless. "You had a lot of people killed. Organized it yourself. Just to—"

"A business decision."

"Yes," Latimer said, "of course."

"I took the decision. No one else knew. But they were happy enough when Hammond died—it seemed a useful coincidence. It was best they should think that. Peddling paintings without being too worried about their origins is one thing—a sort of modern piracy, very flamboyant, a bit like beating the Rhodesian blockade. One or two probably wouldn't have minded about the killings, but

I didn't feel like taking the risk. Just as well, considering what happened. The idea was that the sale would give us access to a new market: which it did. Overseas trade—very important." Warner was smiling; it amused him to be arch.

"Didn't you care?"

They walked in silence for a while. Warner seemed to be thinking the idea through. A jay dipped from tree to tree across a small clearing.

"I don't think so."

"Why?"

Another silence. Finally, Warner said, "People die all the time."

The light that came through the treetops seemed shot through with green, like a depth of water.

"You don't have to say anything. What makes you think you do? I'll take my chances. Who knows how close they'll get?" Warner had called Francis three times that morning and gotten no reply, but it hadn't really begun to worry him until now. He wondered what Latimer wasn't telling him. "If things become difficult, there are ways . . . Just stay quiet. That's all you need to do." Ways out; ways to disappear.

"I know," Latimer said. "I'm not going to."

The jay returned, a flash of brilliance that drew the eye. Warner's hand came out of his pocket to point, arm straight, his hand rising. Latimer had paused, a man with something else to say.

The tire iron landed across his cheek, smashing the bone, and he made a forward step as if he wanted to continue the walk on his own. Then he sat down heavily, traveling a short way down the slope. Warner stood behind him for the next blow. The tire iron thumped into Latimer's skull and stuck; Warner had to pump his hand to get it free.

Latimer fell back. He was flipping like a fish, his body convulsing between shoulders and hips and scooting farther down the hillside. He rattled through a spread of saplings. Warner chased him down, overtaking him, then turning to strike again.

He bent over, standing to one side, and hit out backhanded. Latimer's nose smashed; a band of red sprang up across his eyes like a blindfold. Warner was giving a yell each time, either effort or fury. He laid the iron across Latimer's brow, coming up on his toes for the blow, and a deep trough appeared—a line of fault, like collapsing earthworks. A gigantic muscle spasm flipped Latimer onto his face, neat as an acrobat; he moved off in a lopsided, scuttling crawl.

Warner went after him, wading through screens of brush. When he caught up, he straddled the man and stooped to grab the collar of his coat, as if he were restraining a dog. He brought the iron down twice and there were chunks of bone in Latimer's hair, big as a smashed saucer.

The low, roaring sound was Latimer breathing. On his knees, Warner straddled him. Latimer's mouth was wide open and full of blood. He lifted a hand and groped at Warner's shoulder, at his neck, at his face. Warner got up and walked away, then he paused, his back to Latimer, his head bowed.

Deeper in the wood, the jay screeched. The breathing had become an appalling wet snore.

Warner went back. He wrapped his hand into a clump of grass and tore up the clod, a thick wedge of dark earth on the roots, then knelt down and forced it into Latimer's gaping mouth. Blood welled up past the divot and splashed Warner's hand. He pulled on Latimer's jaw and rammed at the grass with stiffened fingers. Latimer's cheeks bulged. Warner leaned sideways and ripped up another fistful—grass, mud, small stones in among the fibers— and thrust it after the first. Stiff-armed, he pounded at it with a clenched fist.

It was impossible to do more. Warner got up, then stood nearby and watched. Latimer was still except for his arms, which seemed to be working off a different power source, cranking and waving and slapping the ground. Then they stopped. His back arched very slightly and he stared furiously at the sky.

Warner's breathing was a rhythmic gasp and release, the action of someone about to laugh or sneeze. He waited until everything had slowed a little, then he looked down at himself. The waterproof coat was crisscrossed with loops and sashes of blood, like gouts from a hose. He removed it and pulled it across the grass, then folded it on itself and placed it over one arm. He stripped a beech sprout of its leaves and rubbed at the stains on his trousers. It looked as if he'd slipped in the mud.

Before he started up the slope, he pulled Latimer up to the bole of a big tree, patted the man's pockets for his car keys, then rolled him into the bush. He turned twice, coming face-up.

Warner said, "Yes, I thought you would say something like

that." He kicked a trailing foot under the leaf cover. "I thought that's what you were going to say."

He hiked back to the parking lot and drove Latimer's car a couple of miles up the road, parking it in a rest area screened by trees. It would give him a few hours; maybe a day. He returned to his own car and stowed the coat and the tire iron in the trunk. As he pulled onto the road, he picked up his car phone and began to make arrangements.

The wood was full of soft noises: animals and birds, a wind shifting the topmost branches, Edward Latimer's hand among fallen leaves.

The fingers dug and turned, dug and turned, some wintering creature working on its burrow. The creature worked steadily for a time. Then an awful noise came from Latimer's face—a goose-honk—and he died.

Long stalks of grass rose from between his stretched lips. A worm appeared at the corner of his mouth, winding out of a gobbet of earth and blindly nosing the air.

54

IT TOOK TEN MINUTES for Latimer to say what he knew. Protheroe and Culley sat in silence to listen to the dead man. Protheroe was hearing it for the second time. He switched the tape off.

Culley asked, "Have they found him?"

"They've found his car. That's all."

"Who went to collect Warner?"

"Serious Crimes squad. No one home." Protheroe corrected

himself. "No one at either home: London or the country. He's also got a place in Normandy. The French are looking now. I don't think he'll be there."

"There are others we can talk to," Culley reminded him.

"There are?"

"The guy who owns the gallery—Porter. The other directors."

"Latimer said nothing about any of them. He only mentioned Warner."

"Hammond was killed so that two paintings could be routed to America. That's why everyone was killed. Everyone. The gallery deals as any other, but it also deals in works stolen to order. They must know that."

"Some might," Protheroe said. "Some might not. They'll all say they don't."

"We can try." There was an edge to Culley's voice.

"Sure." Protheroe slotted the tape back into its plastic sleeve. "We can try."

Culley tried Alison Travers first. She owned a house in a part of London where most people wouldn't have been able to afford a room. The people who live in such areas always own houses. A man in a gray uniform was washing a dark green Rolls Royce. When Culley walked past, he raised his head, sniffing trouble. He looked back toward the street and saw Dawson, who had gotten out of the car to wait. *Trouble.*

She was blonde and blazingly self-confident, and led Culley through the house as if it were an estate. She gave herself a drink and asked, "What about my father?"

"It's possible that he's been involved in a serious crime."

Alison laughed briefly. Then she said, "What?"

He began to ask her about the gallery and she relaxed slightly. She was thinking: Forgery, tax evasion, smuggling. She even tried to make a small joke. "It runs in the blood, of course. My ancestors were robber barons; stole most of East Anglia." Then she wondered if it had been a good idea and added, "You must know that my father would never support any action that was illegal." She sounded starchy: an official statement in a silk blouse. Culley asked her about the shares.

"I just held them for him. It was a matter of voting, really. Basically, he wanted to own and control the gallery without—" She stopped there.

"Anyone knowing," Culley suggested.

"Is that illegal?"

"No."

"Then what is it that you're accusing him of?"

"Do you know where he is?" Culley asked.

They both waited to have their questions answered. Eventually, Alison said, "Some bureaucratic nicety; some nitpicking rule." Because she had almost become angry, she decided on another drink.

Culley nodded; he might have been considering the issue. "I asked if you know where he is."

She thought about it for a while. "Perhaps I shouldn't say any more without my solicitor being present."

"If you like. It's a simple question."

She continued to think, then said, "No, I don't."

Culley got up to leave and saw Alison relax a little. He'd learned to ask questions on the way out. They often drew answers. "Your shares alone didn't allow your father a controlling interest."

"No." It was all she proposed to say.

As they approached the door, Culley asked, "Do you know someone called Marie Wallace?"

A flush appeared in the hollow of Alison's throat and spread on her collarbones like a yoke. As if it were an answer she said, "You know that my mother is dead?"

"Do you know her?"

"I know of her. We haven't met." She opened the door.

"The Porter Gallery sometimes deals in works of art that have been stolen." Culley was looking away from her, toward the road; he made it sound like an afterthought. "Did you know that?"

Her face opened to him. She said, "Is that what—" Then, "You can't believe—" The door half-closed as she recovered herself. Culley listened while she mentioned her solicitor, then he walked back to his car.

"Well?" Dawson asked.

Culley shook his head. Alison Travers liked the idea of dishonesty, but lacked the nerve for it. Clear on her face, though, had been the knowledge that her father possessed all the nerve it might take.

Marie Wallace had little nerve and even less to say. She sat on the bed and looked at Culley without really knowing who he was. A thirty-five-year-old face on a body ten years older. The room was full of clothes; they were on every surface, on chairbacks, on the floor, on hangers that were hooked to half-open closet doors, on bedrails, on the bed itself. She sat among them wearing a thin housecoat, one bare leg stretched out before her, the other tucked back. Culley tried to find somewhere else to look.

"He told me get ready," she said. "He told me pack."

She was so drunk that she might have been speaking an odd dialect of a language Culley barely knew. He had to concentrate hard on the translation. It took his mind off Marie's pose.

She picked up a glass that was resting lopsidedly on the coverlet and began to cry, shaking, so that she slopped gin into her lap. "It was all . . . But he . . . Wait here; pack . . . I'll come for . . . Then . . . Then . . . Then . . ." Because she was talking at all, Culley strained to listen, though he understood that there was no reason to. She stared at him, her mouth open like a stupid doll, her face blue and gray and red with spoiled make-up, like the dirty iridescence in a spillage of oil.

After a moment, she fell back among the heaps of silks and pastels, and cried as only the truly wretched can. Her robe had divided at the belt, leaving her naked to the waist. Her pubic hair was slick with gin.

"We'll go . . . Wait here . . . I'll come . . . I'll only be . . ."

She had forgotten Culley was there.

The pleasures of solitary living are: Do what you will. The problems are: What will you do?

You make salad for one, you make a very small amount of salad dressing; you grill a single lamb chop, you take a small baked potato from its foil. You can watch TV or read a book—and the great thing about it is, you don't have to ask someone else whether she'd prefer . . . or would she mind if . . . or maybe she'd sooner have lasagne. And no one's going to bitch at you for forgetting to put out the garbage. It can just sit there and rot down to a mulch. That'll be fine. No compromises, no timetables. Nothing.

Culley opened a bottle of wine and threw away the cork. Latimer's tape had said, "I'm sending this to you now, before I reconsider. I shall spend the weekend doing some necessary paperwork. I imagine we will talk to each other on Monday. It won't be necessary to send anyone for me, but I shall quite understand if you do." When Culley remembered the level tone, the nicely chosen phrases, it occurred to him that the search for Latimer might well result in the discovery of a suicide.

Whether or not that was true, he assumed that Latimer had given Warner a head start. Perhaps they'd taken the same route out together. One of the routes open only to the rich. Hugo Kemp's escape didn't even involve movement. The killings had stopped and the man who had committed those crimes was dead. The man who had hired him to commit them had, at least, been identified. To some, it would seem that Culley was winning. As far as he was concerned, he was losing—for the most part, losing people. Ross. Jackson. Latimer. Warner. Helen.

He walked toward the phone and it rang as if she had been thinking of him in the same moment.

"Why not come over?" She sounded constrained. He wondered if she had reached some decision or another, whether it would be better not to go. It made no difference, of course, but he wanted to know what she was thinking.

"For dinner?"

"Yes."

"Shall I bring anything?"

"No." She sounded quite definite about it. "There's enough here for both of us."

He switched off the grill and then he switched off the television. Do what you will.

55

WHEN SHE OPENED UP to him the first thing he saw was the gun. It passed across his eyeline, then stopped an inch or so from the bridge of his nose: a bright blur.

Jackson said, "Lean on it—gently."

Culley tilted forward a few inches and rested his forehead on the barrel. His face was almost touching Helen's. She said, "Oh Christ, I'm sorry."

They backed into the apartment, all three, moving slowly and in unison as if practicing the steps of some bizarre dance; Jackson retreating, his arm around Helen's waist to draw her with him, Culley coming toward them at the same pace, his head thrust forward, seeming to take the lead. Culley wanted to look from side to side in the hope of finding an advantage, but he knew that Jackson was looking directly at him, so he kept his eyes on Helen's. Their heads were so close that it was difficult to focus; her pupils seemed cavernous.

Jackson said, "Stop," and Culley stopped, stranded in the middle of the room. Jackson backed up to an armchair, pulling Helen down so that she sat on his lap. Her left arm was trapped by his bicep, and he gripped her right elbow with his hand; the gun came over her shoulder.

Culley asked, "Why did you kill Eric Ross?"

Jackson smiled and shook his head. He lofted the gun a fraction, and sighted. Then he appeared to change his mind; he said, "Someone asked me to." The remark seemed wittier to him once he'd made it and he gave a brief laugh. Culley saw the gap in his teeth.

"Then you've done the job. Why bother with all this?"

"Ah . . ." Jackson shifted Helen slightly. "I'm afraid you're on the agenda, too."

"We know about Warner. We know about the paintings; and we know where they went." Culley saw nothing of recognition in

Jackson's eyes. He added, "And we're having long conversations with a man called Francis." Jackson shrugged, but his face closed down and Culley saw that he'd made the right connection. "You're not going to get paid for this, so why bother?"

"Well . . ." Jackson made a comic show of thinking things through. "Now that I'm here—it would be foolish not to, wouldn't it?"

"Don't think that by killing me, you stay anonymous. We know who you are. We know all we need to know. Francis told us."

Jackson nodded: a sudden confirmation. "Or Angie Ross."

Culley noticed that a window was half-open and wondered how he might use that. "So what's the point?"

"There's another way of putting that—what's the difference?" Jackson looked at Culley as if he were making up his mind about something. "I saw you at the farm. I was watching. I wondered whether Angie might mention me." He paused. "Just you—I saw you and no one else. I couldn't understand why you'd gone there alone. Later, I worked it out. You didn't expect me to be there. Well, that's reasonable enough. But it would have been standard procedure to take back-up, just in case. Why not? You'd have had men available. Then I realized. You were alone because you hadn't told anyone you knew."

"Why would I do that?" Culley tried to keep the anxiety out of his voice.

"I'm not sure." Jackson sounded genuinely intrigued. "If we had more time, I'd try to find out."

Helen was trembling, her stomach rigid under Jackson's arm; now and then, one shoulder would hop in an involuntary shrug. Her eyes were fixed on Culley as if, at any moment, he might say something that would solve the problem.

What shall I ask? Culley thought. What subject might buy me time? He said, "When you and Ross were—"

Jackson stood up, hoisting Helen with him. "Let's go into the bedroom." After he'd spoken, he ran his tongue up under his lip to cosset the tear in his gum. Clearly, the cavity was paining him. "I'm sure you know where it is. I'd just like you to understand that I know too." He put the gun against Helen's temple. "Walk ahead of me, leaving the doors open. If we get to the bedroom without any silliness, you'll both have lived a little longer, won't you?"

Culley went down the hallway and turned into the bedroom. Jackson and Helen followed. Jackson closed the door, then pushed

Helen toward Culley. They stood side by side, waiting to be told what to do next. Jackson indicated Culley with the gun and said, "Sit on the floor."

Helen raised both arms to waist level, a gesture of supplication though it appeared that she was offering something to Jackson. "Why do you have to do this. I don't understand." She had realized that if Culley was sitting and she was standing, they would divide Jackson's eyeline.

Keep talking, Culley thought.

"Pull the duvet off the bed," Jackson told her.

To deaden the sound. *Keep talking.*

"Don't you see? You'll achieve nothing. You'll still have to hide; still have to run." She pulled the duvet toward her, letting it fold onto the floor.

"No." Jackson shook his head. "Only he knows. And you, now. Drape it over his head."

He'll kill me first, don't you see that? Potentially, I'm more trouble. Me first, then you.

It was a silent scream; Culley's shoulders were locked with tension and effort. He might have been trying to project the words onto the wall.

Do something. Anything. Make any move at all—it doesn't matter what. It's too late to worry about what will happen.

Helen gripped the edge of the duvet and took a half-step toward Culley. Then she swung her arms mightily, bringing the entire quilted sheet around in a fast curve so that it spread and hung in the air like a bullfighter's cape, floating in front of her body and screening Culley. Jackson fired instantly. In the same moment Culley moved forward, staying low.

He took Jackson around the knees and stood up. The duvet had fallen backward over Culley. The only possibility for him was to put Jackson off balance so that the gun couldn't be brought to bear.

When Culley rose, gripping Jackson's legs, he heard another shot. He heaved upward, tumbling them both, and they fell against the wall. Jackson's gun arm came free. Culley got a hand to the weapon and held it clear, his fingers closing over Jackson's. His concentration went to that task and Jackson turned him so that he half-lay with his back to the wall.

As Culley sat up, a spread of fingers covered his face and shoved hard. He heard a sound like an anvil being struck; the room half-dissolved, then swam back together. Jackson got to his knees, wanting to slam Culley's head against the wall a second time. Culley clubbed down with his fist, feeling something break under the blow, and Jackson's grip on the gun loosened. He struck twice more and felt the other man fall away.

The head blow was still affecting him. He thought that the duvet might have fallen on him again, because his eyes seemed to fog. When his vision cleared he was alone in the room and holding the gun.

Jackson stood in the living room close to the open window. He looked at Culley, as if a contract lay between them too complicated for threats or bargains. Culley couldn't tell what was happening for a moment; then he saw how Jackson's arm was stiff with effort and drawn like a hawser toward the outer sill of the open window.

"Give me the gun," Jackson said, "and I'll haul her in."

Culley reversed the gun and took a cautious pace forward. "Start now," he said. "A little for every pace I take."

Jackson put a foot to the wall and leaned back. Helen's forearm appeared, enough for Jackson to grasp with both hands. He had to turn slightly and look back over his shoulder. Helen was hanging over the alleyway that led to the back entrance to her apartment. A man walked past but didn't see her. Two women followed, keeping a low conversation going. Someone appeared at a door with a bin of kitchen waste, then went back in. None of them looked up.

Culley took two more paces. Helen's face appeared above the sill. She was crying and panting with fear. She knew that if she cried out, Jackson would let her fall. The drop was about thirty feet. Culley took another pace, then stopped.

It was a bit like juggling: the important factors were where you rested your eye and how far you were able to trust your judgment of distance and movement. And one other thing—belief. All other aspects could be right, but if you stopped believing that the object leaving your left hand would soon be in your right hand, then everything would clatter down at your feet.

Culley wanted a moment when he was close to Jackson, but with the gun just out of reach; when Helen was all-but safe; when

Jackson was poised between taking the gun and transferring Helen. The trick would be to hold concentration in that moment, since it would be the moment of most distraction for all of them.

He took another step and Jackson lifted Helen a little more. She reached for the windowsill with her free hand, but couldn't turn her body enough to get a good purchase—nothing that would prevent her from falling. Her eyes closed with effort, as if she might conjure up a handhold in her mind, and her fingernails raked downward off the stonework.

Another step. Jackson looked at the gun. Culley said, "She's got to be safe before I give you this. She's got to be in the room."

Jackson shook his head. His arm was trembling; the strain in the bicep was obvious. "I can't hold her forever. It's your decision. Give me the gun and I'll haul her in."

"Will you?" Another step.

"Didn't I say I would?" Jackson's tongue ran to his gum again, swelling his lip. "If we stand here much longer, I'll drop her. If you shoot me, I'll drop her. The only way you win is if you don't mind." He took half a pace toward Culley, drawing Helen with him, and her face rapped the sill. She made a grab at the window-frame, but couldn't find purchase. The attempt seemed wild and weak, as though she didn't have proper control of her arm. Culley saw that her hand and her sleeve were splashed with blood.

Jackson's movement into the room had brought him to within four or five feet of the gun. Culley imagined something leaving his right hand, soon to be gathered with his left; in between was a free-floating object that would remain suspended—controlled—for just long enough. The object in between was Jackson.

He made a further step, extending his hand a little, the giver of gifts. As Jackson reached for the gun, Culley lobbed it through the open window, then went rapidly sideways, grabbing at Helen. Two things filled his mind: to deprive Jackson of the gun and to bring Helen back into the room. There was a vague secondary idea of fending Jackson off with his free hand. Done quickly enough, there might be enough surprise, distraction, and unexpected movement in it to leave Jackson stranded for just long enough.

He didn't really believe it would work and, because of that, it didn't. Culley threw the gun out and Jackson dropped Helen at once.

Culley's momentum took him to the window fast enough to register an almost subliminal image of Helen's moment of impact. She struck the paving, then appeared to rise minutely before her limbs settled with a violent slap and clatter that seemed terrifyingly audible. He saw it like a thought-flash, then turned and took a blow across the temple from Jackson's fist. He stumbled forward, arms outstretched to grapple. There was nothing there. He fumbled, arms still reaching, like someone playing blindman's buff, then sat down heavily.

There was a brief time of blackout. The punch to the temple, together with the blow he'd taken in the bedroom, simply closed him down for a while. When he came to, he was sitting with his legs stretched out, hands in lap, head thrown slightly back, like someone taking the sun.

Six people stood in a ring, all looking down at Helen. No one had touched her. The onlookers were silent and motionless, heads bowed in a mutually agreed solemn gesture of respect. They might have been meditating on the brevity of life.

Culley pushed through, knocking them against each other like skittles. Helen's skirt had ridden up and he tugged at it in a curious fit of jealousy, as if the onlookers were watching her while she slept. There was a little blood, though that had come from a bullet wound in her arm: one of Jackson's shots in the bedroom. Other than that, there was no sign of what damage had been done. Her limbs looked as if they possessed tremendous weight; impossible to lift. Her face was waxy and white.

A siren cut in, startlingly close. As if reminded by the sound, Culley dipped his head and listened for a heartbeat.

A night, a morning, a day. Then another night, another morning. Lines of drizzle advanced from the muddy red of dawn. Clouds were edged with the same livid color; on their undersides, they were dirty purple, like bruised fruit. Another day.

Dawson walked through the corridors with the tails of his raincoat flapping, a briefcase tucked under one arm—the bustle of a man with other things to do. Culley was waiting for him. He took Dawson's arm and steered him toward a rest area close to double windows. The view from the hospital was forlorn clumps of trees trapped between a grid system of arterial roads.

"She's asleep," Culley said. "Maybe tomorrow, if you find the time." He was keeping Helen to himself. Later, she would need other visitors.

Dawson put the briefcase down on a chair. "I've got a message for you."

"From Protheroe."

"That's right."

"Let me guess. He's expecting to see me soon. And he's expecting to see my report." He paused, looking at Dawson to see if there might be more. "Take a holiday?"

"It's personal now," Dawson said, "isn't it?"

Culley glanced toward the briefcase. "Is that you speaking? Or Protheroe?"

"It's a fact."

"What do you think I should do?"

"Well, you could take some leave." Dawson looked away down the hospital corridor. "You'll want to be here a good deal of the time, I expect. I don't know. It's your business." He sounded strange; edgy or impatient. "I shouldn't think anyone's going to worry much about what you do. Or where you are."

Culley said, "Okay, that's what I'll do. Tell Protheroe that." He picked up the briefcase and walked Dawson to the main door. As they were parting, the two men looked at one another. Dawson gave way to a laugh, sudden and explosive, like someone who's been told a joke in church. It died at once. He seemed eager to go.

"Where did you get it?" Culley asked.

Dawson's eyes avoided the briefcase. "Get what?"

Culley watched Dawson retreat through a gray fall of rain, then took the case to his car and locked it into the trunk. The hospital was as deceptive as a hive: featureless walls and blind windows on the outside; inside, all activity and drama. As a child, Culley had never been able to walk past a hospital without looking up and wondering whether someone was dying behind this window or that. The idea had always excited and frightened him. From the parking lot, there was nothing to see or hear. Once inside, you know where you are—the pain factory.

He looked up toward the window of the room where Helen lay, then walked quickly toward the main entrance as if he'd just decided what to do; although in truth the decision had been made before Dawson had brought him the gun.

. . .

Helen woke with a jolt and looked directly at Culley's face. She spoke abruptly. Culley felt he was hearing something from the middle of some lengthy explanation: There was no pause while she emerged from sleep, no drowsiness in the voice.

"I dreamed I was falling." Fear deepened the lines on her face and she half sat up, as if trying to catch what had been said. Then everything about her softened and there seemed to be a second moment of waking. She smiled at Culley and put out a hand. "I suppose that's not surprising."

"No."

"How long have I been asleep?" She meant, How long were you gone?

"Fifteen minutes, perhaps. Not more."

"Did you see Mike?"

"Yes."

"No sign?"

"No sign."

They were talking about Jackson—the man who had made a victim of her. She wanted him caught, bound, locked, sealed. His freedom was like an icy draft at her back, like a death wind.

Culley said, "It'll be a couple of days. Either he's there or he's not. If he's there, he'll be waiting for me."

"Leave it to someone else."

"Is that what you want?"

What she wanted—what she'd asked for—was that Culley would stop. Except that now she also wanted protection. She tried an idea that would let them both off the hook. "He could be anywhere."

"I don't think so," Culley told her.

"You know where to find him? You're sure of that?"

"Pretty sure."

"Then others can do the same." She was arguing against herself, as hard as she knew how. In truth, she suspected that the answer to her fear lay with Culley and Culley's risk.

"I don't think so."

"Why?"

He said something that she would sooner not have heard. "We want each other. We're looking for each other. We expect each other."

Helen reached for a glass of water that stood on a cabinet alongside the bed. Culley helped, cupping the back of her head and bringing the glass to her lips. She drank most of it. When he settled her against the pillow again, her eyes closed.

Culley stood by a window and looked out. Gigantic poles of sun-light radiated from behind a dark cloud, standing between heaven and earth like struts to hold up the sky. Everyone was too busy to notice. They went to and fro in the street with things on their minds.

When he went back, Helen was awake and looking for him. She said, "Did they find Warner?"

He shook his head. "Gone."

"Where?"

"Wherever money takes you. I don't know."

She said, "I think I hate it now, working for the gallery. I don't think I'll go back there. No one cares about the work—you know? It's a cliché, but it's true. A painting is just cash in a frame. I might have been as guilty as any; I'm not sure. I don't even know whether it matters. But Warner . . ." She stopped, as if ordering her thoughts. "How was it possible to do that? To have all those people killed . . ."

"It didn't matter to him," Culley said.

Helen stared because he'd said it as if he understood. "Why not?"

"You don't see it because you're not there. You don't feel grief because you didn't know the person. You don't witness any of the paraphernalia of death—coffins, burials, mourners. It's not to do with human reality, it's to do with patterns and movements. It allows things to go smoothly. Think about it—you're watching TV. There's been an earthquake. Children are buried in the rub-ble. Hundreds dead. Do you cancel your evening out at the the-ater?"

"Warner *caused* it," Helen protested. "They weren't random deaths; he made them happen."

"That's the only difference between your understanding of it and his." Culley shrugged. "You see people beyond the statistic. Statistically, people die all the time."

"So *many*," she said.

"It's relative. It depends what freedoms you allow yourself. So many? If you're fighting a war, it's a case of more equals better. You take a patrol out, engage the enemy, kill twenty. No one says, 'But so *many*.' You drop a bomb and kill a hundred. No one says, 'So *many*.' Lots of people dying is how war works. Warner saw it as a war, I expect. Against competition; in favor of wealth. It's not so unusual. How many does the Mafia kill; the Triads?"

"It doesn't matter what you do as long as you win the war. Is that it?"

"That's it, yes."

A break in the cloud let the sun through and for a minute the window at Helen's back grew slowly opaque, like a cataract. A crumpled rectangle of light appeared on her coverlet and immediately began to fade. They sat in silence for a while. At one point Helen put her hand into Culley's. If she closed her eyes for a while, there was something to hold on to.

"What happened in America? How did you get Ralph Porter's name?"

He told her as much as he'd told anyone else. "I had a guy poking around for me—someone who knew the people, knew the ground. He came up with it."

"What about Kemp?"

"I met him—just briefly."

"And?"

Culley shrugged. "How do you make a judgment about someone with that much money and power? The terms we normally use simply don't apply. They make their own world."

He remembered the aching silences on the phone, then Nina's voice and Kemp's voice: fear and compulsion. He saw Nina's face, pale and questioning. He saw her as she moved about the borrowed apartment, talking of things that were never going to happen.

Helen's hand softened in his. The periods of sleep were lengthening now. Her injuries had weakened her. One of Jackson's bullets had taken a piece out of her upper arm; there would always be a hollow there, dappled with scarring, like a gigantic vaccination mark. The fall had broken an ankle, an arm, two ribs. The doctors had looked for other things expecting to find them; they thought she was lucky. Helen had trouble agreeing with them.

Culley watched her as she dozed. What had happened between him and Nina had begun to seem increasingly real, increasingly oppressive. The dream was then, not now—as if he had woken to discover all the worst parts of a nightmare standing around the bed. In Arizona, she had been a hostage, something to bargain with; cold cash. Now she insisted on being herself. He knew he would have to find ways of guarding himself and Helen against her.

She leaned forward so that he could arrange her pillows. Because she wasn't properly awake, she said, "It isn't flying . . ." then stared after the words in confusion.

Culley lowered her head and stroked her hair for a while. Everyone knew that the bullet wound and the broken bones were beginning to heal; for the most part she was being monitored for the effects of concussion.

Each time she slept, she dreamed the dream of falling, as close and compelling as a vision.

The day darkened; lights flickered on in the long, white corridors. Culley sipped a cup of coffee and lingered on the steps by the hospital's main entrance, eager to go but not sure if the moment was right.

I hate it when you go away.

An ambulance came in at speed, bringing someone who hadn't thought of that when the day began.

"You'd better go," she said. "What's the official story?"

"That I'm coming here each day. Taking a week's leave."

"You want me to lie for you if someone asks me?"

"That's the idea."

"Perhaps it would be better . . ." She shook her head.

"Afterward, we'll go away." He lifted a hand as if indicating the direction they might take. "I meant what I said. I'll find something else to do."

"Brain surgeon," she suggested. "Steeplejack."

"Where do you want to go?"

Instead of answering she said, "If you're going to stop, why not stop now?"—her last attempt to keep him close, despite the instinct that was saying: Protect me from him; guard me; make it safe.

"I'll have to go," he said. "We know that, both of us."

"Both of us." She nodded slowly. "Is that you and me, or you and him?"

. . .

Each little dreamtime ended to find him there. "Will I see you tomorrow morning?" she said.

"I'll be gone by then."

She thought of him driving south as if he were already on the way.

He said, "Where shall we go? Afterward. Where would you like to go?"

She remembered the first year of their marriage, how small the world had seemed, how controllable. She thought it just possible that he meant every word he said.

"We've lost the summer," she said. "Let's go to the sun. Let's go to Figeac."

56

STEPPING ONTO THE MOOR was like shedding a skin. The temperature dropped and the wind grew sharper.

Jackson found the swollen gum with his tongue and tested the inflamed socket. A spike of pain jumped to his eye; he could feel the lumpiness of poison up under his lip and he was rosy-cheeked on that side of his face. It nagged at him and he wished Culley would hurry to be there.

At first light, he had reconnoitered the farm and had seen that it was safe. He had gone down and cooked himself breakfast, then found a silk undershirt and long johns. Autumn might be mellow elsewhere, but the moor was different. Jackson had seen it snow out of a flawlessly blue sky. Already the air was becoming raw.

. . .

He took a wide route toward Bethel Tor, since that was the place Culley was bound to make for. A low bulk of mist was furled under the nearest hill, like a vast bale of hay, or a wave that had peaked but wouldn't drop. Wisps trailed upward from the mass and tangled in the gorse, then rose to film the sky with a pale wash. The sun bled a yolky light into it, yellow through white, the color of antique pearl. Jackson was traveling with nothing more than he needed: good clothing, hardtack, water, compass, gun.

He expected Culley alone. It was simple enough. Two full days had passed and no one had come to the farm. It was clear that Culley hadn't reported Jackson's name. He could be anyone; he could be anywhere. Only Culley would be certain to find him on the moor. If he hadn't shared that information, then surely he would come unaccompanied.

Jackson crossed a stone bridge and skirted a dry stone wall. He checked a compass bearing, then started along the crease of a valley, his shape darkened and blurred by the haze.

Culley was a mile or so ahead of him, following the same route. He topped a rise and surfaced into weak sunlight: a man standing chest-high in mist, deep as a swimmer treading water. Unlike Jackson, he had no compass. The mist was growing heavy, but it was still possible to work off nearby landmarks and a map.

He reached the tor sooner than he'd imagined; it wasn't visible until he was halfway down the slope. There was nothing to do but approach it directly. Culley couldn't see that well, but he assumed he couldn't be seen either.

Great slabs of fallen granite surrounded the base of the tor. Above them, the rock was fissured and craggy for the first third of its height; then it soared away, going smoothly upward for forty feet or more. Culley circled it, his gun drawn, trying to stay close enough to see clearly while not getting in among the apron of scree. The slabs were black and damp from the rub of the mist.

He went twice around the stone, then retraced his steps until he found a wedge of rock set in the turf like a chairback, and settled down against it to listen. The mist was still thickening, though it was a little lighter at ground level. Culley was looking down a green tunnel—the cropped turf going away from him under rafters of mist. Cut off from the rest of the landscape, and illuminated by a dense, pearly light, the tunnel seemed to radiate a vibrant glow.

The moor was windless and hushed, all sound magnified. Culley drew his gun for a sheep that wandered across his vision, then drew it again for the four or five that followed. The splashes of red and blue dye on their fleece were vivid in the strange light. In the two hours that he sat there, Culley thought he must have seen the entire flock, their profiles edging out of the mist and into his gun sights. Eventually, he decided to go down to the tor again, in case Jackson had come in on a different path. When he stood up, he realized that the mist had become a dense fog.

He knew what the dangers were, but he'd never experienced them before: sudden drops in the terrain, wind chill, marsh. The first two were more or less manageable. You could guess at the probability of a drop by the pitch of the ground. Temperature and wind were only a real danger in the winter months. But the marsh could kill you at any time. And in fog it was all risk, no judgment.

He went down toward the tor, trying to use instinct to find the position of the great stone at the bottom of the slope. He knew that it would be possible to pass within a few yards of Jackson and never see the man. He might as well have been blindfolded. The only compensation was that the same was true for Jackson.

Every ten yards or so, he crouched down to gain a slightly clearer view. After a few minutes, he saw the rubble of boulders at the base of the tor and he circled, still crouching, and moving at a half-run. He could see the boulders, and the tor rearing through the fog; nothing else. He decided to get off the moor.

It took him the rest of the day to travel nowhere. Dusk thickened the fog. He had walked for seven hours, his recovery periods growing longer and longer, and had never reached the road nor heard the sound of a car engine. He was exhausted. Whenever he sat down, he fought to keep his eyes open; if they closed, dream images filled his head. Once or twice, he had come upon a stream and decided to follow the watercourse. Each time, it had meandered pointlessly, or else he had felt the ground move under his feet and backtracked at once to get off the marsh. There was no sound. The whole landscape seemed to be holding its breath. Even the streams were silent, as if they were running under ice.

He knew he wouldn't get off the moor that night, and he knew it was pointless to try. He could hope to come across shelter: that was the reason to keep walking. When he found streams, he would drink from them. He had no food.

The fog was a wall without doors; although there were lights suspended amid the hang and curl of it, like streetlamps or the lights above hospital beds. A smell of ether tainted the air and, somewhere in the distance, a bell sounded. The glow grew more intense, fractured by layers of fog, and it seemed that a hundred tiny lights had been drawn together to give each beam. A dark shape appeared just the other side of the white wall: flat and broad, moving slowly, like a ferry being poled across still water. At the back stood the ferryman.

Helen sat up in bed to warn him. Her voice was deadened by the fog, though he could see her lips working. Jackson stood behind the bed, pushing it forward with one hand. In the other, he held a bunch of flowers that seemed to be lit from the inside, each bloom glowing with an eerie incandescence. As he watched, they began to fizz and spark like fireworks. Culley sensed an explosion coming, and instinct started him running; then he remembered Helen and turned back toward her. The lights seemed to withdraw into the fog. He became desperate and began to shout, though he knew that he wouldn't be heard. Helen's face, lit by the burning flowers, shone dimly from the blur of the dark.

He woke with no idea of how long he'd been asleep, though it was night now, and even the ground in front of his feet was blotted out. He stood up and took a step forward, not knowing whether that step might take him over an escarpment or knee-deep into marsh. Nothing to see or hear. If he held his arms out as he walked, nothing to touch. Only the sensation of ground beneath his feet allowed him to feel connected to anything at all. He took a second step and then a third. Like an animal, he wanted something to crawl into, something to put his back against.

Another hour of walking brought him to it: two long granite rocks, propped in an inverted vee and sloping away to where they were partly buried in the ground. He sat on the apex to rest before he discovered their likeness to a ridge tent, higher at the opening than at the blind end and spacious enough to give him room to roll over.

Inside was the dankness of peaty earth and the sour, slightly salty smell of weathered stone. He felt safer once he'd burrowed in. He was hungry, but he scarcely noticed that; tiredness wiped any other need. It wiped caution and it wiped fear. He lay with his face farthest from the opening, worming into the dark, and slept before he could think.

There was nothing Jackson had seen, nothing he'd heard, to let him know that Culley was on the moor. Even so, he was sure. He'd been certain that Culley would come no matter whether Helen had been killed or not. It occurred to him that if she had died, Culley would probably have come at once. So she wasn't dead. And two days was enough; two days was right.

But it was instinct, not reason, that told him Culley was there. During the time of waiting, Jackson had been cautious, but he hadn't really felt at risk. Now, something had changed. The moor was better than five hundred square miles of rock and hill and marsh; suddenly, it felt crowded. He sensed Culley as a creature senses an invader on its territory.

Like Culley, Jackson had scouted the tor. It was a risk, but an acceptable one—he knew the ground; he could fix his position from almost any of the half-buried rocks that littered the slope. But when the fog really set in, he backtracked, using the compass to take him to the stand of conifers he'd been using as a base. The trees would afford protection against wind or rain; they also screened him from anyone on that part of the moor. He carried pretty much all he needed, but he'd stashed a few things there: extra water, food that wouldn't spoil. If he needed to, Jackson could stay on the moor indefinitely with nothing more than basic provisions. Only injury or severe weather could drive him off.

Fog trailed like hanks of rag from tree to tree, snagging and tearing in the low branches. Jackson sat inside the poncho that pegged out like a tent and ate a bar of chocolate, then gave himself a mouthful of brandy from a hip flask, swilling the spirit across his gum so that it flooded the infection and stung. The sounds of the wood settled around him. After a moment, his head lolled forward and he slept.

Earlier in the day, when Culley had been sitting against the stone that was angled like a chairback, he'd drawn his gun and lofted it toward a noise from inside the fogbank. A moment later, another sheep had emerged, staring stupidly at the figure crouching there, arms extended. Culley had made the obvious connection between sheep and noise. He'd been wrong. What he'd heard was Jackson going downhill to the tor.

On three occasions, the men had passed within close range of each other. As Culley had skirted the tor for the second time, Jackson was going away from it; he had only just stepped outside the circumference of Culley's crouching run. At one point, as Culley went wide of the scree, they were back to back with nothing more than twenty feet of fog-bound moorland between them. They heard each other several times, and took the noise to be cattle.

Now they slept with less than a mile between them, Jackson just inside the treeline, wrapped in his poncho, Culley full-length under his stone coffin.

A sound much like a hiss went through the trees and the pine needles shivered.

A note, a low underwater echo, was drawn from the granite lip of Culley's shelter.

He thought he knew what it was. Working backward with his elbows and knees, he emerged from the stone canopy and stood up. The sound still rang in the limitless arches and domes of the fog, then it faded into stillness. After a moment, Culley heard it again, this time recognizing it for what it was, the long sough of a wind off the sea drawing itself over hillcrests and outcrop rock. As he stood there, he felt a coolness on one cheek and the collar of his coat fluttered.

The white walls that surrounded him trembled and shook. At the very highest point, great fissures appeared and something seemed to crumble and collapse, leaving a ragged gap and, beyond it, the hard blue light of a single star.

Jackson woke at dawn and got ready to leave. He ate some more chocolate and a couple of bran bars and washed them down with water. Deeper into the copse, the last of the fog hung from the branches: pale silks furled into skeins, torn sheets of cobweb. He was carrying both his rifle and the handgun he'd used on Ross. It didn't matter much to him whether Culley was a close-range kill or not. He took off the poncho and stowed it in a small, frameless backpack, then pushed his arms through the straps and buckled the waistband.

The wind grew brisker, sweeping the final shreds of fog out of the copse. Storm clouds had appeared on the horizon, moving across the rising sun, so that the eastern sky became a vast pink-black contusion. Jackson emerged from the treeline and started across the open ground at a jog.

After he had woken to the sound of the wind, Culley had crawled back between his angled stones, still feeling the edge of his exhaustion. Now he slept on, his head in a cone of darkness, his dreams all of the man he had come to the moor to find.

57

CULLEY WAS MOVING UNDER LOW purple clouds, under sunshine slanting through rain. The wind was hard enough to bring the storm in from the sea, but not a big enough blow to carry it on. The rain and sun coexisted at the storm's edge; at the center it was night and noise.

A figure appeared on the brow of the next hill, backlit by the mottled storm-light. Jackson seemed to be presenting himself: Here I am; isn't this where you expected to find me? Half a mile apart, the two men seemed to be looking directly at one another. The silhouette changed shape as arms came to shoulder level. Culley dropped, supporting himself on palms and toes, like a man doing push-ups. A hard, flat clang of thunder came off the skyline, a gunshot at its center. When Culley looked up, the figure had disappeared.

He crossed the valley floor and took a direct line to the crest, running hard in case Jackson had circled and was on his flank. The hill leveled out into a broad plateau—more open ground than Culley wanted to look at. To one side, about fifty feet away, was a stone circle, man-sized pillars hunched in silence, preparing to endure the storm. The clouds broke and reformed. For a moment the rain was long mercury lines and the heel stone became glossy with light. He dropped back below the crest and ran along the slope until he was level with the standing stones. Gun up, he came above the skyline once more, sprinted into the circle, and turned. No one. He ran through and turned again. No one. He looked across the plateau and it was empty.

The sky lowered and darkened: a false dusk; the thunderheads went from horizon to horizon. As he crossed the plateau, Culley could hear heavier rain beating up behind him, a wind-driven roar. Jackson could have been anywhere. For the first time, Culley thought: I could die today; I could die at any minute.

On the far side of the open ground, as he came to the slope above Bethel Tor, thunder broke directly overhead, a sound so loud that Culley instinctively dropped. Belly-down, he looked toward the rock, scanning the jumble of boulders around its base. Nothing. He knew that Jackson could be on the far side, waiting to catch him in the open as he approached. He had about a hundred feet of hillside to descend and no real option.

He went crabwise to keep his balance, traveling fast, almost getting airborne where the ground steepened. He was half-way there when the sky went white. There was a vast, rending hiss, then a split second of total deafness as a zigzag switch-back of pure energy arced out of the cloud mass and struck Bethel Tor.

The lightning flung Culley backward. When he got to his feet he could see storm rain barreling in like a sky-high wave, soaking up distances. It arrived with the sound of engines, and engulfed him. The landscape shrank to the apron of ground he stood upon and the tor seemed to be dissolving under the weight of water. Culley stood still for a moment, as if baffled, then continued his sideways lope downhill.

The great electric hiss filled the air again; a jagged blue-white pillar cracked and quivered amid the downpour. The thunder seemed head-high. One of the granite slabs at the base of the tor was thrown back like the lid of a tomb and a man rose from the vault, a rifle up to his shoulder. The sound of the shot seemed to come from miles away.

Culley didn't know whether he'd been hit; the fact that he could run probably meant he'd been lucky. The rain was a partial screen.

He found cover behind a waist-high rock and drew his gun. When he looked at the tor, no one was there. Culley pressed his arms and his torso, knowing that adrenaline could mask a wound. He couldn't raise any pain. He came out of cover and ran straight at the tor, gun in hand.

Jackson's poncho was still there. He had lain under it, the same color as stone in the rain, then had stood up to become a boulder overturned by lightning. Culley went around the tor, looking hard. All the rocks were rocks. He became aware of an odd cessation of sound, like the moment before a wave drops, and realized that the rain had almost stopped and the storm was moving away. The sky lightened and there was a blue wash behind the thinner patches of cloud.

In his mind's eye, Culley followed a comic routine—two men backing around a rock, coming closer and closer but looking the wrong way, their guns trained on thin air, until they bumped and turned with a shared cry of alarm, and the audience howled. The other version was where the two men sat on either side of a rock, each waiting for the other. He calculated that a right-handed man would walk counterclockwise to keep his gun on the outside and make the angle of fire more comfortable. He went clockwise, to counter that move. If Jackson had thought the same, Culley would be leaving his back exposed. He raised the gun to eye level and stayed close to the scree, treading carefully.

Jackson came into view almost immediately. Clearly, he'd intended to cover both options because he was looking over his shoulder. Culley fired and Jackson flipped backward, the rifle going away from him in a high parabola. He got to his feet at once and went after the weapon, running with a sloping back like a sprinter coming off the blocks. Halfway there he overbalanced and pitched forward. One arm was wrapped across his body so that he could grasp his neck. Culley got between Jackson and the rifle, then backed up until he could kick the stock with his heel. He lowered himself slowly, and sat down.

Jackson got up on an elbow, then swung around to sit cross-legged, his hand still on his neck. They looked like the only two people left at a picnic. Blood was oozing between Jackson's fingers and beading on the knuckles before running across the back of his hand. Jackson laughed and lifted his free hand, as if emphasizing some remark he'd already made.

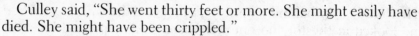

Culley said, "She went thirty feet or more. She might easily have died. She might have been crippled."

"Luck," Jackson said. "It's a gift."

Culley reached back and collected the rifle. He stood up and Jackson stood up too, turning his back and starting to walk away as if they had already discussed what would happen next. Culley lengthened his stride briefly to close the gap. He said, "Wait," and Jackson paused while Culley patted his pockets to locate the hand-gun. Then they began to walk back up the slope.

The sky was clear now, the light glassy and clean all the way to the skyline. You would think the moor had been like that all day. A warm wind turned the grasses.

"You knew him," Culley said. "He was a friend of yours."

Jackson shook his head. "We're not going to talk about that."

It was all Culley wanted to hear about; the only thing Jackson had to offer.

"You don't take contracts for a living. You might have done once. I don't think you do any more." Culley waited and got nothing. "You made an exception to kill your friend."

Jackson walked on in silence. The shoulder and upper sleeve of his coat were black.

They crossed a stone bridge over a stream that was less than six feet wide; the water ran on the stone and lapped their shoes. A spate in the moorland streams was all that was left of the drench.

Culley said, "Do you know why he was killing them?" There was no reply. "He killed a lot of people. There was a reason. Do you know what it was?"

They went a quarter of a mile across turf so bitten back, so thin, that the granite stuck through like starved bones through a pelt.

Jackson said, "I don't fucking care. Do you think I care?" He was very pale and had begun to veer slightly as he walked. Each time, he would pause and correct himself, like a drunk trying to appear sober.

Some things are bad from the start, Jackson thought. Some things are crippled in the egg.

Eric . . .

The after-storm light scoured the landscape like a salt wind, bringing everything close to the eye, bright and raw.

He stumbled and his foot went up to the ankle in a patch of boggy ground. The sudden stop wrenched him and fresh blood welled over the black crust of the old that coated his hand. Culley stood off a way. They were both looking at Jackson's foot, caught and held; he had to put a hand behind his own knee to get it out.

He looked at Culley and laughed. "You don't know what to do with me, do you?"

"The locals can have you," Culley said.

"You shouldn't be here. They'll say you acted on your own. They'll talk about a vendetta."

"Do you think so?"

Jackson smiled and seemed thoughtful. "No, perhaps not." His speech was a little slurred and he lurched more clumsily than before. They had been walking for another ten minutes before Culley realized that Jackson had left his boot in the marsh.

Brightness after rain was drawing all the moorland scents into the air. Culley saw the white snags, like cotton, on the grass and looked left and right for solid ground. Jackson kept walking, throwing his shoulder forward to help his awkwardness. The marsh was pulpy and slick with the new rain, a skim of water gleaming on top of the mosses, and he made small splashes as he went in, trying for the speed that would take him beyond recovery. By the time Culley had shouted a warning, Jackson was twenty feet away. He half-turned, floundering, and sank to his knees.

Culley walked to the edge of the mire, as close as he dared go. Dark water welled up under his feet; he stood in two shallow, black pools. Jackson had gone to his waist.

"Throw me the handgun." He sounded matter-of-fact. Although he'd put himself out of reach, he didn't have to raise his voice.

"Did you think I would?" Culley asked.

Jackson's eyes showed the white, then closed for a moment; it seemed that he might faint. He said, "Throw me the gun."

Culley lobbed it carefully, as you throw a ball to a child, and Jackson caught it with both hands. He looked at Culley and laughed. "You still don't know, do you?" One hand cupped the

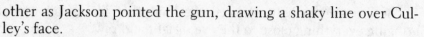

other as Jackson pointed the gun, drawing a shaky line over Culley's face.

Culley stood still, expecting nothing. Not death, not deliverance. Jackson turned the gun and put it into his mouth. His hand was shaking so much that he fired before he meant to. His cheek puffed, as if he had given a great sigh of resignation, and the recoil left the gun three or four feet away to the left. He groped for it and brought it back.

He began to choke and used both hands for the gun, wanting to hurry because the ooze had reached his chest. Even so, his eyes were on Culley.

The wind got up, chasing ripples across the mire. The two men looked at each other as Culley waited for Jackson to get it right.